A PASSION FOR

A DARING HEARTS NOVEL

PLEASURE

New York Times & USA Today Bestselling Author

NINA LANE

SNOW QUEEN

PUBLISHING

An earlier edition of this novel, written under the name Nina Rowan, was
published by Grand Central Publishing in 2013.

Cover Design: Najla Qamber Designs

ISBN: 978-1-954185-11-1

A PASSION FOR PLEASURE
Nina Lane

A brilliant pianist and notorious rake, Sebastian Hall indulges his passion for music and women with equal aplomb. But now that his elder brother has married, his father insists he pursue a respectable path and find a suitable wife.

As a girl, Clara Whitmore quietly loved her piano teacher from afar. Yet her youthful crush cannot compare to the powerful desire she feels when she unexpectedly encounters Sebastian again.

Could the man who once dominated her dreams become the husband she hopes for...and save her from the fate she most fears?

* An earlier edition of this novel was published under the name Nina Rowan.

PROLOGUE

30 September, 1854

My dear brother Sebastian,

I send this via personal courier from Paris to ensure the haste and secrecy of its receipt. Herein is further information regarding my request for your assistance.

When I corresponded with Monsieur Jacques Dupree about his inventions, he revealed the existence of plans he had drawn up for the construction of a machine that creates cryptographs.

I have recently learned that prior to his death, Monsieur Dupree sent the cipher machine specifications to a former apprentice, Mr. Granville Blake, at Blake's Museum of Automata, 20 Old Bond Street, London. It is my belief that

Monsieur Dupree sent him the plans to ensure their safe-keeping.

The machine appears to have numerous wartime uses, but I must study the mechanics, code, and transmission of cipher messages before determining its efficacy. To that effect and with recent difficulties in the Crimea, it is important that you do not tell anyone what you are looking for.

Should you find the plans for me, I will compensate you well. I understand from Grand Duchess Irina that you have returned to London for an indeterminate stay, so it is my hope this task will prove advantageous for us both.

Yours,
Jacob

CHAPTER 1

*S*he was carrying a head.

Sebastian Hall squinted and rubbed his gritty eyes. He blinked and looked again. Definitely a head. Cradled in one arm like a babe. It was a woman's head with neatly coiffed brown hair. Though at this distance he couldn't see her expression, he imagined it to be rather distressed.

He watched as the young woman crossed the empty ballroom to the stage, her steps both quick and measured and her posture straight in spite of her gruesome possession.

Sebastian pushed himself away from the piano. The room swayed a little as he rose, as if he were on the deck of a ship. He had once spent countless hours at the Royal Society of Musicians' Hanover Square building, but now the place felt unfamiliar to him, almost oppressive. A hum, seasick-yellow, droned in his ears. He dragged a hand over his face and scrubbed at his rough jaw as he crossed the room.

The woman didn't appear to see him, her path set unswervingly on her destination. A basket dangled over her left arm.

Sebastian cleared his throat. The guttural noise echoed in the vast room like the growl of a bear.

"Miss." His voice sounded coarse, rusted with disuse.

The woman startled, jerking back and losing her grip on the head, which fell to the floor with a thump and then rolled. A cry of surprise sounded, though in his befuddled state Sebastian couldn't tell from whom it had emerged. He looked down as the head rolled to a stop near his feet like the victim of an execution-er's ax.

A perfect, waxen face stared up at him, wide blue eyes unblinking, pink mouth, her hair beginning to escape a smooth chignon.

After a moment of regarding this turn of events, Sebastian bent to retrieve the head. The woman reached it before he did, scooping it back into her arms and stepping away from him.

"Sir! If you would please—oh."

Sebastian looked up into a pair of rather extraordinary eyes— a combination of blue and violet flecked with gold. Something flickered in his memory, though he couldn't grasp its source.

Where had he—?

"Mr. Hall?" She tucked a stray lock of brown hair behind her ear, hugging the head closer to her chest. "I didn't know you would be here."

She frowned, glancing at his wrinkled clothes, unshaven jaw, and scuffed boots. For an uncomfortable moment, he wanted to squirm under that sharp assessment. He pulled a hand through his hair in a futile effort at tidiness, then experienced a sting of annoyance over his self-consciousness.

"Are you..." He shook his head to try to clear it. "I'm afraid this room is closed until Lady Rossmore's charity ball on Saturday."

She tilted her head. "You don't remember me."

Oh, hell.

Out of sheer habit, Sebastian attempted to muster a charming smile, though it had been so long since one had come naturally to him that his face felt like pulled clay.

"Well, far be it from me to forget a woman as enchanting as yourself," he said. "Your name has slipped my mind, though of course I remember…that is, I must be out of my wits to—"

"For pity's sake." She seemed to be trying hard not to roll her eyes, though a blue-gold thread of amusement wove into her voice. "My name is…was Clara Whitmore. My younger brother and I both took piano lessons from you years ago when we stayed in Dorset."

Sebastian struggled to make his brain work as he looked at her round, pretty face, her curly brown hair pulled into an untidy knot. A streak of grease or oil smudged her cheek. She looked like a thousand other ordinary women—a shopkeeper's daughter, a dressmaker, a governess, a milliner's apprentice.

Except for her eyes. And a tiny black birthmark punctuating the corner of her smooth left eyebrow, like the dot of a question mark.

"I was your student for a scant few months the summer I turned sixteen," Clara continued, as if unaware of his scrutiny. "You weren't much older, but people already spoke highly of your talent. I enjoyed many of your performances at various events in Dorset."

A piece settled into place in Sebastian's mind. Ten years ago he'd lived in Dorset, teaching, performing, and entering contests in an attempt to pay for a trip to the Continent that his father had refused to fund.

"Where did you live in Dorset?" he asked.

"Not far from Weymouth."

"And does your father reside there still?" Sebastian asked.

"No, I'm afraid that property has long been abandoned." Her eyes flickered downward, shading her expression. She shifted the head to her other arm. "So, Mr. Hall, I've continued to hear great things about you over the years. You conducted at Weimar this past summer, did you not?"

The admiring, bright pink note in her voice clawed at him.

The fingers of his right hand flexed, a movement that caused tension to creep up his arm and into the rest of his body.

"Yes." His voice sounded thin, stretched.

Clara blinked, a slight frown tipping her mouth again. Her eyes really were the strangest shade—a trick of the light, surely. No one had eyes that color. He certainly didn't recall having noticed them when she was his student. He didn't even recall having noticed *her*.

Discomfort pinched Sebastian's chest. He wouldn't have noticed her back then. Not when women had flocked to him with bright smiles and hot whispers. Among such birds of paradise, Clara Whitmore—even with her unusual eyes—would have been a plain brown sparrow.

She still is, he told himself. Never mind the knot of regret that he couldn't remember her—Clara Whitmore with the violet eyes that took his measure in one sweeping glance. No one could hide from that assessment. Not even him.

He straightened his shoulders, tucking his right hand into his pocket. He looked at the waxen head with an unspoken question.

"My uncle is introducing an automaton at Lady Rossmore's ball," Clara explained. "Her ladyship thinks it will be great entertainment if Uncle Granville demonstrates one of his musician automata at a Society of Musicians' event. So I'm doing some of the initial preparations for him, as he was called out of town."

A surge of comprehension rolled through Sebastian as the pieces began locking together in his mind.

"Then you are Mr. Granville Blake's niece," he said. "I'd expected…that is, Lady Rossmore said he might be here."

"He'd intended to be, but owing to the circumstances, I'm to carry out his duties." Clara touched the automaton's head, drawing Sebastian's gaze to her long fingers. "This is Millicent, the Musical Lady. Part of her anyhow. She plays four tunes on the harpsichord."

"How"—*ridiculous*—"interesting."   Though   he'd   heard

Granville Blake dabbled in all sorts of mechanical toys and automata, Sebastian was interested in only one of the man's many projects. Not for himself, but for his younger brother Jacob.

And now he apparently had to be interested in Granville Blake's niece, as well.

"You oughtn't be here alone," he told her. "Especially at this hour."

"We've permission to bring in our equipment," she replied. "We must start to assemble Millicent and her harpsichord. And I'm not alone. My uncle's assistant Tom is just outside unloading the remaining crates." She glanced behind him to the piano resting beside the stage. "Are you rehearsing for a performance at the ball?"

His jaw tensed. Six months ago, he might have been here in rehearsal. Now he was here to ensure the safe delivery and tuning of his Broadwood piano, which he had offered for the Society of Musicians' indefinite use. Were it not for the fact that the Rossmores were friends of his father, Sebastian would have spent next Saturday evening wreathed in the smoke and noise of the Eagle Tavern.

"I will be at the ball," he said, "but not performing."

"Oh." Clara Whitmore looked faintly confused. "Well, I do apologize for the interruption. I didn't even know that anyone else would be here. Once Millicent is assembled, we'll leave you to your work."

Work. The piano was all the evidence she needed to assume he'd been working.

He was about to respond with a sharp tone—though he had no idea what he'd say—when a needle of rational thought pierced the fog in his brain.

At the very least, he needed to be civil to Clara Whitmore if he wanted to learn more about her uncle's projects.

Or perhaps he should be more than civil. Women had always

responded to his attentions. Even if now those attentions were corroded with neglect, Miss Whitmore didn't appear the sort who had much to judge them—or him—by.

The thought that she might possess no touchstone by which to judge him was strangely liberating.

"Would you care for a currant muffin?" She opened the basket. "I thought I'd better bring something to eat since I don't know how long Tom and I will be here. We're not quite as adept at assembling Millicent as Uncle Granville is, especially when it comes to the machinery contained within the harpsichord bench. I've also got apples and shortbread, as well as a bit of seed cake left over from tea…"

She kept talking. He stopped listening.

Instead he stared at the curve of her cheek, the graceful slope of her neck revealed by her half-turned head. He watched the movement of her lips—a lovely, full mouth she had—and the way her thick eyelashes swept like feathers to her cheekbones.

She looked up to find him watching her. The hint of a flush spread across her pale skin. With a sudden desire to see that flush darken, Sebastian let his gaze wander from her slender throat down across the curves of her body, her tapered waist, the flare of her hips beneath her full skirt. Then he followed the path back to her face.

There. Color bloomed on her cheeks. Her teeth sank into her lush lower lip. Consternation glinted in her violet eyes. He wondered what she'd look like with her hair unpinned, if it would be long and tangled and thick.

"I…er, I should carry on with my work," Clara went on, ducking her head. "Tom will be in directly, and there's a great deal to do. Please, take a muffin, if you'd like."

Sebastian rolled his shoulders back. A cracking noise split through his neck as he stretched. He realized for the first time that day he'd almost forgotten the headache pressing against his skull.

"Thank you." Again he experienced that wicked urge to provoke a reaction. "I'm not hungry. Not for food."

Her lips parted on a silent little gasp, as if she wasn't certain whether to be offended by his indecorous tone or to ignore it altogether. Expressing offense, of course, meant she'd have to reveal that she had recognized the implications of his words.

She gave a nonchalant shrug and shifted, then held Millicent's head out to him. "If you please, sir—"

"I please, Miss Whitmore." His voice dropped an octave. "Often and well."

He was drunk. Or recently had been.

That didn't explain why Clara's heart beat like an overwound clock, or why the rough undercurrent of Mr. Hall's words heated her skin, but at least it explained *him*.

She tried to breathe evenly. Although ten years had passed since she had last seen him, she recalled with striking clarity the way his presence had made her pulse quicken. She remembered him leaning over her shoulder as he demonstrated the position of his fingers on the piano keys. She remembered the assured tone of his voice as he spoke of quarter notes and major scales...but he'd been distant then, a brilliant pianist, a dashing young man who already attracted beautiful women, who would one day perform for kings and emperors.

Now the distance had closed. He stood before her close enough to touch. Though he could not be over thirty years of age, he seemed older, diminished somehow. Had he...fallen?

An ache pierced Clara's heart. Sebastian Hall had always been disheveled, but in a rather appealing fashion suited to his artistic profession.

I've no time to fuss, his manner had proclaimed. *I've got magic to weave.*

And he had, with kaleidoscope threads and fairy-dust needles. At dinner parties and concerts, Mr. Hall spun music through the air and made Clara's blood echo with notes that had never before moved her.

Not until Sebastian Hall had brought them to life. Sleeves pushed up to his elbows, hair tumbling across his forehead, he'd played the piano with a restless energy that could in no way be contained by the polish of formality.

But now? Now he was just...messy. At least three days' worth of whiskers roughened his jaw, and his clothes looked as if he'd slept in them for even longer than that. Dark circles ringed his eyes. He appeared hollowed out, like a gourd or shell devoid of its essence.

Clara tilted her head to the side and frowned. Although Mr. Hall's eyes were shot through with blood, they contained a sharpness that overindulgence would have blunted. And his movements—they were tense, restless, none of his edges smeared by the taint of spirits.

She stepped a little closer to him. Her nose twitched. No rank smell of ale or brandy wafted from his person. Only...

She breathed deeper.

Ahh.

Crisp night air. Wood smoke. The rich, faintly bitter aroma of coffee. Clara inhaled again, the scent of him sliding deep into her blood and warming a place that had long been frozen over.

"Miss Whitmore?"

His deep voice, threaded with cracks yet still resonant, broke into her brief reverie. Such a pleasure to hear his voice wrap around her former name, evoking the golden days when she had been young, when William and their mother had been alive and sunshine-yellow dandelions colored the hills of Dorset like strokes of paint.

She lifted her gaze to find Mr. Hall watching her, his eyes dark and hooded. Her face warmed.

"Sir, are you…are you ill?" she asked.

The frank question didn't appear to disconcert him. Instead, a vague smile curved his mouth—a smile in which any trace of humor surrendered to wickedness. A faint power crackled around him, as if attempting to break through his crust of lassitude.

"Ill?" he repeated. "Yes, Miss Whitmore, I am ill indeed."

"Oh, I—"

He took a step forward, his hands flexing at his sides. She stepped back. Her heart thumped a restive beat. She glanced at the door, suddenly wishing Tom would hurry and arrive.

"I am ill behaved," Mr. Hall said, his advance so deliberate that Clara had the panicked thought that she would have nowhere to go should he keep moving toward her. Should he reach out and touch her. Her skin prickled with sudden yearning for the act that she had once imagined in her youthful dreams.

She swallowed hard and tried to suppress the memories, reminding herself that she could no longer afford such girlish fancies.

"Ill considered," Mr. Hall continued. Another step. Two. "Ill content. Ill at ease. Ill favored. Ill *fated*—"

"Ill bred?" Clara snapped, forcing her spine to stiffen in denial of her unforeseen anticipation.

Sebastian stopped. Then he chuckled, humor creasing his eyes. An unwelcome fascination rose in her chest as the sound of his deep, rumbling laugh settled alongside the delicious mixture of scents that she knew, even now, she would forever associate with him.

"Ill bred," he repeated, his head cocked to the side. A lock of hair fell across his forehead. "The second son of an earl oughtn't be ill bred, but that's a fair assessment. My elder brother received a more thorough education in social graces." Amusement still glimmered in his expression. "Though I don't suppose he's done that education much justice himself."

Clara had little idea what he was talking about, though she did recall that his elder brother had recently wed. She also knew the Earl of Rushton had petitioned for a divorce from his wife several years ago. Rumors whispered at the edges of her mind, but back then Clara had been too ensnared in her own marriage to be concerned about a scandal involving an earl.

She realized that she'd backed up clear across the room to the stage. Sebastian stopped inches from her, close enough that she could see how the unfastened buttons of his collar revealed an inverted triangle of his skin, the vulnerable hollow of his throat where his pulse tapped.

A prickle skimmed up her forearms, tingling and delicious.

He kept looking at her, then reached into his pocket and removed a silk handkerchief. "May I?"

She shook her head, not certain what he was asking. "I beg your pardon?"

"You have—" He gestured to her cheek. "Dirt or grease."

Before she could turn away, the cloth touched her face. She startled, more from the sensation than the sheer intimacy of the act. Sebastian Hall's fingers were warm, light, and gentle against her face. She wondered, with a suddenness that made her heart throb, what his fingers would feel like on her skin.

He moved closer, a crease of concentration appearing between his dark eyebrows as he wiped the marks from her face with the soft handkerchief. Her breath tangled in the middle of her chest. She stared at the column of his throat, bronze against the pure white of his collar, the coarse stubble roughening the underside of his chin.

She didn't dare raise her gaze high enough to look at his mouth, though she wanted to. Oh, how she wanted to. The urge made her fingers curl tight into her palms, made a strange yearning stretch through her chest.

The muscles of his throat worked as he swallowed, his hand

falling to his side. He stuffed the handkerchief back into his pocket.

With his attention turned away from her, Clara noticed the weariness etched into the corners of his eyes, the brackets around his mouth, the faintly desperate expression in his eyes that had nothing to do with drink and everything to do with fatigue.

Fatigue. That was it. Sebastian Hall was bone-deep exhausted.

He met her gaze.

No. The man was exhausted past his bones and right into his soul.

Why...?

Before she could speak, Sebastian stepped back, turning toward the front of the room. Tom pushed open the doors and maneuvered a trolley loaded with four crates. He glanced up, his face red with exertion. "Almost done."

Clara hurried to meet him. They conferred briefly about how best to organize the various parts of the machine, then she turned back to the stage. Sebastian Hall was gone.

CHAPTER 2

*T*he evening following his encounter with Clara Whitmore, Sebastian stood in the crush of yet another ballroom. Voices rose around him like flocks of multicolored birds. Gentlemen and ladies in their finest evening clothes circled the dance floor, gaslights shining against expanses of silk and satin. A fire crackled in the massive hearth at one end of the room. Music wafted from the quartet seated near the windows.

He shifted his weight, resisting the urge to tug at the knot of his cravat. The music reached his ears in streams of pallid, muted colors. A drop of sweat trickled down his spine. Beside him, his father, the Earl of Rushton, leveled his dark gaze on the crowd like an archer seeking a bull's-eye.

"Lord Smythe," Rushton said, nodding to a lanky gentleman standing near the fire. "Recently appointed by Her Majesty as Ambassador to the Spanish Court. I believe his daughter has returned from a school in Paris. She might be present at Lady Rossmore's charity ball. You are attending, yes?"

"Yes." Sebastian thought of Clara, with her strange eyes and voice flowing with blue and gold. He would see her again at the ball six nights hence, but he hoped she would be at her uncle's museum when he visited the following morning.

"Lord Smythe is also involved with a report on the defects of patent laws and suggestions for reform, both of which you ought to know about," Rushton continued. He drew his eyebrows together, an expression that enhanced the severity of his features. "Since it seems you will be in London for some time now, you must focus on a worthwhile pursuit. I'm glad to see you're finally coming to your senses about what is expected of you."

Of course Rushton was glad. Music had never been a worthwhile pursuit, not in Rushton's eyes. His father didn't even know the truth of Sebastian's resignation from the renowned Court of Weimar. No one did.

If Sebastian didn't tell anyone, perhaps it wouldn't be real.

Not that there was anyone to tell, even if he'd wanted to. Aside from Rushton, their entire family was away from London. Alexander and Lydia now lived in St. Petersburg not far from their younger brother Jacob's own residence on the Fontanka canal. Their sister Tasha had gone to St. Petersburg to visit and assist Lydia, who was expecting a child in the spring. Patrick was...well, no one ever knew exactly where Patrick was.

Maybe Sebastian ought to find out. Patrick would know of a good place to escape.

He flexed his fingers and took a step toward the refreshment table just as a gentleman and young woman approached.

"Miss Butler." Rushton inclined his head toward the woman while his left hand fisted discreetly around the sleeve of Sebastian's coat. "Lovely as ever."

"Thank you, my lord." Pretty as a teacake in a blue lace gown, she encompassed them both with a smile.

Her father, Lord Dalling, beamed with pride. A rotund man with a mustache that curled at the ends like a swine's tail, he favored Sebastian with an approving nod. "Pleasure to see you,

Hall. Rushton here tells us you're thinking of choosing a position with the Patent Office."

Sebastian stifled a sigh and attempted to detach himself from his father's subtle grip. Curious word, that. *Choose.* No, he wouldn't choose any bloody such thing as a position with the Patent Office. He didn't even know if he could carry out a clerk's duties. Not if it meant needing to write a great deal, as he doubted his ability to hold a pen for any length of time.

"Sebastian might take a position as clerk for Lord Russell," Rushton said. "Important to make one's way up, isn't that right, Dalling?"

"Indeed, Rushton, indeed."

"It's a pleasure to see you here, Mr. Hall," Miss Butler said, turning her blue gaze to him. "We missed you over the summer when you were on your grand tour."

"Thank you, Miss Butler." He returned her smile, feeling only a thin shadow of the pleasure he'd once experienced when a woman had looked at him with such a bright, admiring expression. "How is your mother?"

"Very well. Gone off for a stay in the country."

"Champagne, Miss Butler?" Rushton lifted a hand toward a passing server. Actually, he lifted a finger, a quick gesture as if he were flicking aside an insect. A footman hurried toward them, balancing a tray of precariously perched flutes.

Rushton handed glasses to Miss Butler and Lord Dalling. Another bead of sweat rolled down Sebastian's spine. He curved his right hand around the flute his father extended, trying to force his fingers to obey, though his little finger didn't move at all. His teeth came together hard when a cramp seized his hand, freezing the rest of his fingers into a clawlike position.

He grasped the glass with his left hand and steadied a sudden tumble of anxiety.

No one knows. No one knows.

"Oh, a waltz," Miss Butler remarked as the musicians began a new piece. "I do so love the waltz."

Rushton shot him a pointed glance, which Sebastian recognized well. He looked at the couples circling the dance floor. He had always liked dancing. Last spring, he wouldn't have hesitated to ask Miss Butler to accompany him onto the floor, and he'd have ensured they both enjoyed every step and turn.

But Sebastian hadn't danced once in the past five months, and he couldn't start again now. Not when he could no longer count on his ability to guide his partner with accuracy.

An awkward silence fell. Dalling cleared his throat. Miss Butler smiled again.

"Mr. Hall, aren't you recently returned from Germany?" she asked, her heart-shaped face turned up like an open flower. "My father said you had a rather prestigious position at Weimar at the invitation of Monsieur Liszt himself."

"I did, yes."

"But left due to a quarrel with the musical committee?"

"They wanted to alter one of my operas. I objected."

"Of course you did." She giggled with delight, as if she would have expected no less of him. "Though I can't imagine working at the Patent Office will be quite as thrilling as performing for the Court of Weimar."

"No. Not quite."

"Do you intend to return to performing, then?"

"One day."

He intended to. Whether or not he *could* was another matter entirely.

Sebastian knew what rumor said about his resignation—he'd stormed away from the position as director of the court theater in a fiery pique over creative control of his work. The committee members had pleaded for him to return. He'd refused and fled to the home of the Grand Duchess Irina Pavlova, the woman who had recommended him to Liszt for the position in the first place, so that he could work in peace. And, of course, everyone thought she was his lover, the celebrated grand duchess a decade his senior.

None of it was true, but society loved tossing the romantic story about as if it were a balloon bouncing on currents of air.

That, Sebastian thought, was both his saving grace and his downfall. The gossip was friendly, amused, intrigued—nothing like the horrific shock that had followed his parents' divorce after the countess had had an affair and deserted her family.

Rushton, however, now reestablishing himself both politically and socially almost three years after the scandal, would hasten to forestall the glare of any gossip, no matter how good-natured.

Lord Dalling and his daughter soon made their excuses and went to the refreshment table. Sebastian felt his father's gaze, weighted with displeasure.

"Why did you not ask her to dance?" Rushton asked.

Sebastian didn't respond.

"She is also an excellent prospect for marriage," his father continued. "Well educated, respectable. Her father is purported to be the next Secretary of State for Foreign Affairs. You would do quite well with her." Rushton studied him, his eyes narrowing. "Or seek out Smythe's daughter at Lady Rossmore's ball. Unless you intend to be occupied with one of your performances?"

The mild note of condescension in his father's voice grated against Sebastian's nerves. "No."

"Why did you go to all the trouble of having your piano delivered to the Society of Musicians?"

"The Society's piano needs repairs, so I offered to loan them mine." That was the truth, at least, though Sebastian couldn't tell his father the actual reason he'd sought out Granville Blake at the Hanover Square rooms last night. Not without betraying the confidence of his brother Jacob.

Do not tell anyone what you are looking for.

The sentence in Jacob's letter tangled through his brain. The order wouldn't be difficult to follow, considering he *had* very little idea what he was looking for. He didn't much care either. After his furtive visits to several doctors and then the expense of a surgery that had permanently damaged his finger, Sebastian cared only that Jacob would compensate him enough to settle the remainder of his medical obligations.

He still felt his father's gaze. Although Rushton's staid expression often concealed his thoughts, the man possessed a stare that could peel one like an apple. Having been the recipient of that sharp look more times than he cared to remember, Sebastian attempted to deflect it by turning away.

Rushton grasped his arm. "What is the matter with you?"

"Something must be the matter because I don't care to marry an insipid debutante?"

"You used to *chase* insipid debutantes," Rushton snapped. "And since returning from Weimar, you've been sullen as a whipped dog. I refuse to have people talk about what a bad-mannered malingerer you've become."

"You refuse to have people talk about anything," Sebastian said, yanking his arm from his father's grip. "You've become worse than Alexander, though at least he managed to avoid scandal."

He braced himself for his father's anger, but Rushton only shook his head.

"Alexander escaped scandal because of Lydia."

"He wouldn't have courted scandal if he hadn't met Lydia," Sebastian retorted, then swallowed hard against the shame filling his throat.

He'd been the one to encourage Alexander's interest in the brilliant, beautiful mathematician—the rest of the world be damned. He'd known his brother needed someone like Lydia, and the fact that the enamored couple had emerged from potential scandal unscathed—not to mention ridiculously happy—was more than a testament to the strength of their relationship. It was a goddamn miracle.

A strange tightness wound through Sebastian's chest. He wanted to walk away from his father, but a cluster of people blocked the doorway of the ballroom. The musicians began a cotillion that sounded unpleasant and reedy. He flexed his hand, rubbing his thumb against his crooked finger and the scar that curled over his palm.

"Alexander found the right woman for him," Rushton said. "A woman who made him better than he was, who made him a better man. I suggest you do the same."

"As you did?" A red, caustic note colored Sebastian's voice. He wished his father would flare with anger, give him an adversary against which to battle. Instead a dark emotion suffused Rushton's eyes as he stared at the twirling couples on the dance floor.

"No," he replied, his neck cording with tension. "Not as I did. Your mother didn't care what people thought, and she didn't care how her decisions affected others."

He gave a bitter laugh and took a swallow of his drink. "Hell, in the end, she didn't even care about her family, did she?"

Sebastian couldn't disagree. No one had heard from the former Countess of Rushton, who had disgraced their family by having an affair with a Russian soldier. After Rushton divorced her, she had fled England and her children to live in sin with her lover. No one knew where she was now.

The woman was dead as far as Alexander was concerned. The earl hadn't spoken of her in the years following the divorce, not until now. All traces of her were long gone from every property in Rushton's domain. Tasha no longer mentioned her. Patrick... well, no one ever knew where his loyalties lay, except perhaps Jacob, but the distance of oceans had long separated the twins.

Sebastian wondered if his brothers and sister thought of their mother anymore. Almost three years later, he was still twisting the thing around and around in his mind, like unraveling a knotted ball of twine. He would never have expected such betrayal from his mother, who had seemed both faultless and distant.

The countess—indeed, the earl as well—had left the rearing of their five children to nurses and governesses before sending the boys off to school. Nothing about the utter correctness of their upbringing and their parents' marriage had prepared the Hall children for the consequences of their mother's affair and the subsequent divorce.

Catherine, Countess of Rushton, had been possessed of a lovely perfection that one could gaze upon but never touch. She'd been like a window decorated with spangles and curls of ice, cold against one's fingertips, impenetrable.

Except for when she played the piano.

"Find a woman who is the opposite of your mother," Rushton said, "and you'll begin your marriage on a far stronger foundation than I did."

When Sebastian didn't respond, Rushton stepped closer, his mouth compressing. "In fact, Bastian, I suggest you seriously consider my words. Do not think I'm averse to withholding your allowance, or indeed, even your inheritance, should you continue following this ignominious path on which you have embarked."

Rushton turned and strode toward the card room. Sebastian smothered a flare of anger, hating that his father's threat could affect him now. Five months ago, he'd have laughed and gone off to flirt with any woman, respectable or not, who happened to catch his eye. Nothing Rushton said would have altered his desire to live as he pleased.

Now he could no longer do that, even if his father hadn't issued a command.

Finding it difficult to draw in air, Sebastian headed through the adjoining room toward the gardens. Alexander would help him financially if he asked. But asking meant he would have to divulge more than he wanted. Asking would mean disrupting

Alexander's own life, now finally one of happiness and content-
ment. Asking would mean defying Rushton and forcing
Alexander to do the same.

Asking would mean eliciting his brother's pity.

Not for the first time, Sebastian experienced a pang of envy at
the thought of his elder brother.

Alexander *fixed* things. If he were in Sebastian's position, he
would force things back into place—by the strength of his will
alone if there were no other method. He wouldn't capitulate to
their father's wishes because he had no other choice.

Then again, Rushton wouldn't give Alexander an ultimatum
of any kind. Since the scandal and divorce, Alexander's successes
had only illuminated Rushton's failings as both a peer and a
father. Now that Rushton's new appointment as Undersecretary
at the Home Office had garnered a degree of prestige among his
fellow peers, he intended to ensure that the rest of his family fell
into a straight and precise line right behind Alexander.

Starting with Sebastian.

CHAPTER 3

*S*he dreamed of him again. For two nights after seeing Sebastian Hall for the first time in a decade, Clara's slumberous mind filled with images of the man she remembered from her past. The handsome young musician whose eyes creased with smiles, whose graceful hands flew across the piano keys like soaring birds. She dreamed of herself, so many years ago when she, William, and their mother had lived within the enchanted land of Wakefield House, when they had greedily seized those summer days like children grabbing cream-filled cakes.

She dreamed of the grassy hills cresting around the warm, rustic stones of Wakefield House, the wildflowers popping up in fragrant clusters, the gliding foam of the sea as it surged forth to meet the sandstone cliffs hugging the coast.

Sebastian Hall was inextricably woven into the fabric of those very memories because it was there, in Dorset, where Clara had first encountered him in all his vibrant, unruly glory. At balls and dinner parties, he'd enticed people with the beauty of his performances and the allure of his attention.

She'd watched him from a distance, delighted by the way his

charm seemed so genuine. He looked directly at people when he spoke to them. He listened. He laughed. He wore his prestige and talent like a cloak that had been bequeathed to him—not as if he deserved the honor but as if he knew he was fortunate to have received it.

And when she woke from the secret warmth of such dreams, the ash-colored light of London spilling into her room, Clara remembered that in the past ten years, all of that had fallen away.

For her. And now, it seemed, for him. But why? How?

Her encounter with Sebastian in the Hanover Square rooms had kindled an intense curiosity to know the truth of what had happened to him. Now, with dreams still clinging to her like threads, that curiosity almost eclipsed her persistent ache of loss.

She dressed quickly and splashed cold water on her face, the shock of it returning her to her senses. Nothing could divert her from her purpose, not even memories of a man who had once seemed the epitome of everything she wanted. Everything good and kind.

She scrubbed a towel over her face and took a wooden box from her dressing table. She removed the lid and looked at the contents—a dozen satin ribbons jumbled together in a rainbow of colors.

Red, yellow, blue, green. She dumped them onto the scarred table. The ribbons spilled into a heap like the tangled cobweb of a vivid, exotic spider.

Clara rubbed the length of a red ribbon between her fingers, then a green one. Although she knew it wasn't the case, she imagined that each ribbon felt different. The red ribbon was slippery and warm, the green smooth-textured like a new leaf, the yellow coarse like the rind of a lemon, the blue polished as a tissue-paper sky.

As she stood looking at the ribbons, a threadlike sunbeam sliced through the fog and shone against the vibrant satin. More recent memories flashed through her. She pushed aside the dark ones in favor of happier thoughts of her boy with his chestnut hair and missing front tooth. When she thought of Andrew like this, she could almost believe she would one day hold him in her arms again and live within the folds of joy and safety.

Clara tucked the ribbons back into the box and went downstairs. Tom had lit fires in the hearth and turned on the lamps in the drawing room, which served as the main exhibition room of Blake's Museum of Automata. Years ago, her uncle had purchased the town house as both his residence and workshop, but when word of his creations began to grow, he opened the house to visitors.

Dozens of his automata and mechanical toys were displayed on shelves, alongside various machine parts, wires, and tools that Clara was forever trying to contain. Since coming to live with her uncle over a year ago, she had tried to make the museum more of a profitable business, which meant turning the main rooms into exhibition spaces and trying to convince Uncle Granville to keep the mechanics in his workshop.

She opened the curtains in the drawing room and parlor, admitting a watery grayish light. Shelves lined the walls, cluttered with adjustable animals, painted musical boxes, novelty clocks with moving pictures, and mechanical performers and musicians. She straightened the objects, cleared away a tangle of wires her uncle had left on a table, and dusted the surfaces.

"Mrs. Shepherd?" A woman's voice drifted from the foyer.

Clara left the room, schooling her features into a polite expression of cordiality. Mrs. Rosemary Fox stood in the foyer, which also served as the reception room for the museum. She pulled off her rain-speckled cloak, her tall figure slender and rigid as a tree branch.

"Is it nine already?" Clara glanced at the clock, a bit disconcerted to think she'd lost track of time.

"Only just." Mrs. Fox rubbed her gloved hands together and shivered. Her skin was bleached of color, her sharp, elegant features pinched from the dreariness and cold. "I don't expect we'll receive many visitors in this weather."

"Mrs. Marshall hasn't arrived yet, but I'll fetch you a pot of tea."

"There's no need to bother."

"I wouldn't have offered if it was a bother." Clara went to the kitchen while Mrs. Fox began straightening the papers and ledgers that covered the front desk.

After brewing the tea, Clara found several currant buns and put them on the tray along with a cup and saucer. She brought it all to Mrs. Fox and placed it on the desk, where the other woman had stacked the museum's admission receipts.

"Any word from Mr. Blake?" Mrs. Fox poured her own tea and added sugar.

"Yes, he's expected to return tomorrow, thank goodness, so he'll be at Lady Rossmore's ball. It would be a great misfortune if we missed the opportunity to secure her patronage."

After seeing one of Granville's mechanical toys on display at a gallery on Regent Street, Lady Rossmore had paid a visit to his Museum of Automata. She'd been utterly delighted with Granville's creations and insisted that he create something entirely new and astonishing for debut at one of her famous balls in support of the Society of Musicians. Only after Clara had convinced him had Uncle Granville agreed to present Millicent, the Musical Lady, an automaton on which he had been working for months.

"Lady Rossmore has already expressed interest in commissioning an automaton with dancing dolls," Clara said.

Mrs. Fox's expression didn't change, but her dark-lashed eyes flickered upward for an instant. "I believe it's more important that Mr. Blake continues to work as he wishes, rather than be indebted to a patron."

"He won't be able to work without patronage," Clara replied, her voice tart. "We've several appointments next week to discuss special commissions, so it's important that Uncle Granville be present."

"I'm certain Mr. Blake views no other meeting as important as that of consoling and assisting Monsieur Dupree's bereaved family." Mrs. Fox held her teacup in both hands, as if attempting to warm her chilled fingers. Her eyes remained steady on Clara's face.

Clara stepped back. Shame curdled in her stomach. Of course, Rosemary Fox was right. Her uncle had remained close to Monsieur Dupree and his family in the twenty years since completing his apprenticeship. When Granville received word that his mentor and former teacher had died, he'd wasted no time in procuring a ticket to Paris.

"Yes, well, he'll return in time to conduct the demonstration, so that's what matters," Clara said. "I expect Millicent will garner a significant amount of attention from her ladyship's guests as well."

"If you believe that is for the best, then I shall not argue," Mrs. Fox murmured.

Clara's shoulders tightened with irritation. In the thirteen months since she had come to live with Uncle Granville, Clara had found that though Mrs. Fox was sometimes circumspect with her opinions, every flicker of her gaze, every nuance of her expression, carried a weight of meaning.

Self-righteous meaning, Clara thought. Mrs. Fox possessed the air of a woman who had never done anything wrong in her life, who shaped herself to the world rather than expecting the world to accommodate her.

Safe though it might be, how one actually accomplished anything with such a manner, Clara had not the faintest idea. Then again, Mrs. Fox likely had little reason to harbor fear so caustic it would forever scrape her throat like saltwater.

Feeling as if the scales of balance had tipped decisively in

Rosemary Fox's direction during this conversation, Clara nodded toward the array of ledgers and papers on the desk.

"I've ordered new curtains for the front room. Please ensure the bill is listed in the museum accounts and not those of the household."

"Very well." Mrs. Fox nudged a stack of letters toward her. "The morning's post, I believe."

Clara leafed through the stack. Her heart stuttered when she saw one stamped with the seal of her uncle's solicitor. Clutching the letter in her fist, she hurried toward the music room.

With shaking fingers, she tore open the letter.

Dear Mr. Blake and Mrs. Shepherd,

We regret to inform you of the final ruling handed down 4 October, 1854, by the Court of Chancery at Lincoln's Inn Hall, Chancery Lane, regarding the ownership of Wakefield House, a property located at...

Several neat rows of writing swept across the page, but individual phrases jumped out and stabbed one by one into Clara's heart.

Upheld conditions of the trust...possession of the house remains in the hands of Mrs. Clara Shepherd...prohibited from selling or bequeathing the house...

Regret.

Our deepest apologies.

Final ruling.

No further recourse.

The letter fluttered from Clara's limp fingers. She stared at a table piled high with layers of silk and tangled ribbons. For a moment, she was numb, trying to deflect the emotions converging upon her with the force of a battering ram.

Wakefield House was the only point of advantage she had against her father, the only thing she possessed that Lord Fairfax wanted. The financial obligations of Manley Park, including a new studhorse and the cost of a new wing he'd added onto the house, as well as the mortgages of his other properties, had left him facing bankruptcy.

If Wakefield House were transferred to his name, Fairfax could then sell it and use the funds to settle some of his debts. But the terms of the trust forbade Clara from either selling or signing over the property to anyone, which meant she could not offer it to her father with the proposal that he relinquish custody of Andrew in exchange.

Now the courts had made the terms of the trust inviolable.

Regret... apologies.... regret... no further recourse...

Clara's heart was crushed like a piece of paper. Anguish roiled through her. The clock chimed. She clenched her hands as a gleaming image of her son rose through her despair.

She *had* to think of another strategy to get him back. She had no other choice. There would never be another choice except to fight and fight and fight again.

Her father's soul had twisted long ago like tangled ivy choking the breath from a tree. And if Clara didn't do something now, Fairfax's grip would suffocate both her and her son.

CHAPTER 4

*S*ebastian stepped from the carriage in front of Blake's Museum of Automata. He hadn't expected that helping Jacob locate the plans for some incomprehensible machine—plans purported to be at this museum—would mean an excuse to see Clara Whitmore again. That alone lent his task a new and welcome sense of purpose.

Anticipation flickered to life in him as he thought of his encounter with her two nights prior. He couldn't ask her outright about the machine plans that Jacob sought, but perhaps he could convince her to reveal what she knew.

If anything.

Even if his efforts came to naught, the moment to approach her could not have been better—she knew him from her past, and he might see her again at Lady Rossmore's ball. Like a cat seeking entry into a garden mousehole, all he needed to do was paw at the opening until it widened just enough.

A fence wrapped around the front garden of what appeared to be a former town house. Wrought-iron balconies and pedimented windows perforated the façade of the building, and a crooked metal sign hung on the fence proclaiming the museum's hours.

Sebastian knocked on the door and waited, hunching his shoulders against the cold morning drizzle. He knocked again, louder. He checked his pocket watch, then turned the door handle and stepped inside.

A single light glowed in the foyer, illuminating a long desk covered with papers. The doors to what had once been the dining and drawing rooms stood open. Mechanical toys, boxes, and clock parts cluttered the tables and shelves along with an array of tools—saws, chisels, planes, hammers—and limbs of porcelain dolls and animals.

Eerie place with its dismembered dolls, twisted bits of metal, and frayed wires. Dirty windows. Faded wallpaper, peeling paint. Musty smell, greenish brown like decaying moss.

Not wanting to hear the sound of his own voice in the silence, Sebastian ventured farther. Another door stood open at the end of a corridor, spilling light onto the worn carpet. Placing his hand on the door, he pushed it open.

And stopped. Sunlight bloomed through the vast windows of what must have once been the music room. Tables were strewn with brilliant fabrics—green silk, red velvet, blue satin. Ribbons and gold braid cascaded from their spools, spilling onto the floor in colorful puddles. Paintbrushes, wires, balls of thread, and pots of paint cluttered a shelf, along with feathers, flowers, bits of tulle and gauze, garlands.

In the midst of this bright wonderland, Clara Whitmore sat, her dark head bent as she worked a needle through a piece of cloth. She wore a plain cotton dress protected by a white apron. Stripes of blue and red paint smeared the bodice. The coil of hair at the back of her head had loosened, streaming tendrils over her nape.

Something crackled through Sebastian at the sight of her, an energy that made his spine straighten and his blood warm.

He cleared his throat. She didn't move.

"Miss Whitmore?"

She looked up. "Oh, I'm sorry." She put down her sewing and hurried around the table. "I didn't know anyone was here."

"I knocked."

"I didn't hear. Mrs. Fox must have stepped out." She stopped, as if suddenly aware who had entered. "Mr. Hall."

"Good morning, Miss Whitmore." He glanced at her paint-covered apron. "New fashion, is it?"

She gave him an odd look, as if he'd said something entirely stupid. Which he supposed he had.

Rubbing the back of his neck, he crushed a swell of embarrassment. He'd have to scrape the rust off his once-effortless charm, abandoned in recent months, if he intended to beguile this woman.

"Shepherd," she said.

"I beg your pardon?"

"My surname is Shepherd." Her jaw tensed. "I am Mrs. Clara Shepherd."

A stone sank in Sebastian's stomach. "Ah. I apologize. I wasn't aware."

"I am a widow, Mr. Hall. My husband passed away over a year ago." Just as it had the other day when he asked about her father, a shutter closed over her features, rebuffing further query. She reached behind her to unfasten the ties of her apron. "Now how may I assist you?"

He knew well enough not to press her. Not now, at least.

"Have you word on your uncle's return?" he asked.

"I expect him back tomorrow."

If Sebastian had thought the lights of the Hanover Square building were responsible for the strange color of her eyes, he'd been mistaken. Sunlight exposed the truth of all appearances, and even now, Clara Shepherd's eyes gleamed with violet and blue flecks.

Then those unusual eyes flickered to look at his mouth...and lingered. Her intent perusal affected him with a tangible power, warming his skin like the caress of fingertips and making him want to feel that rich gaze sliding across the rest of his body.

She lifted her eyes back to his. Faint color crested on her cheekbones, as if she'd done something she shouldn't do. As if she'd thought something she shouldn't think.

Sebastian hoped she had. Certainly his goal would prove easier to attain if Mrs. Clara Shepherd were intrigued by him from the outset. Not to mention that he rather enjoyed her disconcerted reaction, the touch of heat in her eyes and the blush surging across her pale skin.

Yet he also needed to ensure she was at ease in his presence. To deflect her embarrassment, he swept a hand behind him to encompass the house.

"In your uncle's absence, perhaps you would be good enough to provide me with a tour?" he asked.

"Yes, of course." She placed her apron on a table and slipped past him to the corridor.

Sebastian followed. Cold air swirled in from the foyer. Before him, Clara stopped at the sight of an older woman removing her cloak. She turned to look at Clara. As their gazes met, a tension brittle as spun sugar threaded the air.

"Mrs. Fox, please do inform me should you step out," Clara said.

"I beg your pardon, Mrs. Shepherd." The other woman's tone was the dry, brownish yellow color of a dead leaf. She tossed a newspaper onto the front desk. "I went to fetch a paper since it appears Tom forgot to this morning."

She swept to the desk, adjusting her skirts as she settled behind it like a queen taking to her throne. She lifted a ledger from a stack with long, gloved hands and proceeded to open the thick tome and peruse the pages.

Sebastian saw irritation lace across Clara's straight shoulders.

He stared at the nape of her neck, the slender white column soft-ened by wisps of hair, cupped by the collar of her gown. Her supple muscles tightened as she strode forward into the space between her and Mrs. Fox.

"This is Mr. Sebastian Hall." Clara spoke with precise formal-ity. "I shall be providing him with a tour of the museum. If you would please inform Mrs. Marshall, we'll take tea after the tour is concluded."

Mrs. Fox gave a short nod. "Of course." She ran her finger over a column in the ledger. "You've not recorded the admission."

"Mr. Hall is here as my guest."

"Nonetheless." Mrs. Fox gave Sebastian a look sharp enough to slice through leather. "The admission fee, sir, is one shilling."

"I've no coin at present, but my footman—"

"You needn't pay, Mr. Hall," Clara hastened to assure him. "Please, do come into the drawing room. We'll begin there."

"Mrs. Shepherd, I must protest your decision to allow a visitor to enter without paying the admission fee," Mrs. Fox said.

"And I must protest your concern." Clara opened the door and bade Sebastian precede her. "In my uncle's absence, my decisions are not to be countermanded and my guests are certainly not to be insulted. Please inform Mrs. Marshall about the tea tray."

Sebastian ducked past the older woman's aura of disapproval and into the safety of the drawing room. Clara half-closed the door behind her.

"I apologize," she said. "Mrs. Fox possesses an unfortunate tendency to believe she knows best. Her departed husband used to be Uncle Granville's assistant."

"I don't wish to cause ill feelings between you," Sebastian said, though it was clear such acrimony already lived between the two women. "I'll tell my footman to—"

"No. I've said you are my guest, and my guest you shall remain. Mrs. Fox handles the museum's accounts, but she has no authority in the running of the place."

She spread her hands over the front of her dress. Uncertainty flashed in her violet-blue eyes for an instant, belying the confidence of her tone. "Well. Let us begin with the mechanical toys. My uncle sells them at the bazaar and gives them to children's homes."

She stepped forward to a shelf lined with toys and proceeded to show him how the turn of a key prompted a monkey to beat a tiny drum, a clown to whirl around a trapeze, a pair of geese to glide over a pond crafted of glass.

Rather in spite of himself, Sebastian was charmed by the movements of the little creatures, the delicacy of their painted faces, and costumes of bright ribbons and gauze.

"My uncle devotes most of his time to the larger automata, like Millicent," Clara explained. "But he still derives great enjoyment from toys such as these. This one is my favorite. A colleague of Uncle Granville's made it, which is why the musical element works well. Uncle Granville hasn't yet perfected that in his own creations."

She reached behind a flower-laced birdcage to twist a key, then stepped back. Two lemon-yellow canaries inside leapt from bar to bar as their beaks opened and closed in accompaniment to a melodious, chirping tune.

"Lovely, isn't it?" Clara asked. She smiled with evident pleasure as she watched the birds perform another dance.

"Indeed."

She glanced up to find him watching her. Her smile faded into an expression of disconcertion, warmth again coloring her pale skin. She turned away from him, her hands twisting the folds of her skirt.

"If you'll follow me, I'll show you my uncle's workshop and the room where we display the larger automata," she said.

They went into the foyer and past the redoubtable Mrs. Fox, who gave Sebastian another of her keen glances. He responded with an engaging smile that had the impact of a feather against stone, for all of Mrs. Fox's reaction to it.

Pity, Sebastian thought. The older woman had thick-lashed eyes and fine, elegant features that might be quite pleasing if softened with even a scrap of affability.

As he followed Clara down another corridor, a pulse swept through his chest, diluting the anxiety that had plagued him since he'd discovered the unnerving disability of his right hand. Now pleasure subsumed that dismay, sparked by the anticipation of something new.

His instincts told him that Clara Shepherd was intrigued by him. That meant a few well-placed, sweet words and persuasive smiles would have her revealing what he wanted to know before the week's end.

Five months ago, he'd have ensured she revealed it before the day's end.

They entered a former library, larger than the music room and cluttered with gears, wires, and the entrails of various machines. Clara paused beside a metal-framed figure seated on a bench.

"My uncle is currently working on this," she said, placing her hand on the curved bow of the top. "It's to be a scribe writing at a desk. Uncle Granville is planning to have him write three different poems in both English and French."

Sebastian lifted a brow. That sounded impressive, even to him. "He's ambitious, your uncle."

She didn't respond, and for a moment he didn't think she'd heard. He repeated the remark.

Clara glanced at him. "I'm sorry?"

"Your uncle. I said he was ambitious."

"Yes. You spoke earlier, didn't you?" She waved her hand beside her ear, as if batting at a pesky fly. "I don't hear very well with my left ear, so if I'm turned away I sometimes miss things."

Sebastian didn't recall her having a hearing loss when she'd been his student. Then again, he reminded himself, he didn't recall much about her at all. Shame flickered in the pit of his stomach.

"At any rate, yes," Clara said. "Uncle Granville is constantly thinking of ways to make his inventions ever more complex and unique. His mentor was a very renowned toy and clockmaker. Perhaps you've heard of him, Monsieur Jacques Dupree?"

Sebastian made a noncommittal noise in the back of his throat. Clara moved on to a different automaton.

"I'm afraid you'll have to speak with my uncle to learn about the actual mechanics involved," she said. "This one will be a couple dancing."

"Does your uncle make such things only for amusement's sake?" Sebastian asked, selecting his words with care.

"He makes clocks on occasion, which of course are eminently practical."

Aha. And Jacob had told Sebastian that coding machines contain similar mechanisms as clocks. So if Granville Blake did indeed possess the plans for the blasted thing, then he would not discuss it with just anyone.

And if Clara knew about it, she certainly would not come right out and tell him.

Yet.

"But for the most part, yes," she continued. "Uncle Granville invents the automata for his own enjoyment. We are hoping that after Saturday evening's demonstration, Lady Rossmore will offer her patronage to the museum."

"Your uncle is seeking a patron?"

"He receives a number of commissions, but a patron is always a benefit," Clara admitted. "In the meantime...perhaps I ought not to chide poor Mrs. Fox for insisting our guests pay the admission fee."

"My footman will—"

She laughed—lush, dark purple—a sound so unexpected that

Sebastian's heart twisted with both bewilderment and delight, as if he beheld a rainbow in a thunderstorm. Clara's eyes crinkled with warmth, and a quick shake of her head made curls of hair dance against her neck.

God, but she was lovely.

"I do hope your footman considers himself fortunate to be entrusted with the care of your purse," she said. "But really, Mr. Hall, I didn't intend to cause you any guilt. There is no need for you to pay the fee. Now please, join me for tea before you depart."

Sebastian followed her to the parlor, his heart still strumming with the echo of her laughter.

Ah, yes. Mustering the desire to charm Clara Shepherd would require no effort at all. He couldn't remember the last time he'd so looked forward to something.

CHAPTER 5

*W*hat does he want?

Clara concentrated on the task of pouring tea as the question revolved around her mind.

She couldn't quite believe Sebastian Hall was here solely to view the automata and mechanical toys. She had thought that the case when he first arrived, but his reaction to the inventions was curious at best, as if he appreciated their novelty but had little interest in the technical details of the machinery.

But why else would he want to speak with Uncle Granville? If he were considering commissioning a piece or patronizing the museum, then he would have simply said so.

Wouldn't he?

A scratching noise made her turn. Sebastian stood before a shelf, studying a copper cricket that rubbed its wings together and produced a sound akin to a nail scraping over glass.

"That's what I referred to when I said my uncle hasn't yet perfected the accompaniment of music to his inventions," Clara explained.

"Clearly."

"Are you...ah, may I ask the reason you need to speak with him?" She placed a cup on the table.

He turned, sliding his hands into his pockets with a pianist's grace. "Lady Rossmore spoke so highly of his work that I thought to see it for myself." He glanced back at the cricket. "Perhaps I can offer him advice on the musical component."

"If you'll leave your card, I would be happy to give it to my uncle upon his return. I'm certain he'll contact you straightaway to arrange an appointment."

She waited for him to agree and take his departure. Instead he stood looking at her, an intense gaze that appeared to contain more than mere scrutiny.

His perusal skimmed over her body, heating her from the inside out like hot cocoa on a snowy night. A tingle of warmth skimmed up her arms. Clara's heart pulsed, a light, gentle tapping reminding her of raindrops on a windowpane.

Oh, what a pleasure. So different from the thump of dread that constantly beat through her, drowning her in fear. Now, here in this moment with Sebastian Hall watching her with those warm, appreciative brown eyes, a waterfall of light spilled across the black of her soul. His look even seemed powerful enough to soothe her still-blistering knowledge of the court's final ruling about Wakefield House.

He stepped closer. His delicious scent filled her nose, sliding into her veins, awakening a spark that spread through her entire body.

Her gaze slipped from his eyes to his mouth. She could not help but be fascinated by the shape of his mouth, the curve of his smile, the tilt of his lips. She wondered how it would feel, that beautiful mouth pressed against hers, his whiskers scraping her cheek.

Oh, dear Lord.

What was she thinking? What kind of woman was she to

imagine such things when all she wanted, the *only* thing she wanted was to have…

He touched her. Sebastian slipped his left hand beneath her chin and raised her head so that she had to meet his eyes again. His palm was warm, cupping her chin with the same gentleness he might use to hold a jeweled music box. He studied her face as if he were assessing the value of a rare artifact, his dark brows drawn together, his eyes filled with curiosity.

Questions lingered in his expression. Clara did not know how to answer them, but her body responded with a quickening tempo that made her breath uncoil in her chest.

Kiss me.

The wish bloomed hard, a bright, red rose in midwinter, filling her with the glow of anticipation.

Kiss me and banish the fear.

She blinked against the sting in her eyes. Her throat tightened. She curled her fingers around Sebastian's wrist, though whether to ease his hand away or urge him to keep touching her, she did not know.

She did know that his wrist was strong in her grip, his pulse beating against her fingertips. She imagined his blood ran hot and swift through his veins, inciting his force, his intensity. She wanted to slide her hand farther up his forearm, to feel the taut muscles and sinews, the brush of coarse dark hairs across her palm.

He didn't move away. She didn't release him.

And then he lowered his head and kissed her. So warm, so light was the touch of his mouth that the center of Clara's being melted like ice sliding over a hot pane of glass.

She swallowed, parting her lips to draw in a breath. His nearness, his rough energy, sank into her blood and filled her with sensation, heat, and a yearning for something she had never known.

"Oh." Her whisper slipped like a delicacy into his mouth.

He slid his hand around to the back of her neck, drawing her closer. Her breasts brushed against his chest. Their breath mingled. He tasted like cinnamon. His tongue darted out to touch the corner of her lips, a delicious swipe that made shivers cascade through Clara's entire body.

Who have you become?

She remembered him so well from all those years ago, that affable, talented young man who could keep company with both kings and peasants. Now he was different, like a creature from mythology, filled with complexities that she could not begin to untangle. Exuding an allure that she could not resist. Wrapping her in a heat that felt instinctively comforting and *safe.*

She curled her fingers around the lapels of his coat and sank into the kiss as if it could last forever, and in that instant, she wanted it to. She wanted to stand here for all eternity with Sebastian's hand cupping her neck and his mouth caressing hers because once he stopped, once he lifted his head away from her, she knew the anguish would swamp her once again.

Her grip on him tightened. His kiss deepened. Her blood exploded with colors and light, born from the memories of who they had once been—a girl holding fast to the good in the world, and a young man of such patience and kindness.

That man would help her now, if he still existed. Clara grasped the truth of that belief as if it were sacred, and a spiral of hope filled her. She spread one hand over his broad chest, feeling his heart thump against her palm through the material of his shirt and coat. His teeth closed gently over her lower lip, whisking heat over her nerves.

The middle of her soul softened at Sebastian's nearness, the warm strength he exuded, at the nascent longing that he might prove her ally in the desperate pursuit to reclaim her son.

Andrew.

Coldness swept down her spine at the unbidden thought. Shame cut through her desire like a blade ripping into silk. She yanked herself away from Sebastian, holding her hands to her blazing cheeks as she turned away. Her heart hammered in her throat.

She had forgotten. For one brief, aching moment she had forgotten her son.

Clara inhaled a deep breath to quell her turbulent emotions before she turned back to face Sebastian. His eyes sparked with both lingering heat and wariness, as if her abrupt withdrawal had incited his own confusion.

Her heart still pounded. Oh, heavens. As a young woman, she had imagined what it would feel like to be kissed by Sebastian Hall, but she had never dreamed it would be like this.

And never had her imagination conjured the intricate weaving of emotions binding her now, all securing the strange but firm knowledge that he could somehow help her.

"I...I think you'd best go now," she stammered.

"Shall I return tomorrow?"

"My uncle should be back in the morning. If you'd like to speak with him, you are welcome to return."

"My card." His composure again intact, Sebastian removed a card from his breast pocket and placed it on the table. "Thank you for your time, Mrs. Shepherd."

Clara nodded and watched him leave. Her heartbeat began to calm. She moved closer to the door so that she could hear his voice rumble from the foyer as he exchanged a few words with Mrs. Fox, and then the front door closed.

She hurried to the window, ducking into the shadows as she watched his tall figure descend the steps. He moved with ease and a masculine grace, as if he were comfortable in his skin. He spoke to the footman, then clapped the man on the shoulder before climbing into the waiting carriage.

Odd behavior to bestow upon a footman, but such familiarity seemed suited to a man like Sebastian. He'd never appeared to be the sort concerned with propriety or the opinions of others—

though clearly something had happened in recent months to fray the edges of his character.

He is still the son of an earl. Powerful, surely, in his own right.

Anticipation flared in Clara's heart, burning away the shame of the thought. For so many years, she had tried so hard to be good, to be the woman her father and husband wanted so that, God willing, their lives would be free from turmoil.

She had agreed to marry Richard Shepherd, a man thirteen years her senior, because her father wanted to seal a business partnership and because her father's status would aid Richard's bid for a parliamentary seat.

And while the marriage had allowed Clara to escape her father's house, she remained firmly within his domain. Only by being an exemplary wife and daughter—quiet, practical, polite—could she avoid inciting her father's anger.

But when Andrew was born, Clara discovered how love could overwhelm all practical thought, like a waterfall thundering over a rocky cliff. She learned how emotion could fill her heart to bursting, how joy and fear could tangle her soul into inextricable knots. She knew what it meant to love another person without condition, without thought. She knew what her own mother had felt.

For the sole purpose of being with her son again, however, Clara would suppress even the memory of such emotions and be as calculating, as shrewd, as was necessary.

If she dared.

CHAPTER 6

"All has gone well thus far with Lady Rossmore?" Granville Blake asked. He opened the cherrywood case of a clock whose face was decorated with a landscape scene and a moving windmill.

"Indeed." Perched on a nearby stool, Clara watched her uncle fiddle with the springs and chronometer contained inside the clock. Having Uncle Granville back at home restored her sense of balance and purpose, which had been so askew since Sebastian Hall had reentered her life.

"Tom and I brought Millicent and the bench to the Hanover Square rooms," she continued, "so it's just the harpsichord now. Lady Rossmore said you could assemble the rest on Friday afternoon."

"Good, good." Granville pulled at a pinion wire and picked up a small lathe. Tufts of blond hair fell over his forehead as he frowned at an uncooperative mechanism.

Warmth spun through Clara's heart as she watched him. Her love for her uncle was stronger than ever, unstained by anger and bitterness. For many years he had tried so hard to protect her and her mother from Fairfax. Granville had kept Wakefield House out of Fairfax's hands. He had hired solicitors to wrestle Fairfax in the courts and written countless letters to her father pleading her case.

All to no avail, but Clara knew her uncle would pound a stone wall until his hands were broken and bleeding if it meant she would have her son back.

A delicate cough came from the doorway. Mrs. Fox stood there with her ramrod shoulders and cold, elegant face.

"Good morning, Mrs. Fox."

"Mrs. Shepherd." She nodded at Granville. "Welcome home, Mr. Blake."

"Yes, yes, thank you, Mrs. Fox." Granville wrenched at a part inside the clock, tossing her a quick glance over the tops of his glasses.

"How is Monsieur Dupree's family?" Mrs. Fox inquired.

"Grieving, but well," Granville replied. "Monsieur Dupree's son is shipping several more crates of machinery and supplies to me. Should arrive within a week or so. He thought I could make good use of them."

"Kind of him, especially considering the circumstances," Mrs. Fox murmured. She glanced at Clara again. "You've had no visitors yet?"

"We've been open only fifteen minutes," Clara replied.

"Yes, but the front desk should be staffed at all times during open hours."

"Uncle Granville would hear the front bell if anyone comes in."

"Anyone who enters should not be obliged to wait for someone to welcome them." Mrs. Fox turned to Granville. "And Mr. Blake, I'm certain you wish to rest after your long journey."

Granville muttered something under his breath, his attention on the entrails of the clock.

"Your bags have been brought upstairs," Mrs. Fox continued.

"And Tom is filling a bath. I suggest you make haste before the water cools. Mr. Blake. Mr. Blake!"

At the heightened pitch to her voice, Granville glanced up. "Oh, er, much obliged, Mrs. Fox."

He picked up a scape wheel and examined the pointed teeth at the edges as he walked to the door. After he'd left the room, Mrs. Fox turned to Clara.

"I've rescheduled an appointment this morning so that Mr. Blake might have a bit of time to rest," she said.

"Not Mr. Hall?"

Mrs. Fox frowned. "Mr. Hall is not listed in the appointment book."

"He told me he would come sometime this morning." Clara couldn't prevent the surge of anticipation at the thought of seeing him again, even with the memory of their kiss burning like a dark star in the back of her mind.

"Well, really, this is not terribly convenient," Mrs. Fox said. "Shall I send word to Mr. Hall to postpone the appointment?"

"No. He has been wanting to speak with Uncle Granville for several days."

"Very well, then." Mrs. Fox narrowed her eyes with disapproval and swept from the room with her skirts trailing like coal dust behind her.

Annoyance prickled at Clara's spine as she returned to the studio. She picked up her sewing again and was soon immersed in the rhythmic motion of pushing and pulling the needle through the heavy silk, a cadence that allowed her to focus on the task and empty her mind of thought.

"Meant to give this to you."

Granville came into the room and extended a mechanical toy. "From Monsieur Dupree's wife. She said he'd been intending to send it to you as soon as he finished it."

Curious, Clara took the toy. A slender male figure wearing a harlequin's costume and ruffled collar balanced on his hands atop a narrow table.

She found the key at the base of the platform and twisted it. The acrobat braced his hands on the table and lifted his body into the air, then executed a graceful somersault that curled his entire form before vaulting back to his original position.

She laughed, delighted by the intricate, whimsical action.

"For your collection," Granville said, his smile edged with sadness.

Clara dragged a large wooden chest out from beneath a table and unlatched the lock. Several dozen toys lay inside the chest, some mechanical inventions that sprang into action at the turn of a key and others well-crafted stationary figures.

All were decorated with great care, bearing costumes of silk and satin, tiny jewels and buttons, intricately painted faces. There were ducks that waddled and quacked, dancing animals, wooden trains, singing birds, spinning tops, a shepherd who piped a tune on a flute, and a Turkish conjurer who concealed three silver balls beneath golden goblets.

"I'll write Madame Dupree a letter of thanks this afternoon," she said.

"She'll appreciate that." Granville gazed at her. "I'm sorry, Clara. I've instructed my solicitor to look into the matter of selling or transferring Wakefield House to your father again, but there's not much one can do against a final ruling."

She gripped the acrobat. "Perhaps we could appeal to the justices themselves?"

Granville just looked at her, his blue eyes swimming with sympathy. Clara's heart closed in on itself as she sank down onto a chair and rested her face in her hands. A second later, her uncle's arm circled her shoulders.

"Never give up hope, my dear," he murmured.

"Such a fool I am," she whispered, swallowing hard against a rush of tears.

"No mother is a fool who wants her child back," Granville said.

No, but she was a fool to think she could ever appease her father into giving up custody of Andrew.

No further recourse, the solicitor claimed.

Clara could not believe it. She could not fathom a world in which a defenseless boy, her *son,* would be condemned to a life of isolation. And that she, as his mother, would have *no further recourse.*

Not wanting her uncle to bear witness to her dismay yet again, she pushed herself upright. She swiped at a stray tear and straightened her skirts. "Well, we'd best get back to work. There's a great deal to do before Lady Rossmore's event."

Granville looked as if he wanted to say more, but of course they both knew there was nothing left to say.

After Granville returned to his workshop, Clara picked up the acrobat and turned the key again to watch the dexterous flip and spin. How Andrew would love such a creation. For once, a flutter of happiness rather than pain followed the thought.

She put the acrobat on a nearby table so she could see it from her sewing chair. She sat down and picked up the green silk again.

Push, pull. Push, pull. Don't think. Don't remember.

"I believe she might have granted me a smile."

The deep, clear voice came from the doorway. Clara looked up with a start. Sebastian Hall stood with one hand on the jamb.

"What…oh." She embedded the needle into the silk. "Do you refer to the formidable Mrs. Fox?"

"I do indeed. At least, I think it was a smile. Might have been more of a grimace, now that I think on it."

Clara smiled. She felt his appreciative gaze from across the room, heating her like sunshine.

"Now *that,*" he said, "is most assuredly a smile, which I could never mistake for something else."

A surge of pleasure reddened Clara's cheeks. Oh, but he was still charming, wasn't he? Even with that combination of fatigue and restlessness clinging to him, his eyes warmed as he looked at her.

And she was glad of it. Glad of the evidence that Sebastian Hall's allure still appeared intact, though buried beneath his soul-weary exterior.

"You're here to see my uncle," she said, putting the sewing aside.

Disconcertion flashed across his features. "Your uncle has returned already?"

"Yes, just several hours ago." Clara suppressed the sudden thought...no, the *hope*...that perhaps Sebastian had come to see her and not Uncle Granville. Again, that hope was followed by the instinctive sense that he could prove her ally, even if as yet she had no idea how.

Sebastian continued to watch her as she rose and smoothed her apron. He paused beside a table covered with folds of silk and satin and sank his gloved hand into a swath of orange silk.

She watched his long fingers caress the material, then slid her gaze over the length of his arm, across his shoulder to his face. He looked much as he had yesterday—clad in a forest-green, superfine coat and snow-white linen shirt, but still with shadows smudging his dark eyes, and furrows bracketing his mouth.

What does he want?

The question sprang into her mind again, a riddle she couldn't solve. Sebastian might well enjoy the spectacle of the automata, but she could not believe he held the mechanisms in abiding interest. He'd hardly cast Millicent a glance when they'd first met in the Hanover Square building.

Perhaps that had been because he'd been too occupied looking at Clara.

Warmth suffused her entire body as she recalled his tangible scrutiny. She couldn't recall another man, not even Richard, appraising her with such blatant thoroughness.

And appearing to like what he saw.

Pushing aside the unexpected pleasure of the thought, she ducked her head and hurried past him. "If you'll wait here, please, I'll fetch my uncle. I told him to expect you."

She went to seek out Granville and found him opening several boxes of machine parts Tom had delivered yesterday. Upon hearing of their visitor, he washed the dust from his hands and accompanied her back to the studio.

"Mr. Hall, welcome to our museum." Granville extended his hand.

"A pleasure to make your acquaintance, Mr. Blake." Sebastian greeted him with a nod, ignoring the other man's outstretched hand.

A frown tugged at Clara's mouth as an awkward pause filled the air before Granville lowered his arm back to his side.

Sebastian spoke in a pleasant tone, as if nothing untoward had just occurred. "Your niece has been most accommodating in your absence."

"Pleased to hear it," Granville said. "How else might I assist you?"

"I'm interested in learning more about how the automata are actually put together. And how you intend to use music in an auxiliary fashion to correspond with the actions of the figures."

Clara blinked. Perhaps she was wrong about Sebastian's interest in mechanics.

Out of curiosity, she followed him and Granville back to his workshop, where Granville proceeded to drone on about clock-work mechanisms, bellows, pin joints, and cylinders. He took Sebastian to the former dining room of the town house, where he drafted his diagrams, and unfurled scrolls etched with detailed plans for toys and automata.

Sebastian nodded as Granville waved his hand over the drawings and explained how he intended to bring them to fruition.

"Your niece mentioned you also make clocks?" he asked.

"On occasion, yes. Usually when commissioned. Not quite as interesting as automata, I've found, though often the mechanisms are similar."

"And do you construct anything else?"

Granville shrugged. "I could make anything, I suppose, with the right plans. Why? Have you got something in mind?"

"I've a sister-in-law who is a mathematician," Sebastian said. "She and my brother live abroad now, but she once told me there are machines that can calculate sums. Have you heard of such a thing?"

"Certainly," Granville said. "Quite interesting. My mentor, Monsieur Dupree, has done a bit of work with arithmometers, but there's some difficulty with the multiplying element. Did you wish to commission such a machine?"

"Possibly, though I'm also inquiring for my younger brother Jacob. He lives in St. Petersburg as well and is far more mechanically minded than I am."

Ah. That explained it a bit, then, Clara thought.

"Jacob heard there are also machines that can transmit messages in cipher," Sebastian continued. "Do you know about those?"

"Not in any detail, no," Granville said. "Though if you'd like, I can give you the address of a gentleman who lives in Southwark. He knows more than I do about machines such as those. Perhaps your brother might like to correspond directly with him."

"I'd be much obliged."

As Sebastian turned away from the table, Clara swore she saw frustration flash in his dark eyes.

"If you'll both go into the drawing room, I'll bring tea in," she suggested. "You can discuss this further."

Thoughts tumbled through her mind as she went to find Mrs.

Marshall. Again she was seized by the sense that Sebastian could prove useful. She didn't know how, but surely the son of an earl would have access to resources she lacked. And she was not too proud to plead for anything, not where Andrew was concerned.

She brought the tray into the drawing room and began to pour the tea. Sebastian twisted the key on a mechanical birdcage that Uncle Granville had been working on. The birds whistled a reedy melody that seemed at odds with the delicacy of the feathered larks.

"You ought to use Haydn," Sebastian remarked.

"Haydn?" Granville repeated.

"'The Lark' Quartet, opus sixty-four, number five," Sebastian said. "The first violin imitates the call of larks, which would be more suitable than...what is that supposed to be? A cello?"

Granville straightened and scratched his head. "I don't know. Found it at a music shop and tried to translate it into the engineering mechanism. Doesn't quite work, does it?"

"Not quite, no."

Sebastian glanced at Clara, his brown eyes crinkling with warm amusement. The sight arced pleasure through her, evoking memories of the dashing, vital pianist who had made her heart sing.

The glimpses of that young man made her wonder if *her* former self, the girl who'd once plucked wildflowers from the grassy hills of Dorset and felt the sea foam around her bare feet, hadn't been entirely extinguished.

No. She pushed the thought aside as she returned to the studio. There was no sense in such useless imaginings. Whether or not that girl still existed made no difference in her current life, which was wholly focused on reclaiming Andrew.

And in order to achieve that goal, she needed to formulate a new plan. One that might somehow include Sebastian Hall.

CHAPTER 7

A half hour passed after Clara left the drawing room. Her uncle's exhaustive knowledge of machinery and automata appeared endless, and while Sebastian recognized the innovation in what the man was doing, he couldn't muster the slightest interest in auxiliary levers and polar coordinates.

Whatever those were.

"It's the bellows mechanism that produces sound," Granville continued, "and a certain degree of pressure articulates the vowels and consonants, then if one controls the valve with a cam attached to a crank…"

Bloody hell.

Sebastian crushed a yawn between his teeth. "What are your thoughts on the current political climate, Mr. Blake?" he interrupted.

The other man looked startled, as well he probably should considering the abruptness of the question.

"Oh, er, the war, you mean? Just read the report about the Battle of the Alma, which seems to have been quite a decisive allied victory. They even took two Russian generals prisoner. No offense intended."

"None taken." Sebastian held no strong loyalty to Russia, though he'd spent much time there as a child and on several concert tours. Now his desire to return to the country sprang from the fact that two of his brothers and his sister-in-law lived in St. Petersburg. "I've just read a report that Alma is considered a precursor to the rapid fall of Sebastopol."

"I hadn't heard that."

Sebastian studied the other man. Clearly Granville's unassuming demeanor concealed a sharp intelligence, but how far did he extend that intelligence? Granville hadn't expressed much interest in...what had he called them?...arithmometers, which made Sebastian wonder if he even knew about the cipher machine plans.

Sebastian set his cup down with a force that rattled the saucer. He thanked Granville for his time and the sharing of his very comprehensive knowledge, then went in search of Clara again.

He returned to the studio and paused in the doorway. Clara knelt on the floor, her skirts pooled around her and her head bent as she rummaged through a wooden chest.

He admired her for a moment, casting his glance over the delicate curves of her profile and the arch of her pretty neck gilded with loose chestnut tendrils. He liked the way her pins and ribbons seemed unable to contain the length of her hair, making it necessary for her brush the locks back with a sweep of her elegant hand.

And that refinement concealed a steel-like resolve evident in the determined line of her chin and unflinching gaze.

She turned to look at him. An unexpected smile widened her mouth, creating two shallow dimples in her cheeks. Warmth uncurled in Sebastian's chest.

"Has Uncle Granville bored you to tears yet?" she asked.

"Not at all," Sebastian lied. "We were discussing the machines that solve mathematical problems."

"Is that so? Well, if anyone would know about such things, it would certainly be Uncle Granville." She rose to her feet. "Did you find what you were looking for?"

Not exactly. But I might have found something I wasn't looking for.

"I hope I soon shall," he replied, advancing with certain but careful steps. He still did not know how best to approach her, a circumstance he attributed to her incongruity rather than his tarnished charm.

He paused in front of her and reached up to flick a strand of hair away from her cheek, pale as cream. Instead of surrendering to a blush this time, Clara gazed at him with somewhat startling directness.

"You have...ah, you have extraordinary eyes," Sebastian said, studying the pearly color of her irises.

"My grandfather used to call them the eyes of a witch, though he meant it in a fond way." She arched a brow in amusement. "I think."

"I'm sure of it. They're quite beguiling."

"Thank you." She slanted those eyes to his mouth, her glance like the brush of silk. Not the first time he had caught her looking at his mouth. He wondered what she found so interesting about it.

If anything. Perhaps she just didn't know where else to look, though he suspected that thought wouldn't have occurred to him with any other woman. If Clara Shepherd didn't know where else to look, she'd stare at the wall behind him. She wasn't coy.

He glanced at the interior of the chest in which numerous toys were packed with care.

"Your uncle's creations?" he asked.

"Yes." She placed her hand on the lid and closed it. "I keep them for my son."

"You have a son?"

"His name is Andrew." She pushed the chest away with a hard

shove. Wood screeched against the floor. "He is seven years old. He lives with my father on his Surrey estate."

Though Sebastian wanted to know more, the tone of her voice repelled further inquiry. He heard the emotions beneath her surface-thin remark, like a veneer of ocean ice, and he sensed the effort it took her to keep that façade from breaking. He knew because the very same struggle now ruled his own life.

"What do you want?" Clara asked, lifting her dark lashes once again.

His heart thumped hard against his rib cage. "What do I want?"

"From my uncle. From…from me."

"I—"

She gave a quick, dismissive shake of her head. "Do not tell me you want to understand the functioning of the automata. I saw you try to conceal a yawn at least three times during Uncle Granville's lengthy discourse."

"It's true that I'd rather have been speaking with you."

"You'd rather have been speaking with anyone, as long as the topic was of interest to you." She swept a hand behind her head to tuck a lock of hair back into place. "And why do you seek to flatter me so often? Why did you kiss me? What do you want?"

Sebastian fought a brief battle with himself. If he told her the truth, that he was seeking plans for a secret project, she could very well banish him from the museum, and then he'd never find the plans.

On the other hand, this circumventing was getting him nowhere, and he had a better chance with Clara than he did with Granville.

Her eyes steadied on his face. He detected a faint tremor in the full line of her mouth, a tremor she tried to suppress by pressing her lips together.

"I might be able to help you," she said, "but you must tell me the truth."

The truth. His right hand flexed, the fingers tightening. No one knew the truth.

Emotions swayed in Clara's strange eyes. Eyes of a witch, indeed. They pulled him in like an undertow, drawing him toward their fathomless depths. His intention to charm her into revealing her knowledge of the cipher machine faded to transparency. He could no more mislead this woman than he could stay away from her. He no longer wanted to.

He did, however, want to know her secrets. He almost burned with the desire to explore all the pleats and folds of the tumultuous soul he sensed lay beneath her lovely façade.

He took a breath, felt his pulse pounding in his throat. His brother had asked him to keep a confidence, but Sebastian needed to earn Clara's trust. And honesty was the only way he could achieve that.

"I am seeking the specifications for a certain machine," he finally said. "I've word that your uncle might have them in his possession. The machine was invented by Jacques Dupree, and I have reason to believe he sent the plans to your uncle shortly before his death."

"How do you know such a thing?"

He didn't actually *know* much of anything. "My younger brother told me about them. He lives in St. Petersburg and corresponded with Monsieur Dupree about his inventions."

"What type of machine is it?"

"One that transmits telegraphic messages," Sebastian said. "Apparently in an…innovative fashion."

"But why would Monsieur Dupree have sent the plans to my uncle?"

"I don't know," Sebastian admitted. "Jacob said it was likely to ensure their safe-keeping. You don't know anything about them?"

"I do not." Even though her words were forceful, a faint tremble shuddered beneath them. "But if I did, why would I give them to you?"

"I will pay you for them."

"That decision would be Uncle Granville's, not mine." Her gaze slid past him then, and Sebastian sensed the presence of her uncle.

He turned. Granville looked from Clara to him, concern darkening his eyes behind his glasses.

"Everything all right, Clara?" Granville asked.

"Yes."

Sebastian expected Clara to ask her uncle about the machine's plans. She didn't. His eyes met hers. She stared at him, as if willing him not to reveal his intentions. He gave a slight shake of his head. A smile tugged at her lips.

There it was again, that astute gleam in her eyes, as if she was twisting his revelation around in her mind and examining it from all angles. As if she was trying to determine how she might use his goal to her own advantage.

Rather than be unnerved by the thought, an odd warmth spun through Sebastian. By telling Clara about his need for the plans, he sensed he had given her something she sought. And whatever she chose to ask in return, he thought he would surely grant her wish. No matter what it was.

Clara watched Sebastian through the window as he strode down the steps to the waiting carriage. A heavy curtain seemed to part inside her, allowing streamers of light to filter through. The nascent hope she'd experienced since he had kissed her now bloomed into something tangible and real.

She had so desperately wanted to believe he could help her, yet that belief had been tangled up in her memories of his goodness and generosity. And while she still believed he would assist her in any way he could, for she could not imagine anything less of him, she needed more from him than he might be prepared to give.

Unless she could offer him something in return, and now he had told her exactly what that might be. If she found the plans he sought, she had all the pieces necessary to strike a bargain with him.

Wakefield House belonged to her. Although the courts had decreed that she couldn't sell it or bequeath it to anyone else, she could ensure that the law transfer it to someone else's name.

Sebastian's name. There was nothing to prohibit *him* from then giving the property to her father with the proposition that he release Andrew to her custody.

Clara pressed a hand to her chest. A tremble, both exhilarating and terrifying, swept through her down to her toes.

She needed to marry Sebastian Hall.

CHAPTER 8

"Uncle Granville, they must be here." Clara peeled back the flaps of the box and looked inside. She had spent most of the afternoon since Sebastian's departure rummaging through the boxes and crates stacked in her uncle's workshop.

"My dear, if Monsieur Dupree intended to send me something important, he certainly would have given me some forewarning," Granville said.

"There was no letter?" She lifted a stack of papers from the box.

"Not that I'm aware of." Granville cracked open a crate to reveal several coils of copper wire and drawplates. "Could be any number of things, really. Bit of a collector, Dupree. He always said he never knew when he might need something, so he wasn't apt to throw things away."

"He gave things away, though." Clara removed another sheaf of papers from the box and leafed through them. "To you, at least. Do you think he sent anything to his other apprentices?"

"Couldn't say." Granville shrugged. "He had a number of them, though, so it's certainly likely. But plans for a telegraph machine..." He shook his head. "Can't think of a reason he'd send them to me, in all honesty. I'm sure several of his other apprentices were more well-versed in telegraph machines and the like."

"Do you correspond with the others?" Clara asked, even though her heart began a steady drop to her stomach. "Can we write and ask them if they've received any such specifications?"

"We can try, yes." Granville frowned.

They both knew that such a course would take an indeterminate amount of time, and the result might well prove fruitless. And the more time they wasted, the longer Andrew would remain under Fairfax's hand.

Clara gripped the side of a crate so hard that a splinter pierced her palm. She gripped harder, welcoming the pain to try to distract the wave of rage. She did not know how much longer she could bear it—not knowing how her father was treating Andrew or even how her son fared.

"Uncle Granville."

"Yes?"

She detached her hand from the crate and rubbed the bleeding wound in her palm. "I must find the plans." She waved a hand to encompass the numerous crates and boxes cluttering the room. "I don't know that I'll even recognize them if I find them, but I have to look."

"Yes, of course. I'll help." Granville straightened and removed his glasses, polishing the lenses on his shirt. "But if Monsieur Dupree did send me the plans, he had a reason for doing so. I'm not certain handing them over to Sebastian Hall is a wise idea."

"What if it helps me get Andrew back?"

"How can Mr. Hall help you get Andrew back?"

"I don't know that he can." Clara bit her bottom lip, unsettled by the confession. As simple as the arrangement sounded, there was no guarantee her father would actually accept Wakefield House in exchange for Andrew.

On the other hand, Fairfax had been fighting hard to get his hands on the property. And Clara had nothing left to lose.

"Go to your father first," Granville urged, his blue eyes filled with concern. "Ask him to agree to the bargain. You needn't take such drastic measures yet."

"He won't see me," Clara said. "Even if he did, what if he took exception to Sebastian's involvement? What if he tried to stop it?" She shook her head. "No. When I approach my father again, I *must* to be able to offer him Wakefield House. If I have no leverage, he'll think nothing of shutting me out again."

She opened another box, a fresh resolve spurring her forward. She tried not to think that if she found the plans, she would have what Sebastian wanted and could then make her proposal.

For *marriage.*

Her heart stumbled as a wave of heat and trepidation swept through her. Even if it was for practical ends as her union with Richard had been, Clara could not imagine herself wedded to a man like Sebastian with his rough, restless energy and coiled secrets. With his charm, which warmed her blood, and his devilish smile, which made her melt.

But it didn't matter what she could imagine, did it? The swirls of heat and color evoked by Sebastian's presence alone didn't matter. Only one thing mattered.

"I must find the plans," she repeated, half to herself and half to Granville. "And when I do, I'll marry Sebastian Hall and get my son back."

But first she had to convince Sebastian. Now that she knew what he wanted, she could approach him with a proposal from which they each benefited. She just had to pray he wanted the plans badly enough not to reject her outlandish request.

Several hours later, after Granville had gone to bed, Clara conceded defeat for the day. Weariness clenched her muscles tight as she dampened all the hearths and ensured the candles were extinguished, except for the one she used to light the path to her bedchamber. She placed the flickering candle on her bedside table, then washed in cold water and changed into a shift.

After combing the tangles from her hair, she climbed into bed. Her arms ached from prying open crates and boxes, and her hands were sore and dry. Even as exhaustion claimed her body, her mind twisted around and around the idea of marriage to Sebastian and all the implications buried within.

At the heart of it lay the bright, polished jewel of her son, a treasure long concealed by a veil of darkness. And after struggling for so many months to futile ends, Clara feared to hope that this time might be different. Perhaps not even Sebastian could rip away the obstacles keeping her from Andrew, but she held fast to her instinctive trust in him.

She pressed a hand to her chest and felt the rhythm of her heartbeat. Even as her mind sought to convince her that marriage to Sebastian Hall would be no different from her union with Richard in its practicality, Clara's heart vehemently protested such a comparison.

On the surface, perhaps, it would be a pragmatic arrangement, one that might lead to the fulfillment of her deepest, most powerful wish, but beneath the veneer of convenience, such a marriage would be laced with the restless, unnerving sensations Sebastian aroused in her with every look, every touch.

Marriage to him would be complex, dangerous. She would be required to make choices—present herself as an exemplary but complacent wife or attempt to peel back all his layers to reveal the center of his soul?

For with Sebastian, there could be no middle ground. He would have all of her or nothing. Even now, Clara knew the truth of it.

Dawn broke, red as old roses fading into the grayish blue sky. The sounds of the world filtered into the drawing room—the rattle of a carriage on the street, a boy hawking newspapers, the faint whistle of a bird. Sebastian scrubbed a hand over his rough-ened face, pulling himself from a brief, restless slumber. His eyes burned.

"Mr. Hall?" A footman paused in the doorway, bearing a silver tray. "A note arrived for you."

Sebastian pushed himself upright as Giles crossed the room. He took the folded letter. His name spread across the front in a ribbonlike, feminine hand. Clara.

The footman straightened, slanting his gaze over Sebastian's rumpled clothes and unshaven features. "Shall I draw you a bath, sir, or would you prefer to break your fast first?"

"Just bring me coffee, Giles."

"Yes, sir."

Sebastian put Clara's letter on his lap and stared at it with the sense that it contained a message of great import.

Giles arrived with a tray and poured coffee. Although the footman didn't speak, Sebastian was aware of his exasperation. In fact, he was growing accustomed to the faintly critical demeanor surrounding his brother's staff.

He couldn't blame them. Alexander had been so proper, even rigid, in the way he ran his household, his life. He always appeared for breakfast precisely at seven, clean-shaven, impec-cably dressed. The staff's schedule accorded with his predictable, daily habits.

Since Alexander and his wife left for St. Petersburg, Sebas-tian had come to live in his brother's Mount Street town house. The staff was still adjusting to the rather radical change in routine.

So was Sebastian. He thought he'd want Alexander's vast house to himself, but the bloody place was so magnificent, replete with plush furniture, velvet curtains, priceless paintings, that Sebastian felt like a blemish marring an expanse of flawless skin. And nothing here was his; these quarters were fit for royalty.

He grabbed the letter and broke open the seal. Bits of wax fell to his lap as he opened the page and read the short message:

Dear Mr. Hall,

I would like to request your presence at Blake's Museum of Automata at three o'clock Thursday afternoon. There is a matter of some urgency I wish to discuss.

Yours truly,
Mrs. Clara Shepherd

A matter of some urgency…?

Could she have found the plans already? Was today Thursday?

He shook his head to clear his mind. Yes. He'd told Clara yesterday about the plans, so there was certainly time for her to have found them. But if she had, he knew a woman as clever as Clara would not relinquish them without expecting something in return. He suspected he would find out at three o'clock exactly what that *something* was.

He shoved away from the chair and went upstairs. He rang for a bath, then washed and dressed in a fawn-colored morning coat and silk cravat. As he headed back down for breakfast, the doorbell rang.

Waving the footman away, Sebastian went to answer it. A dark-haired man stood outside, his eyes keenly intelligent behind wire-rimmed glasses, his woolen greatcoat buttoned up to his neck.

Sebastian stared in astonishment at his brother Jacob.

"Hello, Bastian." Faint amusement crackled across Jacob's

expression. "Are you going to invite me in or leave me standing here?"

Any other time, Sebastian would have greeted his brother with an embrace. Now, as he remembered the pain of recent months, followed by Jacob's implacable certainty that Sebastian would do as he requested—which proved to be the truth, owing to his new infirmity—anger bubbled into his throat.

"What are you doing here?"

"I arrived two days ago," Jacob said, his voice the cool blue of a lake undisturbed by waves. "I think it's best if Rushton doesn't yet know I'm here, so I'm staying at the Albion for the time being."

Jacob shed his greatcoat, then moved past Sebastian into the drawing room. With no other choice, Sebastian stalked after his brother.

"What are you doing here?" he repeated, closing the door behind them.

"I thought you'd have found the cipher machine plans by now."

Sebastian twisted his neck to the side, tempted to tell Jacob exactly what he could do with his blasted plans. "No."

Jacob's penetrating gaze raked over him. Sebastian fought the urge to shift with discomfort, knowing well the assessments and conclusions locking together in his brother's analytical mind.

To deflect that assessment, he asked, "Have you heard from Patrick of late?"

Jacob's mouth compressed as he gave a quick shake of his head. "Alexander is well, though. Besotted with his wife and greatly anticipating the birth of his child. Tasha laughs every time she imagines what he'll be like when the babe is born."

Sebastian almost smiled at the thought, which eased some of his anger. No father would be as fiercely protective and devoted as Alexander. Again Sebastian was glad he hadn't surrendered to his desperation and asked his elder brother for financial assistance.

Alexander would have helped him in any way he could, but not without demanding a full explanation of Sebastian's troubles. And the last thing Sebastian wanted was to cast a shadow over his brother's newfound happiness by revealing his medical obligations and the reasons behind the end of his career.

Alexander was happy. For that, at least, Sebastian was deeply grateful.

"How is Jane?" he asked.

"Delightful girl," Jacob said. "Excited beyond measure at the idea of being an older sister. You'll be glad to know she's taken up piano lessons again, though she still prefers to spend her time with insects."

"I'd expect no less of her." Sebastian was pleased at the news of his family. While at Weimar, he had planned a trip to St. Petersburg to visit them himself, but had canceled shortly after discovering the problem with his hand. He'd never be able to hide such a disability from Alexander.

He studied his younger brother. "Why don't you want Rushton to know you're here?"

"He won't like the reason for it," Jacob said.

"The cipher machine plans?"

"Among other things," Jacob replied. He went to the tray and poured a cup of now-cold coffee. "Have you found them?"

"Not yet." Unease tightened Sebastian's chest over the vagueness of his brother's response. "Why couldn't you look for them yourself?"

"Because I haven't been in London for almost four years," Jacob replied, his voice touched with impatience. "And I was certain you would know how best to approach Granville Blake or Clara Shepherd."

Sebastian curled his left hand into a fist. "How do you know about Mrs. Shepherd?"

"From Jacques Dupree's wife, actually," Jacob said. "She is quite fond of Mrs. Shepherd."

"When did you meet Madame Dupree?"

"Last spring the Duprees came to St. Petersburg at the behest of the governor, who wanted to commission a clock as a present for his daughter," Jacob explained. "I met them at a dinner party and told Dupree I was interested in learning more about his inventions. He was agreeable, and we began a lengthy correspondence.

"Once I'd apparently gained his trust, he revealed his plans for the cipher machine, but warned me that he did not want it to end up in Russian hands. After he fell ill, his wife wrote to me and explained that he had sent many of his belongings, including the plans, to Granville Blake. She told me about Mrs. Shepherd as well, and that she'd recently come to live at the museum and assist her uncle."

Jacob sipped his cold coffee, grimaced, and set the cup aside.

"I understand Mrs. Shepherd is quite lovely," he continued. "Perhaps now that I am in London, I ought to free you from your promise and pursue the plans myself."

Possessive anger filled Sebastian's chest at the idea of his brother approaching Clara and interacting with her. His suspicion flared anew. Jacob was not the sort of man to openly reveal his interest in a woman, so for him to speak of Clara—

His fists clenched as his gaze clashed with his brother's. Though Jacob's expression remained impassive, a faint smile tugged at his mouth.

The breath escaped Sebastian's lungs on a hard rush.

"Asshead," he muttered, forcing his fingers to relax.

Jacob's smile widened. "I'd wager ten guineas you didn't anticipate encountering someone like her when you agreed to my offer."

"She's a means to an end," Sebastian said, painfully aware of the hollow tone to his words. "Nothing more."

"Are you certain of that?"

Sebastian glowered, disliking the reminder that his brother

perceived so much more than he wanted to reveal. It made him wonder what other secrets Jacob might detect. Secrets he needed to keep concealed.

He shoved his right hand into his pocket and paced to the window. Frustration tightened his chest.

He spun on his heel and gave his brother a defiant glare.

"I told Mrs. Shepherd what I was looking for," he said.

Jacob blinked, and for an instant Sebastian thought he'd succeeded in rousing his brother's annoyance. But then Jacob merely lifted an eyebrow.

"And what did she say?" he asked.

"You specifically instructed me not to tell anyone."

"Yes, but I did not expect you to find the plans yourself or steal them," Jacob replied. "I assumed you would have to discuss the matter with Mr. Blake or Mrs. Shepherd. Must admit I'd have chosen Mrs. Shepherd as my confidante as well."

Chosen. The word struck Sebastian hard, overshadowing his irritation. Had that been what he had done? Had he chosen Clara?

After so many months of feeling as if circumstances had been forced upon him—the infirmity and resignation, the failure of the surgery, the position with the Patent Office, Rushton's ultimatum—Sebastian welcomed the idea that he had chosen to confide in Clara.

"She has no idea where the plans are," he told Jacob. "Or even if her uncle has them."

"Yet it won't be a hardship for you to continue searching." Jacob removed a folded note from his pocket. "Contact me here when you find them. I'll need them by the middle of next week, and I promise to compensate you handsomely."

"Why next week?"

"The Home Office has already appointed members for a select committee on wartime correspondence," Jacob explained. "If I can secure the funds, I want to construct the machine before their next meeting. First, however, I need to analyze the plans and determine if construction is even possible." He extended the note to Sebastian. "It's an important machine, Bastian, one that might prove extraordinarily effective in both war and as part of telegraph and railway systems. That is precisely why Jacques Dupree wanted to ensure its secrecy."

Sebastian took the note. Suspicion flared beneath his heart, adding fuel to the fire that had burned since he'd received Jacob's initial letter. Never had he been given cause to suspect one of his brothers of malice, but Jacob's evasiveness left too many unanswered questions.

Then again, Sebastian hadn't been truthful of late either.

He sighed. Since their parents' divorce, secrets had begun to spear through his relationships with his brothers, cracking walls that had once seemed indestructible.

He turned away from Jacob, trying to smother his suspicions. He'd never have even felt suspicious of his own brother had it not been for their mother's betrayal. She'd been the one to incite doubts in all of them, for if the Countess of Rushton, the very epitome of the *haut ton,* could conceal such a reprehensible secret, were not the rest of the Halls capable of hiding secrets?

None of them had talked much about the former countess. Though Sebastian knew that Alexander and Tasha had renounced all mention of their mother, he'd had little opportunity to learn Jacob's thoughts on the matter.

Then again, discerning Jacob's thoughts was like attempting to read and understand the Rosetta stone.

Sebastian shook his head as a humorless laugh stuck in his throat. God in heaven. The rest of the world was done with it. His brothers and sister were done with it. What would it take for Sebastian to bury the past?

CHAPTER 9

Clara stared at herself in the mirror. The bodice of her merino gown enclosed her curves in a close embrace, then cascaded over a wide crinoline. Mrs. Marshall had proven her skill with a comb by arranging Clara's hair in a smooth chignon softened by tendrils that curled over her bare neck. Jet earrings matched the brooch pinned to her collar.

She looked well, but her expression betrayed her nerves—her eyes dark, her jaw tight with tension, her skin pale as milk.

She smoothed her skirts and turned to go downstairs. The sound of the doorbell rang faintly in her good ear. Her stomach jumped. She stopped in the corridor, out of sight, as Mrs. Marshall opened the door to admit their visitor.

Sebastian's deep voice rumbled from the foyer as he greeted the housekeeper. Clara strained to hear.

"Lovely day out, Mrs. Marshall," Sebastian said. "I suggest you pay a visit to the park if you've got a moment." He paused, apparently to remove his greatcoat and hat. "Is that your exquisite apple cake I smell? I hope I'm fortunate enough to be offered a piece."

A teasing lilt in his deep tone had Clara pressing a hand to her chest, the thump of her heart like a bird's wing against her palm.

Such a thing of beauty was the man's voice, especially when edged with that beguiling note that spoke of pleasure. Even with the recent struggles that had disheartened him, whatever they might be, Sebastian still found pleasure in a warm autumn day, the scent of baking, making an elderly housekeeper blush. He still found pleasure in life.

Although Clara was fiercely glad that those qualities she had so admired as a young woman were very much a part of Sebastian Hall, she didn't believe they would advance her cause. A man like him would see no purpose in agreeing to a marriage based on practical ends. A man like him would desire a marriage of attraction. A joyous union of love and passion.

A flush swept up her neck to sting her cheeks. She could offer him none of those things, and for a moment she faltered in her resolve. This was a fool's errand, a—

"I'll just fetch Mrs. Shepherd, if you'll wait in the parlor, sir," Mrs. Marshall said. "I thought she'd be down by now, so prompt she usually is."

Clara inhaled a hard breath and straightened her spine. She descended the stairs with measured steps, nerves twisting through her belly.

"Good afternoon, Mr. Hall." For the housekeeper's benefit, Clara managed to keep her voice steady, pitched low, edged with just the right amount of warmth one would use with any welcomed visitor. "Do forgive my tardiness."

Sebastian watched her approach the foyer, his dark brown gaze sweeping her from head to toe in an appraisal that sent ripples of heat over her skin. "The two minutes I've been standing here were worth the wait."

She tried to resist the pull of his compliment, but the pleasure of it lightened her heart just a bit, easing her tension. She paused at the foot of the stairs and allowed herself to look at him. His morning coat was pressed and his boots shining, his face shaved clean of whiskers to reveal the hard edges of his cheekbones and jaw. And yet that rough energy still emanated from him with crackling force, as if proclaiming that this man could never be contained by propriety.

"Do come in." Clara gestured to the parlor. "Tea, please, Mrs. Marshall."

"Yes, ma'am." The housekeeper puffed off toward the kitchen.

Clara led Sebastian inside and bade him sit. Her eyes traveled swiftly over the room, though she had spent the morning instructing Mrs. Marshall and Tom on how best to clean and arrange the furnishings.

Now it appeared perfect—the windows gleaming, every surface clean of dust, the wood polished to a shine. Several vases of flowers bloomed, perfuming the air with sweetness. The bouquets were an expense the household could ill afford, but Clara had only one chance at this, and she needed all the weapons at her disposal. Flowers brightened the room, adding splashes of color that pleased the eye, and their fragrance could soothe an intemperate disposition.

Moreover, not five minutes ago Sebastian had encouraged Mrs. Marshall to enjoy the unseasonably warm weather, so surely the man would appreciate the beauty of the bouquets.

Clara swept her hand over the surface of a table, collecting a few shed petals in her palm. She walked to the settee, dropping the petals discreetly into a Grecian urn before taking her place across from her guest.

"Thank you for coming," she said.

He nodded. Although his clothing was pressed to perfection, his hair was still over-long and mussed by the wind. He lifted his left hand as if to drag it through the dark strands, then seemed to think better of the gesture and lowered his hand to his knee. His right hand remained tucked into his pocket. "Is your uncle here?"

"No." Now her heart began to pound tangibly. "I don't expect

Uncle Granville back until supper. And Mrs. Fox has gone to the shops."

"Ah, well." He shifted, his shoulders moving beneath the stretch of his coat. A shallow crease formed between his eyes. "So what is this about then, Clara?"

She loved the way he said her name, as if his voice were embracing it.

Heat suffused her. She rose in a rustle of skirts and went to the door to hide her discomfort.

"Let's have tea first, shall we?" She forced herself to sound casual and airy as she peered into the foyer. "Ah, here we are. Thank you, Mrs. Marshall. Apple cake too, how lovely." She waited for the housekeeper to depart, leaving the door ajar, before returning to the sitting area.

She concentrated on pouring the tea before extending a cup and saucer toward Sebastian. She glanced up and saw that he was watching the movement of her hands.

Her lips parted, but no words emerged. Her body reacted as if he were touching her, heat searing across her skin. She put the cup down on the table in front of him. The cup rattled in the saucer, betraying her slight tremor.

She sat back and curled her fingers into her palms. Her corset and bodice constricted around her, shortening her breath. She watched Sebastian as he brought the teacup to his mouth, his lips closing over the paper-thin rim.

The heat intensified. Clara tore her gaze away. Not daring to lift her own cup for fear of revealing the unsteadiness of her hands, she rose again and went to the windows. She waited a few heartbeats for him to enjoy his tea and a slice of cake. Wouldn't do to have the man hungry as well as shocked.

"I...I've asked you here for a specific reason." Her voice, at least, remained even. She waited for him to set his cup down and turn to face her.

Again, no surprise flashed across his features, only a faint curiosity. "And what reason is that?"

She had rehearsed this. She had a speech prepared. For hours last night, she'd lain in her bed and practiced it over and over again in her mind. She knew where to start, where to pause for effect, how to list her reasons in a tone that was both persuasive and practical. She intended to call upon every determined technique she possessed in order to convince Sebastian Hall that he must agree to marry her.

And yet all her intentions fell away as she blurted out the words with hasty desperation. "Sebastian, I wish to present you with a marriage proposition."

There it was. The shock he hadn't yet exhibited now flared in his eyes, spread across his features. He blinked. His mouth opened and closed.

Clara clenched her fists and cursed inwardly. Now he'd think she was mad. She held up a hand to forestall his stammered response.

"Please, hear me out." She forced a wry note into her voice. "I didn't mean to surprise you, though I can't imagine what other reaction I expected."

He stared at her for a second, then barked out a laugh. "Of all the reasons I could imagine for you inviting me here, that most certainly was not one of them."

He chuckled again and shook his head, reaching for his teacup. He took a sip and looked at the contents as if wishing they were something much stronger, then set the cup aside and rose.

Clara stepped forward, not wanting to give him the opportunity to bolt from the room before she'd had a chance to present her case.

"Sebastian." His name flowed like honey across her tongue. She swallowed and felt the sound warm her chest from the inside out. "Please allow me to explain. This involves my son, Andrew, whom I have not seen in over a year."

He frowned. "You told me he lives with your father in Surrey."

"Yes. My father is his legal guardian." Clara could not prevent the bitter tone underscoring her voice. "He keeps me from Andrew...or keeps Andrew from me, as the case may be. He has very rigid ideas about how Andrew ought to be raised and does not care for my interference.

"My late husband, Richard, God rest his soul, left his money for Andrew's inheritance, which of course is as it should be. However, he also returned to me a property that once belonged to my mother. Wakefield House."

"He returned it to you?" Sebastian asked.

"Prior to our marriage, Wakefield House belonged to me," Clara explained. "It was handed down in trust from my grandfather with Uncle Granville designated as the trustee. When I wed Richard, Wakefield House was transferred to him but he returned it to me in his will. And my father would very much like to own it."

"Why?"

"Because he's been in rather dire financial straits since my husband died," Clara admitted. "Wakefield House is an extensive property. It's been long deserted, but with the right management and repairs, it could sell for a substantial sum. Of course, in order to sell it, my father first must own it."

"Can you sell it?" Sebastian asked.

Clara shook her head. "A condition of the trust is that the house be bequeathed to my firstborn. I am not allowed to sell it."

"And Wakefield House is the sole reason your father keeps your son from you?"

"No." She couldn't confess the darkest reason behind her father's severance of their relationship. She would not be able to bear it if Sebastian looked at her with suspicion or, worse, revulsion.

"My father was quite close to Richard," she explained. "They were both great sportsmen and shared the same interests. It was easy for them, natural."

"And yet it was not so for you."

Clara gave a quick shake of her head and spoke the words she'd repeated to herself so often, the phrase whose truth lodged like a burr in her chest.

"Nothing for me was easy with my father."

"What happened?"

"Richard died after being thrown from his horse while out riding." Her eyes stung. "I was shocked to learn that he had designated my father as Andrew's guardian. When I resisted my father's rules, he threatened to send me away to America. I left Manley Park before he could.

"I arrived here at my uncle's determined to find a way to regain custody of Andrew. All my and Uncle Granville's efforts have come to naught. We attempted to try to sell Wakefield House in the hopes of appeasing my father, but by the terms of the trust and inheritance, I'm unable to do so.

"However"—she inhaled a hard breath—"if I were to marry again, the house would transfer into my husband's name and *he* would be allowed to sell it."

For a moment that seemed to stretch forever, Sebastian looked at her. A swath of hair fell across his forehead, almost into his eyes. Clara was seized by the urge to brush away the thick strands, to tunnel her fingers into the dark mass of his hair.

She clenched her fists tighter.

"So," Sebastian finally said. "You want to marry me so I can give Wakefield House to your father."

He spoke with a straightforwardness that made Clara jerk her gaze to his. Perhaps she needn't have rehearsed her speech after all.

"I've one thing to offer you in exchange," she said.

His brows rose as he waited for her to continue.

"The plans for the cipher machine you seek."

Sebastian's breath hissed out in a rush. "You told me you've no knowledge of it."

"I didn't. I still don't. But before his death, Jacques Dupree sent my uncle numerous crates and boxes of machinery and plans. His son sent even more after Monsieur Dupree died. It's entirely possible the cipher machine plans are among those possessions. If so, I will find them."

"And if they aren't there?"

"Then you are free to terminate our agreement." Clara spoke with a bravado she didn't feel. She spread her hands, glad that the tremors in them had eased. "Have you anything to lose?"

Except your freedom?

Sebastian didn't speak, didn't turn his gaze from her face.

He hadn't rejected her. The realization shone like sunlight through her fog of anger and despair. She clung to that thread of hope and used it to force down the rage, to prevent it from boiling into her blood.

"I ask...no, I *beg* for your help in getting Andrew back," she said, hating the desperate note in her voice. "I have no claim to him. My father is his sole and legal guardian." She paused for breath. "Wakefield House is the only asset I have, and it's one that my father wants. If I can offer it to him *through you,* I have a chance of getting my son back."

Sebastian rubbed his right hand with his left, a movement that appeared unconscious. Clara watched him for a moment before he stopped and pushed his hand into his pocket abruptly. "Have you gone to the courts to seek custody of your son?"

"I considered it, but the risk is too great. It would be scandalous for my father's reputation, not to mention my own, regardless of the outcome. We might not be a well-connected family, but gossip has never surrounded us. I certainly cannot cause any now."

She drew in a ragged breath. The misshapen difference

between society's view of her life and the brutal reality still had the power to unnerve her, even as she recognized her good fortune in the distortion. If her behavior had caused scandal to erupt in Fairfax's domain, Andrew would truly be lost to her forever.

"Not even my falling-out with my father caused a whisper in society," she admitted. "Ask anyone of consequence in Surrey and you'll hear of my husband's tragic accident, how brilliant he would have been had he been elected to Parliament, how magnanimous my father was in taking him under his wing, and how devastated he was to have lost the young man he'd considered his second son. You'll hear how my father dotes upon his grandson, and how fortunate Andrew is to have such a devoted grandfather."

Clara stopped, shocked by the bitterness discoloring her voice. She turned her back to Sebastian and stepped to the windows, fighting to calm her inner turmoil.

A lengthy silence stretched, almost vibrating with tension.

"And you?" His deep voice was close. Too close. Clara could almost feel the heat of his body behind her. She wrapped her arms around her middle and struggled to contain her shaking.

"Me?" she whispered.

"What would anyone of consequence in Surrey have to say about Mrs. Clara Shepherd, should I ask?"

She stared unseeing out the window. Her reflection in the glass stared back at her. "They would tell you she was so distraught by her husband's untimely death that she fled to London for recuperation. They would tell you that she sees her son regularly when Lord Fairfax brings the boy to London. They would tell you she has crafted a quiet, respectable life for herself in honor and memory of her beloved husband."

Silence again, as if Sebastian were analyzing all she said, working it through his mind like a mill separating the wheat from the chaff.

"But," he said quietly, "they would all be horribly wrong."

"Does it matter?"

No. To anyone else, it mattered not a whit. The story was romantic and tragic, and they all loved to speak of it as if it were something from a penny novel and not ripped from the pages of Clara's life. As if it hadn't burned her soul to ashes.

She whirled around, a rush of hot anger crawling up her throat.

"It doesn't matter at all, not to them," she snapped, some part of her shocked by the way she allowed control to slip so easily through her fingers. "If you agree to this, you would marry a virtuous, well-bred widow, a peer's daughter whose son lives a fine life with his grandfather in Surrey. No one would know anything of Wakefield House or my desperation to have Andrew again. Except…"

"Us," Sebastian finished.

Us. The word flowered in Clara's soul, pushing a fresh stalk of green through the dry, cracked dirt.

"Us," she whispered.

No. There could be no *us* in a marriage of practical ends.

Could there?

Sebastian stepped closer, his gaze fixed on her. He moved with a confidence that belied his initial surprise, as if her revelations had yielded for him some conclusion. As if he'd already decided upon his response.

"It could…it could be a marriage in name only," Clara stammered, voicing the thought that had twisted her dreams, the condition she already knew he would never accept.

"Name…" He stared at her for a moment, then gave a short laugh. "That's what you think, is it? That I would assent to a marriage in name only?"

"Well, a p-pragmatic union is one that…"

Her remark faded as he stepped closer, studying her in that unnerving way he had, as if she were some unusual species of insect that he'd happened to find flitting about the house. She stared at his cravat, the perfect knot nestled at the base of his throat.

"Make no mistake, Clara," he said, a low warning rippling beneath his words. "I desire neither a marriage in name only, nor one that holds even the faintest possibility of separation."

Her heart throbbed. "I…I understand."

"Five days, then."

"Five…?"

"My brother wants the plans by Tuesday next," Sebastian said. "If you find them by then, I will consider marrying you."

"You will *consider* marrying me?" Her spine stiffened. "Why should I agree to help you without any commitment on your part?"

"Because this gives you time to reappraise your request," Sebastian said. "If you conclude that my conditions are unacceptable, you may change your mind and withdraw your proposal."

He stepped away from her and turned to the door. "You must be very certain you know what you ask of me, Clara. And what I shall ask in return."

CHAPTER 10

*S*moke and noise coated the air of the Eagle Tavern. Tankards thumped against the wood of the trestle tables, voices rose in argument over card games, the fire hissed and snapped. The familiarity of the disorder eased some of Sebastian's apprehension over Clara's proposal earlier in the day. Despite all she had revealed, he couldn't prevent the sense that she had not told him the entirety of her story.

He sat hunched over the piano, trailing his left hand over the keys without thought or pleasure. He put his right hand into position on the keys and sounded a C-major chord, then waited for the strings' reverberations to cease. He played the chord again in its first inversion, then again in its second. He imagined a melodic line in the bass, something dark and menacing like the advance of gray fog at twilight.

For as long as Sebastian could remember, sound had been infused with color. Voices, noise from the street, the crackle of a fire. In music, every note had its own color, and color and shape were inexorably linked in his compositions. The various tones, harmonies, and pitches wove through his mind in endless patterns. As he wrote his compositions, guided by what colors and shapes fit together, he saw the music as moving paintings.

Since losing the use of his right hand, he still saw a shadow of those patterns, felt the intense yellow of major C, the pink of the E note, the rich brown of G...but the colors were pallid now, faded, like bright linens left too long in the sun.

He played another chord. Then it happened again—his fourth and fifth fingers faltered as if the strength had suddenly drained from them. Sebastian kept his hand on the keys and tried to repeat the octave. The two fingers resisted control, curling toward his palm instead of obeying his internal command. The muscles of his forearms snarled and contracted clear up to his shoulder.

Sebastian swore and slammed his hand flat on the keyboard. The crash caused several patrons to glance up.

He twisted his neck from side to side and shook his arm to ease the tension. Forcing the thin remnants of color away, he rose from the piano stool and went to the taproom, where Jacob sat. He slumped down at the table across from his brother, clots of smoke stinging his eyes.

Jacob slid a tankard of ale across to him. Sebastian grabbed it with his left hand and took a swallow, then wiped his mouth.

"Didn't you once play here regularly?" Jacob asked. "Annoyed Alexander to no end, if I recall correctly."

"Indeed. Probably one of the reasons I did it."

Amusement flashed across his brother's expression. "Does Pater know you still come here?"

"No. He's occupied with his own work these days." Sebastian realized only then the truth of the remark. "For the first time since his wife left, the old bird is out and about again. Has a new position with the Home Office. Spends time at his club, the theater, balls. And he seems to have earned himself a bit of attention from the ladies."

"Good." Jacob swallowed some ale and leaned back, his gaze narrowing. "And you?"

"Me?"

"You're not quite well, are you?"

Dammit. Sebastian curled his right hand into a fist. Of course he shouldn't have expected to hide anything from Jacob. For all of his brother's impassivity, Jacob was like a hawk who, with one sweep of his keen eyes, missed nothing. Not unlike Rushton.

"I'm fine," Sebastian said. Ridiculous word. *Fine*. Thin and watery, ashen blue.

His brother's attention remained steady, unwavering. "Why did you resign the Weimar position?"

"Didn't you hear?" Sebastian flexed his fingers. "They wanted to amend one of my compositions."

"You would not dishonor your patrons or Monsieur Liszt by resigning over such a trivial matter. Especially after the debacle of our parents' divorce."

Wary, Sebastian reached for his ale. He knew his brothers. Knew their temperaments, their idiosyncrasies. Jacob was the practical, level-headed twin who could sense both deception and danger like a bloodhound following a scent to ground. And when he came upon it, he would stare the threat down, his calculating brain assessing risks and tactics with military precision before he made his move.

A reluctant smile tugged at Sebastian's mouth. Their brother Patrick would react in the opposite manner, plunging headlong into the fray with neither evaluation nor decorum. Even as boys, the twins had complemented each other with an accuracy that mimicked the riposte and parry action of a fencing match.

"You've not spoken with Rushton recently?" he asked.

Jacob shook his head. "Last time I did, I asked about the countess. A mistake, obviously. Rushton ordered me never to speak of her again and left the room." He paused, then rerouted

the conversation neatly back to Sebastian. "I heard that the grand
duchess still wishes to fund a tour of the Continent for you."

Sharp longing twisted through Sebastian. He shook his head.

"Appears as if it would do you some good," Jacob remarked.
"And the payment is substantial."

"No." Not long ago he'd have grabbed the opportunity and not
looked back.

"Then what?" Impatience wove through his brother's usually
placid tone. "You've no intention of reviving your career? You're
not even teaching anymore. What do you intend to do?"

"I'm helping you, aren't I?"

"Why?"

Rushton's ultimatum crashed through Sebastian's mind—
marry or risk his allowance and possibly even his inheritance.
Rushton didn't know about his medical debts, or his attempt to
restore his funds by helping Jacob.

Yet his brother's promise of compensation for the cipher
machine specifications hinged on one uncertain premise—Sebastian had to actually find the plans. If he failed, and without the
income from concerts and investors, he was destined for that
clerk position with the Patent Office. And if he succeeded, if
Clara succeeded, he would be bound to accept her proposal.

An outcome that became more tempting every time Sebastian
thought about it. Marrying Clara would solve his troubles, but
beyond that he would gain a lovely, intelligent wife with violet-
colored eyes that seared him with each glance, whose full lips
laced him with arousal. A woman who reminded him of the
power of unflinching determination.

And certainly no one would expect him to marry someone
like her, especially not his father, which made the notion even
more appealing. He might have done such a thing ages ago, long
before events of the past year had numbed the genial rebellious-
ness he'd once possessed.

He took another gulp of ale. A restive urge vibrated inside

him, like a hammer striking a piano string over and over again. He wondered if his mother had felt like this before she'd fled for another life.

"Clara Shepherd asked me to marry her," he confessed.

Jacob blinked. "Why on earth would she do that?"

Sebastian almost grinned at the incredulity in his brother's voice. "I am, after all, the second son of an earl and still rather known for my dashing ways."

"Exactly so," Jacob replied. "And I understand that Mrs. Shepherd is the quiet sort not given to swooning over men like you. So I fail to fathom why she would propose such an alliance. Unless..." His eyes sharpened behind his glasses. "Has this anything to do with the cipher machine plans?"

"More to do with Rushton's insistence that I marry soon."

Yet Clara's proposal was so tangled up with other reasons that Sebastian could no longer find the thread of his father's ultimatum. He needed the cipher machine plans, he needed money to pay off his debts, he needed to find his way out of the bleakness following the end of his career, he needed to help Clara....

Sebastian took another drink. A waltz played at the back of his mind, but the chords and notes blurred into the sound of Clara's blue-gold voice, the steady cadence of which could not conceal the turbulence of her suppressed emotions.

"And Mrs. Shepherd knows about Pater's decree?" Jacob asked.

Sebastian shook his head, unwilling to divulge Clara's secrets. "She asked me to marry her for reasons of her own. I told her I would consider it."

Jacob stared at him for an instant, then threw back his head and laughed. "You're considering marriage because a woman proposed to you? That was all it took? How many women have set their caps at you over the years, but stood waiting for *you* to be the one to ask?"

Amusement flickered to life in Sebastian. "There is a great

deal more to Clara than her forthrightness, though you are welcome to spread the word that *all* she did was propose. I'd find the resulting gossip very diverting."

He would, too. There would be no disgrace attached to light-hearted speculation about his potential engagement, and it might even obscure the lingering questions about his abandonment of his music career. Not to mention giving Rushton a bone to chew on.

Still grinning, Jacob tilted his head in acknowledgment. "Be assured I will do my utmost to ensure people know that Sebastian Hall has been caught in parson's mousetrap. My only hope is that Mrs. Shepherd proves worth your capitulation."

She already has.

The thought startled Sebastian. He shook his head.

"I haven't yet capitulated," he said.

"Yet?" Jacob's keen perception shone through his amusement. "This is the first time you have ever considered marriage. Is she the reason you refuse to embark on a new tour?"

"No." Sebastian frowned, suddenly wishing he'd kept quiet. "If I do marry Clara Shepherd, it would be for practical reasons."

"You never do anything for practical reasons." Jacob reached for his tankard. "You only ever do things because you want to."

That had once been the truth. Sebastian wrapped his left hand around his right, squeezing it into a fist. In the adjoining room, a man began playing a lively tune on the piano. The sound drifted into Sebastian's ears in ribbons of yellow and white.

Although he had no wish to respond to his brother's probing, Sebastian realized he was somewhat grateful for it. Jacob knew him. Sebastian disliked the secrets that snaked through his family now, but his brothers and sister remained his only solid ground in the turmoil of the past five months.

And as his brothers knew him, he knew his brothers. Jacob's motivations for doing anything were rarely as simple as they first appeared.

"You're here for more than the cipher machine plans, aren't you?" Sebastian asked. "Why?"

"Bring me the plans." Jacob skimmed his sharp gaze over him again. "Eight o'clock next Tuesday. I'll explain then."

Sebastian pushed his chair away from the table and left without looking back. He walked down the street, skirting around pedestrians. Carts and horses rattled on the cobblestones, and lights began to glow in the windows of the braziers' workshops lining Houndsditch. He hired a cab and instructed the driver to leave him at Blake's Museum of Automata on Old Bond Street.

Mrs. Fox was pulling on her cloak when he entered the foyer, and she gave him a somewhat severe frown. "I'm sorry, Mr. Hall, but the museum is closing. I intend to lock the door behind me."

"That's fine, Mrs. Fox, as I'm not here for a tour. Are Mr. Blake and Mrs. Shepherd available?"

She sighed. "You'll have to go look for yourself. Mrs. Marshall is fixing dinner, so you'd best not disturb her."

Sebastian nodded, flinging his hat and greatcoat onto the rack before heading into the depths of the museum. He found both the music room and parlor empty, then paced to Granville's workshop, which was cluttered with boxes and machine parts.

Clara knelt beside an opened crate, leaves of creased paper and disordered notebooks scattered around her. Dust covered her apron. Her sleeves were rolled up to the elbows, and long tendrils of hair had escaped their pins to wind around her throat.

Sebastian's fervent urge from earlier returned, this time thumping in time with the beat of his heart.

"Hello, Clara."

"Oh." She started and rose to her feet. She rubbed her cheek with the back of her hand, leaving a smear of dirt. "I didn't know you were here."

"Just arrived. Nearly skewered by Mrs. Fox's glare. Deadly as a poisoned arrow."

She smiled. He thought he'd do anything, including stand on his head and whistle a tune, if she would continue to smile at him like that. He moved closer. Close enough that her skirts brushed his legs like the glide of fingertips.

"Why have you come back?" she asked.

"I wanted to see you," Sebastian said, only recognizing the truth of the statement after he spoke. With her standing in front of him, all other reasons and motivations faded away and left only the bright, shining possibility of Clara becoming his wife.

She looked at him. He inhaled her scent and lifted his left hand to wind a stray lock of hair around his fingers. He brushed his thumb against her neck and felt the quickening beat of her delicate pulse even through his glove.

"Do you trust me?" he asked. He was so close to her he could have counted her eyelashes. The color of her eyes was muted, but the blue flecks in her irises sparkled like light on snow.

She was silent, her gaze skimming across his mouth, warming his lips. A tremble coursed through her, vibrating against his palm. His breath almost stopped as he waited for her response.

"Do you?" he repeated.

"Yes." The word escaped her on a whisper. She lifted her hand to his mouth. Heat pooled low in his body at the touch of her fingertips, the stroke of her thumb in the indentation beneath his lower lip.

He captured her hand in his and turned her palm upward. Rough scrapes lined her skin, gritty with dust. She closed her fingers and tried to pull her hand from his. He didn't allow it, stroking his forefinger over the thin scratches. "You haven't found them."

"I will." A tremble shuddered in her voice despite the declaration. "Uncle Granville is helping, but there are at least twenty crates and boxes to inspect, not to mention the sheer number of papers and diagrams. If Monsieur Dupree didn't write down the purpose of his inventions, I have to ask Granville to interpret them for me. It all takes...time."

Time that neither of them had.

Sebastian looked at the scratches on her hand, disliking the evidence of her pain. He brought her wrist up and pressed his mouth against the middle of her palm.

Clara gasped, her arm jerking in reflex even as her other hand closed around the lapel of his coat. Warmth spread through Sebastian's chest, untangling the ache of fatigue and restlessness. He lifted his right hand to cover hers, forcing his fingers into the position he would use on a keyboard.

His fingers contracted, then froze. Tension pinched through his forearm. He struggled to make his hand close over Clara's, but the muscles seized.

She stared at his hand, his fingers stiffened into a claw that refused to curl around hers. Fear and dismay roiled in his stomach as he watched the dark comprehension cloud her violet eyes.

"What happened?" she whispered.

"I don't know."

"You don't..."

Her fingers closed around his. Warmth flowed up his arm, easing the persistent constriction of his muscles.

"You don't know?" she repeated.

Sebastian shook his head and forced the confession from his tight throat. "It started a few months ago, right after I took the Weimar position. My right hand wouldn't do what I wanted it to, almost as if it weren't even part of me anymore. Whenever I tried to play the piano, my fingers froze and curled toward my palm. I went to several doctors, one of whom referred me to a surgeon who said it was a muscle problem. Did a surgery that bent this finger permanently."

He touched his little finger, which was bent at a right angle.

Even if he could regain control over the rest of his hand, he'd have to undergo another surgery to try to fix the damaged joint.

Clara sighed, her eyes veiled by her lashes. She didn't release his hand. Instead she rubbed her fingers over his, as if soothing the ruffled feathers of a bird. His breath eased a little.

"I'm sorry," she murmured.

He lifted a hand to her ear. "You?"

Shadows filled her expression, her mouth tightening. "Do you remember my brother, William? He also took piano lessons from you when we stayed in Dorset. He died when he was fifteen. I was seventeen. We were boating on a lake when a storm came up. A wind blew my hat into the water. I leaned too far to retrieve it and tipped the boat over. William hit his head and I couldn't…"

The words crumbled beneath the weight of sorrow. Sebastian pulled her into his arms, breathing in the sweet smell of her hair.

"The days following were horrible," Clara continued. "The grief tore us apart. My mother refused to leave her room. I developed a terrible pain in my ear and a ringing noise that wouldn't cease. I didn't tell anyone. I…I wanted to hide. I knew they all blamed me for William's death. By the time the inflammation was treated with poultices and tinctures, my hearing was already damaged."

Sebastian touched the delicate shell of her ear. He brushed his lips across her temple, across the soft strands of hair that had escaped their pins, and to the black birthmark at the corner of her eyebrow. Then lower, down to her cheekbone, before descending to capture her mouth.

Clara murmured his name and turned her head to meet him in a kiss that quivered with suppressed longing. He covered her lips, heat blooming in his blood as she opened for him without hesitation. He probed the warmth of her mouth, slid his tongue across her teeth. His damaged hand stiffened against her hip as her body curved against his.

He wanted to crush her to him, to pull her clothes off so he could touch the bare smoothness of her skin. Urgency pulsed through him like a heartbeat as her hands came up to cup his cheeks, angling his head to deepen their kiss.

A vibrant energy crackled from her into him, searing him with pleasure and something remarkably akin to happiness. Like cool, fresh water she poured into his desiccated soul and brought him to flourishing life again.

With her, he almost felt as if he could be himself again. As if he could reclaim everything that was pleasant and joyous of his former life.

Clara moved her lips to his jaw and gave a husky laugh, her breath fanning against his skin. "You never imagined this would happen, did you?"

"Did you?" Sebastian flexed his fingers against her waist.

"Oh, yes." She parted from him, her hands sliding down to his neck. Warm amusement creased her eyes, bright above her flushed cheeks. "When we were in Dorset. When I watched you weave your music while surrounded by beautiful, admiring women....Oh, I imagined it. I *hoped* for it....I wanted you to look at me, dance with me, speak with me."

He lifted his good hand to her face and rubbed his thumb across her full lower lip. When he first encountered her in the Hanover Square ballroom, he thought he didn't remember her.

He had been wrong.

Her revelations brought an image to the surface, like the burn of a constellation in a night sky. She'd been a quiet, pleasant, young woman who hovered on the periphery of the crowds, circling the ballrooms and parlors. A sparrow, yes, but one whose plumage shone with colors of rich brown, ocher, snow-white.

He turned toward a birdcage automaton resting on a work-bench and found the key at the base. With a few twists, he wound the machine and released it. A metallic but pleasant tune drifted from the mechanism.

He lifted Clara's right hand and placed it in his. Nerves tightened in his chest, but he curled his fingers around hers and willed his hand not to falter. Then he slipped his other hand around her waist and pulled her closer.

"May I have this dance?" he asked.

Clara smiled, her eyes sparking with colors as she put her hand on his shoulder. "I'd be delighted."

Sebastian guided her into a slow waltz. Although they were hampered by the scattered tables, she followed his lead with ease, matching her steps to his in time to the thin music and the chatter of the automated birds.

He turned, drawing her to him. His apprehension faded into the pleasure of the simultaneous movement, the ease of letting the music be his guide, the sheer enjoyment of holding Clara in his arms.

"You're a wonderful dancer." She looked up at him. "I remember that too."

"I haven't danced in months."

"I haven't either," she admitted. "Not in the last year."

Her eyes skimmed across his face, down to his mouth and lower to his neck. Sebastian's blood warmed at the caress of her gaze. The automaton music wound down, the final strains filtering into the dusky air. He drew Clara to a slow halt. She remained within the circle of his arms, her hand still clasping his. For the first time in months, he realized he had forgotten about his disability.

An emotion tugged at him that he didn't recognize, something rich and saturated with all the colors of the rainbow. His breathing shortened.

He stared at Clara's lovely eyes. Eyes of a witch. Surely they had beguiled him into considering her proposal, for he could have conceived a dozen other ways of obtaining the cipher machine plans. Yet when she had laid out the terms, he knew it was the quickest way to obtain her assistance, to appease his father, to settle with Jacob.

To make Clara his alone.

Apprehension rose to dilute his unforeseen emotions. Her approach to this agreement was calculated and practical. She needed Wakefield House transferred to his name. She spoke of warm feelings toward him, but her admiration had been directed toward the man he once was. Not the man he was now. Whereas he was drawn to all the complexities and turmoil of Mrs. Clara Shepherd, the woman who had sustained suffering and still burned with vital determination.

He remembered the young woman she had once been. He only wished he'd looked beyond himself far enough to actually see her.

He lowered his head to her damaged ear and spoke in a whisper that he knew she would not hear. "Now I see no other woman except you."

She turned, her forehead creasing. "I'm sorry?"

No, he couldn't allow her to hear such a confession. Not when her admiration for him was so misguided.

He released her and stepped back, unsettled. "I will come back tomorrow to help you look for the plans."

A flicker of confusion passed across her expression before she glanced away. "Yes, of course. I...I've explained to my uncle about Wakefield House. He remains cautious, but as trustee he would not hinder the transfer of the property to you. Should we come to an agreement."

Her voice leveled out into a practical tone, as if she sought to remind them both of the conditions underlying her proposal. And yet even with that reminder, Sebastian could not forget his caveat that their marriage would be both real and immutable.

Heat coursed down his spine. He would bind his emotions tightly because he would not lay himself bare before a woman who looked at him through the lens of the past, whose desire to marry him sprang from a practical and desperate purpose. And he would not lose sight of his own agreement with Jacob, now laced with suspicions about his brother's motives.

"Tomorrow then." He fisted his right hand and headed for the foyer.

"Tomorrow," Clara echoed.

He gave a short nod and opened the door.

"Sebastian?"

He stopped, but didn't turn to face her.

"Thank you." Clara paused, then added, "I'm glad we both remember how to dance."

CHAPTER 11

*C*lara didn't want to believe it.

Not him. Not the talented performer who wove music like an intricate tapestry. Not the man who drew people into the warmth of his disarming presence. Not the man who had colored her Wakefield House days with brilliant strokes of red, green, and purple. Not the man who danced with a lean, masculine grace that made her feel as if she were floating.

Not him. Her heart ached, even as she knew the captivating man of her youth was still there, locked behind the despair of a new and indescribable infirmity.

She threw an empty box into the corner of the room and wiped her forehead with the back of her hand. Perspiration trickled down her backbone. Her hands were dry and grimy from breaking open crates and boxes, rummaging through machine parts and papers that made no sense to her.

Disappointment roiled through her. Monsieur Dupree might have written pages and pages of hieroglyphics, for all she could understand of his notes.

Every time she found a diagram that appeared to resemble a

machine, she handed it to Uncle Granville for translation. Every time he shook his head.

"Music box," he said, placing another drawing atop the pile already at his side. "A clock made of a birdcage. Letter keyboard. A cabinet with chimes. Look for a drawing that contains a cylinder and a rotating circuit wheel."

"I *am* looking," Clara replied with a touch of annoyance. They had been looking all morning, and so far had found nothing resembling a telegraph machine. "Perhaps he didn't send them to you after all."

Granville didn't respond, which Clara interpreted as agreement. She thrust another empty crate to the side and reached for a box.

"Mrs. Marshall has breakfast prepared, if you're both hungry." Mrs. Fox appeared in the doorway, her eyes skimming the room in one glance. "Have you found what you're looking for?"

"Not yet." Granville stood and stretched, pressing a hand to his lower back. "Clara, come break your fast. You've been up since dawn."

"You go. I'll be in later."

Granville's hand closed on her shoulder. "Don't make yourself ill over this."

She whirled to pin him with a glare. "I've *been* ill since the moment I left Manley Park, Uncle Granville."

Pain flashed behind his glasses. His grip tightened on her shoulder. "I know."

He glanced at Mrs. Fox. "Please tell Mrs. Marshall we'll take breakfast later."

Mrs. Fox gave a crisp nod and turned. A few minutes later, she returned. "Perhaps I can be of some assistance. I've locked the front door, so visitors will have to ring for entry."

Clara and Granville exchanged glances. At her nod, he told Mrs. Fox what they were searching for. The other woman pulled a chair to the table and began unrolling a stack of scrolls.

Clara's hands stung with cuts from the wooden crates, and a layer of dust coated her apron. She wiped her hands on a cloth.

She tried not to think beyond this one goal, the desperate need to find the machine specifications. She tried not to think of what would happen if she didn't find them.

Sunlight began to press against the windows, making it easier to see in the dusty storeroom. Mrs. Fox stopped once to return to the foyer, then came back with Sebastian behind her.

Clara's heart jumped at the sight of his tall figure, his thick, black hair rumpled from the scrape of his fingers.

"Good morning." His deep voice rumbled over her skin.

She could not help delighting in the sensations he aroused in her, not only because of *him,* but because they were such a pleasurable reprieve from her ever-present fear. Seeing Sebastian, being near him, was like taking a breath of fresh, clean air after escaping a smoke-filled room. Yesterday she had thought she would never want to leave the protective circle of his arms.

She rose, experiencing a new surge of hope as Sebastian greeted Granville and explained the reason for his presence. Her uncle responded with wariness, which Clara knew sprang from his concern about her new plan.

Yet even cautious Uncle Granville could not deny the plan might very well *work.*

She guided Sebastian to a stack of boxes in the corner and explained the organizational procedure they had devised—machinery parts went into the adjoining room, diagrams for toys, clocks, musical items, and larger automata were divided into stacks on the table, and undecipherable plans and notebooks were placed on a sideboard for Granville's perusal.

Sebastian began unpacking one of the boxes. Several hours passed, with only the sounds of shuffling paper, creaking wood and metal, and occasional questions breaking the silence. Mrs. Marshall appeared with a tea tray and plate of muffins, which she left on a side table.

Clara went to the table where Mrs. Fox sat examining note-books. She took a scroll from a pile and removed the string. A sheaf of papers unfurled onto the table, a stack of notes embedded in the center. She smoothed her hand over the curling edges of the diagram and weighted them with books so the scroll would lie flat.

The intricate diagram resembled a music box, with gears attached to a central wheel. Notes decorated the paper like the margins on an illuminated manuscript—elegant boxes of Monsieur Dupree's penmanship.

"What about this one?" Clara asked Uncle Granville.

After a brief inspection, he shook his head and started to turn away, then paused. He put his hands flat on the table and bent to look more closely at the drawing. His forehead wrinkled.

"What is it?" she asked.

"I don't know. But I've never seen its like before." Granville reached for the pages that contained Dupree's writings. "Get me a pencil, please, Clara."

She hurried to find a pencil and paper, which she placed on the table beside her uncle. She glanced at Mrs. Fox, who was watching Granville with her unwavering gaze. Sebastian came to stand next to her.

Granville muttered something to himself as he examined the diagram and read the papers, then began scribbling incompre-hensible notes. Clara's fingers curled into her palms as she waited, sensing her uncle's flare of curiosity. He rubbed a hand through his hair and wrote a series of letters in the form of a square.

"Uncle Granville, what is it?" Clara finally asked after a good half hour of his muttering and scribbling. Impatience tightened in her chest. "Is it the telegraph machine?"

"No. It's a machine meant for transmitting messages, but via some sort of cipher."

"That's it."

They turned to stare at Sebastian. "What?"

"That's the machine." Sebastian's spine straightened. "It transmits telegraphic messages through some form of secret writing. I believe some call it cryptology."

Granville frowned at the drawing. "I can only conclude that Monsieur Dupree would have sent such specifications to me in the hopes I'd know what to do with them." He looked at Sebastian, the reflection of sunlight on his glasses enhancing the suspicion in his eyes. "Clara tells me you sought the plans for your brother?"

"Yes." Sebastian rubbed a hand over the back of his neck, discomfort flashing across his expression. "He wrote to me from St. Petersburg asking for my help. He has since come to London. He wants to present the constructed machine to the Home Office, with full credit to Monsieur Dupree as the inventor. I would venture to say that should a patron wish to fund the project, Jacob will ensure the profits go to Monsieur Dupree's family."

Granville regarded him steadily. For a moment, a wealth of questions and answers seemed to pass between the two men, heightening Clara's impatience.

The devil himself could have the plans, for all she cared. *Anyone* could have them if it meant a chance she would be reunited with her son.

"So that's it, then," she said. "Give them to your brother and have the whole thing done with."

Granville placed his hand on the diagrams, the stack of notes. "Clara, please understand Monsieur Dupree must have sent them to me for safe-keeping. I cannot allow the originals to leave my possession."

"Make copies, then," she said. "You can do that, can't you?"

Granville didn't respond, his forehead creasing. Clara clenched her fists.

"Please," she said.

Her uncle looked at her. His eyes flashed with a wavering combination of reluctance and concern.

"Only for you," Granville said, "will I agree to this." He turned to look at the notes and diagrams, then nodded. "I'll start right now. Should take me a day or two."

Relief flooded Clara alongside a strange apprehension—the portent of what finding the machine plans actually meant to her future. The uncertainty of it all undulated before her like heat rising from cobblestones, hazy and indistinct.

She stared at Sebastian. A thin stream of light glinted off his dark hair and illuminated the golden flecks in his brown eyes.

He began questioning Granville about the cipher alphabet and transmission methods, his voice a deep cascade over the dusty sunlight.

Clara took the opportunity to escape the room. Her heart pounded like a wind-whipped leaf. Her breath came rapidly as she stopped in the foyer and struggled to calm her turmoil of emotions.

"Counterpoint."

His voice echoed against the walls. Settled into her blood, her bones. She turned to watch him approach, his footfalls oddly silent on the marble floor. He stopped before her, his dark gaze intent.

"I beg your pardon?" Clara said.

"In music, counterpoint involves independent melodic lines that harmonize when played together," Sebastian explained. "As in our situation, we can now give each other what we desire."

Clara's shoulders tensed, even as the word *desire* rippled through her.

"Have…" She swallowed past the dryness in her mouth. "Have you considered all the implications of marriage to me?"

"I have, indeed. And you know my expectations?"

Her breath burned her throat. She knew the expectations. She'd known of them since the idea of marriage had first occurred to her. She knew, because Sebastian Hall was not the type of man who would accept a platonic marriage, even one based on calculated ends.

She knew because thoughts of these *expectations* had seared her mind as she lay in bed at night, the thin sheets twisting around her legs, her body pulsing with restless palpitations she could not comprehend.

She told herself again she could do it. She could agree because Sebastian was a good man who would fulfill his part of the agreement. All she needed to do was give him copies of the plans. All she needed to do was take her vows and prove a loyal, good wife.

All she needed to do was share his bed.

A hot flush flooded her cheeks. She turned away to collect her composure.

Really, it wasn't as if she hadn't known a man before. It wasn't as if she didn't know what to expect. If Sebastian Hall was anything like Richard, he would climb beneath the coverlet, push her nightdress up to her hips, then have the whole business over and done with in a scant few minutes.

All she needed to do was lie there and wait for him to finish.

So why was apprehension swirling through her belly at the mere idea? Why could she not erase the image of Sebastian from her mind—him looming above her in the dark, the weight of his body heavy atop hers, his long-fingered hands brushing her bare skin as he slid her gown over her thighs…

Oh, God. Clara closed her eyes. She could not fathom the source of such imaginings. What on earth would the man think if he knew about them? If he knew how her body reacted to such thoughts of him?

"It distresses you so much, does it?" He was directly behind her, his voice a deep rumble spilling like warm water over her skin. "The idea of being my wife in all capacities?"

"No." The word had a bit of force behind it, to Clara's relief. She did not want Sebastian to think she wavered in her determination. She turned to face him, her pulse hammering. Unable to bring herself to look into his eyes, she stared at his mouth.

A mistake. His beautiful mouth—the shape of his upper lip marked by a slight indent, the smooth curve of his lower lip with the shadowy notch hiding beneath it like a secret—made untold longings spiral through her blood.

God in heaven. Did she want to marry him for more than the need to sell Wakefield House?

She lifted her head and found him watching her, intent but wary, as if he knew a false move would send her scurrying off. She looked away and gathered her resolve.

"I will be your wife in all capacities, Sebastian," she said.

"You don't even sound appalled at the prospect."

"Should I be?"

"Not to my knowledge." He stepped into the space between them and slid his hand beneath her chin, turning to her face him. "You needn't be frightened of me. I will uphold my part of the agreement, but I will not marry for practical reasons alone. I will not tolerate a marriage in name only. We will be husband and wife both in public and in private."

A tremble rippled through her. "I understand."

His hand dropped away from her, and he stepped back. A faint consternation flickered across his features, as if he didn't quite know what to make of her response. "I shall make the arrangements. We will be married next week."

CHAPTER 12

"*L*adies and gentlemen." Lady Rossmore climbed the steps to the stage of the Hanover Square ballroom and clapped her hands, raising her voice above the din. "May I have your attention, please? I welcome you all and would like to begin a demonstration of an automaton created by the esteemed inventor Mr. Granville Blake."

Sebastian pushed his right hand into his pocket and maneuvered through the crowd closer to the stage. He stopped beside his father, who stood with his fellow secretary Lord Margrave. Onstage, Lady Rossmore continued her lengthy discourse on Granville Blake's genius. She then stepped aside when the curtains parted to reveal Granville and the automaton.

Sebastian's breath stuck in the middle of his chest as his gaze skirted to Clara. She stood beside the harpsichord in a dark blue gown that was at least a year out of fashion but whose color reflected the light and cast a sheen of pink on her pale skin.

"Thank you for the lovely introduction, Lady Rossmore," Granville said, smoothing wrinkles from his coat with a sweep of his hand as he stepped forward to address the audience. "My niece, Mrs. Clara Shepherd, and I are honored to be here to demonstrate our newest creation, Millicent, the Musical Lady."

The crowd laughed at the name. Clara placed her hand on the shoulder of the mannequin, who sat at a small harpsichord, her porcelain fingers unmoving over the keys, her head bent. The mannequin wore a crimson silk gown edged in lace and accented by gold earrings and an ivory cameo. Her face was a model of feminine perfection, her cheeks and lips tinged with pink, her long eyelashes lowered in perfect feathery crescents.

"Millicent is an automaton who plays four tunes on the harpsichord," Granville continued. "We will demonstrate with three tunes and ask that you watch her carefully, as she moves her fingers, feet, and even her eyes with the utmost accuracy. After the demonstration, I invite you to examine the very intricate mechanisms more closely."

The audience rustled with interest, several women straining on tiptoe for a better view of the stage. Granville moved to the side of the harpsichord and took hold of the crank handle to wind the machine. He turned it halfway. The crank stuck.

Murmurs buzzed like insects from the audience. Clara moved to her uncle's side as he pulled the crank back into position and started to wind it again. It jerked at the same sticking point, then rotated. The bellows inside the instrument released an audible expulsion of compressed air, and the wheels began to turn.

Relief flashed across Clara's face. Granville wound the machine twice more and stepped back to watch Millicent perform. The mannequin's chest expanded as if she were inhaling air into her lungs, and then her fingers began to move across the keys. A tinny but pleasing melody drifted from the harpsichord.

Gasps and applause rose from the guests as they shifted to obtain a better view. Clara smiled.

Millicent seemed to preen at the attention, her elegant head sweeping back and forth as she watched the keys, her foot tapping in time to the music. After the first tune concluded, she gave a slight bow before starting to play again.

"I heard tell that Lady Rossmore intends to offer her patronage to Blake's Museum." Lord Margrave scratched his bristling side whiskers as he peered at Millicent. "Apparently Fairfax's daughter is Blake's new assistant, so her ladyship believes he ought to have the means to exhibit more of his work."

Sebastian slanted his gaze to Margrave. "You know Mrs. Shepherd?"

"Indeed. Her husband was quite a promising young fellow. Tragic death in a hunting accident. Fairfax has been good enough to take the son under his wing."

He returned his attention to the stage as Granville concluded the demonstration and the audience began buzzing with excitement and questions. Several people crowded up to the stage to look at Millicent more closely, while others drifted toward the refreshment table.

Sebastian's heart thumped against his rib cage as he saw Clara weaving through the crowd. As if sensing his presence, she turned her head and smiled, then diverted her path to approach him.

"It went well, don't you think?" she asked. "Lady Rossmore was quite pleased."

Sebastian nodded, acutely aware of his father's presence. "Mrs. Shepherd, this is my father, the Earl of Rushton."

"Oh." A flush painted her cheeks as she realized the familiarity of her remark. "Lord Rushton, it's a pleasure to make your acquaintance."

"Yours as well, Mrs. Shepherd." Rushton studied her with his apple-peeling gaze. "Quite a unique demonstration, I must say."

"Thank you, my lord. My uncle has a number of—" Her eyes skidded to Margrave. "Er, good evening, Lord Margrave."

Though he didn't know the reason for her sudden unease,

Sebastian moved closer to her, resisting the urge to pull her protectively to his side.

"Mrs. Shepherd." Margrave gave her a short nod. "I saw your father not three weeks ago at a steeplechase. Visited Manley Park recently, have you?"

"No...no, not for some time, my lord." She paused, glanced at Rushton, then back to Margrave. "Have you been to Manley Park, my lord?"

"This past summer, yes," Margrave replied. "Your father invited Lady Margrave and myself for a Saturday to Monday visit. He's procured a very impressive studhorse."

"I've heard, yes." Tension threaded her voice. "Was Andrew Shepherd present, my lord?"

Sebastian saw a slight frown tug at Rushton's mouth, but the implications of the question appeared lost on Margrave.

"No, no, didn't see him, unfortunately. Fairfax said the boy wasn't well." Margrave shook his head. "He's back in London now, I think, Fairfax is. Must speak to him about the railway investments he was considering. Might have brought the boy along. Beg your pardon, there's Lord Crombie. Rushton, I'll see you at the club, yes?"

Clara took a step back, her skin white as paper. Margrave bid them a good evening and pushed through the crowd.

"Well, Mrs. Shepherd, if your father is in town, I'd be pleased to make his acquaintance," Rushton remarked.

Sebastian slipped his hand beneath her elbow. "Clara?"

"Excuse me. I...I need some air." She pulled from his grip and hurried toward the doors leading to the street.

Sebastian and Rushton exchanged glances before Sebastian went after her. He caught her on the steps, reaching out with his right hand to grasp her arm. Momentarily startled, he watched his hand obey his instinctive command to draw her to a halt.

She spun around. "What? *What?*"

He cupped her cheek with his other hand, easing her face upward to look at him. "Why are you so afraid of your father?"

"He has my son, Sebastian. And if he comes to London, he won't allow me to see Andrew." She pressed her hands to her face and closed her eyes. "Lord Margrave said Andrew wasn't well. What does that mean? What's wrong with him?"

She shivered, hugging her arms around herself. Sebastian removed his coat and slipped it around her shoulders as protection against the cold night air.

Help her.

The command fell through his mind like a stone into a lake, expanding outward in foaming waves. He slipped his hand to her neck. Her pulse beat strong and rapid. He eased his thumb to touch the soft, vulnerable hollow just beneath her jaw. He wanted to remove his glove, feel the softness of her skin against his thumb.

She still hadn't told him everything. He'd sensed it when she'd first proposed, but he had told himself it didn't matter, since the marriage would fulfill their practical goals. Now, seeing the distress written so plainly across Clara's face, Sebastian wanted her to trust him enough to confide in him.

"Have you tried to see Andrew in Surrey?" he asked.

She shook her head. "Fairfax has banned me from Manley Park."

"Why?" He wound a lock of her hair around his forefinger. "Why is your father so vehement about keeping Andrew from you?"

Clara's eyes skidded to meet his. A dark red bloomed in their depths, like the molten heat of an incipient volcano. When she spoke, her voice was even, cold as glass in winter and edged with black.

"Because he thinks I killed my husband."

Sebastian recoiled in shock. A thousand years passed in the

instant between her utterance of the dark confession and his absorption of her words. He stared at her, knowing the falsity of such an accusation and yet unable to fathom the reason for its very existence.

"It's why I was forced to leave," Clara said. "Richard and I had a contentious marriage, one in which my father frequently intervened on Richard's behalf. My father despised what he considered my lack of deference and chastised me for it daily. One weekend Richard and I argued about Andrew accompanying them on a hunting excursion. I didn't want Andrew to go because the weather looked threatening, but Richard insisted. I accompanied them because I thought I could at least return to the house with Andrew if a storm approached.

"We were gone for an hour when I realized Andrew had forgotten his satchel. I went back for it, and when I returned I found Richard had fallen from his horse and hit his head. He was still breathing, but..."

Tears spilled down her cheeks. She looked away, the burn of despair darkening. "Neither my father nor Andrew was there. I didn't know what had happened. I started shouting Andrew's name, which is how my father found me. I don't know what he thought at that moment, but he hauled Richard's body onto his horse and rode back to the house to send for the constable. I think by the time he arrived at home, he'd already decided I was somehow responsible for Richard's death."

Sebastian's heart thumped against his ribs. "He had no evidence that you were."

"No. He also had no evidence that I wasn't." Clara dashed a hand across her eyes. "We found Andrew at the house when we returned. He'd ridden back on his own. He said he hadn't seen what happened to Richard. Everything was a blur after that. The constable came. We had funeral arrangements. And a week after we discovered Richard had left custody of Andrew to my father, he threatened to send me away. That was when I left Manley Park. To this day, my father remains certain that I had a hand in Richard's death. He believed I surrendered to a rash act of mutiny caused by my unbalanced sensibilities."

An ugly question rose to Sebastian's mind. He didn't want to ask, but for the sake of all that his family had endured, he had to. "Did he make a public accusation?"

"No." Clara expelled her breath on a heavy sigh. "He knew there was no evidence, but he wanted to separate me from my son. And so he has."

Sebastian grasped his right hand with his left, curling his fingers into a fist. Anger and tension knotted the back of his neck.

"Why didn't you tell me this sooner?"

"Because I was afraid you wouldn't help me." She shook her head. "I'm sorry. You shouldn't marry me."

"I've already agreed to your proposal," Sebastian said. "More than that, I want to marry you."

Clara's lips parted, drawing his attention to the full line of her mouth. Heat twisted through his lower body, the urge to kiss her seizing his blood even as his mind wrestled with his blunt admission.

He wanted to help her beyond conducting the transfer of Wakefield House. He just had no idea what else he could do. Blackness swamped his chest, threatened to pull him under. He knew the feeling well and hated it as much now as he had the night he'd stood in front of the Weimar musicians and Franz Liszt to resign his position.

He lowered his head to her left ear, the one that was lost in silence.

"I will find a way," he whispered, the promise made to himself and not her. Not yet. Only when he could confirm his ability to carry it through would she hear his vow.

Clara turned her head, as if she sought to remind him he spoke into her damaged ear. The movement brought their mouths perilously close together, so close her breath swept across his lips.

"I'm scared," she confessed.

"So am I." He understood it, her fear about something over which she both blamed herself and yet had no control. He understood it because the same fear seethed beneath his own skin.

"You?" She gave a husky laugh. "What are you afraid of?"

He pressed his forehead against hers. She closed her eyes and curled her hand around the lapel of his coat. The smells of machine oil and perfume clung to her, but beneath it he detected the scent of oranges and spice, a strangely tropical aroma that sweetened his bitter thoughts.

Her lips brushed his. So soft. So gentle. Her fear seemed to dissolve into the tenderness of her sigh, the unwinding of tension from her body. He laced his hands around her waist, drew her closer, deepened the kiss until she arched like a supple willow against him.

The icy thoughts thawed, melting into the heat of their kiss, the press of their bodies. Warmth filled Sebastian, twined through his blood. A vital energy surged from her into him, a spark of electricity that ignited a fresh resolve.

Clara placed her hand flat on his chest and eased herself away from him. Urgency threaded her voice. "I must find out what happened to Andrew, Sebastian. I will not lose sight of him."

"Nor will I."

They stared at each other, the bloom of night between them, the sounds of the ball filtering through the open doorways of the building. In that moment, a strange, reckless impulse seized Sebastian hard—the urge to grab his world and force it upright, to find his footing again, to repair everything that had been broken.

For him. And now for her.

"Bastian." Rushton's voice carried through the night air.

Clara stepped away, then turned and fled back into the building. Sebastian took a breath and faced his father, whose keen gaze followed the woman.

"You've a particular interest in Mrs. Shepherd," Rushton remarked.

"I ought to," Sebastian said. "I'm going to marry her."

Grim satisfaction filled him as his father blinked with evident surprise. Sebastian's pronouncement hung in the air. Rushton cleared his throat.

"Bastian, she is an assistant in an automata museum who—"

"She is lovely and respectable, and she..." His voice tangled suddenly as he recited his father's own words about finding a wife who would make him a better man. "You gave me both an ultimatum and a suggestion, my lord. Marriage to Mrs. Shepherd will fulfill both."

The mention of Rushton's ultimatum left a sour taste on Sebastian's tongue, as if such a calculated motive somehow diminished the intensity of his feelings for Clara. Marriage to her would do more than fulfill a condition. Sebastian suspected it would somehow fulfill *him*, though he could hardly explain that to himself, let alone his father.

"You have recommended several young women who would serve as a suitable match for me, sir," he said, his voice sharpening with determination. "Yet you have neglected to take into account my view on the matter. You now have my response to your decree. I *choose* to marry Clara Shepherd."

They looked at each other, Rushton's dark eyes penetrating the dusky light. A flood of questions and answers seemed to fill the space between them, reminders of the countess, of all their family had lost and still sought to regain. Sebastian steeled himself for a battle, prepared to defend his decision with every ounce of his being, but then...rather to his shock...his father stepped back.

"Very well," Rushton said. "If Mrs. Shepherd is your choice, then I trust you to fulfill your obligations with the honor that befits the son of an earl." He turned toward the door leading back to the drawing room. "I hope she will, at the very least, remind you of what nobler qualities you can possess. Only by improving oneself can a man sustain a good and rewarding marriage."

CHAPTER 13

*C*lara looked at the clock. Nearly four. Mrs. Fox's voice came from the parlor, where she was explaining the history of Uncle Granville's inventions to a visitor. Granville was back in the workshop continuing his task of copying the intricate details of the cipher machine plans.

Without informing either of them of her intentions, Clara pulled on her cloak and left the museum. As she hurried toward the cab stand, the clatter of horses' hooves and carriage wheels neared.

She stepped aside as a black carriage came to a halt beside her. The door opened, and Sebastian descended with a sense of purpose, as if he'd come directly for her.

"Where are you going?" he asked.

Trepidation tightened her throat. She had not had an opportunity to speak to him in private since Lady Rossmore's charity ball two nights before. It was for the best, she tried to tell herself, as after her confession she feared that any conversation might result in his withdrawal from their agreement.

"I've...I've a few errands to run," she explained. "Why are you here?"

"I've come to tell you my father has given his assent for our marriage," Sebastian said. "Had he not done so, I still would have married you, but his approval will sanctify the union for the benefit of society."

"Very...very well." Lord Rushton's approval was, Clara knew, the last element needed for the marriage to proceed smoothly. Now they needed only to speak their vows.

"I'll accompany you on your errands, then." Sebastian stepped aside to allow her to precede him to the curb. "We'll take my carriage."

"That's not necessary. There's a cab stand at the end of the street."

Sebastian frowned. "It's growing dark. Where have you to go?"

Clara stared at the looming interior of the carriage. She'd already told him everything. And he had not retreated. She felt her resolve to keep him at a distance slipping away like raindrops on a windowpane. Not even to herself she could deny her gratitude for his presence, his insistence on remaining by her side.

"My father stays in Belgravia when he is in London," she said. "I...I sometimes wait outside his town house to see if he's brought Andrew with him. Thus far, I haven't caught a glimpse of him."

His left hand tightened on her arm. "What is the address?"

Swimming suddenly in the need for companionship so she would not have to face the predictable disappointment alone, Clara recited the street number and allowed Sebastian to hand her into the carriage. His deep voice rumbled as he relayed the address to his driver, then climbed in after her. Dusky light slanted across his strong features, his dark eyes glittering as he watched her from the opposite seat.

Clara folded her arms around herself and swallowed hard, her blood pulsing with the troubled urge to close the distance between them, to slide onto the bench beside him and curl her body tight against his. She could almost feel him—the hard, lean length of his muscles, his broad chest, the weight of his arm as he draped it across her shoulders and pulled her closer.

She wanted the haven of his warmth and strength, a safety she had never known. Her untold longing was made all the more potent by the knowledge that he would not turn her away. Not physically, at least.

Clara forced her gaze to the window, aware of the danger Sebastian Hall posed. Her soul was already so threaded with cracks, brittle from repeated breakage and vain attempts at repair. If she allowed him to slide between those cracks and find his way into her heart, she would then give him the power to deliver a fatal, crushing blow.

And yet she would not renege on her proposition, dangerous as it was to her very being. She could not retreat now, did not want to, or everything would be lost.

She stared at the passing streets. Shadows and waning light skated across the storefronts, the narrow tenement buildings, the fruit stalls and horse-drawn carts. Before long, elegant town houses swept into view, the brick façades adorned with curved balconies and slender pilasters.

The carriage shuddered to a halt. Clara leaned forward, sliding the curtain farther aside to enhance her view of the house across the street. A gleaming black door barred the entrance, and the windows blinked like eyes in the reddish light. A menacing silence seemed to emanate from the house, as if warning passersby that nothing good lurked within.

No lamps shone through the windows. The expected disappointment pierced her heart, sharp as a driven nail.

"They're not at home," she murmured. "Or *he's* not at home."

Sebastian leaned across and settled his hand on her knee. The heat of his palm burned clear through her skirts and petticoats.

Clara made a fist to prevent herself from placing her hand atop his and tracing the long lines of his fingers.

She continued watching her father's house. An ache built in her throat. She heard Sebastian's breath, the sound weaving into her ear alongside the increased beat of her heart.

He did not take his hand from her leg. After an interminable period of time, she relaxed her tight fist and allowed her hand to spread over his. Not looking at him, she pulled off her gloves. He turned his palm upward. His strong fingers knotted with hers.

Desire sheared into her soul like the clip of scissors, both the physical reaction of warmth and the longing not to feel so utterly alone anymore. Even her beloved uncle with his unflagging support could not ease her sense of cold isolation.

But the clasp of Sebastian's hand in hers reminded her of his presence and assuaged the loneliness. Just a bit. Just for now.

She tightened her fingers on his as a black carriage pulled in front of the town house. She recognized the matching grays that came to a stop, their sleek manes rippling in the twilight, their polished hooves stamping the cobblestones.

Her spine stiffened. In one swift movement, Sebastian was beside her, peering past her through the window. "Is that your father?"

"H-his carriage."

Fairfax's driver had parked at an angle that allowed her to see the space between the carriage and the front of the town house. When the footman swung open the carriage door, Clara gripped Sebastian's hand so tightly her knuckles burned.

Her father stepped down—a tall, slender figure in a blue greatcoat and hat, his gloves white as bone in the diminishing light. Fairfax carried himself with an elegance that masked his brutal streak, like a gleaming sharp sword concealed within an ivory-tipped cane.

Even as dark memories and anger rushed at her in a torrent, Clara's heart wrenched at the sight of the man who had sired her, clothed and fed her, the man who might still, somewhere, harbor an emotion resembling love for her.

Fairfax spoke to the footman. No one followed him down from the carriage.

Clara tried to deflect the arrow of disappointment, realizing only in that moment of bitter dejection how much she had hoped today would be different from all the other times she had sat in desperate surveillance, wishing for one glimpse of her son.

She turned to Sebastian, seeking his eyes, needing his assurance. "You can tell your dri—"

"Clara." Holding her gaze, he nodded to the window.

She looked…and gasped. The footman held the door of the carriage again to allow a brown-haired boy to exit. Andrew grasped the handle as he navigated the steps and stopped not far from where Fairfax stood.

Clara's heart pounded wildly, her blood filling with a chaotic mixture of joy and despair. She couldn't breathe, couldn't think past the single desperate thought that her son stood a scant distance away and had no idea she was *right here.*

Fairfax turned, lifting his arm as a breeze threatened to tip his hat from his head.

In that instant, Clara saw it. Andrew flinched, hunching his shoulders into his coat and taking a half-step back. The movement was almost unnoticeable, or at the very least attributable to a gust of cold air or unpleasant odor…but Clara knew her son's reaction for what it was, and the very marrow of her bones froze to ice.

"No." The word scraped her throat like rusted metal. *"No."*

She wrenched her hand from Sebastian's grip and flung open the carriage door. Rage swamped her so fast, so hard, that murder felt within her grasp. She plunged with reckless abandon across the street. "Andrew!"

"Clara!" Sebastian shouted from behind her.

A screeching noise filled the air, the yell of a cart driver, the whinnying cry of a frightened horse.

"Andrew!"

Her father and son both turned. Fairfax moved with the swiftness of a lizard, shoving Andrew toward the town house steps and snapping orders at one of the footmen. The man rushed between Clara and Andrew, blocking the boy from her line of sight.

"No!" Blinded by tears, Clara reached the other side of the street the instant the town house door opened and the second footman pushed Andrew inside. "I won't let you do this! I won't let you keep him from me!"

"Stay away, Clara." Fairfax faced her, pointing his forefinger as if to condemn her. "You have no right to him."

"I do have a right to him!" Her chest burned with anguish. "I'm his mother. Andrew!"

The footman at the door grunted suddenly and grabbed his shin. A small figure darted around him and back down the steps.

Tears streamed down Clara's cheeks as Andrew approached closer…closer…a few more steps and he would be in her unbreakable embrace, his arms around her neck, and she would run and run and keep running….

"Stop." Fairfax flung his arm out to arrest the boy's flight. Andrew slammed into the barrier and stumbled backward, his wide-eyed gaze locked to Clara's. Even then, she saw the desperation seething in his young soul.

Before she could move forward again, the footman hurried down the steps to grasp Andrew's shoulder and pull him back toward the house.

Fairfax stepped in front of Clara. Her breath lodged in her throat as she lifted her terrified gaze to her father. Cold laced his expression, his features as immovable as the rocky outcropping of a cliff.

"Please…" She whispered the desperate, broken plea. Sebastian's hand closed over her arm.

Her father didn't acknowledge the other man's presence. Fairfax stood rigidly, feet apart, the stance of a man of power. He stared at Clara, his eyes stamped with utter detachment, stark and hard as a fossil.

In that instant, she knew whatever love he might have once felt for her had dissolved into nothing. Just as she knew her own heart had long ago cast him out.

A second footman stepped in front of her.

"Get out of my way." A flame of renewed fury spilled over her. She lunged at the man, clawing at his face, kicking his shins, but he was an unbreachable wall until his big hands closed over her shoulders and pulled her toward the dark interior of her father's carriage.

Another pair of arms closed around Clara from behind, yanking her from the footman's grip. Sebastian half-dragged, half-carried her away as she frantically struggled to get loose.

People had stopped to gape at the commotion, but there was no sign of a seven-year-old boy with eyes the color of toffee…

The black door of the town house slammed shut.

He was gone.

Clara collapsed to the ground, sobs wrenching her, every breath pulsing anguish through her entire body. Sebastian pulled her closer, his arms tightening, the wall of his chest solid against her back. He was saying something, she felt the movement of his lips against her hair, but she couldn't hear him past the sobbing inside her head.

Finally, when her last cries had left her wrung out and empty, she let him guide her back to his carriage and crumpled against the seat. She wanted to beat on the town house door until her knuckles bled, but no amount of screaming would convince her father to admit her.

Just the opposite. Now that she'd caused a scene, Fairfax might very well fortify his stronghold around Andrew.

A fresh wash of tears streamed down her face. Sebastian sat beside her as the carriage rattled into motion. She stared at him, the hard set of his jaw, the burn of his dark eyes. Contained energy vibrated from him, as if he sought to keep leashed a vivid anger.

Awareness seared through Clara's despair—the memory of his touch, his mouth, the cloak of forgetting he offered her without the slightest knowledge that he held such power.

The carriage lurched to the right, tossing her closer to him, and the length of his thigh pressing through her skirts sent a bolt of need arcing through her. Clara released the tight breath from her lungs, forced the anguish down into an icy ball, burning it beneath the simmering heat Sebastian's presence wrought in her.

He will banish all that is painful and leave nothing but pleasure.

There could be, Clara knew, a fragile thread between pain and pleasure, a thread broken with a brush of fingertips. But she alone could withstand Sebastian's ability to cause her pain by sealing her heart against him, even as she opened her body to him.

With a muffled groan, she twisted on the seat to face him, her skirts tangling as she clambered to her knees and wound her arms around his neck. Shock rippled through his lean, muscled frame as he started to speak, his left hand grasping her hip to steady her in the shaking carriage.

Clara slanted her lips hard over his, relief billowing in her at the first touch of his beautiful mouth, the scrape of his whiskers delicious against her palms as she positioned herself to deepen the kiss. Thought fell away, subsumed by the heat breaking over her skin.

Sebastian's fingers tightened on her hip, the strength of his hand burning clear through her skirts. She thrust her hands into his hair and relished the glide of the thick strands against her palms. She moaned against his mouth and shifted to straddle his hard thighs, pressing herself against him.

He cursed, the sound deep and guttural between them. She gripped his shoulders as if he were the only secure element in a sea foaming with angry waves. His breath was hot, his restraint evident in the tight muscles of his arms, the stiffness of his grip as he sought to keep space between them. Not wanting to allow it, she thrust her tongue past his lips, drank him in, and reveled in the sizzling desire traversing her every nerve.

Desire. That was it, the elusive sensation that had spiraled inside her from the moment he'd first allowed his dark, apprecia-tive eyes to peruse her body. From the moment she had stared at his throat and wondered what it would feel like to press her lips to the smooth, taut column.

She gasped, breaking the kiss as her fingers fumbled to unravel the bonds of his cravat, to release the buttons of his collar and bare his skin to her seeking lips.

Sebastian's hands enveloped hers, his breath brushing the fine hairs sweeping across her temple. "Clara."

"No." She ripped at the cravat, sent the buttons of his shirt clattering to the carriage floor. Even in the dusky light she saw the hollow of his throat pulsing with the beat of his heart, betraying the response of his body.

She pressed her mouth to that hot indentation at the base of his throat, clenching her fingers into his arms as she flicked her tongue out to taste the salt of his skin. Sebastian groaned, low and rough, a sound that rippled through her blood.

Emboldened, she thrust herself against the muscled planes of his thighs. Her knees hugged his hips. Shocked pleasure cascaded upward when the core of her body shifted to enfold the hard swell in his trousers, her thighs clenching around him with instinctive need.

Heat shot across her skin. And then, eliciting a burst of triumph, Sebastian was kissing her in return, his mouth rough and desperate, his hands yanking up the folds of her skirts and petticoats to grasp her thighs and press her more tightly against that male arousal that had never before evoked such a sharp, sudden yearning in her.

She shifted, writhed, her mouth locked to his. She smoothed her hands over his chest, imprinting the feel of his muscles in her mind, the heat of his skin burning through the fine linen of his shirt.

He stroked his tongue over her lower lip and grasped the coil of hair at the base of her scalp. With a few tugs, her hair unraveled in a long skein down her back. Sebastian muttered another oath and speared his hands into the thick mass, angling her head to allow him access to the innermost recesses of her mouth.

She melted inside, her tongue tangling with his, her body pulsing with urgency. Sebastian pushed his hips upward and rubbed against some secret, throbbing place at her core, heat building like a kindled fire poised to erupt into flames.

Clara lifted her head, her breath steaming as she stared into his blazing eyes. Her breasts strained against her corset, her dress heavy and stifling in the dark heat of the carriage.

"What..." She couldn't voice the question as her hips shifted again. She flared with the desire to be free of clothing, to feel the glide of his erection against the shell of her body, to reach whatever completion lay beyond her grasp.

Sebastian's fingers tightened on her thighs, his own lean frame still vibrating with restraint. Uncertain, Clara felt her body strain for more, sensing that all these uncoiling sensations would compel her toward a shattering pleasure she had never before known.

She clutched the fabric of his shirt in her fists, her throat rippling with a hard swallow as she sought the pleasures of his mouth again. His stubbled jaw scraped her cheek as he shifted, his lips brushing the corner of her mouth on a path to her left ear. He spoke then, his chest rumbled with the sound, but whatever words he voiced were lost in the silence of her damaged ear.

She tightened her grip on him, panic mushrooming in her belly to subsume the taut urgency of lust. She clenched her thighs around his hips and fought again to seize the hot, silken threads she already felt slipping from her grasp.

Sebastian's hands cupped either side of her face, his thumbs easing away the lingering dampness on her cheeks. His resolve was conquering his lust; Clara saw the evidence in the set of his jaw and the flare of regret brewing in his eyes.

She gripped his shirt harder, tears spilling over when he slid his hands from her thighs, allowing her skirts and petticoats to flood back over her legs and conceal her wantonness.

Hating her desperation, she crushed her mouth to his again, pressing her breasts to his chest, fighting for his response. He closed his hands around her waist and began to lift her away from him.

"No." The word broke between them, frantic and shattered.

Clara clung to him, refusing to unclench her fists from his shirt, locking her legs around his hips. Fear pierced her to the bones, for she knew that if she released him, if she let him break this blinding hot spell of passion, then the isolation would descend upon her and freeze her soul to ice.

Sebastian tugged at her grasping hands, pulled her legs from their circled clamp around him. A muscle throbbed in his clenched jaw, betraying his own inner fight. But he was so much bigger, stronger, that Clara already knew she stood no chance against his determination to separate them.

A bolt of rage pierced her. She forced herself to sever her body from his, shoving at his chest as she flung herself across the bench and away from him. She huddled against the opposite side of the carriage and wrapped her arms around herself, smothering the new sobs welling in her throat.

For a long moment, the rasp of their hard breathing sliced

through the noise of the carriage. Then Sebastian swore again, a sound of pained frustration, and scraped a hand roughly through his hair. He turned to her, eyes glittering with banked lust.

"Not here." Steel threads of determination wove through his hoarse voice. "Not like this."

Clara wrenched her gaze from him and stared out the window, unseeing, blinded by tears. Cold slithered across her skin from the inside out.

"Goddamn you," she whispered.

A humorless laugh shattered the brittle air. "He already has."

CHAPTER 14

"*W*hat is he doing with Clara?" Lord Fairfax lifted his head, stretching the corded muscles of his neck. Pressure collected behind his eyes, causing a throb of pain.

Saunders, his secretary, shifted his weight as a glimmer of discomfort rose in his expression. "Er, it seems as if they are to be wed, my lord. Mr. Hall applied for a special license last week."

"Wed?" Something knotted at the back of Fairfax's mind, though he couldn't focus well enough to unravel it. "How long have they been acquainted?"

"I couldn't say, my lord."

Fairfax drummed his pen on the desk. Clara had a reckless streak to her, a regrettable inheritance from her mother. The same impulse had sent Elizabeth into more than one untenable situation, requiring Fairfax to set things right by whatever means necessary.

"Well." He dismissed Saunders with a wave of his hand. "Ensure she does not plan anything foolish."

Though accosting him screaming in the streets was the height of foolishness, as far as Fairfax was concerned.

Stupid girl. If she'd thought to gain anything by such rash behavior, she would be sorely disappointed.

"Yes, my lord." Saunders bowed slightly and turned to leave, pausing when he saw the small figure of Andrew hovering in the doorway. Davies the butler stood behind him.

Fairfax frowned. Andrew was thin and pale, nothing like his son, William, had been. William had also inherited Elizabeth's rash impulses, but at least he'd had a robust constitution and strength of will, which Fairfax knew was a result of his firm upbringing. He'd raised his son well, ensuring he knew how to fight, to defend himself. As a result, William had been strong and fearless.

Fairfax suspected he wouldn't be so fortunate with his grandson. Already Andrew was weak, preferring picture books and drawing to hunting. The boy couldn't fire a gun to save his life. Richard would be appalled if he knew his son still flinched at the mere neighing of a horse.

A painful longing pierced him, born from William's death at too young an age. Fairfax wanted a true son again, one he could count as a companion, one whom he could mold into his own image. A young man of cunning and strength and sportsmanship. One who would prove loyal and obliging to the bitter end.

He stared at Andrew. Not like this introspective boy, who looked as if his fate should lie within the stagnant confines of a church or university.

Pathetic.

"What?" Fairfax asked his grandson, his voice sharp with regret and disappointment.

Andrew didn't respond, not that Fairfax expected him to. Thin relief curled through him, but not enough to assuage the fear that had burned in his gut since he'd heard Andrew speak to his tutor less than a month ago. Just one word, a whispered answer to a geography question, but it was enough.

As far as Fairfax knew, the boy hadn't said anything before or since, but he would not risk the chance that Andrew would regain use of his voice for good. For if Andrew were to speak again, his words could prove damning.

Davies cleared his throat. "I believe Master Andrew wishes to see his mother, my lord."

"Your mother abandoned you," Fairfax snapped at Andrew. "And do not think you can escape unnoticed and find her. Try to do so, and I'll flay the skin from your back."

Andrew flinched. Even Davies looked appalled, as if such a vicious threat had physically struck him. The pain behind Fairfax's eyes stabbed harder, fueling his anger. Weak lot, all of them.

"Get out," he ordered. "Both of you. And remember this, Andrew. Your mother is dead."

CHAPTER 15

*M*oonlight shone gray and pallid through the fog. Sebastian dragged his fingers across the piano keys, the resulting cacophony echoing the restless pulse of his blood. Colors tumbled together, as if they were spinning inside a storm. He slammed both hands down on the keys with a crash. A cramp knotted the fingers of his right hand. He shoved away from the piano, then paced to the hearth.

A mistake. The whole bloody thing was a mistake—his reckless capitulation to his father's demand, his agreement to help Jacob, his acceptance of Clara's proposal, which had seemed so practical at the time and was swiftly becoming fraught with more complications than he could bear.

The most prominent being that he wanted to kill Fairfax himself.

A brittle fiber of level-headedness, one that would have made Jacob proud, had prevented Sebastian from attacking the baron and forcing his surrender to Clara's pleas. He knew they required an advantage before Fairfax would agree to speak to them—and even then, Sebastian doubted the man's willingness to negotiate.

Didn't appear likely, given Fairfax's reaction to seeing Clara.

Bastard.

Breath billowed from Sebastian's lungs as if someone had punched him in the gut.

The front bell rang, bringing his attention to the clock. Nearly seven. He waved off one of the footmen, then went to the door and opened it. The folds of a hood shadowed Clara's features, but could not conceal the resolve burning in her violet eyes. Unease lanced through Sebastian as he glanced behind her to the black cab waiting at the curb.

"What are you doing here?" he asked.

"Uncle Granville finished the copies just after dinner," Clara said. Her voice shook, a shiver of pale blue-gold.

Sebastian pulled a hand down his face as a curse ruptured his thoughts. Emotions flared in him—anticipation, relief, disquiet, pleasure. Fear.

"Where is your uncle now?" he asked.

"At home. He'd planned to deliver the plans to you tomorrow. I hadn't told him you need them tonight."

"Did you come here alone?" Sebastian yanked open the door and ushered her in.

Clara stepped into the foyer. With a trembling hand, she brushed her hood back from her head. The folds cascaded into a puddle around her long, slender neck, drawing Sebastian's gaze to the hollow of her throat. The sight of her pale skin roused his lust, which he had fought to keep contained since their encounter in his carriage yesterday.

Arousal coiled through his lower body. Heated memories swept his mind in flashes of color—the hot cavern of Clara's mouth, the delicious press of her thighs against his aching erection, the tight way she'd locked her legs around him and clung as if she would never let go, as if she belonged to him and him alone...

Christ. Heaviness settled low in his groin. Although he knew he'd done the right thing in putting a stop to matters, he bitterly regretted the circumstances that had forced him to take such measures.

Because God knew he wanted her. Not even the restless sting of half-sleep could smother the desire that burned him during the night, the hot imaginings twisting through his mind of Clara splayed beneath him with her hands gripping his naked back and her gasps hot against his ear.

With every breath, he wanted her more.

And he *would* have her. One day soon, he would have her until the earth fell away beneath them.

He swallowed, his agitation tempered by the knowledge that they now had an agreement. If he thought it a mistake, he could not retreat now, even if he wanted to. And with Clara standing in front of him, the folds of her cloak draping over her slender curves, her unpainted lips full and parted, a pulse tapping in her lovely throat...Sebastian knew he would sell his soul to the devil if it meant having her as his wife.

She watched him warily. "Do you still intend to meet with Jacob?"

"Yes."

"And give him the plans?"

"Yes."

"Then you won't..."

"I have no intention of reneging on our agreement."

Her throat rippled with a swallow. "What about your father?"

Sebastian's jaw tightened. "He has approved of our engagement and no doubt learned whatever he could about you and your father from the members of his club. We owe him no further information." He forced his fingers to unclench from the doorjamb. "I will return you to the museum before meeting with Jacob."

"I want to go with you."

Sebastian jerked his gaze to hers. Alarm split through him at the unyielding determination in her expression.

"Why?" he asked.

"Monsieur Dupree entrusted the plans to my uncle," Clara said. "And though Uncle Granville would never admit this, I know he feels as if he has somehow betrayed his mentor by making copies of the plans. Yet he did it for me, because he trusts me. I will not see his faith in me misplaced. I must insist upon knowing more about what your brother intends to do."

Bloody hell. Even Sebastian didn't know all the details of what Jacob intended to do. He would find out tonight. But because he was suspicious of his brother's hidden motives, Sebastian did not want Clara to hear anything directly from Jacob. He didn't want her to know that Jacob had promised to compensate him financially. And he especially did not want to subject her to his brother's knife-edged perception.

"You can't go with me," he said.

"Why not?" She stepped forward. "I'm to be your wife. You made it quite clear we will not wed in name only, so I've a right to accompany you."

Sebastian's teeth came together hard. "I will tell you what you want to know after—"

"No. I want to go with you. If you do not allow it, rest assured I will follow you." She paused. "And I will not give you the plans until we arrive at our destination."

He stared at her for a long minute, convinced this was some form of punishment for having arrested things in the carriage the previous day.

"Where are the plans?" he asked.

"I'll give them to you when we arrive at the meeting," she repeated, turning back to the door. "I've told the driver to wait, but we'd best hurry so we're not late."

Sebastian swore aloud this time, his fists clenching as he glanced at the clock. Whatever game Clara was playing, he had no time for it, not if he intended to settle the bargain with his brother. And settle it he must, for he hadn't gone to such drastic lengths—the promise of *marriage*, for the love of God—to risk the whole thing going to hell now.

He yanked his greatcoat from the rack and stalked after Clara to the carriage. The plans had to be inside. Once he had them, he'd pay the driver a handsome sum to ensure Clara's safe return to the museum.

He gripped the door and hauled himself into the cab, throwing Clara a dark and fulminating glare. She merely blinked at him.

"Where are the plans?" Sebastian asked through gritted teeth.

"I told you when I would give them to you." She tilted her head and gave him a look that was both amused and considering. "And I thought I was the one with the hearing loss."

A growl rumbled in Sebastian's throat as he leaned out to snap the address at the driver. Then he slammed the door as the cab jolted into motion. Clara looked out the window, her expression impassive as porcelain—the polar opposite of her heated desperation the last time they had shared a carriage.

Sebastian grimaced, shifting as the memory rushed heat through his lower body. What did the infuriating woman hope to accomplish with this? Whatever it was, in any case, he ought to leave her at the museum. Wake Granville and tell him not to let Clara from his sight until Sebastian had settled with his brother.

Except that he couldn't settle anything with Jacob unless he had the goddamned plans.

Right. Everything about the whole affair was a mistake. And he was a bloody fool to have thought any differently.

He folded his arms across his chest and stared at Clara through the shadowed light, thrusting aside the knowledge of what their agreement would entail. If he allowed himself to imagine her as his wife, his brain would flood with intoxicating images of all the acts sanctified by the marriage covenant—and several especially gratifying ones that weren't.

An unwelcome speculation surfaced regarding her previous

marriage. What had been the true nature of her relationship with Richard Shepherd? Had the man made her happy? Had he satisfied her?

Sebastian's fingers dug into his palms, anger cording his back at the idea of another man, even a former husband, touching Clara.

Mine.

The word exploded like a star behind his eyes, drenching him in feelings of possession, lust, want, *need…*

"You look a bit peaked tonight," Clara remarked.

A hoarse laugh shook his chest. "Do I?"

"Haven't you slept well?"

"I never sleep well." Irritated by her implacable calm, especially in the face of the storm foaming and cresting inside him, he shoved across and fell beside her on the bench. "And with thoughts of you invading my mind at every turn, I'm not certain I even want to sleep. Why invite unwanted dreams when I can lie awake and imagine in perfect, crisp detail all the erotic things I want to do to you, all the places I intend to put my hands, my mouth—"

"Sebastian!" Clara's intake of breath stirred his grim satisfaction. "You speak indecently."

"I will act even more indecently," Sebastian assured her, "when you are naked and trembling in my arms with your—"

"Stop." She whirled to face him, her calm dissolving in the violet turbulence of her eyes. Their breath mingled in the heated space between them, energy crackling in the air.

"I gave you the opportunity, did I not?" Clara hissed, her gaze sweeping down to stroke his mouth. "I threw myself at you and acted a perfect wanton. You quickly forestalled the entire incident, so don't think now you can shock maidenly blushes from me with your lewd remarks."

Sebastian grabbed the folds of her cloak and pulled with such force that she fell against him with a gasp. His mouth descended on hers with an utter lack of decency, heat firing his nerves. Clara's body arched back like a strung bow, her hands splaying over his chest to prevent his advance. He deepened the kiss, swiping his tongue across her lower lip, pulling a moan from her that went straight to his blood.

The tension slid from her frame like melting honey. She parted her lips and whispered his name, drawing him into her. He forgot himself, sank into the warm, sweet haven of her mouth, inhaled the essence of her skin. She thrust her fingers into his hair, angling her head so their mouths locked together seamlessly.

Mine. The word burst through him again, but it wasn't just a word. It was a vow, an assertion, a command.

A truth.

"Sir? Sir." A rap thumped the cab from above.

Sebastian surfaced from the haze of passion, aware the vehicle had ceased moving. He cursed on a breath of frustration and shoved to his feet, blocking Clara from sight in case the driver had descended from the bench.

Shoving open the door, Sebastian sucked in a lungful of cold air and fought for control. Light smeared the dirty windows of the Eagle Tavern. Patrons lurched outside, voices thick with drink, laughter gathering like rain clouds.

Clara's voice came from behind him, clear and steady. He turned as she spoke to the driver and held out a pouch weighty with coin. The driver doffed his cap and clambered back to the bench. He opened the box and withdrew a scroll of papers, which he extended to Clara as if it were a sword, both fearsome and precious.

She nodded her gratitude and approached Sebastian. He tried, and failed, to smother revived anger. His fist crushed the scroll as he took it from her.

"Wait in the cab," he said, then added through the pain of a clenched jaw, "Please."

She shook her head, the folds of her cloak rippling like a stream. She pivoted and started toward the tavern.

Sebastian grabbed her arm too hard in his haste to delay her. Her soft skin yielded under his grasp, but her spine straightened with determination. Her eyes flashed as she met his thundering glare.

"All right then," he snapped. "But keep silent and do as I say."

Still holding her arm, he strode into the tavern. Noise swelled through the hot, smoke-drenched interior—shouting, arguments about card games, the shrill whistle of a pipe. A fire blazed in the hearth, logs shifting and crackling.

One sweeping glance told Sebastian that Jacob had not yet arrived. He shoved two chairs away from a table strewn with smudged, empty cups, and spills of drink. After seating Clara with a firm hand to her shoulder, he gestured to the barman for two ales. A serving girl came to clear the table and plunked down the foaming tankards.

Sebastian downed half the ale in three swallows and swiped the back of his hand across his mouth.

"For what it's worth," he said, "I do enjoy your maidenly blushes."

Clara's eyebrows rose, a mixture of surprise and unexpected pleasure flashing blue-violet in her eyes. She parted her lips to speak just as the lanky figure of Jacob approached, weaving like a needle through the tapestry of jumbled tables.

"I wasn't certain you'd come." Jacob slid into the opposite chair, his gaze arcing from Sebastian to Clara. "Mrs. Shepherd, isn't it? I certainly did not expect you, but find your presence most agreeable. I welcome the opportunity to thank you in person for your assistance with my request."

"You are welcome." Her brows pulled together, caution evident in the corded lines of her neck. "Mr. Hall."

"Jacob, please."

"Jacob."

Jacob smiled, clearly pleased by the way his name swam through her voice. He took her hand in greeting. Jealousy rustled in Sebastian's gut. He rose to his feet, wrenching his brother's hand away from Clara.

"Why here?" he asked Jacob bluntly.

"Away from the possibility of Rushton's discovery," his brother replied.

"Why are you so goddamned intent on avoiding Rushton?" Sebastian snapped. "What are you hiding?"

Clara cupped her hand beneath Sebastian's elbow, silently urging him to sit. He did, fighting the burn still crawling across his chest.

"You have the plans?" Jacob asked.

Sebastian tossed the scroll onto the table. The pages scattered like leaves, absorbing puddles of spilled ale before Jacob rescued them from damage with a sweep of his hand.

"We'll pay a visit to the bank tomorrow," he said. "I'll transfer funds into your account."

Sebastian no longer cared about the funds. He restrained the urge to grasp Jacob's arm again. "Tell me what's going on or I'll tell Rushton you're here."

Jacob sat back. Behind his glasses, his gaze was unflinching. "Catherine Leskovna."

"Catherine…"

"Our mother. She wants to see you again."

Sebastian couldn't have been more surprised if the roof had fallen in. Past the sudden shock, he heard Clara's intake of breath.

Christ. He didn't want her here. Didn't want her to know anything about his godforsaken mother.

He swallowed another gulp of ale and then, as if an epiphany burst within him, he had the answer. So obvious. If he'd taken a half-second to actually think, it might have occurred to him much sooner.

"Where is she?" he asked his brother in Russian. The language crunched between his teeth, unfamiliar and stale with neglect.

Jacob's eyebrow arched in surprise, but he responded in kind. "Dare I suspect Mrs. Shepherd does not speak Russian?"

Sebastian leaned forward, tension knotting his shoulders. Beside him, Clara shifted. He felt the exasperation building in her. Her own damned fault for insisting on this foolishness.

"Where is our mother?" he asked. "What do you know of her?"

"She found me in St. Petersburg earlier this year." Jacob heaved out a sigh and sat back. "She remarried and is now known as Catherine Leskovna. She contacted me because she suspected I would be the only one to agree to a meeting."

"She was right," Sebastian muttered. Alexander and Tasha would have refused to see her, and Sebastian had no reason to react any differently. Certainly their mother had no way of contacting Patrick or even knowing where he was. Jacob, on the other hand, would allow his intellectual curiosity about their mother to conquer any remnants of anger and hurt.

"She has been following your career," Jacob continued, "and wanted to seek you out after your resignation from Weimar, but feared causing further disruption."

Sebastian laughed without humor. "Did she consider that when she had a blasted affair?"

"She then approached me asking if I knew what had happened, as she suspected more than a conflict with the Weimar committee."

Anger twisted hard in Sebastian's chest. *Bloody, bloody hell.*

He'd not been any closer to their remote mother than his brothers or sister, but he and Catherine had shared an unspoken love for music—a love Catherine had kept private. Even now, Sebastian remembered hovering in the shadows of the doorway as a child while his mother played the piano to an empty drawing room. Unaware that her son was her only audience.

Sebastian jerked his head toward the scroll Jacob had set on an empty chair. "That's what this was about? Why didn't you just tell me?"

"I knew your loyalty to Alexander would preclude you from even hearing me out," Jacob said. "And while it's true that I believe the cipher machine has numerous uses, I also wanted to know if you would agree to my proposition."

"Why?"

"If you did, it meant that you had nothing else to do. No plans for another tour, no income from concerts or teaching, no work with the Society of Musicians. It verified that you withdrew not only from your public career but from any association whatsoever with music. And your acceptance of financial compensation indicated you were in need of funds, which I'd suspected after I saw Grand Duchess Irina last summer. She informed me you'd refused her further patronage and returned to London without explanation."

Jacob sat back, his gaze flickering to Clara before settling again on Sebastian. No satisfaction over the proof of his deductions appeared in his expression. Rather he appeared dispirited, a shade of sorrow veiling his eyes.

"And that," he said, reaching for the tankard, "also led me to believe our mother's suspicions were correct."

Anger over his brother's duplicity churned in Sebastian's gut. He hated the idea that Jacob had approached the harshest crisis of Sebastian's life with logical calculation, as if he were a puzzle that required solving.

Yet still Sebastian was unable to prevent himself from voicing the question that had burned in all their minds for nearly three years.

"What happened to her?" he asked.

"After her affair came to light," Jacob said, "she fled first to France with her...paramour...then returned to Russia."

"So she did go back." How often had Sebastian wondered that?

"Yes. She lived on her father's estate in Vyborg when her lover was deployed to the Urals."

"Who was he?"

"A common soldier," Jacob said. "Alexei Leskov. They met during one of her visits to St. Petersburg. They married shortly before he left for the Urals. Her family opposed, of course, and insisted she remain at their country estate so as not to cause talk in the city. Leskov returned for a time, but last spring was sent to the Baltic Sea. This time, rather than remain confined to the Vyborg estate, Catherine accompanied him."

"She went with him to war?" Good Lord. Had Sebastian known nothing at all about his own mother?

"She volunteered to assist the nurses. She had no training, but wished to learn because she wanted to help the Russian troops in whatever way she could. At the Battle of Bomarsund against the English and French forces, her husband was killed."

Jacob paused, as if waiting for that revelation to sink into the quicksand of Sebastian's soul. Sebastian downed another swallow of ale to conceal his reaction of surprise and, to his confusion, sorrow.

He wiped his mouth on his sleeve. "Then what?"

"She returned to Russia to live with her sister in Kuskovo," Jacob said.

"And where is she now?"

Jacob looked at him for a moment, appearing poised to respond, and then his gaze landed on Clara like a hornet seeking a vulnerable place to sting. He finally spoke in English. "She is in London."

Clara's courage had faltered as currents of Russian arced between the two men. She sensed Sebastian's growing agitation, a simmering pot close to boiling over the course of a half hour, but she began to question her own heedlessness in forcing her presence on him.

Her justifications to herself had seemed so rational and significant not two hours ago—Monsieur Dupree had sent the plans to her uncle, so they were entitled to know the details of the exchange. She wanted to know as much as possible about her soon-to-be husband. She *needed* to know more about him, because God knew she had laid bare every raw fold of her soul to him...and still she remained bewildered by his incongruities, his restlessness and unease.

But this she had not anticipated.

In the strained hush following Jacob's revelation about their mother's whereabouts, Clara sought Sebastian's hand beneath the table. His fingers gripped his thigh, and she splayed her hand across his and pressed. Tension vibrated through his long frame, a violin strung too tight, and before she could speak a word, Sebastian lunged to his feet and clenched his left fist around his brother's collar.

"You lied to me."

"I did not lie." Jacob met his gaze unflinchingly. "What would you have done had I contacted you just to tell you our mother wants to see you?"

Sebastian loosened his grip slightly, pulling back. Even Clara knew he would have ripped the letter up and tossed it to the flames.

Jacob unclenched Sebastian's fingers from his collar and pushed his hand aside. "If anyone is lying, Bastian, that person appears to be you."

Clara's throat closed. Sebastian hadn't told his brother about his disability. Had he told anyone besides her?

Jacob caught her gaze. "My apologies for bringing you into this, Mrs. Shepherd. Bastian, Catherine Leskovna is staying at the Albion. I ask only that you consider a meeting."

Sebastian shoved away from the table and strode to the door, pushing aside obstacles in his path and leaving behind a chaotic maze of overturned chairs and displaced tables.

Clara hurried after him, nearly colliding into his solid back when she stepped outside. He stood with his shoulders hunched, his fists curled at his sides. She searched the shadows, relief welcome when she saw the cab rolling along the other side of the street. The driver had kept his word to wait.

When the cab was rattling through the streets, Clara gazed at Sebastian across from her, shards of light and shadow slanting across the hard planes of his face, his eyes burning, the black of his hair indistinct against the night.

"Don't allow her to leave without seeing you again." Her words came out as a whisper, floating on the dark air.

He didn't respond, his jaw tight.

"Sebastian. She is your mother."

"She betrayed us all. She can rot in hell, for all I care."

"If you..." Her throat constricted. "If you do not give her the chance to make amends, you will regret it forever."

"I have no reason for regret. She does."

Pleas twisted through Clara's mind. She knew nothing about the former Countess of Rushton—only that the other woman was a mother anxious to see her son again. Although Clara could not fathom the reasons behind Catherine Leskovna's decision to leave her family, she knew all too well how it felt to long for one's child. And to have that wish thwarted.

Clara started to speak again, but Sebastian held up a hand to forestall her. Words, pleas, faded in her throat.

When they reached the museum, he pushed open the door and strode to the front steps. She fitted the key into the lock and went inside, then turned and watched as he strode away, his back straight and stiff as metal.

CHAPTER 16

*S*ebastian paced to the hearth. He'd spent a sleepless night wrestling with everything Jacob had told him the previous evening. By morning he had still come to no satisfying conclusion. So rather than dissect the problem of his mother until his brain ached more than it already did, or surrender to his festering anger toward his brother, Sebastian would concentrate on the fact that he was to marry Clara Shepherd two days hence.

Ought to be interesting explaining that to the rest of his family.

He gave a hoarse chuckle and scrubbed his sore eyes. It might have been better if all his relations had remained in London. Then none of this would have happened.

Clara wouldn't have happened.

His heart stung. He dragged a hand across his chest, his mind flaring with pictures of her blue-violet eyes shimmering with heat and determination. He didn't want to imagine his life if she hadn't entered it. Couldn't.

Sebastian ordered the carriage, shoving his arms into his greatcoat as he descended the steps. A half hour later he was opening the door of Blake's Museum of Automata and facing Mrs. Fox, who rose like a dark sun from behind her desk.

"Welcome to Blake's...oh. Mr. Hall." A gray thread of disapproval knotted her voice.

"Good morning, Mrs. Fox." His attempt at a smile felt as if it might crack his face. "Lovely to see you again. Is Mrs. Shepherd at home?"

"She's in the studio, as usual."

He started down the corridor. With a swiftness that belied her redoubtable severity, Mrs. Fox stepped into his path.

"The fee, Mr. Hall," she said, "is one shilling."

Sebastian laughed, undiluted amusement coursing through him. It was the first genuine laugh he'd experienced in more than an age. The sound of it, booming and sudden, startled Mrs. Fox, who retreated a step and stared at him in astonishment.

Still chuckling, Sebastian went back to the carriage. He retrieved five shillings from the footman and returned to Mrs. Fox. He pressed the coins into her gloved hand and closed her fingers around them.

"Well worth the cost of admission," he assured her with a wink.

The woman gaped at him, a pink blush bringing a welcome color to her pallid cheeks.

Sebastian's spine straightened as he continued to the studio. He found Clara folding swaths of silk and stacking them in colorful squares onto a shelf. Granville sat at a table, adjusting an automaton of a crouching tiger. Brilliant stripes of black and orange decorated the animal, its pointed teeth gleaming white and its face twisted into a snarl.

They both looked up at Sebastian's entrance. A faint tension crackled the air as they exchanged glances. In an instant, Sebastian knew Clara had confided all to her uncle.

Irritation needled him. Unwarranted, he knew. He himself

had solicited their aid in not only finding the plans, but relinquishing them to him.

He leaned his shoulder against the doorjamb and folded his arms. "I don't intend to see my mother again," he said. "My only hope is that her presence in London remains a secret so as not to cause my family further harm."

Granville wiped his greasy hands on a cloth, his gaze on the machine. "We've no one to tell, Mr. Hall."

"Even if we'd wanted to," Clara added.

The snarled knot in Sebastian's chest loosened, easing the tightness of apprehension. He couldn't confess any of these recent events to his brothers, but here stood two people with whom he'd been acquainted for less than a fortnight...and he knew to his bones that Clara and Granville would guard his confidences with steadfast dedication.

Words of gratitude stalled in his throat. He gave a short nod and turned to leave, forgetting the reason he'd come.

"Come in," Clara said. She smoothed wrinkles from a bolt of silk and beckoned him to sit. "Have you taken breakfast yet?"

"I...no."

"I'll ask Mrs. Marshall to set another place." Granville twisted a key on the automaton. The tiger pushed back on its hind legs, then lunged forward across the circular platform on which it crouched. A tiny door in the platform sprang open, and a delicate, painted gazelle leapt out in a graceful arc. A growl emerged from the mechanism as the tiger landed on the hapless creature, bringing it to the ground between two large paws.

"Well," Clara remarked, "at least it works."

Granville chuckled. "Commissioned for a man who enjoys hunting, I suspect. He's sending someone to pick it up later this morning."

He pushed away from the table and left in search of Mrs. Marshall.

"I'm sorry," Clara murmured to Sebastian after her uncle was gone. "I shouldn't have forced you to take me with you last night."

No, she shouldn't have, but she knew the truth now—and perhaps that was for the best, considering she was poised to become his wife. He'd been the one to insist the marriage would encompass more than mere legal ties.

Now revealed secrets scattered between them like packages ripped open, surrounded with torn paper and bits of string. Now there was nothing left to hide.

Sebastian went to the automaton and rewound it to watch the gruesome scene play out again.

"Why don't you want to see her?" Clara asked.

"Because she ruined my family."

"Your brother appears to be granting her another chance."

"My brother is a fool if he thinks anything good will come of this."

Clara was quiet for a moment, though he felt her perceptive gaze peeling through all the hardened layers of his soul. "Don't make a decision now that you will later regret, Sebastian. Especially where your mother is concerned."

"For God's sake." An old, long-buried anger surfaced. "If anyone should regret their decisions, it is Catherine Leskovna. Not me."

"That may be so, but when someone has wronged you and then wishes to make amends…"

"What makes you think she wishes to make amends?"

"If she'd wanted to hurt you, she wouldn't have gone to Jacob first and asked him to facilitate a meeting. She's giving you the chance to refuse, even though I'm certain she wants more than anything to speak with you again."

"What makes you so certain?"

"I'm a mother. And I would give my blood to have my son again."

Sebastian lifted his head to look at her. A pang cut through his chest at the sight of the fathoms-deep longing coloring her eyes.

"You…" A curious knot tightened his throat. "You are nothing like my mother. You did not make the choice to desert your family. Aside from separation, there are no similarities between my relationship with her and your relationship with Andrew."

"Separation is a breach, no matter the cause. You have the opportunity to cross it and see your mother again. Andrew does not."

A choice. Sebastian's fingers curled into his palm. He hadn't chosen to end his career. Wouldn't have chosen marriage had it not been for his father's threats. Hadn't had much of a choice to help Jacob, not when he'd needed the money and, as his brother had bluntly reminded him, he'd had little else with which to occupy his time.

He had, however, chosen Clara. A brilliant, glowing fact he still feared to fully acknowledge in the event it was taken from him.

She was right that he now had a choice to see his mother again. The idea that he had another choice felt good, even if he had no plans to take a step in her direction.

The tiger folded back onto its haunches. Sebastian set the machine aside and moved to where Clara stood. He put his left hand on her warm nape, rubbing the tight muscles. A sigh escaped her as she tilted her head to the side to encourage the manipulation of his fingers.

He stepped closer, inhaling her scent of oranges and spice. The muscles of her neck became pliable, softening under his touch and easing a soft groan from her throat.

He pressed his mouth to her temple, right beside the birth-mark at the corner of her eyebrow. The pulse there, quick as a sparrow's heartbeat, strummed against his lips. Warmth unfurled in his blood along with something else, something more, that rich, sea-blue satisfaction of knowing, even before their vows, that Clara was his. And that, even if she didn't yet realize it, he belonged to her.

The idea of belonging to a woman would have wrung a laugh from him a year ago. He'd never have allowed anyone to weave into his soul the way Clara had, never have gone to any lengths to help her, never have admitted she could fell him with a harsh word.

But now he had. And he would. And God knew she could.

She shifted, stretching her body upward to press her cool cheek against his. She murmured something against his stubbled jaw, then turned her face and sought his mouth with hers. He slipped his hand to her shoulders, his fingers kneading the tension still lacing her supple muscles, and yielded to the sensations washing over him.

Clara wound her arms around his waist, splaying her hands over his lower back as she angled her head to allow him to deepen the kiss. Her body softened against his. Heat arced into his groin as her breasts pressed into his chest and her tongue danced with his.

Sebastian curled his right hand into her side, crushing the fabric of her skirts and petticoats. He stepped forward and guided her back against the wall, then pushed his hips against her. The hard ridge of his cock nudged her skirts, an ache already building at the base of his spine. He wanted her naked, wanted to rub his stiff flesh against her bare thighs, wanted her cool hands sliding over his skin...

She gasped, her mouth breaking from his with a rush of hot breath. She tucked her face against his shoulder, her body rippling with a moan before she slid her hand down to curve with tentative curiosity around his erection.

He winced, bracing one hand on the wall behind her as the warmth of her hand burned clear through his trousers. His breath stirred the loose tendrils of hair at her temple. He struggled against the urgent need to thrust against her grip, to allow her to wind the tension to breaking point and then let go.

He placed his hand on the curve where her shoulder met the upward sweep of her neck. She eased her head back, her eyes dark purple with arousal.

"Two days," he whispered.

A shudder rocked her. "Two days."

He forced himself to step away. Just in time, as well, since Granville reentered the room and announced that Mrs. Marshall had a late breakfast prepared for them.

As Sebastian and Clara followed him from the studio, her gaze met his. Warmth still glimmered in the depths of her eyes, and her flushed lips curved with the promise of a shared secret.

A foreign sensation curled into Sebastian's heart, skeins of color woven into a smooth, endless braid. He sat with Clara and Granville at a wooden table in the morning room, the air warm and scented with fresh-baked bread, while they ate muffins and drank coffee...and he surrendered to the feeling as it spread through his blood, into his soul, and warmed every part of his being.

lowers bloomed from vases around the drawing room of the Mount Street town house. The morning sun lanced through the curtains, glinting off the rose tucked into the lapel of Sebastian's dark blue morning coat. Clara kept her attention on the flower as the minister blessed their union, his voice deep and solemn.

"Be pleased, O Lord, to regard in much mercy and goodness the parties now before Thee..."

She lifted her eyes to find Sebastian watching her. Her heart thumped. A slight smile curved his mouth, the reassuring promise that they had both chosen wisely and well.

"You will please take each other by the right hand," the minister requested.

Clara, her gaze locked to Sebastian's, reached for his right hand. She expected him to hesitate for fear that his muscles would falter, but his long fingers closed around hers without wavering. Relief spilled through her, her own anxiety eased by the warmth brewing in his dark eyes and his absolute lack of uncertainty.

"I do," he said, before Clara realized the minister had moved on to address her.

She gripped the folds of her pearl-gray gown with her other hand in an attempt to still the nervous shudders elicited by the gravity of the minister's words—*"a wife shall love her husband"*—but her right hand, the one tucked securely in Sebastian's large, warm palm, did not tremble.

"I do," she whispered when the minister stopped speaking.

Her fingers tightened around Sebastian's. Memory flashed through her—the elaborate spectacle of her wedding to Richard, also a union based on practical ends but one launched with a display of wealth and celebration.

The numerous guests, the music, the extravagant feasting—it had been the opposite of this quiet ceremony in Sebastian's drawing room with only Lord Rushton, Uncle Granville, and Mrs. Fox in attendance, all sitting with twin lines etched on their foreheads.

Clara avoided looking at them until the minister had pronounced her Sebastian's wife. Her heart caught when he bent to brush his mouth against hers. She allowed herself to feel the pleasure of the contact for an instant before turning to her uncle. Granville moved to embrace her. She gripped his arms and swallowed past the tightness in her throat.

"I promise you I'm doing what is best for us," Clara whispered.

"Should you need anything," he murmured in her ear, "you know where to find me. I will do whatever I can to help you. I regret that I have not done more."

Sadness swelled in Clara's chest.

"You gave me a place to live," she said. "You tried to help with Andrew. There was nothing more you could have done."

"I only hope that this decision"—Granville glanced at Sebastian—"will yield the result you desire."

So did she. The portent of failure loomed before her. She'd

devised no strategy for what to do should she encounter it. She couldn't. Black as oil, impenetrable, failure would swamp her under and take her last breath.

She looked to where Sebastian stood speaking with Lord Rushton. The earl glanced her way and approached. "Congratulations, Mrs. Hall. I wish you and my son much happiness."

"Thank you, my lord." Although Clara had no idea how Lord Rushton truly felt about this union, the fact that he approved of their marriage made the idea of having an earl as a father-in-law less intimidating.

Sebastian moved beside Clara, cupping his left hand beneath her elbow with easy grace. "If you'll all join us in the dining room, I believe there's quite an elaborate breakfast waiting."

For Clara, the next few hours passed with rabbitlike speed, although they lingered over breakfast and then, at Granville's suggestion, went for a walk in the garden of Grosvenor Square to benefit from the brisk autumn day. Rushton returned to his Piccadilly residence, while the rest of the party took some air.

Clara, knowing quite well what awaited her upon their return to Sebastian's town house, proposed they take the carriage to visit the Regent Street shops for a few hours. They had lunch at Verrey's restaurant, then went to the Portland Gallery to view the array of paintings and sculptures, an excursion that she hoped would take the remainder of the afternoon.

Embarrassment still scorched her when she remembered her behavior in Sebastian's carriage, the way she'd thrown herself at him with an utterly wanton lack of restraint. Although Sebastian had given her no reason to feel ashamed, she knew well that her behavior fell far outside the bounds of decency.

She couldn't fathom how Richard might have reacted, had she conducted herself in such a manner with him. Then again, nothing about Richard and his detached, stoic presence had ever inspired so much as a modicum of desire in Clara. She hadn't even wanted to kiss him.

But Sebastian? He was a man who could turn her insides into molten heat with one brush of his fingertips, one intent look from his dark eyes. All she needed to do was gaze at his beautiful mouth, and she was seized by the urge to press her lips to his, feel the sweep of his tongue, drink the hot sweetness of his breath.

She shivered at the very idea, turning to study a landscape painting as she attempted to entrap all her wild, furtive imaginings.

Lock your heart, she reminded herself even as she slanted a glance toward her new husband, so disarmingly handsome in a crisp morning coat and a cravat the color of a sweeping, cobalt-blue Dorset sky. The breeze had mussed his unruly black hair and a corner of his cravat had escaped the lapel of his coat, the loose edge rumpling his appearance just enough to remind the world he would not be contained like other men.

A sudden and sharp ache of tenderness constricted Clara's chest. She averted her gaze from him and tried to focus on the painting.

Lock your heart lest you give him the power to damage it.

And with Sebastian, she knew, the damage would shatter her beyond repair.

She hurried to fall into step beside her uncle as they left the gallery and went back outside. The sunlight was beginning to dim and the shadows to lengthen by the time Mrs. Fox remarked that she ought to be returning home, and Granville summoned a cab for her. After she'd gone, he glanced at Sebastian before turning a worried gaze on Clara.

For whatever reason, her uncle's concern eased Clara's own apprehension. After all, it wasn't as if she'd wed an ogre. Quite the opposite, in fact. She became acutely aware of Sebastian beside her, his tall, quiet presence comforting rather than fearsome.

She kissed Uncle Granville's cheek. "I'll call on you tomorrow, yes? I've still the sewing to finish for your dancing couple, and I'd like to start on the adornments for the next birdcage."

"You needn't—"

"I'll be there at ten."

Sebastian stepped aside to open the door of another cab. Granville squeezed Clara's hands in farewell. Before Granville entered the cab, Sebastian lowered his head and spoke to the other man.

A breeze whisked the words from Clara's ear, but her uncle nodded with what appeared to be satisfaction, then clapped his hand firmly on Sebastian's shoulder in a gesture of approval.

"What did you say to him?" Clara asked when Sebastian returned to her side.

"That I'll contact your father tomorrow to discuss the matter of Wakefield House," Sebastian said.

"Already?"

He nodded, brushing a coil of hair away from her forehead. "My brother's solicitor has already started to draw up the papers. I told him to do so the day you proposed."

"What if I hadn't found the plans?"

A warm, wicked light flared in his eyes. "Then I would have devised another way to make you my wife."

CHAPTER 18

*D*arkness fell. Clara watched the curve of the moon melt against the sky. Her pulse shimmered through her veins, settling into the nervous beat of her heart. She slid her hand across the worn, wooden box resting on the table beside her and unfastened the catch. The tangle of ribbons inside gleamed incandescent, like a pearl embedded in an oyster.

Clara lifted the ribbons from the box, pooling them in a colorful mass on the table. The door clicked open behind her, and then she was no longer alone.

She turned. He wasn't looking at her. His dark head was bent, a swath of thick hair covering his forehead, his attention on the knot of his cravat as he tugged at it with his left hand. His right hand remained at his side, the fingers curled toward his palm.

Clara allowed her gaze to wander over him—the breadth of his shoulders and length of his strong legs, the way his waistcoat hugged his lean torso, the drape of his coat, which had managed to collect numerous wrinkles over the course of the day.

A slight smile pulled at her mouth. Good thing she hadn't expected him to deck himself out in all sorts of finery for their wedding night.

Not that she had, either. Until this moment she hadn't considered he might expect her to wear a fashionable peignoir of silk
and lace. Unnerved, Clara tugged her dressing gown more
securely over her plain cotton shift and waited.

He twisted the catch of the pin holding his cravat in place.
The fastening gave way, allowing him to tug again at the knot
close to his throat. As the folds of cobalt-blue silk spilled into his
hand, his eyes met hers. He pulled the silk from his collar and
dropped it to the floor before approaching.

"From the studio?" He scooped the ribbons into his left hand
and let them stream through his fingers.

"They were my mother's. She had very beautiful, dark hair
and she loved to wear colorful ribbons."

A cherry-red ribbon trailed from his hand as he held it against
her burnished hair. "Do you wear them?"

"Sometimes. More often when I was a girl."

She remembered that her mother had liked to tie the ribbons
into Clara's hair as well, how perfectly she was able to shape the
bows. Clara cupped her hand beneath Sebastian's, catching the
tangle of fabric as it fell from his fingers. She dropped the
ribbons into the box and closed the lid.

His dark gaze swept her from head to foot and back, lingering
on the neckline of her gown, which exposed a shallow curve of
bare skin. He was close enough that she could see the gleaming
dampness of his hair, his smooth, clean-shaven jaw that she
wanted to stroke with her lips.

A tremble coursed through her blood. She'd be lying if she
said she had not imagined this moment, the taut, fevered space
just before the consummation of their union. But her speculations had been pointlessly twisted with memories of Richard,
tangling the fearful, young virgin she'd been with the woman she
was now. No longer young. No longer a virgin.

But fearful...?

Sebastian cupped his left palm around her nape, his fingers

warm and strong, then reached to loosen the pins restraining her hair. In moments, her hair uncoiled in long skeins around her shoulders. Warm appreciation glowed in his eyes. Her heart hammered.

Fearful still, yes. Not because the dire portent of physical intimacy stretched between them and the bed, but because he aroused such a flurry of emotions, like butterflies spiraling and cascading through her very soul.

Because she *wanted* him.

Clara still didn't understand it. She didn't know its source or its end, this desire sparking in her blood, at once exhilarating and terrifying. All she knew was that it made her crave his lips, his hands on her bare skin, made her yearn with the need to touch him in return.

Sebastian dragged his fingers through a swath of her hair, softly pulling the tangles free. His brows drew together.

"Did he hurt you?" He spoke in a gentle voice, but the implications of his question corded the words with anger.

Clara shook her head, unable to speak past the knot in her throat. No, Richard hadn't hurt her. Not physically. He'd been dispassionate and methodical and she'd felt like a vessel rather than his wife, but he'd hurt her only after he died.

And never once had he made her feel like *this*—restless and hot and wanting more, wanting something she couldn't name.

Before she could speak, Sebastian captured her fingers in his and, with unmistakable intent, brought her hand to the buttons of his shirt.

Clara skirted her gaze to her husband, her pulse jumping at the heat already brewing in his eyes. No swift rut beneath the covers for this man. She steeled her courage, though her hands shook as she unfastened the first button to reveal the triangle of skin at his throat.

If she didn't look directly at him…she forced her fingers to work as she slipped each button from its entrapment. When the folds of his shirt began to part, she stepped back, her breath quickening in pace as she watched his long fingers release the final two buttons before he pulled the shirt over his head. Mesmerized by the dexterity of his movements, the graceful lift of his shoulders, she could hardly muster any shock as his shirt pooled to the floor.

A riot of sensations fluttered inside her as she gazed at his half-naked form. So utterly different from Richard's slender torso, which Clara had seen bare only several times during their six-year marriage.

She stared at the expanse of Sebastian's flat stomach, the layer of dark hair over the sculpted planes of his chest, the smooth musculature of his shoulders. A strange, urgent pulse flared in her belly.

Dear God, but the man was beautiful.

He closed the scant distance between them, his hand moving to cup her face and draw her closer.

"I promise," he murmured in the instant before his lips touched hers, "I will only bring you pleasure."

And then she was in his arms, his mouth crushed to hers, her hands trapped between their bodies. Clara breathed in a gasp and sank against him, opening her mouth to allow him access, drowning in the flood of sensations that swept over her. She unclenched her fists and let her hands spread tentatively over the expanse of his naked chest.

Warm, taut skin and soft hairs tickled her fingers as she pressed her hands against him and slid them upward. The steady beat of his heart quickened against her palms, delighting her with the knowledge that her touch could inspire his reaction.

The pulse in her belly beat harder, sliding heat through her veins and winding around her lower body. Sebastian's hands stroked her hips, his fingers digging in as he urged her even closer, close enough that the bulge in his trousers nudged against her belly.

Rather than alarm her, the sensation flared a new spiral of heat. He wound the thick mass of her hair around his hand, tugging her head back for ease in deepening his potent kiss. His tongue slid into her mouth as his hand grasped her wrist and guided her to touch the hardening evidence of his arousal.

She hesitated, uncertainty warring with desire, before she allowed her fingers to curve around him. A hiss of pleasure escaped him, hot against her lips, and the sound emboldened her to tighten her hold. Even through the material of his trousers, he throbbed heavy and hard against her palm. A blaze of white-hot lust coursed across her skin. She moaned into his mouth, closing her teeth on his lower lip, swimming in the increasing urgency to see him stripped naked.

Tension rippled through his lean frame as he lifted his mouth from hers. His eyes burned. He yanked at the ties of her dressing gown, the knots surrendering easily to his adept fingers, and pushed it away from her shoulders. A part of Clara's mind remained aware that he was using only his left hand, his right immobile at his side, but so deft were his movements that his infirmity seemed negligible.

Although her shift concealed her from chest to calves, Clara had never stood before a man wearing so little. Sebastian's gaze moved lower, to where the fabric outlined the taut points of her breasts. Her breath hitched as she moved to cross her arms, but he was swifter and caught her wrist in his hand to prevent the concealment.

"Oh, no," he murmured. "This time, I will see everything."

Everything?

A shudder shook Clara to her core. Sebastian began to retreat, still grasping her wrist, compelling her to match his footsteps as he guided them both to the bed. He fell backward, bringing her down on top of his long body and locking his mouth to hers once again.

Her blood quaked as her breasts rubbed against his chest. Her hair fell in thick veils on either side of his face, enclosing them both in shadows dappled with shards of light. When she lifted her mouth from his to draw in air, she placed her trembling hands on his cheeks and stared down at him.

His dark eyes flared with heat—no self-restraint this time, only the hot, heady burn of desire. For her.

He captured her hand again and guided her palm over his chest, down his muscled torso to the thickness straining between them. Again she spread her fingers over his hardness, a fever filling her throat as he swelled against her hand.

"Take them off," he murmured, moving her fingers to the buttons.

Clara's breath hissed out in a rush. She sidled downward, her hair trailing like a paintbrush over his bare chest before she straightened, her bottom pressed to his thighs and her hands placed flat on his hips.

He was watching her. She felt his gaze like a hot kiss as he cast it across her crimson skin and the curves of her body beneath her shift. The faint thought surfaced that he was giving her a measure of control, as if to atone for the helpless subservience that had pervaded her life.

Until now. Until she'd purposefully asked Sebastian to marry her.

With a tremulous gathering of courage, she released the fastenings of his trousers, her urgency and trepidation stretching, then snapping like an electric wire. She let the trousers drop to the floor, a strange mixture of shock, curiosity, and pure want filling her like a cloud.

Sparks flew through her body when he nodded at her questioning glance, and she curled her hand around his smooth, taut shaft. They both watched her fingers, slender and white against his flesh, as she moved them in a hesitant rhythm that soon had Sebastian pushing his hips upward.

He made a muffled noise, half-groan and half-laugh, and flung his arm across his eyes. "Wait."

Clara stopped, enthralled by the push-and-pull cadence of her stroking and his thrusts. "Are you all right?"

He gave another hoarse laugh and reached to ease her fingers from him. "More than all right. Come back here."

She stretched the length of her body beside his, pressing her thighs together to quell the ceaseless throbbing that had begun the moment she unfastened the first button of his shirt.

Then he gathered the folds of her shift in his hand, his eyes never leaving hers as he pulled the cotton over her calves, her thighs, her hips…higher…higher…

Cool air brushed against her skin, knotting a tangle of trepidation in her belly. She'd never been so exposed, her slender limbs and hips bared to the dancing firelight and the heat of Sebastian's perusal. He put his hand on her thigh, the intimate contact wringing a gasp of stunned pleasure from her as his fingers brushed the dark curls between her thighs then circled the shallow indentation of her navel.

Then he stopped suddenly, a ripple of tension coursing through his body, and Clara knew without needing to ask what had happened. She surfaced from the haze of passion and reached for his right hand, rubbing and kneading the stiff muscles until his fingers became pliable under her touch.

Holding his gaze, she placed his hand back on her body in a silent urge for him to continue his sensual ministrations. He did, his shoulders relaxing as he stroked his hand back down to the apex of her thighs.

God in heaven, she had never known the touch of a man could wind such a tight spooling of bliss. Her body strained as heat consumed her, beading perspiration on her brow and in the valley between her breasts. She wanted to arch against Sebastian, rub their naked bodies together with heedless abandon, beg him to touch her in shockingly intimate places. She wanted him to fill her and soothe the aching emptiness.

He murmured a request, lost in the sound of her heartbeat pulsing inside her head, but she knew what he asked and lifted her arms so he could slide the shift up over her head. He tossed the garment aside and levered his weight onto one elbow, a hard breath expelling from his lungs as he gave her body a slow and thorough appraisal.

Clara crushed the bedcovers in her fists, fighting the urge to cover herself—an urge that dissolved like salt in hot water when hunger fired in Sebastian's eyes.

Then, in a movement taut with masculine grace, he rolled to straddle her, his knees hugging her hips, his lean, muscular body rippling with carnal tension above her.

She gasped, succumbing to her body's urge to squirm beneath him, swimming in arousal at the sensation of his shaft throbbing hard and ready against her belly. She cried out when his long-fingered hand cupped her breast. Pleasure spiraled into her core as he caressed her tight nipples, rubbed his fingers into the warm crevice beneath her breasts.

He shifted on top of her, uncoiling the length of his body as his knee eased between her thighs. Placing his hands on either side of her head, he levered his weight onto his forearms and pressed his mouth to her right ear.

"Open for me," he whispered, his breath a hot shiver against her neck.

Clara's throat quivered with a swallow as she curved her hands against his hips and parted her thighs to allow him to ease into place. His hard, slick length breached her body, eliciting a sharp intake of breath from them both. Sebastian paused, sweat beading his chest, the cords of his neck taut with restraint.

She couldn't speak past the burn cascading through her. She coiled her legs around his in invitation and gripped his hips, knowing that only he could ease the urgent ache expanding outward like surging waves. Then with a muffled groan, he pushed forward, filling her, stretching her in one smooth motion.

"Oh!" Clara gasped, her eyes seeking his, stunned to the depths of her being by the desire crackling from him and into her, the promise of untold pleasures evoked by the thrust of his hips, the pressure collecting in her loins.

He lowered himself onto her, sealing their damp bodies together as he buried his face in her neck and thrust harder. Drowning in sensations and heat, she instinctively arched her body to meet his, her broken cries flowing through the crackling air. She clenched her fingers into the smooth muscles of his back, reveling in the flex and pull of his body as he urged them both toward an explosion of pleasure that Clara knew would be her undoing.

When it happened, a cry tore from her throat as a tide of bliss overwhelmed her, as her world distilled to nothing but the rocking of their bodies together, the grip of his hands and delicious, increasing press of his shaft inside her. His own groan was muffled against her neck at the moment of his hot release, his hands digging into her thighs to spread her more fully for his final thrust.

His weight collapsed on top of her, his chest hairs abrading the tender skin of her breasts as their bodies heaved together. When Sebastian eased aside, an odd sense of bereftness fluttered in Clara until he curved an arm around her and pulled her against him again. Their breathing quieted. The logs cracked and sparked.

She closed her eyes, as if by doing so, she could banish the wealth of emotions rising in her chest, the certain and painful realization that no matter her efforts, Sebastian was winding into her like a plume of brilliant, shattering fire.

Her body fit against his, her curves yielding to the hard planes of his muscles, her leg sliding between his. He brushed his lips across her forehead. Clara's throat closed.

The cold isolation in which she had lived for so long seemed to be melting. And in its place flourished the warm knowledge that she need never be alone again, that she could live the rest of her days with the reassurance of having Sebastian by her side.

Yet she did not want to imagine the cost of such a haven. If she allowed herself to acknowledge all the emotions beating at her heart, like birds struggling to escape a cage, she could lose sight of the reason she had married him in the first place.

What if loving Sebastian weakened her resolve to reclaim Andrew? What if she lost the sharp edge of her determination, the anger and desperation that had fueled her for the past year?

Lock your heart, she reminded herself. But even now she knew it was a futile command.

She couldn't lock her heart against Sebastian, for he alone held the key.

he low crash of chords reverberated in Sebastian's head, woven into a long, spiraling braid of blue and brown. In the early morning hours of his wedding night, he'd left Clara sleeping and come downstairs to sit at his piano. He let the fingers of his left hand extract the notes of Mozart's Concerto in G Major. The harmonies faded into the still night air. He played them again and added two octaves, struck by the sudden sense that the notes formed a counterpoint.

He'd always loved the melodic interactions of counterpoint. He loved the multicolored texture and structure of it, the challenge it presented to a composer.

He played the lines again, then improvised and added a new line that had a life and purpose all its own yet fit snugly against the other. Counterpoint. A melodic relationship between two independent lines. Two lines played together creating a harmony.

An image of Clara flowed over the echo of music. Warmth spread through his blood as he pictured her sprawled asleep, the sheets winding around her pale limbs, her hair spilling in ribbons across the pillows. His body stirred. Tempted though he was to return upstairs and wake her, he hunched his shoulders and glided his left hand over the keys again.

A movement at the corner of his eye caught his attention. His hand stilled as he turned. A cast of light framed Clara, caution etched in her quiet steps as she approached. Sebastian let his gaze wander over her, appreciation swelling as he noticed the satiation beneath her wariness, the lingering flush painting her skin, the tousle of her hair that she'd leashed back with a trailing ribbon.

Clara slid her tapered hand over the glossy surface of the piano. "Didn't you give this to the Society of Musicians?"

"They returned it after theirs was repaired."

She pressed an A on the keyboard. "The last time I heard you play, I was seventeen years old. I'd taken lessons the summer before."

"You didn't care for the lessons, I gather?" Sebastian asked.

She lifted her shoulders in a slight shrug. "I never had much of an ear for music." Her mouth twisted with wry amusement. "Even before I lost part of my hearing."

He swallowed a tide of anger, hating what had happened to her. Wanting to make things right for her. Wanting to fix them.

"Ah, well." He straightened, letting his hands slip from the keys. "No doubt I wasn't much of an instructor back then."

"Do you still teach?"

"No. I'd intended to return to it this past summer. Then came the Weimar position and the difficulty with my hand...my former students and their parents have asked if I intend to teach again but I don't see how it's possible."

If his students returned, he'd be a terrible instructor these days. He could hardly remember tetrachord exercises, much less how best to teach them.

"Your left hand still works," Clara said. She smiled at him, a pink blush coloring her cheeks. "As I well know."

He returned her smile, heat rising in his chest. Only because of her had he begun to feel emotions other than despair and anger again. Welcome emotions—pleasure and hope and satisfaction. Happiness.

She reached out a hand as if to touch his hair, then lowered it again to the piano surface. "You don't sleep much, do you?"

He shook his head, rubbing his rough jaw. Despite the satiation of his body, he was loath to admit to his inability to grasp even a sliver of restful slumber.

"Doesn't matter."

"What do you do, then?" She pressed a C. "Compose?"

"Haven't in some time."

If he'd expected sympathy—and to his embarrassment, he suspected he had—he was disappointed when Clara gave him a mild glare.

"You've stopped composing as well?" she asked. "Why?"

"I haven't got any ideas. Can't hear any music. Not even a melody."

"You were just playing something that sounded like music to me."

"That doesn't mean it was good."

Her breath expelled on a hiss of exasperation. "So you'll just give up? You didn't achieve your success by not working at it, did you?"

"Clara, I can't play the piano anymore," Sebastian said, his jaw tensing.

"Why can't someone else play while you write the music?"

He flexed his hand. He didn't know if he could bear watching someone else do what he wanted to do. What he *should* do himself.

"It's not what you're accustomed to," Clara said, "but that doesn't mean you lack the courage."

"It has nothing to do with courage."

"Of course it has to do with courage," she retorted. "Any idea, any change, takes courage to implement. Uncle Granville is

constantly testing his ideas, trying new mechanisms and connections and all that sort of thing. He'd never know if something
would work if he didn't attempt it."

"That's fine if you've got the ideas to begin with." Irritation
prickled Sebastian's spine as he thought of the courage he knew
it cost her to confront her father. "I thank you for your thoughts
on the matter."

"No, you don't." Her eyes burned with determination. "This is
the first true obstacle you've faced, isn't it? Not even the scandal
of your parents' divorce affected you the way it did your brothers. In fact, if it weren't for Alexander's renunciation of your
mother, you wouldn't have resisted seeing her, would you?"

Sebastian slammed his fists onto the keys with such force that
she jumped. The resounding crash vibrated through the room in
a distortion of dark colors. He shoved away from the piano and
stalked to the sideboard, where a decanter of brandy sat. He
downed a glass, appreciating the burn as it seeped into his blood,
then poured another and strode to the hearth.

"You know you can do it," Clara said, her voice quiet but resolute. "You're just afraid to."

Bloody hell. He hated the shame crawling up his throat, the
bitter taste of truth. Self-directed rage speared through him.

He clenched his hand on the glass and threw it at the flames.
The glass shattered against the stone hearth, the liquor bursting
into a fireball as the shards crashed against the logs and began to
blacken.

Clara's hand settled on his back, the heat of her palm burning
through the linen of his shirt. No apology appeared forthcoming
from her, and for that, oddly enough, Sebastian was glad. He did
not want his wife to apologize for speaking the truth.

"You're not a coward," she murmured, sliding her hand
beneath the loose shirttails to touch the naked skin of his lower
back. "Don't let anyone believe you are. Don't believe it of
yourself."

She let out a long breath and shifted behind him. Her warm hands curved around his waist to interlace across his stomach. She pressed her forehead against his back and tightened her arms, her body locked soft and warm to his. He covered her hands with his left hand and stared at leaping flames.

A humorless laugh rose in his throat. He had anticipated none of this when he agreed to marry Clara Shepherd. And he was not at all comfortable with the realization that she could illuminate the darkest corners of his soul and reveal things he didn't even want to acknowledge to himself.

"Rather than concerning yourself with me, we should concentrate on reaching an agreement with your father," he said, leveling his voice into a flat, practical tone. "That's the reason we married."

He felt her stiffen against his back, and then her warmth left him as she stepped away. Her hand slid across his torso in a lingering caress.

"That isn't the only reason we married," she murmured.

Sebastian's chest constricted. An odd recollection pushed at the back of his mind—a memory of the day he'd encouraged Alexander to do something that would make him happy. Sebastian had known that *something* meant pursuing Lydia Kellaway. At the time, he had been happy with his own life, performing in both concert halls and taverns, courting pretty women and attending social events as if their family had suffered no scandal whatsoever.

He wanted that again, though he knew it had nothing to do with the accolades and everything to do with the fact that his music had once brought people pleasure. It had once brought him pleasure.

He turned to face Clara, forcing his right hand to the side of her face. He didn't like the way she was looking at him, with a soft admiration that he no longer deserved.

"Do not imagine I am the man you once admired," he whispered, his voice rough. "I am not. If you thought you were marrying that man, then you'd best rid yourself of any romantic notions immediately."

She covered his hand with hers. "I once thought I loved you. And I did, from afar. I loved everything I thought you were, loved everything that was bright and glowing about you, but I never really knew you. Not the way a woman should know the man she loves."

A foreign sensation threaded through Sebastian's pounding heart. The strength spilled from his right hand, his fingers stiffening against Clara's smooth cheek. He tried to pull away. She tightened her hold.

"I know you now," she whispered. "I know the sorrow you've locked inside your heart. I know the depths of your loyalty. I know you are still the man you once were, but also that you've irrevocably changed. I know you the way a woman knows the man she loves."

He stared at her. The sound of his pulse filled his head. Clara turned her face to press her lips against the palm of his damaged hand. Warmth skimmed up his arm, into his blood. A ribbon of hair trailed over her neck as she kissed the crooked angle of his finger.

Different. She was so different from the women he had once known. Those women would never have dared to unearth the dark shame of his fear and challenge him not to surrender. They would not have forced him to question his decision to shun music altogether.

And none of them would have made him feel this way— hopeful and wary and determined, all at the same time. Clara made him want to succeed, for her sake if not his own. She made him want to fix the broken parts, to believe he could find his way back to music again. She made him want to be as loyal to himself as he was to his brothers and to her.

She made him want to be a better man.

A bolt of vitality arced between them, sudden as a lightning strike. He lowered his head as their mouths collided fiercely. The world dropped away, subsumed by the supple warmth of Clara in his arms, the press of her lips and soft bow of her body.

Sebastian cupped the back of her neck to deepen the kiss, a rich, blue wave swelling beneath his heart. A sigh escaped her as her unfettered breasts crushed against his chest. Arousal spiraled into him, pooled in his lower body. She shifted, rubbing his rough cheek with her smooth one, sliding her mouth to his ear. Her breath caressed his neck.

"I want so badly to love you," she murmured into his ear.

Sebastian's heart jolted. He pressed his lips against her right ear and whispered, "Me? Or the man I once was?"

"*You.* But I can't."

The remorse coloring her tone sliced into him, killing the fresh hope elicited by her words of love. Clara lifted her head, a veil descending over her expressive eyes, and he felt her severance from him as tangibly as if she had walked away from him.

"You can't," he repeated.

She shook her head, fixing her gaze on the unfastened buttons of his collar. She placed a trembling hand on his chest. "Whenever I am with you," she said, "when I think about what I feel for you, when I allow myself to *feel* it, I am not thinking about my son."

"That does not mean you care any less for him."

"And yet for the past year I've thought of nothing but him. Until I met you."

"Clara, you asked me to marry you for the sole purpose of regaining custody of Andrew."

"That wasn't the sole purpose." She spoke beneath her breath, almost a whisper, not looking at him.

"Clara." He tucked his hand beneath her chin and lifted her face to his. "You are not abandoning Andrew by casting your thoughts elsewhere. You are abandoning despair and hopelessness. You are believing in something more. Since I met you, I have thought less and less about all I've lost with the injury to my hand. Instead I remember that I would not have met you had I still been at Weimar. Had I still been performing."

Her gaze searched his, her eyes luminous. A dark understanding passed between them—the realization that they also would not have met had she remained at Manley Park with Andrew.

Beneath his fear, like a seed buried in the soil, Sebastian knew they had a chance at happiness. He had known that since the moment Clara proposed. He wouldn't have agreed otherwise, wouldn't have insisted that their marriage be real.

Yet that chance of happiness was contingent upon the results of their meeting with Fairfax, because Clara would never let herself be happy knowing her son remained under Fairfax's control.

Sebastian cupped her face again with his damaged hand, his disability now inconsequential in the shadow of his resolve. He would not only help Clara prevail over Fairfax; he would also prove worthy of the love she kept leashed in her heart. And he would start by being as honest with her as he knew how to be.

"I love you, Clara. And one day, when we have Andrew back, I hope you will allow yourself to love me in return."

CHAPTER 20

"The inner alphabet on the cipher disk contains the original twenty-six letters," Granville explained, pulling a stool up to the table in the museum's studio. "And the exterior contains twenty-six numbers as well, plus the integers two through eight inclusive, for a total of thirty-three."

"So the openings on this plate"—Jacob tapped his finger on the drawing of a brass disk—"align both the plaintext and the ciphertext equivalents."

"And the gears inside the box rotate the disks," Granville said.

Both men peered at the diagrams if they were maps to a hidden treasure.

Clara smiled slightly at the sight of them, furrows of concentration lining their foreheads. Though Jacob needed the funds of a patron before constructing the machine and presenting it to the Home Office committee, he had enlisted Uncle Granville's help in translating the diagrams. The men had spent all their time studying the plans in the two days since Clara and Sebastian's wedding.

"The alphabet code is very precise," Granville explained. "And it requires a different keyword for each correspondent. Wait a moment. Let me get the notes I made about Monsieur Dupree's calculations and we can see if they work."

He left to return to his workshop. In the ensuing silence, Clara remembered Sebastian's words, his declaration of love that wound through her like bright ribbons. Oh, how desperately she wanted to return the avowal, to admit to all the feelings that had been locked inside her for so many years—her youthful adoration now flourishing into a brilliant, richly complex love that both thrilled and frightened her. A love she could not yet acknowledge.

A shuddering breath escaped her. She looked at Jacob, who was watching her across the misty sunlight. A hint of sympathy eased the impassivity of his features.

Clara swallowed and placed her sewing on a nearby table.

"Did Sebastian tell you about my son?" she asked.

Jacob nodded. "He will help you in whatever way he can."

"He already has." A touch of nervousness wound through her. "Were you terribly shocked when he told you of our agreement?"

"No, because I know my brothers." Jacob rubbed a hand across his hair and studied the notebook in front of him. Behind his glasses, his eyes took on a distant cast. "Sebastian is not like Alexander or Patrick. Or me, for that matter. Alexander forces things to fit the way he wants them to. Patrick breaks them, if need be."

"And you?" Clara asked.

He shrugged and leaned forward to make a notation on a page. "Sebastian is more...surreptitious," he continued. "He used to merely charm people into doing what he wanted, but now it seems he needs to find a different approach. And he *will* find it, Clara, make no mistake. Loyalty is his greatest strength."

A smile tugged at her mouth. "And his greatest weakness?"

"The same."

"Why?"

He put the pencil down, a frown etched on his brow. "Because he sometimes finds it necessary to lie in order to protect those he loves."

Clara knew he spoke of the way Sebastian had kept secret the infirmity of his hand, which Jacob must have sensed even if he didn't know the full truth. Yet Sebastian had told *her* about it shortly after her proposal, as if he knew the secret would be safe with her.

"Here it is." Granville returned, his head bent as he leafed through a tattered notebook. "I expect one of these codes will work."

He and Jacob began conferring over the specifications again. Clara pushed up from her chair and went to the foyer, where Mrs. Fox sat penning numbers into her account books.

"Any word from Mr. Hall?" Clara asked.

"No, Mrs. Hall." Mrs. Fox peered at her from above the half-moons of her reading glasses. "You said you were expecting him before supper, and it's not yet tea."

"Yes, I know." Clara twisted her hands into her apron. Sebastian had gone to a meeting with his brother's solicitor, Mr. Findlay, in order to finish the contract to convey Wakefield House to Lord Fairfax. As soon as the terms were established, and both Clara and Granville, as trustee, signed the papers, they could approach Fairfax with the proposal. Despite Clara's wish to accompany Sebastian, he wanted to ensure the impermeability of the terms first before she and Granville reviewed the contract.

"You'll let me know if he returns or sends a message?" she asked Mrs. Fox.

"Of course." The other woman returned to her ledger.

Clara went into the drawing room and tried to busy herself by straightening the displays and testing a few of the automata. She twisted the key of a mechanical toy and watched a little bear beating on a drum. When it wound down, she turned it again.

Restlessness seethed in her, born of both Sebastian's admission and the physical pleasure she had experienced at her husband's touch. She could not reconcile the two most essential needs she had ever known—her desire for Sebastian and her desperation to have her son back. In allowing herself to surrender to the former, she feared she weakened the force of the latter.

And yet both heat and tenderness billowed through her every time she allowed herself to relive those moments in Sebastian's arms, the flex of his muscles beneath her hands, the glide of flesh against flesh. The sensation of his heart beating against hers.

"Mrs. Hall?" Mrs. Fox's voice came from the doorway. "A visitor has just arrived."

Clara forced down the tangle of emotions and schooled her features into impassivity before she turned to face Mrs. Fox.

"Have they requested a tour?" she asked.

"She has requested to speak with you," Mrs. Fox replied, her severe expression mitigated by a faint air of confusion.

With a frown, Clara followed her to the foyer. A tall, dark-haired woman, clad in a plain black cloak and hat, stood beside the desk. Her large, dark eyes were framed by thick eyelashes, and her skin appeared bronzed from the sun.

The instant Clara met her gaze, she knew the identity of the woman. Her heart crashed against her ribs as she stepped forward.

"Mrs....?" Her voice faltered.

"Leskovna." The woman extended an elegant hand, her eyes sweeping Clara from head to toe. "You are Mrs. Sebastian Hall?"

"I am."

A strained silence fell. Mrs. Fox cleared her throat delicately.

"Mrs. Hall, if you'd care to bring your guest into the parlor, I will have tea brought in."

"Yes, of course. Thank you, Mrs. Fox." Grateful for the direction, Clara gestured for Sebastian's mother to follow her and closed the door behind them. "Mrs. Leskovna, I'm glad to make your acquaintance. Jacob is in the studio with my uncle, but I'm afraid Sebastian isn't here."

"I know. It's the only reason I dared visit you." Catherine Leskovna tugged off her gloves. She cast a glance around at the automata and mechanical toys. "I feared Sebastian might have me thrown out otherwise."

Clara's chest constricted as she murmured, "He wouldn't do that."

Yet her words did not have the ring of conviction, and clearly Catherine sensed its lack. Clara waited, guarded, uncertain of the reason the woman would have come here knowing Sebastian was elsewhere.

"I'm certain you know the reasons my children have renounced me," Catherine said. "When I heard about Sebastian's resignation from Weimar, I could not believe it. I was convinced something disastrous had befallen him. Sebastian would never abandon his patrons and supporters on the basis of a disagreement over his work. I had to learn the truth of what had happened to him."

"Why did you not approach him first, then?"

"If I'd thought he would speak to me, I would have. And perhaps he might have considered it, were he not so loyal to Alexander. Even as children, he and Alexander had a bond that would not be broken. And I know..." She paused and looked down at the floor, only the slight tremble in her voice disclosing her emotions. "I know Alexander has forsaken my very existence. Sebastian would not betray his brother by opening the door to me."

"Yet Jacob did."

Catherine gave a sad smile. "Jacob is ruled by his head rather than his heart. Not unlike his father. Though he might feel hurt by my actions, Jacob would not allow his emotions to overrule his intellectual curiosity. Not to mention his appreciation of a good challenge. And so when I approached him and explained the situation, he conceded to my request. Yet Sebastian continues to refuse a meeting with me."

"Surely you understand the reasons why."

"Yes. But I cannot remain in London much longer, Mrs. Hall. I am aware of the scandal I created, and in its aftermath I thought I would leave England forever. Certainly that was the least I could do considering the wreckage I created. I returned solely for the purpose of seeing Sebastian again, but I will not allow my presence here to cause renewed gossip."

A brief knock announced Mrs. Marshall arriving with the tea tray. After the housekeeper left, Clara poured the tea and sat back to study Sebastian's mother. Catherine Leskovna had lost the refined elegance of a countess, but she possessed a kind of self-assurance, a calmness, that seemed at odds with the disgrace of her infidelity.

Though Clara had encouraged Sebastian to visit his mother, a flare of anger swept through her chest suddenly. How dare Catherine Leskovna not flay herself with remorse over what she had done? How dare she sit here with such graceful stillness, as if she did not regret anything? How dare she seem to be *at peace*?

Clara's fingers tightened on her cup. "Why are you so insistent upon seeing Sebastian? Haven't you caused him enough pain?"

Catherine lowered her gaze to her teacup, concealing whatever reaction she had to the barbed question. When she spoke, her voice was soft. "Of all five of my children, Sebastian is the one most likely to understand why I did what I did."

"Why Sebastian?"

"Because he has always followed his heart, his instincts, regardless of what people have said. He has always been so confident in his decisions. In his place in the world. He has never done anything unless he was certain he wanted to."

Clara's throat tightened as she remembered Sebastian's words of love. Even when she first proposed, had he truly wanted to marry her? Had he followed his heart?

She pressed a hand to her chest, feeling her own heart, which had taken such a tangled, labyrinthine path during the past year. She had once believed that path could lead her only to Andrew, but now she had to confront the very real possibility that Sebastian, too, stood at the end of her heart's journey.

But at what cost to Andrew?

Clara blinked away the sting of tears. "Do...do you think Sebastian could be a liaison to your other children, then?" she asked. "That if you make him understand your decisions, he might defend you to the rest of them?"

"No. I need no one to defend me, Mrs. Hall. I've long become accustomed to doing that myself."

A somewhat unwelcome twist of admiration went through Clara as she met the other woman's resolute gaze. "Then why are you here?"

"When Jacob told me Sebastian had married at Rushton's urging, I couldn't help but wonder if this union was somehow related to the reason he left Weimar." Catherine took a sip of tea. "Forgive me, but neither his resignation nor his marriage accord with the man I know Sebastian to be."

"Perhaps he's changed." Clara set her cup down and paced to the windows, her shoulders stiff with tension. "Do you believe he resigned from Weimar because of our marriage?"

"Did he?"

"He resigned last spring, Mrs. Leskovna. I knew Sebastian when I was younger, but did not make his acquaintance again until recently. No. I had nothing to do with his resignation."

A mild surprise flashed in the other woman's eyes. "I didn't think *you* had a hand in it. I was speaking of your father."

"My...my father?"

"Forgive me for recalling that he was not the kindest of men."

"How on earth do you know that?"

"I knew your mother, Mrs. Hall."

Clara's knees weakened as shock bolted through her. She sank into a chair, buffeted by a sudden rush of memories. "I…I was not aware of that."

"We were not close friends, but we shared an interest in several of the same charities and saw each other often at various meetings and teas. I regret to say that the other ladies often remarked on Lord Fairfax's reputation, though your mother had the grace never to discuss personal matters. I found her to be a kind and thoughtful woman. So did many other ladies of my acquaintance."

Clara's jaw tightened as she struggled against another wash of tears. She nodded her gratitude, not trusting herself to speak.

"So when Jacob told me Sebastian had married you rather suddenly," Catherine continued, "I remembered both your mother and the rumors about your father. And while I fully recognize this is none of my business, especially in the shadow of my own decisions, I was concerned about Lord Fairfax's hand in your hasty engagement."

"My father did have a hand in our engagement," Clara admitted, forcing the words past her tight throat. "Though not in the way you think."

With images of her mother flowing through her mind, Clara found herself confessing everything to Catherine Leskovna—Richard's death, the will that had granted Fairfax custody of Andrew, Wakefield House, and the reasons behind her proposal to Sebastian. Catherine listened without expression, but smiled when Clara explained that Sebastian had agreed to marry her in part to satisfy his father's ultimatum.

"I believe Lord Rushton capable of such an ultimatum," Catherine said. "But Sebastian would not have agreed to marry you had he not wanted to, regardless of Rushton's threats. I hope you know that."

Clara did. She'd known the moment Sebastian told her their

union would be both real and permanent. And in a very secret corner of her heart, she had wanted that too.

"Have you asked for Rushton's assistance in the matter with your father?" Catherine asked.

"No. Sebastian would not hear of it."

"No, I imagine he wouldn't." A crease marred Catherine's forehead. "I wish I could offer you advice or assistance, but I've lost whatever connections I possessed in London. And I don't dare contact anyone lest I cause trouble for Jacob. I owe him a great deal."

"When Jacob told us the true reason for his return to London, I attempted to convince Sebastian to agree to meet you," Clara admitted. "Although I know very little about what happened, I do believe he should not deny you the opportunity to explain."

Clara realized that her wish extended beyond the fact that Catherine was Sebastian's mother. Clara herself knew well what it felt like to have one's efforts at reconciliation thwarted, and she did not want that pain for Catherine Leskovna. Questionable though Catherine's choices might have been, her feelings for her children were genuine.

"I am extraordinarily grateful to you, then." Catherine set down her teacup and rose. Such calm infused her gestures, even the air around her. Despite the turmoil Catherine Leskovna had both caused and sustained, she appeared unrepentant, as if something had soothed the sting of her deceit.

Clara wondered what it was. And she wondered if she would ever know that kind of peace following the storms that had battered her over the past year.

Catherine approached to take Clara's hand. A kind smile curved her lips. "Jacob believes you are a good match for Sebastian. I must say I agree with him. Your mother would be proud of you."

"Thank you." She tightened her hand on the other woman's.

Her mother would not have censured Catherine without having known the truth of the rumors, and so Clara would not either. "You don't know how much that means to me."

Catherine smiled. "I do know."

CHAPTER 21

*S*ebastian pushed his right hand into his pocket and watched his father clip dead leaves from a plant. The humid, musty air of the greenhouse filled his nose with the smells of damp soil and moss. Flowers flourished throughout the glass-encased house—asters, roses, lilacs. Only here among his plants did Rushton ever seem relaxed, at his ease. Elsewhere, the earl still wore an air of caution, as if he knew the restoration of his family's standing remained somewhat fragile.

"Bastian, stir the soil in those pots, would you?" Rushton nodded toward a row of Botany Bay plants lined up on a shelf. "Just the surface. And open the window sashes to let some air in."

Sebastian picked up a trowel and proceeded to dig into the pots. For a few moments, they worked in silence before Rushton set down his clippers and wiped his hands on his apron.

"She's not what I'd expected," he finally said, "but she is suitable enough and appears to be very well mannered."

Sebastian almost smiled.

"She is suitable indeed," he agreed.

Rushton picked up a water syringe and began misting the

plants. "I understand her father is visiting town. Thought I would invite him to dine one evening."

Sebastian turned away so Rushton wouldn't see the tightening of his expression. Two days hence, he and Clara would approach Fairfax with the completed proposition about Wakefield House. Then they would know if she would finally have Andrew back.

"I've explained that Clara and her father are estranged," he told his father.

"Still, it would be in good form if I were to introduce myself to Fairfax. And bring Mrs. Hall for tea one day soon," Rushton suggested. "Her uncle as well. I'd be interested to speak with him more about his rather unusual creations."

"I'm certain he would be pleased to accept."

"You ought to tell Jacob about his inventions as well." Rushton began putting the tools away. "Have you written to him and Alexander with the news of your marriage?"

"I intend to do so later this week." The lie stuck in his throat, for he could not tell Alexander anything until he had settled the matter of Clara's son.

And he knew Jacob had not told their father he was back in London. The secrecy of his brother's presence, not to mention that of the former countess, continued to poke at Sebastian like a thorn. Hadn't their family harbored enough secrets in recent years?

He completed the task Rushton had given him, then left to return to the Mount Street town house. He removed his great-coat and hat before entering the drawing room, where Clara and Jacob sat conversing.

Sebastian let his gaze wander over his wife, appreciating the curves beneath her dark green dress, the coils of hair spilling around her neck, the warmth in her eyes as she rose to greet him. A mixture of tenderness and unease churned through him.

"I was just telling Mrs. Hall I regret not having attended your wedding," Jacob said. "But owing to the circumstances..."

"What are you doing here?"

The abruptness of the question didn't appear to offend his brother. Jacob settled back into his chair, a grave expression steadying across his face.

"Catherine Leskovna leaves at the end of the month." Jacob folded one leg over the other and studied the brandy in his glass as if it were a specimen under a microscope. "I'd suggest you pay her a visit before she pays you one."

"She wouldn't dare."

"She might. She just wants to speak with you, Bastian. What harm is there in that?"

Sebastian felt Clara's gaze as if she were touching him, felt her silent urging. Although he knew it would be his doom, he turned his head to meet her violet eyes.

Dammit.

He shot his brother a pointed look. Jacob pushed himself to standing and murmured a farewell to Clara before seeing himself out.

"Please don't deny her this," Clara said the moment the door closed.

"You know nothing about her."

"She came to see me this afternoon."

Sebastian's spine stiffened with wariness. "What?"

"She wanted to learn the details of our marriage. She also knows of my father's reputation for cruelty. While I revealed nothing about your resignation from Weimar, I did tell her the circumstances that led to my estrangement from Fairfax."

"She doesn't deserve to know anything."

"She is still your mother," Clara said. "Whatever she's done, you cannot deny her the opportunity to see her son again."

"After what she did, I can deny her anything," Sebastian snapped.

Clara studied him a moment, then approached and curled her hand around the lapel of his coat. "You're not the slightest bit curious to hear what she would say to you? Are there no questions you wish to ask her? Nothing you want to tell her?"

Sebastian's heart pulsed against his rib cage. For almost three years, questions had amassed in his mind until his head ached with them. And beneath it all lay the pervasive memory of listening to his mother play the piano and knowing he was the only one of his family who understood how music could soothe all the rough edges of one's life. The only one who understood, somehow, that his mother's seemingly flawless life might actually *have* rough edges.

He had tried to rid himself of that memory, not wanting to remember anything that would soften his anger toward her, but still it remained, like fresh grass buried beneath layers of hard winter ice.

"You know I would give anything to see my son again," Clara said. "I cannot believe your mother doesn't feel the same way. And trust me when I tell you that you will regret it if you do not grant her a meeting before she leaves London. What if you're never given an opportunity again?"

Sebastian tried to smother the anger roiling in his chest. He wrapped a lock of her long hair around his finger. "If I agree to meet her, what will you give me?"

Startled, Clara drew back to look up at him. "What will I give you?"

"Mmm." He rubbed his thumb along the soft strands of hair. "You devised all the arrangements for our marriage. I'd help you transfer Wakefield House if you helped me find the cipher machine plans. So if I agree to see my mother, what boon will you grant me in return?"

"You..." Her breath shortened, her violet eyes darkening. "You insisted upon your own conditions to our agreement. Do you not recall?"

"Oh, I recall." He wished now he'd insisted on a few more

conditions. Creative ones. "This, however, is a new request that requires new conditions."

She frowned. "You are trying to divert my attention from the subject at hand."

"Is it working?"

"Sebastian." Clara lifted a hand to cover his. Though her voice was stern, a smile twitched her lips. "You know I will give you anything you wish in return. But please don't make a decision based on that. Make a decision based on what your heart tells you to do."

"That was not how you made your decision to propose," Sebastian reminded her.

Clara looked at him, her gaze skimming across his face, her fingers tightening on his.

"Oh yes," she whispered. "It was."

His heart thumped.

"It seems to me that you have experienced enough regrets in recent months," she said. "I do not wish for you to endure more of them."

Neither did he. He'd had so few regrets in his life prior to the difficulty with his hand, simply because he'd always done as he pleased. He'd made a career of doing the very thing he loved to do.

He sighed and looked at Clara, her eyes filled with wary hope. He hated the idea of being the source of yet another disappointment for her. He flexed his right hand and tried to imagine seeing his mother again. A mixture of doubt and, surprisingly, anticipation rose in him.

"All right," he finally said. "I will pay my mother a visit."

CHAPTER 22

"*A*ndrew is out with his tutor today." Clara gripped the curtain in her fist as she stared out the carriage window at Fairfax's town house. The day following her wedding, she had sent her father a note requesting an interview. He had agreed to see her at precisely three o'clock on Tuesday, and now all the events of the past three days—the wedding, Sebastian's admission of love, Catherine Leskovna's visit, and now this meeting—collided in Clara's mind like crashing stones.

Fear shuddered through her. "I suspect my father wouldn't have agreed to see us if Andrew were at home. Especially not after—"

Sebastian settled his large hand on the back of her neck, stopping her words. "It's done," he said. "We have what he wants. All he needs to do is agree and sign the papers."

Not wanting to risk granting the baron any time to rethink his decision, Sebastian had had his brother's solicitor draw up the papers for the transfer of Wakefield House to Fairfax's name. Even if Fairfax agreed to the terms, Clara knew her father wouldn't sign the contract without his own solicitor's review, but at least they could shorten the duration of the transaction.

Sebastian tucked the file of papers beneath his arm and stepped from the carriage. He helped Clara descend, holding her trembling hand in his as they approached the townhouse and rang the bell.

The gray-haired butler Davies admitted them, rigid as a stone column, his gaze cold as it skirted over Clara. No light of recognition flashed over his impassive features, even though he had known her since she was a child and had always treated her with kind respect.

Sorrow congealed in Clara's throat. "Hello, Davies."

"Mrs.…Hall. Your father awaits."

Apprehension shuddered through her as she saw the half-open door of Fairfax's study, a triangle of light edging from the room. Davies divested Sebastian of his greatcoat and Clara of her cloak before preceding them down the corridor.

Her father stood beside the hearth, his lean frame sheathed in a black morning coat and gray waistcoat, his white hair furrowed with comb marks. Like a tree in winter, stark and unyielding.

Clara smothered the urge to remain within the comfort of Sebastian's presence. She made a quick gesture indicating he should remain by the door. Though protest vibrated from him, he came to a stop.

Clara's heart slammed against her ribs as she forced herself to take measured steps across the carpet. Never had a room felt so vast, so cavernous, as she made her way to where her father stood. Sweat collected on her nape when she finally halted and lifted her head to meet his cool, gray eyes.

"My lord." Her voice shook. She swallowed and tried to conceal the shades of panic coloring her words. "Thank you for agreeing to see me. I beg your forgiveness for my rash and imprudent behavior earlier this month."

Fairfax didn't reply. He slanted his gaze past her. "You, there. What did you hope to gain by marrying her?"

"A good wife." Sebastian's deep voice rang close behind Clara.

Relief rippled through her at his nearness, despite her mandate that he remain by the door.

"Mr. Hall did us both a great service with this union," Clara said. A bead of sweat rolled down her spine as she continued to hold her father's flinty gaze. "The day we wed, Wakefield House transferred into his name."

Satisfaction clenched in her as a flash of surprise glinted in Fairfax's expression. Papers rustled. Sebastian placed the contract on the low table between them.

"What is that?" Fairfax jerked his chin to the papers.

"A contract granting you ownership of Wakefield House and the surrounding property," Clara said, "if you will release custody of Andrew to me."

She took an involuntary step back, as if the proposal would ignite a bolt of fury in her father, but Fairfax didn't move. An eerie calm collected around him, like a coat perfectly tailored to his form.

"That is the reason you married him," he said.

Clara nodded, finding no purpose in lying. "You've been attempting to gain ownership of Wakefield House for months," she reminded her father. "I would have given it to you the day I left Manley Park, had the courts allowed it. But now I can give it to you through Mr. Hall. I'm certain your solicitor will find the papers entirely in order."

When her father didn't respond, Clara pressed on with a growing sense of desperation. "My lord, it's worth a substantial sum, even with the house in disrepair. I'm certain the proceeds from a sale would go a long way toward assuaging any financial difficulties you may—"

"Do shut up, Clara." Fairfax flicked open a silver box seated on the mantel. He pressed tobacco into a curved, fluted pipe of polished teak, then used the tongs to extract a burning twig from the fire. Smoke billowed from the cup of the pipe as he puffed.

He squinted at Sebastian through the haze. "Your father is Lord Rushton."

"Benjamin Hall, the Earl of Rushton. Yes."

An arrow of tension lanced through Sebastian's tall frame, tightening his shoulders and stirring Clara's unease. She moved closer to him, appearances be damned, and watched her father warily.

Fairfax drew on his pipe again and released the smoke on a long exhale. "And you both think *this*"—he flicked the contract with blunt fingers—"is enough for me to surrender custody of my grandson?"

Clara's heart plummeted. "But you...you've been wanting Wakefield House for months and now..."

"Oh, I'll accept Wakefield House. Sell it to the first hapless buyer who offers enough. But Andrew is worth so much more than a decrepit old house, isn't he, Clara?"

Sebastian's tension crystallized into anger, lacing him with fury. He closed the distance between himself and Fairfax, and for a heart-stopping instant Clara thought surely he would strike her father.

No. Anger vivid but leashed, Sebastian glared down at Fairfax. "How much more do you want?"

"More than you have, my boy."

Clara gasped. Still Sebastian did not lash out, though a visible current of rage vibrated through him. Fairfax puffed on the pipe and met Clara's gaze over her husband's shoulder.

"I commend your efforts, my dear. But Andrew will remain within my custody, as I refuse to jeopardize his safety in your presence. You will not see your son again."

Clara started to shake. Her father's final remark opened a wide, black pit inside her that she dared not face for fear she would fall into the endless darkness.

"There...there is nothing that will change your mind?" she

asked, her voice weakening under the onslaught of suppressed emotions.

"I am not doing this to be cruel, Clara," Fairfax said. "Andrew has been in a prolonged state of shock since his father's death. I am sending him to an institution where he can receive proper treatment."

"A...an institution? Why—" Clara's voice broke as she recalled Lord Margrave telling her that Andrew hadn't been "well" during his visit to Manley Park.

"The institution is in Switzerland, near Interlaken," Fairfax continued. "I have corresponded with a Swiss physician who has studied afflictions of children, and agreed to work with Andrew. The institution has wards dedicated to children's care. I'm certain Andrew will receive the help he needs there."

"What kind of help does he need?" Clara cried, her spine so tight it felt like it would break in two. "Why do you want to send him to a physician? What is wrong with him?"

Fairfax slanted Sebastian a glance. "Please take Mrs. Hall out before she becomes hysterical. Or before I have her removed."

"You will not get away with this," Sebastian snapped.

Before Clara could shove words past her constricted throat, Sebastian grabbed the papers from the table, then took her arm and led her into the foyer. Davies stood near the door, his expression impassive even as tension poured from the room.

"Davies, what do you know of this?" Clara grasped the man's sleeve in desperation. "Why is my father sending Andrew away? What's happened to him?"

Something wavered in the butler's eyes, but he shook his head. "I do not know, Mrs. Hall."

"Please tell me! You've known me since I was a child, Davies, you know I only want the best for my son. What is *wrong*?"

"Lord Fairfax has requested that you depart, Mrs. Hall," he replied.

Sebastian cursed. He tossed Clara's cloak around her shoulders and grabbed his greatcoat, stalking to the carriage with a hard, determined stride.

Clara hurried beside him, fighting for breath and calm. Sebastian handed her into the carriage and ordered the driver to return to Mount Street. Shaking with cold, she lunged across the space to collapse onto the seat beside him. Her chest rattled with dry, wrenching sobs.

He locked an arm around her, pulling her body hard against his. She pressed her face into his shoulder and absorbed his warmth. Yet not even Sebastian could rid her of the new, icy reality shearing into her soul.

She had nothing left to offer.

Bastard.

Now more than ever, bloodlust gripped Sebastian. He not only wanted to kill Fairfax—he first wanted to see the man suffer. He wanted to induce the suffering himself. The feeling clawed at him as he wrestled for a solution in the midnight hours following their confrontation with Fairfax.

Sebastian stared at the papers he'd spread out on the desk—accounts, expenses, budgets, bills. His father afforded him a generous allowance, the funds of which would continue owing to his marriage to Clara. Sebastian also had Jacob's payment for the cipher machine plans, and he'd a small fund left from the proceeds of his tours and performances. Still, even if he didn't use the money to pay the remainder of his medical obligations, he doubted it would be enough to appease Fairfax. And money was all he could think of with which to bargain.

He groaned, clamping the bridge of his nose between his fingers. God in heaven. What chaotic hell would flare if his father and elder brother discovered the truth of all this?

He'd crush his pride to sand if he thought begging would generate their help. A portion of Rushton's and Alexander's combined fortunes would cover Fairfax's debts, no matter how dire.

But that would mean confessing all. And once Rushton and Alexander learned about Catherine Leskovna...

"I won't let you do this."

Clara's gentle voice swam into his thoughts. He dragged a hand through his hair and straightened, watching her approach. A deep russet, merino dress trimmed in brown enclosed her slender figure, and her chestnut hair cascaded in a long ribbon over her shoulder. She looked like a wood sprite, pale and delicate, her unusual eyes veiled with caution.

An ache gripped Sebastian's throat. More than anything, even more than wanting the use of his hand again, he wanted to help her. He wanted to give her that which she desired most. He wanted to ease her pain, to make her happy. He wanted to protect her.

He'd failed spectacularly at doing any of those things.

Her warm hand slid beneath his chin, guiding his face toward hers. "I won't let you," she repeated. "You will not ruin yourself because of my father's threats."

"Then what? You'll let him send your son away?"

Clara drew back, her hand dropping away from him. Sebastian sighed and snared her wrist. "Sorry."

She twisted her wrist from his grip and tangled her fingers with his. He pushed the chair away from the desk, putting his hand at her back to draw her closer. She lowered herself to his lap, her knees hugging his hips, her orange-spice scent flavoring the air. He grasped the streamer of her hair and let the loose tendrils glide through his fingers.

She placed her hands on his cheeks and stared into his eyes. "I never wanted this. Never meant to drag you into the vile swamp of my father's domain. I honestly hoped he would accede to my request, that he wanted Wakefield House enough to release Andrew."

She shook her head and bit her lower lip, creating little indentations Sebastian wanted to soothe with a sweep of his tongue.

"He thinks Andrew will never be worth anything," Clara said. "Andrew is a quiet boy, studious. He likes to read and draw. He likes animals. He's skilled at archery and fencing, but my father insisted that he learn shooting, hawking, riding, wrestling...he thought Andrew should be adept at all such masculine pursuits, even at seven years of age."

She sighed. "Richard would have thought the same, had he lived."

Sebastian understood the boy's inclinations. He'd never been one for hunting or wrestling himself, though between his father and three brothers he'd become accomplished at all sports.

"Was that the source of your arguments?" he asked.

"Some of them. Others involved Andrew's education, the fact that Richard wanted to send Andrew away to school...I'm sorry to say we disagreed on a great deal. Sometimes I acquiesced to Richard's demands in order to maintain peace but neither he nor my father appreciated any sign of dissent. I suppose it oughtn't have been a surprise that Richard believed my father a more suitable guardian. My father also had very exacting ideas about how Andrew should be raised, especially since he is the only grandchild. I suspect things might have been different had Richard and I been blessed with more children."

"Brothers and sisters are a blessing," Sebastian agreed, "though it is sometimes difficult to conform to the standards they might set."

She studied him from beneath her dark eyelashes. "You've never conformed."

No, and that too had set him apart from his family. The distinction brought an unwelcome thought of his mother to mind, that clandestine sense that he shared something with her that no one else in his family had. She must have known it as well, or she wouldn't have sought him out after the Weimar disaster.

Certainly none of his brothers had comprehended his proclivity for music, though they eventually came to appreciate the flock of admiring women his success attracted.

Now Sebastian couldn't remember any of the women who had peppered his life over the years. Like paper dolls, they were flimsy and impermanent, strung together with brittle thread.

Nothing like Clara Shepherd, who blazed with life and fire and determination.

He stroked his thumb across her lower lip, rubbing away the painful little notches caused by her teeth. "You will have your son again."

She twisted the ends of his cravat between her fingers, her downcast eyelashes painting crescents on her pale cheeks. She spoke no words of agreement, but she didn't refute his statement either. That must mean she still had hope.

Of course she still hoped. Nothing would ever extinguish Clara's essential belief that she would one day be reunited with her son. That spark would burn in her until she held Andrew in her arms once again. No matter how long it took. No matter what she was forced to do.

She lifted her lashes to look at him, then leaned forward to press her mouth against his. A soft heat spilled through him at the touch of her full lips, the breathy sigh easing from her throat. He tightened his hands on her waist, his left hand curling against the stiffness of her corset. His right fingers seized and refused to move. He tensed and started to pull away from her, hating his inability to control the way he touched his own wife.

Clara covered his disabled hand, tucking her fingers between his. She parted her lips to deepen their kiss and moved his hand up to her bare throat.

"Touch me," she whispered.

His fingers remained rigid, locked into place, but he felt the softness of her skin, the pulse tapping at the hollow of her throat. Warmth skimmed from his fingertips up the length of his arm.

She speared her hands in his hair and tilted his head back, her mouth urgent, her hips pushing against him. She shifted closer. Her bottom slid against his lap until his groin nestled within the enclosing arch of her legs.

He grasped the pleats of her skirt with his other hand and drew them up. The heat of her skin burned his palm. She wiggled closer, pulling at the knot of his cravat until his throat was bared to the caress of her warm lips. He breathed her in, stroking his fingers over the supple length of her thigh. Clara dropped her hands to his trousers and unfastened the buttons.

Lust sparked and flared in him. Clara cast him a quick glance, a smile curving her lips as she felt the bulge pressing against her fingers. He shifted to allow her easier access, wincing with pleasure at the touch of her hand against his hot flesh. Clara flicked her tongue against the side of his neck as she moved her hand over him, her body softening with readiness.

Sebastian's blood pulsed. He gripped her thigh with his left hand to encourage her positioning, already aching to sheathe himself within the tight clasp of her body.

"Sebastian…" Uncertainty rippled through her.

"Slow." His voice rasped from his chest. He slid his hand up to the juncture of her thighs and stroked. She gasped, trembling as she steadied herself with a hand on his shoulder. Her violet eyes searched his as she poised herself above him and then eased down, enclosing him by scant degrees. When he was fully embedded in her, throbbing, he tightened his hand again.

"Oh." Clara shifted experimentally, her hips writhing. "Should I…"

"You should move." Sebastian struggled to maintain what little control was left to him. "Right now."

She did, her hands fisting on his shoulders as she lifted her body and brought it down again, driving their pleasure higher. She convulsed around him with a cry the instant before his tension broke. He thrust upward with a groan, spilling inside her as her inner muscles rippled around his shaft.

Clara's mouth descended on his as the final shudders undulated through them. She pressed her hands to the sides of his face and leaned her forehead against his.

"I count that evening in the Hanover Street rooms," she whispered, "as one of the luckiest days of my life."

Sebastian rubbed his finger across her lower lip. "Yet still you have not gotten what you want."

"With you, I have." The words seemed to slip from her involuntarily. A sheen of dismay colored her eyes as she straightened to separate herself from him. She stroked a lingering hand across his neck. "But I meant it when I said I would not allow you to ruin yourself over this."

"No, I won't. But I will find a way to defeat him."

She studied him, her expression veiled with a sudden guardedness. "Will you not approach your father?"

A humorless laugh stuck in Sebastian's throat. "No."

"Surely Lord Rushton could—"

"My father threatened my inheritance unless I wed, Clara." Anger built in Sebastian's chest as he recalled the threats of both his father and hers. "Rushton could not have cared less that my career failed so badly. He never even asked what happened. He has spent the past six months reestablishing himself in society and attempting to convince me to take a position with the Patent Office, of all bloody places. No. I will not involve him in a matter such as this."

"But even your mother knew about Fairfax's reputation," Clara persisted. "If your father were to approach him, Fairfax might at least listen, if not relent to some degree."

"No." Unease twined with his anger as he refastened his shirt, cursing inwardly at the awkwardness of attempting the buttons with his left hand. "My father stays out of this."

"All right, then." She drew away from him and allowed her skirts to pool around her legs, regaining her modesty. Notes of both frustration and finality, blood-red, colored her voice. "We'd best find another solution, then."

CHAPTER 23

Clara descended the cab in front of Fairfax's town house. The tall buildings concealed the descending sun, and a red-orange light glowed like fire on the horizon. Gas lamps burned, smears of yellow flickering through the smoky glass.

No fear compressed Clara's body. Not anymore. For two days following her conflict with her father, she had battled overwhelming fear as she tried to formulate a plan. Now, weary of being afraid, she had woken that morning with the sharp, new intention to confront her father alone. Sebastian had been gone most of the day, apparently in a lengthy meeting with Mr. Findlay, his brother Alexander's solicitor. Clara knew she had to resolve matters before her husband set plans into motion that would result in his inevitable ruin.

"Welcome again, Mrs. Hall." The butler reached to take her cloak.

"Hardly welcome, I'm certain, Davies," Clara murmured.

His mouth turned down at the corners and a faint sorrow flashed in his eyes before he schooled his expression back to impassivity. After hanging her cloak on a rack, Davies ushered her into the study.

Fairfax sat behind his desk, his fingers pressed to his temple and his features lined with pain.

Clara waited for him to acknowledge her. She held her shoulders stiff and straight, forced emotion from her face, restrained the urge to tremble. Once again, she would prove herself dutiful and obedient, even if the effort killed her. Which seemed likely, given the speed at which her heart was racing.

Fairfax lifted his head. The sly malice that had colored his eyes during their previous meeting had faded, leaving a bleak, hollow look Clara had never seen before.

Momentarily startled, she couldn't find her voice. Then, as if by the force of the man's will alone, his look dissolved into hard irritation.

"If you are not here to accede to my wishes and agree to stay away from Andrew for good, then get out," he said.

Clara could do neither, but she couldn't very well tell him that. Her spine lengthened as she approached his desk, her skirts rustling softly, her slippers soundless against the carpet.

"I beg you to tell me why Andrew needs a physician. Why you want to send him away."

Fairfax's mouth thinned. "I told you. He has suffered prolonged shock over the death of his father. I am doing what is best for him."

"Will you allow me to accompany him to Switzerland?" Not until the question left her mouth did Clara realize she had even thought of it.

"No."

"I will go under whatever conditions you impose." She placed her hands flat on the desk and leaned forward, a tremor of urgency threading her bones. She pushed aside thoughts of Sebastian, ignored the ache building around her heart.

"Andrew needs a mother," she said. "I regret that my behavior forced you to cast me out when you did. I will no longer disrespect your upbringing of my son. I will obey your rules. No one will say an unkind word against me, for they will never again see such a dutiful and loyal daughter. All I ask is to be near my son again."

"Why should I allow you to be anywhere near him after what you have done?"

"Perhaps you shouldn't." Clara struggled against a wave of cold. "But I beg you to give me another chance. Imagine what people will say. How kind Lord Fairfax is to shelter his aggrieved daughter and reunite her with her son. Look at what care he bestows upon her and her son following Mr. Shepherd's tragic death."

Fairfax studied her for a moment from beneath hooded lids. "The death for which you were responsible."

She shook her head, unable to voice the denials that had boiled inside her for so long. She jerked back when her father slammed a big hand onto the desk, the resounding crash vibrating up her arms.

"Foolish girl," Fairfax snapped, pressing his fingers against his temple again. "You think you are worth what your useless husband can beg from his father? You think I would take *you* over an earl's fortune?"

No. She hadn't thought that for one second. But she was desperate enough to attempt anything. The black pit of hopelessness inside her widened, threatening to pull her into its endless depths.

No. No. No.

"Sebastian won't just give you a fortune, you bastard," Clara hissed, anger exploding like a cannon inside her head. "Not without Andrew in return."

"You will never have Andrew again."

"And you will rot in hell."

"Get out," Fairfax said, his expression hardening to stone. "And mark my words. Should you interfere again, I will not hesitate to tell people exactly what kind of woman the Earl of Rushton's son married."

Shock filled Clara's throat. In her desperation, she had not foreseen the danger of such a threat. Unable to counter it, she turned and fled, the door banging shut behind her.

Run.

The command pulsed like a heartbeat through her brain as she hurried into the safety of the carriage. She stared at her father's town house as the carriage rolled away from the building's thin, narrow reach.

Although no shadows blurred the windows, Clara sensed Fairfax watching her retreat with the grim satisfaction of a general driving back enemy forces. There would be no compromise.

Run.

No other solution took shape beneath the windstorms whipping against the walls of her heart and soul. She had to seize her son and flee as if the hounds of hell would tear after them. She had to rescue them all from the quicksand of Fairfax's power or the man would choke the very breath from their throats.

A strange, brittle calm settled into her bones as she entered the Mount Street town house and allowed a maid to take her cloak. The door to Sebastian's study sat half-open, his deep voice, laced with urgency, rolling into the foyer. Clara paused just outside the door.

Another male voice joined Sebastian's. Clara recognized it as belonging to Mr. Findlay, who had been drawing up the ineffectual contracts.

Tension gripped her shoulders when she realized the two men were discussing Sebastian's finances and the possibility of liquidating several assets, selling stocks, and draining a fund he had established to provide music scholarships to worthy students.

Clara closed her eyes and pressed her forehead against the cold wall.

What had she done?

In her desperation to have Andrew back, she had dragged Sebastian into a situation so tangled and fraught with peril that even the hope of escape was frail at best.

She pushed away from the wall and tried to draw air into her constricted chest.

She had to leave her husband. If she managed to seize Andrew and run away, Fairfax might turn his attention toward pursuing them and leave Sebastian alone.

Dear God, let him leave Sebastian alone. She could break the tenuous prayer with a breath, so thin and slight were its chances of being answered, but Clara had nothing else. She *would* succeed in this rash, dangerous escape for no other reason than to save her son and protect the man she loved beyond measure.

She pressed her hands to her eyes and allowed the strong, lovely pleasure of that admission to ease her simmering agony. Leaving the flow of conversation behind her, she went to her bedchamber and sat at the secretary.

A plan. She needed to sever her emotions and employ every particle of intellect and cunning she possessed in order to implement a plan. She dipped a pen into the inkwell and began to write.

She would defeat Fairfax. She had to defeat Fairfax, even if no one had ever done so before.

CHAPTER 24

*T*here was a regimen to Fairfax's household. Clara had lived within its boundaries for most of her life, so she knew her father adhered to strict routines and behaviors. Both times she had gone to the Belgravia town house, in the late afternoon, Andrew and his tutor had ostensibly been on an outing to the public garden.

Clara would give herself three days to determine the schedule. She could afford to wait no longer than that. Fairfax might leave London at the end of next week, and if Andrew were once again confined to Manley Park or, God forbid, an institution in Switzerland, Clara knew she could never breach such impenetrable walls.

This was her only chance. The day following Fairfax's threat, she hired a cab just before tea, making excuses to Sebastian that she needed to run some errands and would prefer to leave him the carriage since she didn't know when she expected to return.

Not quite a lie, any part of it.

She didn't dare venture close to Fairfax's town house and instead instructed the cab driver to stop at the edge of Belgrave

Square Garden. If Andrew and his tutor walked to the park from the town house, they would likely take Chapel Street. Hands knotted together, sweat trickling down her back, Clara waited.

She watched birds pecking at bits of grass. Pedestrians strolled along the pathways. Smoke wafted from a coal fire at the meat-pie stand situated on the corner of the street. The vendor, a man with whom Clara had conversed that morning, caught her eye and gave a short nod.

A humorless laugh lodged in Clara's throat. The man's pockets bulged with the small fortune she'd given him in advance for his assistance. Never had she imagined she would be in league with a meat-pie vendor.

A wan-faced girl trudged past the cab, her thin fingers clenched around an open box of ribbons, scraps of fabric, and spools of snarled thread.

Through a canopy of tree leaves, sunlight fell onto the box and sparked against the shiny waves of ribbons. On impulse, Clara pushed the door open. "Miss? Miss!"

The girl turned, regarding her through weary eyes. "Thread, ma'am?"

"The ribbons." Clara dug into her pocket for the remainder of the coins. "How much are they?"

"A penny apiece, ma'am."

"Give me all of them, please."

The girl's eyebrows lifted in surprise, but she quickly gathered the trailing ribbons. Clara gave the girl several shillings, then closed her hand around the ribbons and shut the cab door. The ribbons slithered between her fingers, bright and shiny. She tucked the spilling mass into her pocket and returned her attention to the window.

Her heart stumbled over itself as a familiar figure rounded the corner.

Not Andrew. Not Fairfax.

Sebastian strode to the cab as if it were his intended destination, his steps long and determined, the breeze ruffling his dark hair beneath his hat. Clara shrank back and tried to dissolve into the shadows, but a spear of sunlight flared against her as he wrenched open the door.

Their gazes clashed for an instant before the driver shouted down at him.

"I'm her husband," Sebastian replied curtly, tossing his hat onto the seat. "Leave off and there's a crown in it for you."

The driver fell silent. Clara's fingernails dug into her palms as Sebastian entered the cab and slammed the door behind him.

"What are you doing?" he asked, his voice edged with steel.

"I...I thought to catch a glimpse of Andrew again."

Sebastian slanted his gaze to the window. "Here?"

"He seems to have a...a scheduled routine. I believe he comes here with his tutor at this time of day if the weather allows."

He frowned at her, his wrinkled clothes and messy hair making him appear rough and dangerous in the dim confines of the cab. Clara pressed a hand to her chest to quiet the throb of her heart.

"How did you know I was here?" she asked.

"Followed you." He folded his arms over his chest, grooves of displeasure bracketing his mouth. "Did you think I would believe your flimsy excuse? Why didn't you tell me?"

She couldn't look at him and lie, so Clara stared at the garden, the expanse of grass carpeted with fallen leaves. "I didn't want to take your carriage in the event my father saw and recognized it."

"That's not an answer to my question."

"I didn't want to risk you thinking me a fool for attempting this again."

"I would never think you a fool." No softness cushioned the remark, but the words eased some of Clara's trepidation.

She fought the sudden urge to confide everything to him. A black-edged dream bloomed in her mind—she would tell Sebastian her plan, he would help her, together they would take Andrew and flee far, far away...to the edge of the earth.

They would find a tropical island canopied with a crystal-blue sky, enveloped by water, and abundant with trees bearing ripe fruit and coconuts. A place where sea dragons and monstrous creatures would billow from the sea to protect them forever.

Her very blood ached with the wish that such a dream could come true. And that its fulfillment would not mean the utter destruction of Sebastian's family.

Clara clenched her teeth. If Sebastian escaped with her—and she knew with a churning mixture of longing and sorrow that, should she confess, he would accept no other course of action— then news of his departure would spread like a virulent infection.

God alone knew what havoc Fairfax would attempt to wreak upon the Earl of Rushton and his family. Powerful though Rushton was, the earl had been crushed by scandal before and might not withstand it again. And if Sebastian left London with Clara under such circumstances—by law, the kidnapping of her son—he could never return.

Just like his mother.

Clara's resolve steeled. She would protect both her husband and her son or die trying.

There. She straightened, eagerness crackling along her spine as a slender young man approached one of the garden's pathways. Andrew walked beside him, dressed in a dark blue jacket and short pants, his thick chestnut hair hidden beneath a cap. Both man and boy walked with sedate, measured strides, the tutor turning or gesturing with an occasional remark.

Sebastian leaned forward, as if anticipating Clara might dash heedlessly toward her son again. Though the urge to do so shook her to the bone, she dug her fingers into the seat cushion and watched as Andrew and his tutor paused to look a flock of birds rustling through the hedges.

The tutor spoke for a few minutes, then they continued

walking along a different path. Clara didn't take her eyes from her son until he and the gentleman rounded a corner and disappeared behind a row of trees.

She drew in a shuddering breath and unclamped her fists from the cushion. Sebastian had shifted to sit beside her. Wariness flashed in his expression as he looked from the garden to her.

Clara pulled a faint smile to her mouth. "So. I didn't lose my reason this time."

"No one would blame you if you had." He rapped on the roof and the cab lurched into motion. "When do they leave London?"

"At the end of next week, I believe, though I don't know if they are returning to Manley Park or leaving for the Continent. My father had planned to stay in London for a fortnight."

There was still plenty of time for Fairfax to concoct and then present further demands. But not nearly enough time for Clara to construct all the details of her plan, save for the most skeletal framework. Staying with Uncle Granville during the past year had allowed her to save the jointure funds from her marriage to Richard. Clara needed the money now more than ever.

Armed with breath, desperation, and a prayer, two days hence she would intercept Andrew in the garden while the meat-pie vendor diverted the boy's tutor by whatever means necessary. Clara would hasten Andrew to a cab and speed into the maze of streets before the tutor had a chance to follow or even bear witness to which direction they'd gone.

They would catch the Brighton line at the London Bridge station and take the train to the coast, then procure two tickets to cross the Channel to Dieppe. There, by God's will, she would be able to purchase tickets on a passenger freighter before Fairfax discovered where they had gone.

And then she and Andrew would sail across the sea to where the vast wilderness of America would enclose them in long, sweeping arms and hide them forever.

Something was wrong. Very wrong. Something even beyond the catastrophic failure of their strategy.

Sebastian watched Clara as she entered the morning room, looking lovely with her hair gleaming in a smooth coil, her dark blue gown sprigged with flowers.

"Good morning." She smiled at him and took her seat, arranging her skirts on the chair, her back stiff. She lifted her coffee cup to her lips, then set it back on the saucer with a rattle that betrayed the tremble of her hand.

Sebastian's gaze narrowed. Hovering on the clouded edges of Fairfax's threats, Clara had been unnaturally brittle since their confrontation with her father, as if she held herself together with only glue and string. Her observation of Andrew the previous day had further diminished her, casting a haunted shadow over her brilliant eyes.

What is she plotting?

The question slithered with unpleasant implications into his mind. He hated the idea that his own wife hadn't told him the full truth yesterday of her attempt to see her son. Had she thought he'd try to prevent her from doing so?

"What are your plans for the day?" he asked in a conciliatory tone.

"Oh." She swept a ribbon of hair away from her neck. "A visit to Uncle Granville, perhaps. I've been remiss in my duties at the museum, though I don't imagine Mrs. Fox laments my absence."

She picked at a muffin, leaving her plate littered with crumbs, then took a delicate swallow of coffee. "Are you going out? Do you have time to leave me at the museum?"

He nodded. "Will you try to see Andrew again today?"

She fumbled again in the movement of setting her cup on the saucer. The cup tipped, spilling a few drops of coffee onto the pristine tablecloth. "Oh! I'm so sorry."

"Never mind."

She grabbed a napkin and began pressing on the stains. "Silly of me, wasn't it?"

"Clara, leave it." With a mutter of irritation, Sebastian pushed his chair back and went to her side. He grasped her wrist to stop her ineffectual wiping. Her skin was cold, her pulse beating rapidly against his fingers.

"Clara."

She turned to him, a faint wildness darkening her eyes to purple. "I'll just finish getting ready then."

"Will you try to see Andrew again today?" Sebastian repeated.

Her throat rippled with a swallow. She lowered her gaze from his and shook her head. "It was foolish of me to go yesterday. I'm afraid Fairfax will learn of my presence, so it's best if I stay away."

Sebastian tucked his forefinger beneath her chin and lifted her face. He searched her eyes for signs of deception and found none. He found nothing. A transparent shield permitted the colors of her eyes to gleam as vividly as ever, but it concealed the emotions usually storming in their depths.

He stepped away from her. Irritation flared. "All right, then. I'll leave you at the museum before my appointment at the bank."

"Don't do anything foolish." A plea threaded her words. "We'll think of another arrangement, come to different terms."

And yet they both knew Fairfax would accept no other terms. Clara swallowed. For an instant, fear shone in her expression.

"I don't know how much time we have left," she whispered.

Sebastian cupped her face with his left hand and willed her to believe his next words. "I will fix this, Clara. You must trust me."

"But if we don't have the resources to contest my father…"

Her words faded as the doorbell chimed to announce his brother's arrival. Clara stepped away from him and turned to hurry upstairs.

Sebastian watched her go. The resolve that had taken root

when he'd first learned of her dilemma now flourished into something permanent and unyielding.

He strode to the foyer as Giles opened the door to admit Jacob.

"I've made the arrangements for your meeting with Catherine Leskovna," Jacob said as they entered the drawing room. "The day after tomorrow at the dining room of the Albion Hotel."

Sebastian sighed. "I should never have agreed to help you find those bloody plans."

"If you hadn't, you wouldn't have met Clara," Jacob replied mildly.

Sebastian lifted his head to meet his brother's keen gaze. It was an odd sentiment coming from a man ruled by his head rather than his heart.

"Neither would I have put the earldom in jeopardy," he said. "Again."

Jacob shrugged, as if that matter were of no more consequence than a fly in the jam jar. "The earldom is locked tight and secure."

"For now."

"Bear in mind that Fairfax has his own sphere, which I'm certain he wishes to keep free of rumor," Jacob said. "A peer who cast his own daughter from his estate and is effectively holding his grandson hostage while battling back creditors and potential foreclosures...imagine what polite *society* might have to say about such circumstances."

"I'd tell a reporter to print it in the *Morning Post* if I thought Andrew would emerge unscathed," Sebastian said. "As long as Fairfax has the boy, he has the whiphand."

"You don't have to print it in the papers to use the threat as leverage," Jacob pointed out. "Who else knows about this?"

"Findlay. Some of it, at any rate. I've an appointment at the bank later this morning."

"I'll come along," Jacob said. "Fairfax's weakness is your advantage. He needs money. You have money now. And if you dangle it before him, he might very well stumble over his own feet in his haste to seize it."

One could hope, Sebastian thought.

CHAPTER 25

$\mathcal{J}$f it weren't for the gauze of clouds veiling the afternoon sun, the scene would be a repeat of the previous day's. Pedestrians strolled into Belgrave Square Garden, birds splashed in a puddle, a boy rolled a hoop along one of the pathways. The meat-pie vendor was stationed at his stand, casting glances at Clara in between doling out his fragrant pies. Andrew and his tutor rounded the corner at half past three, taking the same path they'd walked yesterday.

Concealed within the cab's interior, Clara again watched her son until he had vanished from her sights.

Tomorrow. Tomorrow she would take him and run.

She instructed the driver to return to Mount Street. After leaving her at Blake's Museum that morning, Sebastian and his brother had gone to an appointment with the expectation that they would return before tea.

Well enough. Time for her to pack a few remaining articles while spooling her torment into a tight, unyielding ball.

Practical. Ruthless. Determined.

She could not afford sentiments of love and regret. She could not think about never seeing Sebastian again. She could not envision how this whole plan might ricochet to hurt him. All she could do was move forward and pray her husband didn't shatter her brittle façade.

Clara spent the next hour readying herself for tea, shaping her appearance with care in order to conceal any trace of distress. She dressed in an emerald-green gown that fell in sweeping folds around her legs and summoned a maid to fix her hair into a smooth chignon laced with green ribbons. She pinched her cheeks in the hopes that the extra color would conceal the tension darkening her eyes.

Male voices rumbled from the foyer. Clara smoothed her skirts and turned, pressing a hand to her belly to try to quell the riot of anxiety. She forced expression to slide from her features like water washing over a rock as she descended the stairs to greet the brothers.

A tiny curl of softness eased past her defenses when she saw them, deep in conversation as they removed their greatcoats and hats. Like two sides of the same coin with their black hair and snapping dark eyes, those Slavic cheekbones arching down to hard-edged jaws. But Jacob was a foil to his elder brother, striking in the precision of his appearance, the crisp dark morning coat and waistcoat deterring wrinkles rather than attracting them the way Sebastian's did.

And Jacob lacked Sebastian's vital energy, the restless impulses that vibrated from his very bones, his essential compulsion, impervious to rumor or scandal, to live and do and *be*.

Only Sebastian possessed those qualities. Only he had a mouth curved at that beautiful angle. Only he had that single lock of hair determined to flop over his forehead no matter how often he pushed it back. Only his eyes contained that beguiling mixture of warmth and wickedness that made Clara's blood run like hot, thick honey.

"You're just in time for tea," she said, descending the

remainder of the stairs. "It's an unusually warm afternoon out, isn't it? Is autumn in St. Petersburg quite this lovely, Jacob?"

"Often, yes, we too are blessed with a colorful autumn, though I consider St. Petersburg lovely any time of the year."

"I should like to hear more about it, then."

Clara didn't know how much Sebastian had told his brother about the snarled mess of their circumstances, so she kept the conversation centered on Jacob as they took tea and cake in the parlor. She quite liked the pragmatic young man, at once so different and yet so similar to Sebastian. His presence made her wish she could become acquainted with the rest of the Hall family.

And yet, God willing, that would never happen.

Suppressing pain at the thought, Clara made her excuses and left the brothers alone as she returned to her bedchamber. She occupied herself with useless tasks—repacking her belongings, unsnarling her ribbons from their tangle, considering and then dismissing the idea of writing Sebastian a letter of explanation. The less he knew, the better.

She then took supper in her room, sending down a claim of fatigue that she knew would not prevent Sebastian from coming to her later that night.

And so he did, a fire crackling in his gaze as he entered her room. "You're not unwell?" he asked.

"Oh, no. I wanted to give you time with your brother. I...I look forward to one day meeting the rest of your family."

"They'll feel the same when Jacob tells them of our marriage." Sebastian tugged at the bonds of his cravat, drawing Clara's eyes to the flex and pull of his long fingers.

Tomorrow. Tomorrow she would leave this man whom she loved and pray her flight kept him safe.

Blinking away the glitter of tears, she rose and approached him. She eased his hands aside and loosened the knot, allowing the silk to glide through her fingers before pulling it free. Crumpling the silk into her palm, she went to her dressing table where her box of ribbons still sat. She dropped the cravat beside the box and returned to Sebastian. She wound her arms around him, put her hand on the back of his neck, and guided his head down.

His mouth descended on hers, his hands smoothing over her sides to her hips. Their bodies pressed together like the pages of a closed book, tight and sealed. Clara parted her lips, drank in Sebastian's murmur of pleasure, stroked her tongue over his lower lip. He moved his left hand to her hair, unfastening the pins and dropping them to the floor while he deepened the kiss to the color of emeralds.

Her eyes drifted closed as he pulled the tangles from her hair with gentle strokes, then cupped her face between his palms and kissed her cheeks, her forehead, her eyelids, the tip of her nose. She grasped his arms and urged him to the bed, wanting his weight on top of her one last time before she broke their world apart.

He spanned her waist with his hands, preventing her from sinking against the coverlet, and turned her back to him. He unfastened the buttons of her dress with the growing dexterity of his left hand, then divested her of her corset and let it fall to the floor.

Clara inhaled, her body softening with the release of her clothes, as her husband continued undressing her until the fire-warmed air caressed her naked skin. His hot eyes slipped over her, tracing the contours of her breasts and hips before he gathered her in his arms again and guided her to the bed.

She thrust her hands into his thick hair, gasping as he kissed a path from her lips to her throat and down to the taut peaks of her breasts. Pleasure bolted through her, pooling into the core of her body. He closed his lips around her nipple, and she arched against him, winding her legs around his thighs. Her skin surged with heat. She wanted this forever, wanted *him* forever.

Rising to her elbows, she watched as he pressed his mouth to the curve of her belly, his whiskers deliciously abrading a path, his tongue swirling into her navel. She closed her fingers around his shoulders, urging him back up the length of her body so that she could unfasten his shirt and ease the linen from his muscular shoulders.

Such a beautiful man. Clara stroked her hands over his arms, down his chest to his trousers.

"Take them off," she whispered, uncertain if she spoke an order or a plea.

He pushed the trousers to the floor. Arousal coiled into her at the sight of his smooth, hard shaft, the empty place at her core aching. She pressed him onto his back and mapped his body with her hands and mouth, kissing and touching every plane and sinew of his chest. His skin burned beneath her lips, his chest rising and falling with the sound of his breaths. Clara traveled a path that she would be forced to leave behind forever while simultaneously wishing, with desperation, that she could traverse it again and again.

She curled her hand around his erection, perspiration dotting her brow as she pressed her thighs together to quell the throbbing ache. Sebastian grasped one of her thighs and urged her legs over his hips so that she straddled his body. A trace of unease lanced into her—this was the posture of a whore, surely—but Sebastian's eyes blazed with such a combination of desire and heat that she trembled with the urge to indulge in this blatantly provocative act.

"Sebastian, I…"

He stopped her words with a tightening of his fingers. One guiding hand on the curve of her hip, he took his shaft in the other hand and poised himself at the entrance of her body. Chestnut hair falling in skeins over her shoulders, Clara braced her hands on the wall of his chest and stared down at him.

"I can't…" She gasped, words falling away at the drenching knowledge that with one shift of her hips, she could plunge downward and savor that hard, delicious thrust of pleasure. The exquisite memory of how it had felt the last time she straddled his lap spilled through her mind.

"You can." Cords tightened in his neck, his fingers flexing against the dip of her waist. "You will."

She did. Tentative at first, she lowered her body until he glided halfway into her and then, with a moan, she sank farther until he was fully inside her. Hot. Hard. Pulsing.

Clara curled her fingers against his damp chest. Her heart pounded against her rib cage, her gasping breaths flowing down to mingle with his.

"Clara." He shifted beneath her, pushing his hips upward to thrust into her with a force that wrung a cry from her throat. "You need to…"

Spurred by recently learned instincts, she lifted her body and lowered it again, soon meeting his upward thrusts with a rhythm that made her blood burn and her body sing. Her arousal spiraled tighter and tighter, winding into the center of her being. Sweat coursed down her spine, into the crevice between her breasts.

She gasped when Sebastian gripped her waist, this time preventing her downward glide. He twisted her onto her back, his body still locked with hers, and surged over her. Clara wound her arms around him, her panting moans hot against his bare shoulder as he pushed into her and drove them both into the sweet, churning storm of bliss.

Afterward, he clasped her in his arms and they lay still and silent as their breathing slowed. She pressed her lips to his chest and closed her eyes.

This was the end. With everything she was, she had to pray for the success of her escape. And while sorrow blackened the circumstances that had led her to such desperation, she could not regret a single moment she had spent with Sebastian. Indeed, a restive joy surged in her with the grace of a bird taking flight—

and she believed she could live a lifetime of undiluted happiness and gratitude that she had known such a man.

She lifted herself to her elbow and looked at him. Heat kindled in Sebastian's eyes along with something else, something more, an emotion that expanded the walls of Clara's soul.

Her heart was still sealed. But with him *inside.* She had locked her heart well and truly—not to keep Sebastian Hall out but to ensure he remained within.

CHAPTER 26

*T*he only sounds in the morning room were the scrape of forks against plates and coffee cups clicking against saucers. Sebastian watched Clara, who sat with a rigid posture in utter contrast to her supple writhings of the previous night. Again that brittleness had encased her, a teacup lined with threadlike cracks.

"So." She patted her lips with a napkin, although she hadn't eaten a bite. "Where is your meeting taking place?"

"I've arranged for us to meet at the dining room of the Albion Hotel," Jacob said. "What are your plans for the day, Clara?"

"I thought I'd visit Mudie's Library, then pay a visit to Uncle Granville." She set her napkin beside her plate. "In fact, I'm running a bit late already, so if you'll both excuse me, I'll finish getting ready."

Both Sebastian and Jacob stood and watched her leave, then exchanged glances. Sebastian was not surprised that his brother sensed the odd tension threading the air. He shoved his chair back and headed upstairs. He found Clara in her bedchamber, closing the wooden box that contained her beloved tangle of ribbons.

He stopped in the doorway. "What is going on?"

"I beg your pardon?"

"You look as if you're close to breaking." He approached her, disliking the utter paleness of her skin and that impassive veil that had once again descended over her expression. "We will deal with Fairfax. I promise you."

Her throat worked with a swallow, her gaze darting to the scarred box. Just before her lashes lowered, a flash of something —disbelief? Guilt?—appeared in her eyes. Sebastian reached out to take the box from her.

Clara started. "What—"

He flipped the lid open. Nestled amid the cobweb of ribbons was the cravat he'd worn yesterday. With a frown, he pulled the blue silk from the box, ribbons spilling away from it, and shifted his gaze to Clara.

Guilt. What the hell did she have to be guilty about? What was she hiding from him?

"It's...ah, you know I keep the ribbons because they're precious to me," she said. "I wanted one of your cravats for the same reason. I hope that's all right."

"Of course it's all right." Disquieted by her reaction, he dropped the cravat back into the box and snapped the lid closed. "All you need do is ask. You shall have anything you want."

Not until the words hovered between them did Sebastian realize he had not yet given her her heart's desire. An oath broke through his mind.

"Come with me to this blasted meeting with my mother," he said. "Since you've met her before, you ought to be there now."

Clara shook her head. "This must be done between you and her. And what if Fairfax sends word about Andrew? Someone needs to be here." She took his right hand and gently ran her fingers across his. "Go speak with your mother, please. I'll be with Uncle Granville most of the day anyway. Everything will be fine."

Her voice was certain, a cool shade of sapphire-blue that belied the darkness shadowing her eyes. She lifted his hand to her lips and pressed a kiss against his wrist, on the fraction of skin below his sleeve. Heat shot through his arm.

He wrapped his other hand around her nape and pulled her to him, lowering his mouth to hers. Her soft gasp slid into his blood, settled in the middle of his chest. He kissed her deeply, driven by some unnamed desire to remind her she belonged to him.

"Sebastian." Clara gripped his lapels, her violet eyes filled with a mixture of emotions that he could not begin to discern. "I want you to remember that you have always meant more to me than you will ever know."

He frowned at the strange finality of her words. "For God's sake, Clara, what are you doing? If you are thinking of approaching Fairfax alone—"

"Bastian." A knock sounded at the closed door, followed by Jacob's voice. "Best be moving along."

"Go," Clara whispered.

With a muttered curse, Sebastian eased away from his wife. Troubled and not knowing how to unravel the source of his apprehension, he pushed his right hand into his pocket and went to the door.

She no longer looked like Catherine Hall, Countess of Rushton, the woman who wore her beauty like delicate armor, whose eyes were cool glass. His nerves taut, Sebastian stopped in the doorway of the dining room at the Albion Hotel as his mother approached.

Her dress was elegant but simple, and she wore no jewelry. Her dark hair was pulled into a neat chignon, a few tendrils lacing her long neck. As she neared, he saw the silver threads streaking her hair and the thin lines radiating from the corners of her eyes. A tan had darkened her porcelain skin, and freckles dotted her nose.

Freckles.

His *mother*?

She stopped in front of him, lifting a hand as if she wanted to touch him and then letting it fall back to her side.

"Sebastian," she whispered.

He cleared his throat, his nerves taut with unease over Clara's behavior and now this meeting with a woman he hardly recognized. "Hello...Catherine."

Beside him, Jacob clamped a hand on his shoulder and squeezed. Then he turned and left, leaving Sebastian alone with their mother.

Mustering a bit of chivalry, Sebastian went to pull a chair from one of the empty tables. "Have you had dinner yet?"

"Not yet, no." She spoke English, though with a bit of hesitation and a more pronounced accent than Sebastian ever remembered hearing. "Thank you for agreeing to see me."

"I didn't want to." He hadn't intended the bitter tone, but it was there, coloring his words like the dark smear of a pencil. A thousand questions bubbled and popped in his mind.

As they sat, he noticed her hands tremble as she brushed a lock of hair from her forehead. She sat back and studied him, her dark gaze—so like his brothers'—both wary and hopeful. "Why did you change your mind?"

"Clara."

A smile tugged at her mouth. "I like her."

"Why did you come back?" Sebastian asked, not wanting to discuss his wife with a woman who had severed her own marriage through infidelity.

"I came back to see you," Catherine said.

"And I'm to be grateful for that?" Anger pierced Sebastian, and he leaned across the table to fix her with a glare. "For the love of God, you caused a scandal and ran away, leaving your family to clean up the mess. You forced the earl to divorce you. You left your daughter with all of society thinking she was no better than her dissolute mother. Did you not once think about what a wreckage you created?"

"Of course I thought about it." Although regret weighted her words, Sebastian detected no trace of shame. His anger hardened at the notion that she would not be ashamed of what she had done.

"I thought about nothing else after it all came to light," she said. "But what else could I have done but leave? If I'd returned to London, it would have made everything worse. I knew that if I fled, everyone would cast blame upon me and claim my children had fallen into misfortune because I was their mother. I *hoped* you would be spared any condemnation."

"We weren't," Sebastian said bluntly. "But we might have withstood it if we'd known what happened."

"Oh, Sebastian." She looked down at her hands. Once soft and white, her hands were now browned and wrinkled. "I wish I could tell you it was a mistake. That I didn't want it to happen. That I never *meant* for it to happen. But when it did, I felt like…I don't know. Like something had broken inside me. Broken open."

Like when I met Clara. Sebastian pushed the thought aside, not wanting to draw any more similarities between him and his mother.

"Catherine." Sebastian tried to keep his voice level. "What *did* happen?"

"I fell in love."

Bloody hell.

"I'd taken a trip back to St. Petersburg," Catherine said. "Do you remember? My sister had an invitation to a Court ceremony for regimental troops. She didn't want to attend, so I went in her stead. I met him there. Alexei. He was a captain in the army, younger than me by six years. He didn't care. He was handsome, bright, courteous. He made me feel like the only woman in the room."

"So you abandoned your family for him."

She almost winced. "It wasn't like that. It wasn't...vulgar."

"A married woman...a *countess*, for God's sake, having an affair is the height of vulgarity."

"To you, perhaps. To society. Not to us. Do you have any idea what it was like being married to Rushton? We never loved each other, not really. I know he is not a cruel man, but he was so... rigid. So strict. He had no life inside him, no fire. Every day I felt as if I had to hold myself together so tightly or I'd otherwise break like glass. I didn't even realize I felt like that until I met Alexei. In that moment, I knew I had to make a choice. I had to either plunge into a world of brilliant, dangerous colors that could shatter us all or return to a life in which I felt dead."

"You didn't think of us?"

"Of course I thought of you. But you were all living your own lives. I rarely saw any of you, did you even realize that?"

"No, but how much did we ever see of you?"

"That didn't mean I didn't love you," Catherine said. "I always loved hearing you play the piano, even when you were a child. Do you remember?"

He cleared his throat. "You used to play as well."

Only when he had watched Catherine play the piano, her hands skimming with such grace over the keys, had she been real to him. Alive.

"I played more for myself than an audience," she said. "I so admired you when you began performing and earned such accolades. I wish I'd had such courage." She traced a scratch on the table with her finger.

"You all grew up so quickly," she continued. "And Alexander became busy with his company, Jacob with his studies, you with your music. Even Tasha spent all her time with friends and charities, and of course Rushton was never there. I drifted around his vast house like a ghost. Until I realized that it would be my tomb if I didn't escape."

Sebastian dragged his hand over his hair, hating the gleam of understanding that sparked to life within him. He knew well what it was like to feel as if you no longer had anything. And that if you didn't *do* something about it, you would cease to exist. It was that urge, like a hammer striking a piano string, reverberating and echoing into his blood.

He looked up. She was watching him, concern and wariness etched into the face that both belonged at once to his mother and a stranger. He wondered if she would have made such a confession to Alexander or Patrick. Or even to Tasha.

"Do you still play the piano?" he asked.

She smiled. "I did. Especially for Alexei. He loved to hear me play."

She didn't have to say that Rushton never seemed to notice. She gestured for one of the servers to bring them more tea, and then she told Sebastian about the man who was apparently the love of her life, a soldier who'd moved up in the army ranks through determination, strength of will, and proficiency in battle. She told Sebastian how she'd waited for him, withstood the disapproval of her family, and longed for Rushton's divorce petition to free her.

She must have loved Alexei Leskov to distraction, Sebastian thought, to have followed the man into battle because she could not bear to be parted from him again. And him too, waiting, then returning to her, asking for her hand in marriage, while knowing he would never be welcomed into her family, that she wore the mantle of disgrace, that she would never bear his children.

They both had known they would be alone together. Just two. And for them, that had been enough.

"I'm sorry," Sebastian finally said. He was still not able to comprehend how she could have cut her life in two with such irrevocability, but a faint understanding wove through him at her confession of overwhelming love.

"I loved Alexei deeply." Sorrow flashed in Catherine's dark eyes. "I was blessed to have known and loved him for as long as I did. I was blessed to have known him at all. You'd have liked him. He had a love of life that was not unlike yours."

Sebastian's hand clenched. Too late, he realized that the subtle movement drew his mother's attention. She lifted a hand as if to cover his, then settled it on the tablecloth.

"And you?" she asked. "I knew the moment I heard about your departure from Weimar that something was wrong. Will you not tell me what happened?"

Realizing there was no reason not to, especially after her confession, Sebastian explained. He pushed his hand into his pocket and told her the entire truth of his disability and resignation. Tears spilled down her cheeks by the time he'd finished the unpleasant tale.

"I knew you wouldn't have forsaken your patrons without a reason," she said. "Did any of them know?"

Sebastian shook his head. Some part of him recognized that he had kept his secret just as she had kept hers, both to protect others and to protect himself. Oddly, the thought was fitting. He realized now that he and Catherine shared certain instincts—foremost the need to be free from the trappings of expectations. It had taken her thirty years of a stifling marriage to discover that.

He, at least, had always lived as he pleased, and his marriage to Clara had reminded him of the importance of such a desire.

Sebastian pushed to his feet. A strange but welcome sense of calm settled over the turmoil of his emotions. His mother came around the table and took his hand in hers. He didn't know if he would see her again, but at least now he finally had answers to the questions that had plagued them all.

"Will you try to see Tasha?" he asked.

The light in Catherine's eyes dimmed. "I don't know. Jacob refuses to facilitate a meeting with Tasha. I fear she must despise me."

Sebastian couldn't reassure her otherwise. They would all impede Catherine's access to Tasha for no other reason than to protect their sister from further hurt.

"Where will you go now?" he asked.

"I'm staying with my sister in Kuskovo. Please know you can always contact me there."

Sebastian nodded. After a moment's hesitation, he bent and brushed his lips across her cheek. Then he turned and left, pulling his hand from his pocket and unclenching his fingers as he stepped back outside.

CHAPTER 27

*R*ain streamed down the arching windows. Charcoal clouds foamed overhead, spilling heavy drops that pooled on the streets into wide, greasy puddles. Inside the studio of Blake's Museum of Automata, the piles of satin and silk appeared muddy in the gray light, the ribbons and streamers dulled, the paint thick and congealed.

Clara pushed a needle through a square of silk and glanced at the clock. Two thirty. Her stomach tightened. The hour between now and the moment when she had to execute her plan seemed almost impenetrable.

She pushed the cloth aside and paced to the window. *Please stop raining.* If the rain didn't cease, Andrew and his tutor wouldn't go to the park...and Clara had no secondary plan in place.

She glanced at the clock again. She couldn't wait another day in the event Fairfax left London sooner or Sebastian discovered the truth. She also had to act before Sebastian returned from the Albion, rain or not.

Although she wanted to know the results of his meeting with his mother, Clara feared that if she saw him again she would capitulate and confess everything. She could only hope that even if a full reconciliation was beyond their reach, Sebastian and his mother could come to an understanding of sorts.

Unlike her and Fairfax.

Pain seized her chest. She stared out the window, allowing images of her mother and brother to form in her mind. How different this all would have been had such tragedy not struck.

The sound of the doorbell rang faintly in her good ear. Her nerves taut with tension, she turned and headed into the foyer, where the housekeeper was greeting a visitor.

Clara stopped at the sight of the Earl of Rushton. His large, broad-shouldered frame seemed to fill the entrance. He shook raindrops from his hat and greatcoat as he removed them and handed them to Mrs. Marshall.

"Welcome to Blake's Museum of Automata, my lord." With a rustle of her skirts, Mrs. Fox approached the earl and swept a hand out to encompass the rooms. "Please have a look around on your own, and should you enjoy a tour, I'll inform Mr. Blake of your presence. The fee is one shilling."

"Mrs. Fox!" Clara hurried forward. "His lordship is most certainly not required to pay the admission fee."

"Visitors are visitors, Mrs. Shep...Hall, and I daresay that his lordship..."

"Mrs. Fox, please." Embarrassment rose to heat Clara's cheeks. "Lord Rushton, welcome to my uncle's museum. I'm sorry we're not better prepared for your visit. Mrs. Marshall, please bring in a tea tray while I seat his lordship in the drawing room."

Rushton, who appeared baffled rather than affronted by their indecorous greeting, gave Mrs. Fox a swift nod before accompanying Clara to the adjoining room.

"I apologize again, my lord, but we weren't expecting you." Clara closed the door and ran her damp palms over her skirt. "Sebastian is away at the moment."

"I didn't come to see him, in any case," Rushton replied. He strolled around the room, examining the automata and mechanical toys lining the shelves and tables. He turned the key on a musical mouse and watched as the creature lifted a flute to its mouth and piped a merry tune.

Rushton's deep chuckle eased the tension from Clara's shoulders. She nodded as Mrs. Marshall entered with tea and poured for both of them.

"As Mrs. Fox explained, my uncle will be glad to provide you with a tour," Clara said after the housekeeper had left.

"I would enjoy that," Rushton agreed. "I was most impressed by the demonstration at Lady Rossmore's charity ball. I've another son who would find your uncle's inventions quite fascinating."

"Jacob?" Clara spoke without thinking, then winced inwardly at her use of his Christian name.

Rushton lifted a bushy eyebrow. "Has Sebastian told you about him? A very fine mind, that boy has always had. Last I heard from St. Petersburg, he and my daughter-in-law were supporting the invention of machines that calculate arithmetic."

Clara nodded. Did Rushton still not know Jacob was back in London?

"I...I look forward to meeting them all one day," she said, unable to prevent the tremor in her voice.

She glanced at the clock. Half an hour. The rain seemed to pound harder, hitting the windows like thousands of pebbles.

A deep sense of foreboding filled her. Andrew would not be at the park. And Clara had no other idea how to reach him.

"My lord, please excuse me while I fetch my uncle." She couldn't stand here conversing with Rushton while her plan shattered around her. "He'll be most pleased to know you're here."

Rushton peered at her. "A moment, Mrs. Hall. I had thought to invite your father for dinner before he returns to Surrey."

Clara's heart plummeted. "Er, my lord, I—"

"However," Rushton continued, "Bastian has told me of your

estrangement. Though he explained it is a personal issue that will not affect my family, I should like your assurance on the matter."

God in heaven. Two weeks ago, she could have granted him such assurance. But now? If Fairfax were to approach Rushton…

Fear gripped her nape. She took a breath and tried to think past the looming sense of hopelessness.

"May I inquire as to what Sebastian told you?" she asked.

"Nothing beyond that," Rushton replied. "That is the reason I am here."

The sound of the rain filled Clara's head. She looked to where water cascaded in sheets over the windows, the clouds a blanket of gray overhead. Thin, pallid light filtered into the room.

"The estrangement involves my son, Andrew, my lord," she confessed, her gaze still on the windows. "I…my deceased husband, Mr. Shepherd, granted my father custody of Andrew upon his death."

"Is this the reason you have not seen the boy recently? I recall you asking Lord Margrave about him."

Clara nodded, her breath burning her throat. She paced to the hearth and back, crushing the folds of her skirt in her fists.

"I love my son, my lord," she said, desperation coloring the words. "Not being able to visit him has broken my heart. I would…I would ask that you please believe me when I tell you I love him more than anything."

"I do not doubt it, Mrs. Hall," Rushton replied. "Yet I fail to understand the reasons for your distance from him."

"My father keeps Andrew from me, my lord."

The earl studied her for a moment, his brow creased into furrows of displeasure. "How is it, then, that Bastian can assure me this separation will not affect my family?"

He can't. The admission clawed at Clara's throat.

She searched frantically for another solution, an escape, but her thoughts ran through a maze and hit one barrier after another.

Until, like a window opening, a possibility appeared.

She turned to stare at the earl. Her heart began to beat faster. The storm had thwarted her first plan, but Lord Rushton would surely have an idea of what she might attempt next. He was the only person she knew who was more powerful than her father.

If she confessed all, would he help her?

"Lord Rushton." She lifted her chin, fighting to keep her voice steady as she plunged into the unknown. "I...I am aware of the scandal your family has suffered. I did believe that the earldom would not be touched by my difficulties. But now I must caution you that my father might approach you in an attempt to circulate false rumors."

Rushton frowned. "Involving you?"

"Yes. It's the reason he forced me to leave Manley Park, though few people knew about it outside of me and my father."

The earl waited, implacable, the very air around him motionless. Clara cast her gaze to the shelf behind him and struggled to gather her courage.

"What is the reason, Mrs. Hall?" Rushton asked.

"I...my father believed I was responsible for my husband's death." Still unable to look at him, she spilled out the whole story —how she'd knelt beside Richard lying on the ground, blood still pooling beneath his head, and how her father had found her there. She told him about Wakefield House, about her proposal to Sebastian, and her hope that Fairfax would surrender custody of Andrew.

"Sebastian...he knew marriage was the last chance I had to regain custody of my son." A knot congealed in Clara's throat. "Unfortunately my father has rejected our proposition and, further, threatened to spread lies should I fail to leave Andrew alone."

"And you did not anticipate such a reaction," Rushton said.

"No, my lord."

"Then, Mrs. Hall," Rushton said, his voice leveling out like a hard piece of wood, "I suggest you do as your father requests and leave your son alone."

Clara's heart squeezed into a tight, hard ball at the note of finality to his words, as if he were verifying that she had no option but to capitulate.

And yet she would never do that. She could never be fully happy with Sebastian, never allow herself to love him as she truly wanted to, all the while knowing Andrew remained under Fairfax's control.

She gripped the back of a chair and fought not to think of Sebastian, of his determination that they would not approach his father. "My lord, the reason I married your son was to try to regain custody of Andrew. You must understand that I cannot surrender that aim."

He peered at her again from beneath his black eyebrows, his features set like those of a king studying a vassal. "If that is the reason you married him," Rushton said, "why did Sebastian marry you?"

"He...he told me you'd expressed a wish that he marry soon."

"He could have married any number of women soon. Why did he choose you?"

The earl might as well have added, *a woman of ordinary means who lives with her uncle in a ramshackle museum and has very little standing left to her?*

A sudden pang speared Clara, as she struggled against a powerful longing to reply with her secret wish. *Sebastian married me because he wanted to. Because he loves me.*

She could not lie to Rushton. Not only because she desperately needed his help, but because he was her father-in-law, and now she could very well pose a threat to the reputation the earl and his family had recently restored.

Clara pressed a hand to her heart and told Rushton about the cipher machine. "Sebastian sought the machine plans for...for Jacob, my lord."

Rushton's sharp gaze flickered. "Why?"

She tried to calm her thoughts. Her very soul felt cloven in two by her desperation to have Andrew back and the intensity of her feelings for her husband.

But never could she allow those feelings to usurp her goal of rescuing Andrew. Everything she had done up until this very moment had been with the intention of reclaiming her son. And if she were to ask Lord Rushton for help, she had to prove herself loyal to him and willing to avoid further scandal.

"Because, my lord," she said, feeling as if she were standing on the edge of a sharp precipice with no idea what lay at the bottom of it, "Jacob wanted to facilitate a meeting between Sebastian and the former Countess of Rushton."

Shock flashed swift and hard across the earl's face. "What?"

"Jacob knew Sebastian would reject the possibility of a meeting, so he sought to establish the truth of his resignation from Weimar by asking for his help finding the cipher machine plans."

"And what is the truth of his resignation, Mrs. Hall?"

His question confirmed what Clara had suspected—that Sebastian had not told his family about the difficulty with his hand. Tears stung her eyes.

"He's suffered a disability in his right hand." She rubbed her thumb against her palm. "He can't use it anymore. Can no longer play the piano. The former countess suspected something was amiss, which was the reason she wanted to see him."

"And what was Sebastian's response?"

"He went to visit her at the Albion Hotel."

She flinched when Rushton slammed his hand on a table. His face reddened with a flush of ire, his eyes hardening into glass. "When did she return to London?"

"I don't know, my lord." She stepped forward and lifted a shaking hand. "I'm telling you because I beg for your help with my son. I must convince my father to return custody of Andrew to me. Lord Fairfax is—"

"Lord Fairfax is the boy's legal guardian!" Rushton snapped, his spine straightening like a ramrod. "How dare you expect me to interfere in another man's raising of a child? If your father has banned you from seeing your son, I suspect he has a very good reason for doing so. And if you think I will risk the potential of gossip by intruding in your father's affairs, then you are sorely mistaken."

"My lord, please…"

"Mrs. Hall, if I had known this prior to your marriage to Sebastian, I would never have allowed the union to take place," Rushton said coldly. "I will tolerate no—"

He stopped suddenly, looking toward the foyer. Clara turned. The drawing room door opened. Her heart closed in on itself as Sebastian and Jacob stepped in.

Sebastian's dark gaze skidded from her to his father. Wariness flashed across his features. Even Jacob faltered for an instant.

"Sebastian." The earl's voice vibrated with barely suppressed anger. "And Jacob. I would like a word with you alone. Now."

"Wait." Clara hurried toward Sebastian, reaching out a hand to touch his arm. He jerked away from her, his eyes clouding. "Please…"

"Mrs. Hall!" Rushton's order thundered through the room. "I ask that you leave us alone."

"My lord, you must let me explain."

"You have explained more than enough." He pointed a finger toward the door. "Please go."

Desperate, Clara cast a glance toward Jacob but found no understanding in his grave expression. An ache welled in her throat. Unable to look at Sebastian again for fear of his censure, she hurried from the room.

Male voices flared in contention as she closed the door behind her. She hugged her arms around herself and tried to contain her bone-shaking trembles. Mrs. Fox looked at her, her expression set with disapproval, but she made no remark about the sudden cacophony.

"W-where is Uncle Granville?" Clara stammered.

"He's gone to oversee the exhibition in St. James's Street," Mrs. Fox replied. She hesitated, pursing her lips. "Would you… I've a bit of brandy in the dining room, if you'd like. You look rather pale."

Clara shook her head. "I'm…I've somewhere I need to be. Please, would you…when you see Sebastian again, tell him I'm sorry."

"Sorry for what?"

"He'll know." Clara grabbed her hat and shoved her arms into her cloak. "Please, just tell him."

"Mrs. Hall, I must say you don't look as if you ought to go anywhere at the moment."

"I have no choice, Mrs. Fox."

Clara wrenched open the door and ran.

CHAPTER 28

"How dare you put our family in peril again?" The very air around Rushton vibrated with anger. "After what she did?"

"She leaves London on Friday," Jacob said, his tone unapologetic. "And never did she intend to inform anyone else of her return."

"As well she shouldn't," Rushton snapped, swinging his hard gaze to Sebastian. "I knew it was a mistake to leave things in your hands, to expect that you would make the right decisions as to your future. Have you any idea of the damage Fairfax could wreak with his accusations against his daughter? When did you learn about this?"

"Before we wed," Sebastian admitted. He stepped back to the door, pulled by the urge to race after Clara. Unease coiled in his gut. "But we had no suspicion that he would make such accusations public. What has he to gain by doing so?"

"His motives do not concern me." Rushton paced to the hearth, his shoulders rigid. "The accusation does."

"We could very well turn this back upon him," Jacob said.

"Fairfax has creditors to appease. He needed money from Sebastian, so if he were granted enough funds…"

"I have no intention of putting myself at the mercy of a man who is strengthened by the accusation of murder," Rushton retorted. "I could give such a man my entire fortune and would still have no guarantee that he would keep his silence." He glowered at Sebastian. "Not to mention that I have no evidence as to the falsity of his claim."

Sebastian's jaw clenched. "Clara did not murder her husband."

"Of course she'd tell you that," Rushton snapped. "You have no evidence to the contrary, do you?"

"I don't need any."

"And *you.*" Rushton spun to confront Jacob, anger tearing through him as he pointed a finger at his other son. "You could be considered an enemy of the state owing to your residence in Russia. And now Mrs. Hall tells me you sought plans for a cipher machine that could be used in wartime? Your loyalties would be called into grave question should the Home Office discover you are in possession of such plans. And what defense would you have should they accuse you of wanting to use such a machine against British troops?"

"They could not do so if you, my lord, finance the construction and testing of the machine for the Home Office."

"Why in the love of God would I finance anything with which you are involved?" Rushton snapped.

"Because it is the most innovative and expedient way of transmitting coded messages between British troops. Granville Blake and I can prove the codes are unbreakable."

Rushton stared at him but before he could respond, a knock came at the door. Sebastian turned as Mrs. Fox poked her head into the room, blinking at the heated tension buffeting the air.

"I beg your pardon, gentlemen." She delicately cleared her throat and looked at Sebastian. "Mr. Hall, may I speak with you for a moment?"

Sebastian strode to the foyer with her. She held out a folded note. "A delivery boy just brought this for Mrs. Hall. He said it was a missive from Lord Fairfax's butler. I thought you should know. Mrs. Hall left in such a hurry, and she did not look well at all."

Foreboding seized him. Sebastian grabbed the note and unfolded it. His heart plummeted.

"Mr. Hall?" A twist of alarm crossed Mrs. Fox's sedate features. "Is everything all right?"

"Tell my brother and Granville." Sebastian threw the paper into the bin and yanked open the door. "Davies says Fairfax has made plans to take Andrew to the Continent. They're leaving tomorrow."

Rain pounded on the roof of the cab. Only a few pedestrians hurried past, umbrellas blooming like mushrooms over their heads and puddles splashing around their feet. Clara peered through the carriage window at the façade of Fairfax's town house, two windows burning with light. No movement shifted behind the water-streaked glass.

Please, she thought. *Please let him come out. Please let them go somewhere, anywhere, just get Andrew away from Fairfax and I'll think of something...*

She slid her gaze to a carriage that rattled over the street and came to a halt at the curb. Her heart stumbled when Sebastian descended and walked toward Fairfax's house with a long, determined stride.

If he intended to confront her father...

Alarm ripped through her. Without thinking, Clara shoved open the door. "Sebastian!"

He stopped and turned, rain streaming off his hat to drench his shoulders. Two seconds later he was pushing her back into the cab, his expression taut with anger and...fear?

"What?" Clara gasped, clutching at the damp sleeves of his greatcoat. "What happened?"

"He leaves tomorrow for Switzerland. With Andrew."

"No." All the strength drained from her bones, pooling into terror. She sank onto the seat, still gripping his sleeves, trying not to shake. "He can't."

"He won't." His mouth set in a grim line, Sebastian eased himself away from her and grasped the door handle. "Wait here."

"No." She tightened her grip. "You can't see him."

"I will—" His voice stopped as he looked to the door of the town house.

Andrew, his tutor, and a footman descended the steps toward a waiting carriage. Sebastian snapped an order at the driver and slammed shut the door of the cab. The cab rattled after the carriage at what seemed an exceedingly slow speed—the dappled mare no match for Fairfax's fresh gray pair. Thankfully the rain had slowed the pace of traffic, and the cab driver was able to keep the carriage within his sights.

When the carriage pulled up to the entrance of the British Museum, Clara tried to dart out before Sebastian, but he curved his gloved hand around her wrist and forced her back. Panic clutched her.

"You can't..."

"Wait here," he ordered, then vaulted from the cab just as Andrew and his tutor climbed out.

Clara's breath stopped. Like a blade slicing through cloth, Sebastian ran across the street. Rain streamed down, splashing against mud-slick cobblestones. He dodged a wagon and a water cart, swerved between two phaetons, and skidded onto the steps of the museum before Andrew.

The boy and his tutor recoiled at the sight of the water-drenched stranger, then the tutor reached for Andrew's shoulder to draw him aside. Sebastian lunged forward. In one movement, he hauled the boy into his arms and ran.

The driver shouted. The white-faced tutor stared. Andrew kicked at Sebastian, twisting and flailing to escape. The footman leapt off the bench and pursued them, his boots sliding on the slippery stones. Sebastian held fast, darting in front of a ragpicker's cart to reach the cab.

A burst of hope cracked open Clara's shell of terror. She threw open the door. "Andrew!"

He twisted in Sebastian's grip at the sound of her voice. And then he was *there.* With a cry, Clara clutched her son as Sebastian pushed him into the cab and followed.

"Go," he shouted at the driver. "Paddington station."

The driver hesitated. The footman neared, face slashed with determination. Sebastian pounded on the roof. The cab lurched forward just as the footman grabbed the door handle. His foot skidded on the slimy gutter, his grip loosening. The cab clattered down the street, picking up speed as it rounded Great Russell Street and headed toward the train station.

Clara hugged Andrew to her chest, hardly daring to believe she was again holding her son. Tension wove through his slender frame before the fear dissipated, and then he sagged against her. His arms crept around her neck. She buried her face in his dark, wet hair and sobbed. Fairfax would have to rip her in two before she'd let her son go again.

Time compressed to nothing when the cab halted in front of the railway station. Sebastian urged them out before him, handing several coins to the driver before he strode toward the ticket booth.

Clara pulled away from Andrew, cupping his face in her hands. She brushed her thumbs across his damp cheeks. "Are you all right?"

He nodded but didn't speak. The train steamed into the station, disgorging clusters of passengers before the conductor called for embarkment. Clara turned to see Sebastian coming toward them, tickets in hand. He handed her two and guided her toward the door.

A sudden shout pierced her like an icicle. She whirled around, pulling Andrew closer. The footman and a police constable pushed through the crowd behind Sebastian. People gasped, parting to give them way.

Clara edged toward the train, her grip tightening on Andrew's shoulder. The constable came closer. A wall of people closed between Clara and the train door. Air squeezed from her lungs. Sebastian's hand slipped away from her.

Her heart slammed against her chest when he pivoted and shoved toward the approaching men. Before Clara could speak, he lunged toward the footman and sent them both to the platform floor. A woman screamed. People scattered.

"Sebastian!" Clara shouted. Panic flooded her as the crowd surged, pushing her toward the train.

She gripped the bar beside the train door. Her breath lodged in her throat when the constable edged around the struggling footman and started toward her.

The train started to move. Sebastian gripped the footman's arm and twisted it behind his back.

The constable shoved aside two men, his expression dark and determined. Clara pushed Andrew ahead of her onto the train. A woman bumped into her from behind.

Then, quick as a cat, Sebastian leapt to his feet. He threw a punch at the footman. The man stumbled back. Sebastian ran for the train, dodging the constable. He grabbed hold of the pull-bar with his left hand and vaulted into the car just as it picked up speed. He slammed the door closed.

Clara clutched his arm. "Are you all right?"

He nodded, his chest heaving as he guided her and Andrew to a seat. He sat across from them, bracing his elbows on his knees as he caught his breath. Clara hugged Andrew closer, a shiver racing down her spine.

"Sebastian, what happened?" she whispered.

"Your father's butler sent a note about their departure." He sat up, pulling a hand through his hair. "It seems he realized Fairfax had planned nothing good."

Beside Clara, Andrew tensed. She looked at her son, brushing his chestnut hair away from his forehead.

"Did you know about this?" she asked. "Why did your grand-father want to take you away?"

Andrew didn't respond. He turned to look out the window, all emotion concealed behind a shield of wariness. A frown tugged at Clara's mouth. She didn't press him for a response, but kept her arm around his shoulders.

"Where can we go?" she asked Sebastian, keeping her voice low to avoid being overheard.

"Our family seat in Devon. We'll stay there while we determine what to do next."

They fell silent as the train rumbled over the tracks. Rain pounded on the windows, blurring the darkening view of the crowded London streets as they gave way to the expanse of the countryside. Shivers continued to ice Clara's skin. The hum of conversation rose from other passengers. A porter came by with tea and biscuits.

When Andrew dozed off, lulled by exhaustion and the rocking motion of the train, Clara looked across at Sebastian again. She dreaded to know the results of his conversation with Rushton, so instead she asked, "Did you see your mother?"

He nodded.

"Will you tell me what happened?"

He sighed and dragged a hand down his unshaven jaw. "Apparently she surrendered all for the sake of love."

"Love?"

An image of Catherine Leskovna came to Clara's mind, the

calm and unrepentant woman who seemed at utter peace with her decisions. Had love been the balm that mended the wounds of her infidelity?

"Will you tell me her story?" she asked Sebastian.

He turned his gaze to the window, but told her about his meeting with Catherine and how a single encounter with a young soldier eventually led her to a love strong enough to break her from her entire family.

Clara had no response when Sebastian fell silent. She, too, had deceived him. She had betrayed him. But she had done so with Andrew at the forefront of her mind. She had done so because she wanted her son back. Catherine Leskovna's deceit and betrayal had separated her from her children, and that Clara would never understand.

Gazing across the distance between the seats, at once a space both too close and inaccessibly remote, Clara loosened her suppressed emotions and allowed them to fill her chest. She looked at the sharp, whiskered planes of Sebastian's face, the wide slash of his mouth, and his thick-lashed eyes, which seemed capable of penetrating all the layers of her soul.

She had committed those acts because she wanted to protect him from her father's wrath. Instead he had joined her on the very pursuit she feared would result in his ruination.

"Do you forgive her?" Clara whispered in a voice so soft she thought he would not hear her.

Sebastian slid his gaze to her, his eyes lacking the warmth to which she had become so accustomed.

"I forgive her," he said, "but I do not expect to ever see her again."

CHAPTER 29

*B*y the light of the moon, the grounds of Floreston Manor spread around the house like an ocean surrounding a ship. Trees stood around the property like soldiers guarding the land, pointing forked branches toward the dark sky.

Upon their arrival after the long train ride, Sebastian explained to the resident servants, a housekeeper and a cook, that he, Clara, and Andrew would be staying for the next couple of days. The housekeeper hurriedly arranged for two maids to come from the village and help with the preparations. After a flurry of activity, even Sebastian managed to sleep a bit in the early morning hours following their hasty flight.

He woke to sunlight glistening on the still-damp grounds and windowpanes. He washed and dressed, then descended the stairs. Clara's voice drifted from the dining room, where she was apparently in conversation with the housekeeper.

Sebastian diverted his steps to the drawing room. Her betrayal coiled inside him, hard and tight, seething beneath his simmering anger. Not even the familiarity of the manor, the place where he had passed many happy hours with his brothers and sister, eased the pain of her disloyalty.

A protective cloth covered the grand piano that dominated the drawing room. He pulled the cloth from the front of the piano and draped it across the lid.

He pushed the bench back and sat, rolling his shoulders to ease the tension knotting his spine. How often had he played this piano over the years? The last time had been in the spring, when he'd come here with Alexander, Lydia, Rushton, Tasha, and their friend Lord Castleford.

Sebastian rubbed his right hand, remembering with a touch of fondness the genial atmosphere of that weekend visit. He'd played a great deal of Mozart, whose music was among Tasha's favorites.

He pushed up the fallboard to expose the shiny black-and-white keys and trailed his left hand over them. He played a sequence from Mozart's Sonata No. 15, the left-handed pattern sustaining harmonies from pale to vivid yellow. After the notes faded, Sebastian played them again. And again. And again. An unexpected flash of light went through him, the crackle of energy incited by music.

He played the sequence twice more before a movement at the door caught his eye. Andrew hovered just inside the room, a book clutched in his arms.

"Come in," Sebastian said. "Have you ever played the piano?"

Andrew shook his head. En route to Floreston Manor, Clara had explained to her son that she and Sebastian were married, but the revelation had prompted no outward response from the boy. In fact, he hadn't spoken a word.

"Come here, then," Sebastian invited.

The boy approached with caution, his eyes darting to the keys.

"Put your hands like this." Sebastian guided Andrew onto the bench and spread his hands on the keys. "This key is called middle C. If you put your thumb on middle C, you can use your other fingers to play D, E, F, and G."

He watched Andrew press the keys and listen to the notes, and then he put his right hand on the keyboard. "Do you know the song *Mary Had a Little Lamb*?"

Andrew nodded. Willing his hand to cooperate, Sebastian played the first few notes and sang the accompanying lyrics. "It starts with your third finger on this key, E. Try just those three notes. Down, then up again."

He straightened as Andrew placed his fingers on the correct keys and played the simple melody.

"Then the second 'little lamb' is right next door on this key, which is D." Sebastian played the note three times. "Do you hear how the sound is a bit lower?"

Andrew put his hand on the keyboard again and played the melody, ending with D. Sebastian then showed him the third "little lamb" on the G key. The instruction came back to him with surprising ease, and a distinct pleasure wound through him when Andrew played the first line correctly.

"Good." Sebastian straightened, glancing at the boy's face. "Did your grandfather provide any music lessons for you?"

Andrew shook his head and concentrated on pressing the G key. He looked toward the door as Clara entered. She paused a short distance from the piano, a shadow of uncertainty passing across her features. Sebastian flexed his fingers and tried to temper the anger toward her that had smoldered inside him for the past day.

"Andrew, would you like to see the conservatory?" she asked.

Andrew shook his head, his attention on the piano keys. Clara twisted her fingers into the folds of her skirt.

"There's also a library at the other end of the manor," she continued. "I'm certain Mr. Hall won't mind if we borrow some books to read."

Andrew didn't respond. Clara bit her lip, her uncertainty darkening into outright worry. Sebastian tried to deflect the sympathy that lanced through him and turned back to the boy.

"Andrew, while we wait for Mrs. White to prepare breakfast, I'll show you the river where my brothers and I used to fish," he said.

The boy pressed his fingers onto the keys again, then pushed to his feet and turned toward the door.

"I'll stay with him," Sebastian told Clara.

He let Andrew precede him to the gardens, then followed along the wet flagstone paths winding around the flower beds where a few late roses still bloomed.

Rather than ask questions that might not provoke a response, Sebastian merely talked—telling Andrew about the summer days he spent here with his brothers and sister, the hoop races they'd had on the grassy inclines, the trees they'd climbed. He pointed out the stables, the road to the village, the field where they'd practiced archery.

Andrew didn't offer any comment, though he appeared to be listening. Sebastian wondered if the boy was unable to speak or chose not to. Either way, this was likely the affliction that had prompted Fairfax to seek a physician.

By the time they returned to the house, Mrs. White had organized a hearty breakfast of bacon, eggs, and toast. After eating in silence, Andrew went out to the garden again, with an admonition from Clara not to wander too far.

She looked at Sebastian, her face pale in a stream of morning sunlight. "I'm sorry."

He couldn't tell her it didn't matter. His right hand clenched inside his pocket.

"Did you think I wouldn't help you?" he asked, his voice tight. *Did you think me incapable of it?*

"I was trying to protect you."

"How is running away protecting me?"

"My father threatened to spread rumors that I was responsible for Richard's death. I hoped that if I left, he would turn his attention to me and leave your family alone."

"He could never prove you had anything to do with Richard's death."

"No one else knows that, do they?" Her voice stretched thin as she stood and paced to the hearth. "Why wouldn't they believe Lord Fairfax, who was so close to his son-in-law and who has been such a dedicated grandfather? What possible recourse do I have against such an accusation?"

"*I* am your recourse, Clara," Sebastian snapped. "Why didn't you trust me when I said I would help you?"

She whirled to face him. "I did trust you!"

"If you had, you wouldn't have gone to my father."

"I didn't go to him," Clara said, spreading her hands in desperation. "He came to the museum to ask about my estrangement from Fairfax, and I…my plans had been thwarted because of the rain. When Lord Rushton started questioning me, I realized he is the only person I know who is more powerful than my father. If he couldn't help me, who could?"

"*I* could."

"We had no time left, Sebastian. If Fairfax had taken Andrew away again, to an *institution* no less, what could either of us have done?"

"So you found it necessary to tell Rushton about my mother." Sebastian's jaw clenched to the point of pain. "And my hand."

Clara pressed her palms to her flushed cheeks. "I'm sorry."

"*Why* did you tell him?"

"Because I was scared! What if Fairfax made good on his threat? When your father spoke of associating with him, I had to warn him that Fairfax might attempt to spread lies about me. I hoped that if I were honest with Lord Rushton about *everything*, he would prove to be my ally instead."

"Yet you gave no thought to the effects of such a revelation."

Despair rose to darken her eyes. "Everything I have done has been for the purpose of reclaiming my son. *That* is the effect I'd hoped for when I spoke to your father. Maybe if he'd offered to help, we'd have found another way."

She sank into a chair, her shoulders slumping with defeat. "I'm sorry, Sebastian. You might still rectify matters if you return to London now. If I'm the one who is vilified…"

Anger boiled through him, propelling him forward in three long strides. "You think I would allow that? Allow you to be slandered for attempting to reclaim your son? God in heaven, Clara, what kind of man do you think I am?"

"I know exactly what kind of man you are! I've known for years, ever since I first met you in Dorset. You're kind and generous and talented. You would do anything to help those you care about. I've never doubted that. But I had no more time left. Telling your father was my last resort. If he'd agreed to help me, I might not have needed to run."

"And where did you plan to go?"

"*Away.* France. Then America, if I could. As far from my father's reach as I could possibly get."

"With no intention of telling me anything."

"The less you knew, the better for all of us." Clara looked past him to the door as it creaked open and Andrew entered, a black-and-white cat struggling to escape his clutches.

Andrew glanced from his mother to Sebastian, hesitant to enter the strained atmosphere. Sebastian forced his shoulders to relax as he crossed to where the boy hovered in the doorway.

"You've found Minou, have you?" He scratched the cat behind its pointed ears, a gesture that eased Minou's agitation. "She's a bit skittish, but becomes quite docile after she's eaten. You can see if Mrs. White has some fish you can give her."

Andrew nodded, tightening his grasp on the squirming cat as he hurried off toward the kitchen. Sebastian took a breath and turned back to Clara. She watched him warily, her violet eyes glittering in the damp sunlight.

"I never meant for any of this to happen," she said. "I only wanted to protect my son."

Sebastian knew that. He'd known that from the beginning, from the moment Clara proposed. He flexed the fingers of his right hand.

"What else did you want?" he asked.

"What else...?"

"Why did you ask me to marry you?" His heart thumped against his rib cage. "Any man would have done, if the transfer of Wakefield House was your only concern."

A delicate blush rose to paint her cheeks. "No, not any man. I didn't even consider the idea until you came back into my life."

"And was it because I am the son of an earl? Did you think even then that my father might have access to resources that you and Granville did not?"

Her flush deepened to a rose-red. "And if I did? Would you not understand that? Would you blame me?"

A flame of renewed anger bolted through Sebastian again. No, he didn't blame her for identifying his father as a source of power. But it would kill him to think that had been her sole motive.

"When you refused to approach him for help, Sebastian, I saw everything falling away. I couldn't allow you to ruin yourself by conceding to my father's demands. I couldn't allow him to ruin you by spreading lies about me. What else could I have done but go to your father?"

"You could have come back to me."

"No." Her throat rippled with a swallow. "Not if it meant putting you at further risk. And that I never wanted to do."

She rose and approached him, placed a trembling hand on his chest. His heart pounded against her palm, the warmth of her hand seeping into his skin.

"I had a hope your father's position would be beneficial," she said. "It would be a lie if I said otherwise. But that is not the only reason I wanted to marry you. And I did want to marry *you*, not any man. I wanted to marry Sebastian Hall, the generous and cheerful pianist who never spoke an unkind word. I wanted to marry the man who made people smile simply because he was near. The man who created music as if it were born from his very being."

Sebastian grabbed her hand so tightly that Clara drew in a breath. Resentment sank claws into his neck.

"That man, Clara," he whispered, his voice taut, "no longer exists."

She met his gaze without flinching. Her eyes burned with resolve. "Yes, he does."

A sharp energy crackled between them. An assault of memories swept through him as he recalled the arid desert of the past few months, a wasteland relieved only by Clara's presence. Only with her had he felt happy and alive again. Only with her had he begun to believe that he could control his own future. That he had a *choice*.

Clara rose onto her toes and pressed her lips hard against his. Sparks jolted through him as her orange-spice scent filled his head. He gripped her waist with his left hand and sank his mouth into hers, their tongues tangling in a sudden collision of heat. Her breasts crushed against his chest, her hands winding around the back of his neck to grip his hair. For an instant he let himself fall into her, let the feel of her obliterate his anger.

"I will love you," Clara whispered against his mouth, her breath hot on his lips, "if you will recognize that the very core of who you are will never change."

A month ago, Sebastian would not have believed the truth of her remark. Yet being back at Floreston Manor did remind him of the pleasures of his youth when anything was possible. For the first time in months, seated at his old piano, he had felt music flow through his blood again.

He stepped away from Clara. He knew the cost of keeping

secrets, but he had entrusted her with his. And he had revealed too much of himself already to give her this fragile admission.

"If you…" His voice tangled around the words. He swallowed and forced them through his throat. "If you will love me, Clara, you must do so without any conditions whatsoever."

CHAPTER 30

*C*atherine Leskovna sat in a private room at the Albion Hotel, her dress a plain black chintz, her graying hair pulled back into a chignon. The set of her shoulders, the tilt of her chin, the firmness of her expression—all spoke of the regal countess she had once been. Only her dark eyes, brewing with untold desires, gave any indication of the impulsive gypsy blood that ran through her veins.

Benjamin Hall, the Earl of Rushton, fought an assault of emotions threatening to overwhelm him. His hands clenched on the rim of his hat as he stood in the doorway and looked at her for the first time in three years.

"Hello, my lord." Catherine's voice sounded uneven, less cultivated. "I assure you no one aside from Jacob and Sebastian...and you...knows I am in London."

"I expect the situation will remain that way, madam." Rushton advanced, anger tightening his shoulders.

"Yes." She rose, as if to put herself on equal footing with him. "I will do nothing to cause further difficulties."

"Forgive me if I find your promises less than assuring."

Catherine studied him, her eyes unnervingly perceptive. "You've been well, Jacob told me. I'm glad to know that."

"I haven't come here to discuss my health. I came to confirm your departure from London, which I expect will occur with great haste now that you have interfered with my family."

"I did nothing of the kind, Rushton. I only wanted to know what happened to Sebastian. Despite everything, they are still my children."

"Your children whom you deserted." Another bolt of anger, this time on behalf of his five children. "Now you know how they all fare, and you can take your leave."

"I want...will you not allow me to remain in contact with them?"

Rushton's teeth came together hard. "They're adults, Catherine. And though I consider you *persona non grata*, I have no way of preventing them from associating with you, should they choose to do so. Clearly this incident with Jacob has proven that. But mark my words, if I hear the slightest hint of rumor, I will denounce you again." Tension knotted his back. "And if you dare do a thing to harm Tasha either personally or publicly, I will find a way to have you thrown into prison."

Catherine's eyes flashed, but she stepped back and nodded. "Tasha would never agree to see me. Neither would Alexander."

"To their everlasting credit." Rushton turned to the door, hating the anger and regret churning inside him. "You've wreaked enough havoc upon their lives. I suggest you never try to contact them again. You have lacerated us all with your deceit."

Although he didn't see her face, he almost felt the cloud of despair that descended over her. He steeled himself against caring. Jacob had told him about the death of Catherine's husband, and while Rushton felt a degree of sorrow for the loss of a young soldier, he could not bring himself to experience any sympathy for his former wife.

"I loved him," she said.

Rushton stilled. *"Him."*

"I didn't know anything about love until I met him," Catherine continued. "I didn't know what love felt like. And I blame myself for that because I never *expected* more. I never thought that either you or I deserved more from our very dull marriage."

Damn her to all hell.

"Our marriage was as it should have been," Rushton said through gritted teeth. They'd had a marriage encased in propriety and respectability, one that produced five children and was the envy of many of his peers.

Rushton crushed the edge of his hat in his fists. His chest ached.

"Exactly," Catherine said, sorrow coloring her voice. "Our marriage was as it should have been. Not as either of us should have wanted it."

Without looking at her again, Rushton stalked from the room. He ordered his driver to return to King Street, battling back memories of his life with Catherine, their marriage of almost thirty years, their five children.

He smothered the persistent and painful belief that if he had done something differently—though what, he had no idea—Catherine might not have done what she did. She might not have turned to another man.

A curse split through his mind. He pushed all such speculations aside, for what good were they now, and descended the carriage in front of his town house. The butler greeted him with the announcement that he had a visitor—Lord Fairfax, who had insisted on waiting for his return to speak with him.

"He claims he has something very important to tell you," Soames said as he collected Rushton's greatcoat and hat. "I asked him to wait in the study, but shall I tell him you are not available?"

"No, that's all right. Thank you, Soames." Rushton smoothed a hand down the front of his waistcoat as he approached the study.

Fairfax stood upon his entry. A slender, hard-faced man, he extended a hand and introduced himself.

"Fairfax, welcome. I regret that we haven't made each other's acquaintance before now."

An odd smile twisted the other man's mouth. "I'm afraid now you might very well regret that we have."

Rushton frowned and moved around the other side of the desk. Fairfax lowered himself into a chair and crossed one leg over the other.

"How is your family, Rushton?" he asked conversationally.

Despite the innocuous tone of the question, wariness flashed through Rushton. "Well enough, thank you."

"I was given to understand that your son has retired from his musical career," Fairfax continued. "Is that correct?"

Regret constricted Rushton's chest. He'd been so angry over the reappearance of his former wife and his sons' disloyalty that he hadn't thought about Sebastian's newfound incapacity. He hadn't wanted to. Despite what Sebastian had kept from him, Rushton never wanted to see any of his children so wretchedly harmed.

"That is correct," he told Fairfax.

"What are Mr. Hall's plans for the future, then?"

"He is considering a clerk's position with the Patent Office."

"Ah. Well, I ought to warn you that the Patent Office will likely not wish to employ him when they learn he is a criminal."

The final word struck Rushton like a blow, snapping his head back as his gaze collided with Fairfax's. "What?"

"My grandson, Andrew, has been abducted," Fairfax said. He paused as if to enhance the effect of his next statement. "Clara and Sebastian are the ones who committed the crime."

An icy chill ran down Rushton's spine. He had known something was wrong when Sebastian had left the house in such haste yesterday. And despite the shock of Fairfax's accusation, Rushton didn't find it necessary to question the other man. Of course

Sebastian would do whatever he could for Clara and her son, even if it meant breaking the law. Sebastian was nothing if not loyal to a fault.

A very grave fault.

Rushton pressed his fingers to the bridge of his nose. "How do you know this?"

"My footman witnessed the abduction and followed them to the Paddington station, but was unable to prevent them from boarding a train. I'd thought it might have been a ruse and they would have returned to London, but they are not at Mr. Blake's museum or your son's town house." Fairfax paused. "I assume they did not attempt to take shelter here?"

"Of course not." Tension threaded the back of Rushton's neck as he attempted to recall everything Clara had told him. "Why would they commit such an act?"

"Clara's husband left Andrew in my custody," Fairfax explained. "He knew she would not be capable of caring for Andrew herself, a supposition that Clara proved when she fled Manley Park in her grief over Mr. Shepherd's death."

"That does not answer my question as to why she would find it necessary to resort to abducting Andrew."

"I have been forced to keep Andrew from her," Fairfax replied, casting his gaze downward. His face furrowed with sadness. "He has been in a terrible state since his father's death. I did not want him further damaged by associating with his unsound mother. Her recent actions have only proven the truth of my judgment."

Rushton studied the other man from beneath lowered brows. Dislike speared his chest, though he could not quite identify its source.

"Both my footman and Andrew's tutor saw Mr. Hall seize Andrew outside the British Museum," Fairfax said. "Then they boarded a train on the Great Western Railway, but I have no way of finding out where they might have disembarked. So I am here to ask you. Do you know where they might have gone?"

The Great Western Railway. Rushton was silent, his gaze fixed on a paperweight that sat at the corner of his desk. He knew where Sebastian had gone. Only one place in the world had served as a sanctuary for them all.

After a moment, Fairfax unfolded himself from the chair and stood.

"If you don't help me retrieve my grandson, Rushton," he said, "I will see your son arrested and hanged."

CHAPTER 31

*F*loreston Manor was as close as they would come to a tropical island protected by sea dragons, but it was enough. The property reminded Clara of Wakefield House, a refuge tucked away from the rest of the world, though still vulnerable to attack. She descended the stairs, her heart thumping against her corset. Fear gripped her, but the emotion was tempered by relief that Andrew was safe.

For now. It would not be long before Fairfax thought to look for them at the Halls' estate.

She stepped into the drawing room, where Andrew sat curled in a chair playing with several chess pieces. Clara gazed at him for a moment, the persistent knot in her belly loosening at the sight of his tousled chestnut hair. He'd grown taller over the past year and his features had sharpened, but he was still every inch her son.

"Are you hungry?" she asked, pausing beside him to brush her hand across his hair. "You didn't eat much for breakfast."

Andrew shook his head.

"Would you like to read a book?"

He shook his head again, his attention on arranging the chess pieces into a battle formation. Concern knotted in Clara's throat as she tunneled her fingers through his hair.

"I know this has been a shock, Andrew, but I assure you Mr. Hall and I will allow no harm to come to you."

She had hoped her revelation that she and Sebastian were married would prompt questions from her son, but his reaction appeared indifferent.

"Since I left Manley Park, I've been trying desperately to see you," she continued. "You know that, don't you? I never wanted to leave you, but I had no choice."

Still no response. Clara tried to calm her rustling unease with the thought that the boy was exhausted. She bent to press her lips to his forehead. Her heart shriveled a bit when he withdrew.

"I'll come and find you when it's time for lunch, all right?" she said. "If you venture outside, please stay close to the house."

She went to find the housekeeper and engaged in a brief discussion about when they would take lunch and dinner. She wrote a letter to Uncle Granville assuring him that she and Andrew were safe, although she made no mention of where they were.

Clara then tried to occupy herself with some reading in order to pass the time, though she could hardly concentrate on the task for the thoughts and worries swimming through her mind. After an hour of staring at one page, she went back downstairs in search of Andrew. As she neared the drawing room, she paused at the sound of piano music. Hesitant, slow, but definitely music.

Concealing herself within the shadows of the doorway, Clara peeked into the room. Sebastian sat beside Andrew at the piano, showing him something on the keys. He used his left hand only, his right tucked into the pocket of his coat, but the glide of his fingers produced a tune that resonated with light. Pleasure creased his eyes as he said something to Andrew and played the phrase again.

Clara pressed a hand to her chest. A memory glowed at the

back of her mind—herself as a younger woman standing in the corner to watch Sebastian Hall play the piano. Delighting in the graceful way he moved his hands over the keyboard, the ease of his posture, the effortlessness of his creation.

She had loved him then. How could she not? He had embodied all that was good and beautiful in the world.

And now? The darkness that had encroached upon him only enhanced his appeal, painting him with nuances of shadows and light. This new chiaroscuro strengthened Clara's love for him, as it seemed to mirror her own soul, the blend of hope and despair that had colored so many of her days.

You must love me without any conditions whatsoever.

Of course she did. She had loved him for years. If Andrew hadn't been taken from her and she had still somehow married Sebastian, the union would have fulfilled every wish that had ever sparked in her young imagination.

She watched as her son put his hands on the piano keys and clumsily reproduced the phrase Sebastian had played earlier. Her heart thrummed as she waited to see if he would turn to Sebastian and say something, but the boy kept his head down and his attention focused on his hands. He listened when Sebastian spoke, responded to the instructions, but said nothing.

What is wrong?

The fear that had lived inside Clara since the moment she discovered Andrew's muteness bloomed into full force. When had her son stopped speaking?

She tried to remember the days following Richard's death, all so filled with shock, grief, and chaos. Then the revelation that Andrew had been left in Fairfax's custody, Clara's desperate attempt to prevent her father from sending her away...yes, she had talked to Andrew many times during those weeks, attempting to comfort and reassure the boy.

She blinked back tears and tried to suppress the ache of regret. She'd been wrong in her assurance that everything would be all right. She had no idea what had happened to her son during their separation. And she feared to her very bones that she might never know.

Sebastian's deep voice resonated in the drawing room as he placed his left hand on the keys and played another scale. Clara ducked from the shadows and hurried back to her room.

Not until this moment did she acknowledge the secret dreams that had taken root in her soul. The dreams in which she and Andrew had closed the distance of their year-long separation with one embrace. The dreams in which they laughed and cried, and she had reassured him she would never let anyone separate them again. And then they sat down and talked about all they had done and made plans for all they would do. Together.

Never in those dreams had Clara believed things would be so different. Never had she imagined that her son, for whom she had desperately fought every minute of her waking hours, would have become a stranger.

"Now remember that the linseed oil has to be dry before you put the paper on the seams." Sebastian lifted the cut pieces of taffeta from the wooden table while Andrew spread the brown paper beneath it. "Put a sheet on the top as well. I'll get the iron."

He went to the fire, where a metal iron sat heating. He brought it back to the table and told Andrew to stand back a little while he ironed the seams. A hiss and crackle rose as the iron pressed the paper, releasing the pungent smell of linseed oil.

Since arriving at Floreston Manor yesterday, Sebastian had tried to occupy Andrew's time with activities that would prevent the boy from worrying. He hadn't told Andrew of his plan to leave the following day for Brixham, where they would stay with a cousin of his before making their way to France.

Sebastian was so intent on his ironing task that the sudden

falter of his hand caught him by surprise. The iron toppled to the side and fell to the floor as his grip weakened, the hot edge hitting the table. Andrew darted forward. He grabbed the handle to straighten the iron and placed it back on the table.

His heart pounding, Sebastian rubbed his hand and stared at the paper. He'd been using his right hand without even realizing it. He swallowed hard and met Andrew's gaze. Although he knew the boy had noticed how little he used his right hand, Sebastian had never called attention to it. Neither had Andrew.

Andrew stepped back and nodded to the iron, as if encouraging Sebastian to finish the task. Sebastian grasped the iron with his left hand and managed to finish ironing all the seams.

After the paper cooled, Andrew tested the seams to ensure they were airtight. He looked up at Sebastian.

"Good," Sebastian said. "We'll give it a coat of varnish and let it dry. The one we did this morning ought to be ready."

He went to the stove where a pot of lime and drying oil sat bubbling. He and Andrew each took a paintbrush and smeared the varnish over the taffeta and paper until it was thoroughly coated.

"We'll leave it over here." Sebastian lifted the material and brought it to a cord he'd strung across a corner of the kitchen. He removed a dried cloth from the line and pinned up the wet one. "Or Mrs. White will have a fit of apoplexy if we take possession of her workspace."

Andrew grinned and brought the bowl of varnish and brushes over to the washbasin. They cleaned the remainder of the mess they'd made, then Andrew took the dried material while Sebastian collected more supplies. They donned their overcoats and hats and went out into the garden. A brisk fall wind swept through the neglected beds, and the sun shone against the clear blue sky. The cold, fresh air sent a renewed energy through Sebastian, a sense of anticipation and pleasure that he thought he'd lost.

He and Andrew walked along the flagstone paths until they came to an area of the garden that was clear of trees. The boy began twisting the material around a hoop and attaching it with cords to a small basket that he had painted emerald-green with yellow stars.

After setting out their supplies, Sebastian dropped a pound of iron filings into a jar filled with water, then picked up a bottle of oil of vitriol with his left hand. As he forced his fingers to close around the top, Andrew appeared at his side. Without looking at him, the boy twisted off the lid of the bottle and grasped the jar.

Something tightened in Sebastian's chest, but it wasn't an unpleasant feeling. No embarrassment or sense that the boy pitied his inability to rely on his hand. Instead Andrew gave him a matter-of-fact nod and pushed the jar closer. After Sebastian poured the vitriol, Andrew stopped the jar with a cork and together they pressed a glass tube through the cork.

"Ready?" Sebastian asked.

The boy nodded and moved closer. They fitted the other end of the tube into the hoop and watched as the gas caused the taffeta to inflate into a balloon. At Sebastian's instruction, Andrew clamped his hand around the material to prevent the gas from escaping. Sebastian removed the tube.

"Now let go," he said.

Andrew released the balloon, which instantly caught a current of air and began to rise, the green basket dangling below. Andrew applauded as it bobbed on the air, rising higher and higher.

A smile broke out across Sebastian's face as the balloon drifted like a bright bubble. He remembered all too well the joy he and his brothers had experienced constructing balloons exactly like this one and setting them aloft. It filled him now, the delight of watching the balloon bounce through the air, the enjoyment of being outside, the pleasure of being concerned only about whether or not the linseed-coated seams would hold.

"Now we have to chase it," he warned Andrew as the balloon drifted farther.

Andrew turned and started to run, a laugh breaking from him suddenly. The sound caught Sebastian by surprise, verifying his suspicion that Andrew's muteness was not the result of any physical affliction. The boy could make sounds. He just chose not to.

Rather than tussle with the question of why, Sebastian raced after Andrew as they followed the path of the balloon. The wind surged cold against his face. His muscles flexed and pulled as he ran, and for a moment his snarled emotions loosened. A new feeling spread through him, a sense of freedom that he'd thought had died with the end of his musical career.

As the gas inside the balloon dispersed, it slowed on the current and began to descend. They chased it to the river, where it floated to snag on a branch jutting out over the water.

"I'll try to grab it." Sebastian hurried down the grassy bank toward the river, but Andrew got there first.

After shucking off his boots, the boy stepped onto the first of several flat stones that provided a path to the opposite bank. The current cascaded over the stones, polishing them to smoothness.

Knowing well how cold the water was, Sebastian grinned as Andrew made his way cautiously to the largest stone in the center, then reached to grab the dangling balloon. Clutching it in one fist, he retraced his path back to Sebastian's side. He held up the deflated balloon with a triumphant smile.

"Well done." Sebastian tousled the boy's hair. "You'd make a fine retriever. Shall we give it another go?"

Andrew nodded, and they walked back to the garden where they had left the supplies. Sebastian mixed another batch of the gas concoction, and they set the balloon aloft again. As the boy ran off to give chase, Sebastian saw Clara coming toward them from the house.

Tension knotted his shoulders as half of his soul urged him closer to her and the other half remained locked behind the wall of his anger. Even understanding the desperation behind her revelations to Rushton made it no easier for Sebastian to accept the fact that Clara hadn't trusted him.

"He seems happy." Clara paused beside him, her smile belied by the strain in her brilliant eyes. She looked to where Andrew ran along the path back down to the river. "I'm so grateful for the time you're spending with him, however short it might be."

"He's good company. Intelligent, curious."

She didn't look at him, her gaze fixed on her son. "Has he said anything to you?"

"No."

Clara's shoulders sagged, as if she had been holding her breath while awaiting his response. Sebastian surrendered to the urge to comfort her and slid his arm around her. A ripple of unease went through her, but she stepped closer to his side.

"I know this is the reason my father wanted to send him away," she said, her voice low, "but I don't understand why Andrew refuses to speak. He must have stopped speaking after I left for London because he had no such affliction when I was still at Manley Park."

"I've heard him laugh," Sebastian said.

She swung her gaze to him. "You heard him laugh? When?"

"Earlier today when we set the balloon aloft. He still has a voice. He just chooses not to use it."

"Have you asked him why?"

Sebastian shook his head. He stared after Andrew, lifting his hand in acknowledgment as the boy held up the deflated balloon.

"I never wanted to be asked about my hand infirmity," he said. "I assume Andrew wouldn't want to be asked why he won't speak."

Clara watched her son. A breeze whipped a loose tendril of hair across her face, and Sebastian couldn't resist brushing it aside. His fingertips stroked the softness of her cheek. An ache clenched his chest as he thought of how drastically his life had changed in the past months.

Clara turned to him again. "What will we do now?"

"I've made arrangements for us to leave tomorrow afternoon. I've sent word to a cousin who lives near Brixham. We can lodge with him for a few days. I've also directed Alexander's solicitor to look into matters again, especially pertaining to the debts your father has incurred. Perhaps we might still come to an agreement with Fairfax."

As much as he wanted to believe his own statement, the words rang hollow.

"He's poisoned my son against me," Clara said.

"What?"

"My father." Her jaw tightened, a pulse thudding along the delicate column of her neck. "He must have said something to Andrew about my being responsible for Richard's death. It's the only explanation I can think of as to why Andrew doesn't want to be near me."

Before Sebastian could respond, Andrew approached, his gaze darting to Clara. Wariness flashed in his blue eyes. He paused uncertainly near Sebastian. Though Clara smiled at the boy, Sebastian felt her close in on herself, felt a strain arcing between mother and son. She stepped away from them.

"I'll…I'll leave you both to your sport, then. Tea will be ready in an hour, if you'd care to join me."

"Of course." Sebastian watched her return to the house, her steps measured and stiff.

Andrew tugged on his sleeve and held up the balloon. Sebastian took it, wanting again that feeling of blithe freedom to conquer his foreboding.

"Let's try it again, shall we?"

CHAPTER 32

*C*lara sat on the edge of the bed, smoothing the blanket over Andrew's legs. He held an open book on his lap, his chestnut hair falling in a swath across his forehead as he examined an illustration of a knight on horseback. She curled her fingers into a fist, suppressing the urge to reach out and stroke the lock of hair back.

"Do you still like the King Arthur tales?" she asked, desperate for any topic that would reconnect her with her son. "I remember we read them often when we were at Manley Park."

Andrew nodded and turned a page. Clara placed a tentative hand on his leg, and experienced a rush of relief when he didn't pull away from her touch.

"Andrew."

He glanced up.

"Whatever…" Her voice tangled into a knot. She took a breath. "Whatever your grandfather has said about me, it's not true. Do you understand?"

He returned his attention to the book. Clara's hand tightened on the bedcovers.

"I never wanted your father to be hurt. I never wanted to

leave you. And I certainly never wanted to give you up to the custody of your grandfather. Will you please believe me?"

He didn't look at her, but gave a nod so slight that Clara might have missed it had she not been gazing at him so intently. She patted his leg and stood. A small reassurance was better than none at all. She bent to kiss his forehead and whisper good night, then returned to her own bedchamber down the corridor.

While she was glad to her bones that Sebastian and Andrew had developed a quick and strong friendship, Clara could not dispel her pervasive sorrow that her son had become so unreachable to her.

She stripped out of her clothes and washed, then unpinned her hair and brushed out the tangles. She crawled into bed with a book of poetry. The words dipped and swam before her unfocused eyes.

Weary, she set the book aside. She hadn't slept well since the confrontation with Fairfax, her thoughts a confusion of memories and fear. Now a vast, black void had opened inside her heart. The lamp on her bedside table flickered, shadows twisting across the ceiling.

The fear that had lived inside her for so long, the despair she had believed would vanish like a puff of smoke the instant she held Andrew in her arms again...it was still there. Slithering into her blood, coiling in the pit of her belly.

Would she never be free of it? And now that Sebastian was inextricably tangled in their circumstances...God alone knew what the future held.

She pushed the covers aside and tugged on her dressing gown, then padded down the corridor to his room. She knocked and pushed the door open when he bade her enter.

He sat beside the fire, still clothed in trousers and a white linen shirt, his long legs stretched out before him. A tingle swept down Clara's spine at the sight of him—the reddish glow burnishing his dark hair, the V of skin revealed by the unfastened buttons of his shirt, the rough whiskers covering his jaw.

"Am I disturbing you?" she asked.

"Yes." His gaze moved over her, a long slow sweep like the glide of his fingertips. "You've disturbed me since I first saw you carrying Millicent's head."

Clara smiled faintly at the memory. She approached him with caution, but there was nothing forbidding in his expression. She lowered herself into the chair across from him, glancing at the paper he held. The penmanship was scrawled, uneven.

"Is that to your brother's solicitor?" she asked.

"Yes." He set the paper and pen on a small table. "He'll likely feel obliged to explain the situation to Alexander, but my hope is that things will be settled by then."

Clara hoped so too, though she had no idea how. Perhaps a different solicitor could offer a solution. She nibbled on her thumbnail and stared at the leaping flames of the fire.

"Will you not dissolve our marriage?" she asked, her voice steady but quiet. She could not bring herself to utter the words *divorce me*.

"No." Sebastian's hand curled into the material of his trousers. "I told you when we first agreed to wed that I would not tolerate even the possibility of separation."

"But surely that would be less troublesome for you than having to contend with our current situation."

"No. There will not be another divorce in my family."

She kept her attention on the fire. All that had occurred in the past week had forged a question at the back of her mind, one she had struggled to ignore because she was afraid of Sebastian's answer. Yet now she forced herself to voice it.

"Do you regret it, then?" she asked. "Agreeing to my proposal? I fear the cost to you has been far greater than you anticipated."

He didn't deny it.

Her heart tightened. She felt his gaze on her, but could not bring herself to face him.

"No," he said. "I do not regret our marriage."

She looked at him. A deep and abiding love swelled beneath her heart. She pressed a hand to her chest, feeling as if her body could not contain all she felt for him.

"I'm so sorry for what I did," she whispered. "Please know it wasn't because I don't love you. I have loved you for years." She rose, hesitant, and went to lower herself into his lap, willing him not to reject her.

He didn't. She tucked herself against him. The heat of his long, muscular body eased the tension from her, like steam smoothing wrinkles from a swath of silk. He lifted his left hand to touch her neck, resting his fingertips in the hollow of her collarbone. Warmth brewed in his eyes behind a shield of guardedness.

"I am no longer the man you once loved," he said.

"Yes, you are." She spread her hand over his chest. "People don't transform completely into someone different. We change, yes, but we remain the same at our very core. You lost the use of your hand, Sebastian. You didn't lose your talent or your kindness. You didn't lose your love of life."

"If that is true"—he tucked his hand beneath her chin and turned her face to his—"what about you?"

"Me?"

"Are you also the same as you once were? During those Wakefield House days when you were happy and filled with hope?"

A warm glow filled Clara's chest as she looked into her husband's beautiful dark eyes. "With you, yes," she whispered. "I am."

She imagined then what it might have been like had they met under different circumstances. If she had somehow already come to terms with her father and been living at Wakefield House with

Andrew. She could have come to Sebastian free of desperate, calculated motives, compelled only by her love for him.

"I never meant for it to come to this," she said.

"You meant to have Andrew again. That's what it came to."

"Will you forgive me for the price we paid?"

"Yes."

The word flowered beneath Clara's heart, though its brightness did not diminish her unease. He would forgive her because he was a good man who tried not to think ill of others, but he would not forget the fact that she had gone against his wishes. He would not forget that she had revealed his secrets to his father.

Her chest hurt. She pressed her forehead to his neck and closed her eyes. Sebastian cupped her chin and urged her to lift her head, his fingers strong and warm. How she loved his hands. The strong, gentle hands that had captivated her from the first moment he touched her. Their lips met in a gentle kiss before he curved her legs around him and rose, holding her against him as he moved to the bed.

The mattress dipped as he lowered her onto it and stretched out beside her, skimming his palm across the expanse of her shift. She reached for his right hand and brought it to her lips, brushing her mouth across the bent angle of his little finger. His eyes burned in the flare of the candlelight, his dark hair sweeping across his forehead as he moved closer.

Clara turned to him, an ache of longing swelling through her, and lifted her arms to allow him to divest her of her dressing gown and pull the shift over her head. She fumbled to remove his trousers, welcoming the shock of arousal that conquered her ever-present fear, like water crashing endlessly over a jagged stone.

He lowered his head to kiss her. Hard, his tongue sweeping into her mouth in a hot caress that tore a moan from her throat. Her head fell back, her mouth opening and body yielding to him all over again. He nipped at her lower lip with his teeth, the slight twinge vibrating across her skin. His tongue tangled with hers, slid over the surface of her teeth, his lips demanding a response that she could give only to him.

Soon, too soon, he lifted his head. He stared at her, then placed his hand between her breasts. Her heartbeat thundered against his palm. His fingers trembled. He leaned in close again, his breath hot against her ear.

"Touch me," he whispered.

Clara's breath caught as she grasped his smooth, hard shaft. He pulsed against her hand, driving her arousal higher. His breath burned against her neck. He palmed her breasts, watched the peaks harden beneath his touch, then smoothed his warm hands over her belly to the apex of her thighs.

He moved lower, his body taut, coiled tight. Clara's heart began to pound slow and hard, her lips parting on an indrawn breath as he pushed his hands between her legs and spread her open. She fisted the bed linens in her hands, pushing aside the instinctive urge to close herself. She had long passed the point of being able to hide. She would forever be stripped bare for him, only him.

Her hips twitched upward. He rose to his knees and pushed his trousers to the floor. Lust pitched and rolled through her, and she arched herself toward him in silent entreaty.

He positioned himself at the entrance to her body and thrust into her once, heavy and fast. She gasped, lifting her arms to wrap them around his shoulders, stroking one hand through his thick hair. He lowered himself on top of her, bracing his hands on either side of her head and locking their bodies together. Slowly, he increased the pace of his plunging, the slick glide filling her repeatedly, and Clara came apart like a bursting star, her hands gripping his back and her body undulating with trembles.

He grasped her right wrist, pinning her hand against the bed. He thrust again, and again, before spilling into her with a low groan that shuddered through her blood. For a moment, he was still.

Breathless, Clara opened her eyes. He was watching her, a sheen of sweat on his face and neck, the carnal satisfaction fading from his expression. She stroked a hand over his jaw, her gaze tracing the sharp planes of his cheekbones that sloped down to his beautiful mouth. His thick-lashed eyes, the color of burned honey in the firelight, gleamed with warmth.

I love him. She knew that to the depths of her being. A braid of fear and pleasure spiraled through her. She stroked his lower lip with her thumb.

Over the past weeks, she had overcome her fear and plunged forward with reckless and daring steps to ensure Andrew's return to her. She had proposed marriage, conceived a calculated agreement, tried to bargain with her father, lied to her husband, plotted the abduction of her son. Yet it had taken every ounce of courage she possessed to tell Sebastian she loved him.

"What's so amusing?" Sebastian asked.

Clara realized she was smiling. She'd had no idea that loving him could be both the most daunting and exhilarating thing of all. "I love you."

Wary hope flashed in his eyes. Before he could respond, she shook her head to forestall him.

"I was so frightened after Richard died," she said, her gaze on his mouth as she continued stroking his lower lip, "and then when my father made his accusations and forced me leave Andrew. For the past year, I've lived with fear as my sole companion. And yet I've realized that the only times I *haven't* been afraid, I've been with you."

For a long, stretched moment he just looked at her, then he took her hand in his. "You're the bravest person I've ever known. And you're the only one who has ever challenged my own courage."

"Because I know who you are. I know what you are capable

of. I do still love the man you once were, Sebastian. I've loved that man for years. He's the brilliant, charming musician who showed everyone, including me, how to find pleasure in life."

She lifted herself onto her elbow, sliding her hand down his neck to his bare chest. "But the man you are now, the man I love with everything I am, is the man I *know*. I know the shadows and light that color your heart because I feel them too. You are the man who has proven that goodness and hope still exist, even in the face of despair. You are the man I love."

A shuddering breath escaped him. Clara's heart thumped hard in the wake of her admission, fear of his rejection rising to the surface. But no. Confirming what she had always believed about him, Sebastian turned to brush his lips across her forehead, down the slope of her cheek to her lips.

And then he kissed her, locking their mouths together in an affirmation of their inseverable union.

Two movements linked together. Sebastian studied the sheet of music and tightened his hand around the pencil. Starting with the woodwinds, then the full orchestra building into a crescendo in preparation for the piano's entry. A stack of fourths. E, A, D, G. Blue, white, yellow, brown. He scribbled the notes and played them with his left hand.

Anticipation flared in his blood. Caution, too, for he didn't quite dare to believe that a one-handed piano part would be any good, much less please an audience. His right hand had always been dominant, its dexterity concealing whatever imperfections lay within the composition. Focusing on his left hand required a perfection of musical balances and dynamic gradations, allowing no room for inadequacy.

He played the notes again. The dark orange bass of the orchestra resounded through his mind. Then the cadenza. He wrote another measure, trying to make his way a few more steps to the end, gritting his teeth when his hand faltered and the pencil dropped to the floor.

Before he could bend to retrieve it, Clara stepped forward. Sebastian straightened, not having known she was in the room. Apprehension tightened his spine.

"How long have you been here?" he asked.

"Just a few minutes." Her gaze skimmed over the papers littering the piano surface. "I heard the music and thought you were here with Andrew."

"He's with Mrs. White in the kitchen." Sebastian reached for the pencil, but Clara moved away and took hold of the arms of a chair. She pulled the chair closer to the piano, then picked up the smudged sheet of paper.

For an instant, Sebastian didn't understand. And then when it hit him, he felt his breath almost stop. He stared at his wife, gripped by an emotion he couldn't name and had never experienced before. Her eyes soft with tenderness, she nodded toward the keys.

"I remember the basics of piano music," she said. "But what I don't know, you can show me."

He swallowed hard and turned back to the piano. He played a chord with his left hand and showed Clara where it should be placed on the staff. She carefully transcribed the notes onto the paper, then looked up at him and waited.

He heard the double bass, the colors of a sunset. Then he listened for the echo and pointed out the structure of the notes so that Clara could write them down. Her penmanship was neat and precise, the notes marching like soldiers across the page. Together they worked for the next half hour, until several lines of music filled the paper.

When Sebastian finally lifted his hands from the keys, a deep satisfaction rose in him, a sense of fulfillment that he hadn't experienced in longer than he cared to remember. He flexed his right hand. His third finger curled toward his palm, but no wrenching despair accompanied the reminder of his disability.

He felt his wife's gaze on him and turned to face her. Warmth filled her eyes and curved her lips.

"It's beautiful," she murmured.

Sebastian stretched his left fingers. He still didn't dare believe that the final composition would be good, but he did know that he would finish it. For the first time in months, he would finish a composition that he could actually perform.

Clara stacked the sheets on top of the piano and brushed her lips across his forehead. "I want to help you."

He caught her arm. "We leave for Brixham at four o'clock. I've arranged for a cab to take us to the train station."

She put her hand over his and tightened her fingers. "Thank you. For everything."

Sebastian watched her leave the room, recalling her admission of love from the previous night. She was the one who reminded him that he was the same man he'd always been, that the loss of his hand didn't diminish his talent. Certainly it couldn't affect his love for music, though he'd tried hard to bury that love under layers of fear.

And what good had it done him? Clara had never allowed fear to hinder her desire to reclaim her son. Even though she *was* afraid, she plunged forward with inflexible resolve, determined to achieve her goal by whatever means necessary.

A noise turned him toward the doorway. Andrew entered the room and approached the piano.

"Is that one of Mrs. White's cream cakes?" Sebastian asked, nodding toward the pastry clutched in Andrew's hand. "When I was a boy, I knew I was having a very good day when Mrs. White offered me a cream cake."

Andrew grinned. An idea occurred to Sebastian. He reached for the pencil and turned a sheet of paper over. Gripping the pencil in a tight fist, he quickly scribbled a sentence and turned it toward Andrew.

You can tell us anything.

Andrew's eyes darkened. He scuffed his feet across the rug.

Sebastian hesitated, loath to drive the boy away but also wanting to assuage Clara's hurt. He held out the pencil in invitation.

For a moment, he thought Andrew might accept the offer of communication, but the boy gestured to the door leading to the foyer.

"Shall we try the balloons again?" Sebastian asked. "Now that we have two, we can have races."

Andrew shook his head and gestured to the foyer again. Sebastian set the pencil and paper aside. He would try again later.

He followed Andrew to the kitchen, where they had worked on preparing and varnishing the balloons. They had also constructed a wooden frame crossed with wires that supported a spindle.

From beside the wall, Andrew retrieved a large wheel constructed of paper and indicated to Sebastian that the paint was dry. The boy had spent most of the morning painting and decorating it with several spiral designs, and now they attached it to the spindle. The paper wheel was further embellished with a pattern of small holes, which they had punched with a dowel.

They fitted the wheel to the spindle and tested the mechanism. After ensuring that all the wires were tight, Sebastian carried the frame into the drawing room and set it before the fire —close enough to achieve the effects of the light, but not close enough to set the paper aflame. He stepped back.

"All right, then. Give it a try."

Andrew held up both hands in the gesture Sebastian had learned to interpret as "Wait a moment." The boy then scurried from the room, returning a few minutes later with a perplexed Clara in tow.

A smile broke loose from Sebastian's heart. Clara cast him a questioning glance before she saw the paper wheel.

"Did you make this?" she asked Andrew. "It's beautiful."

He motioned toward a chair in front of the wheel. Clara sat, shifting her gaze to her son. A guarded hope appeared in her eyes as she realized that Andrew had invited her here to demonstrate their new creation.

Sebastian moved to stand beside her, nodding at Andrew to conduct the performance. Almost vibrating with anticipation, the boy went to the wheel and took hold of the spindle.

With a few hard twists, he set the paper wheel spinning into a kaleidoscope of colors. Firelight flickered and leapt through the pattern of holes, sparking with every rotation of the wheel. The paint shimmered and gleamed under the illumination until the wheel became a blur of colors and light.

"Oh, how lovely!" Clara clapped, charmed by the display. She glanced at Sebastian. "How on earth did you conceive of this?"

"My brothers and I used to make them when our governess banned us from making real fireworks. Tasha usually decorated the wheels, and the rest of us tried to devise ever more dangerous ways to enhance the effects of the light. Andrew did this one almost entirely on his own."

"Andrew, it's brilliant! It's like watching a spinning rainbow. On fire, no less. I've never seen anything like it. Do it again, would you?"

The boy rotated the wheel faster, creating another fireworks display. Then he and Sebastian showed Clara how the mechanism was constructed, with Andrew pointing out the various parts and Sebastian explaining how they worked.

"I'm astonished. I love it." Clara squeezed Andrew's shoulder and started to lean in to embrace him. Then a shadow of wariness crossed her features, and she straightened. "Thank you for showing it to me."

Andrew nudged the frame away from the fire. Clara slipped her hand into Sebastian's.

"Thank you," she whispered. "If it weren't for you…"

Some of Sebastian's tension faded with the trailing off of her voice. He tightened his hand on hers, then went to help Andrew situate the frame near the wall.

"Shall we try our balloon races before lunch?" he asked, glancing out the window. "No rain appears forthcoming."

Andrew nodded. He looked at his mother. Clara twisted a fold of her skirt.

"Will you accompany us?" Sebastian asked.

"I'd be delighted." She kept her attention on her son, her wariness fading beneath a growing hope. "I can ask Mrs. White to pack us a picnic."

Andrew smiled.

CHAPTER 33

*C*lara shaded her eyes from the glare of the sun as she watched a carriage make its way up the drive. Sebastian had arranged for transportation to the train station at four o'clock, but it was too early for the vehicle to arrive. Apprehension flared in her chest at the realization that someone was invading their temporary sanctuary. She let the curtain fall back across the window and hurried from the room.

"Mrs. White, have you seen Mr. Hall anywhere?" Clara stopped the housekeeper en route to the kitchen.

"I believe he's still out with Master Andrew, Mrs. Hall."

Clara headed toward the drawing room. Sebastian's voice resonated from the doors opening to the garden as he and Andrew entered. Their clothes were streaked with dirt, their hair messy from the wind. The area around Clara's heart tightened at the sight of them, at the reminder that her husband and son had developed a strong rapport in less than two days.

"If you apply an extra coat of linseed oil, the seams are even stronger," Sebastian told Andrew in the moment before they looked up and saw her standing there.

Andrew stopped. Sebastian frowned.

"Clara?"

She swallowed past the tightness in her throat and gestured to the foyer. "There's…someone's arrived. I don't know who it is."

Sebastian's frown deepened. He said something to Andrew that Clara didn't hear, and went to the foyer. He wrenched open the door and descended the steps.

Clara followed, putting out a hand to keep Andrew behind her as the boy approached her side. The horses stamped and shuffled as the groom vaulted from the bench to open the door.

Shock froze Clara's blood to ice as her father stepped down from the carriage, followed by the stern, unyielding figure of the Earl of Rushton. Instinctively, she stepped backward, her hand closing around Andrew's shoulder. Panic clawed at her.

"Sebastian." Rushton strode forward, his sharp gaze flickering from Clara to his son. "We've come to reclaim the boy."

A black pit seemed to open beneath Clara's feet. She felt herself falling, falling, spiraling into a darkness that had no beginning or end.

Tension and anger stiffened Sebastian's shoulders. He slanted a glare at Fairfax. "I will not allow Andrew to be removed from his mother or placed in an institution."

"You have no say in the matter," Fairfax snapped, his lean figure rigid with determination. "You have committed a hanging offense by abducting that boy from my custody, and rest assured I will see you charged unless you return him to me."

Clara felt Andrew start to shake. Her throat closed over. She hugged him to her side as the panic clawed harder.

Run. The command beat into her blood again, but this time she had nowhere to go. This time there was no escape.

"Lord Rushton, please." She tightened her grip on her son and focused on the earl, willing him to find some degree of sympathy for their plight. "I want only to be with my son. Lord Fairfax will not allow me anywhere near him, and I—"

"We have discussed this already, Mrs. Hall," Rushton replied curtly. "And the fact remains that Lord Fairfax is Andrew's legal guardian. If you do not yield custody of him at once, your father will make good on his threat to have both you and Sebastian arrested."

Clara knew that. For herself, she didn't care. Even in prison, she would somehow find a way to keep fighting for her son if she had to write letters to every justice in the country and the queen herself. But she could not bear the thought of Sebastian being censured for an act that had been entirely her doing. She could not allow him to take any blame when he had only sought to help her.

Shame split her heart in two. Her breath jolted from her throat when Fairfax strode toward her. She stiffened her spine and clutched Andrew to her side.

"Andrew!" Fairfax's mouth compressed with irritation. "Get in the carriage at once."

The boy shook his head, half-concealed behind the folds of Clara's skirt.

Fairfax pierced Clara with a glare. "What has he said to you?"

"He hasn't said anything!" The admission ripped at her chest. "What have you done to him to make him stop speaking?"

"He has been despondent over his father's death," Fairfax replied. "Andrew, get in the carriage. You know the consequences should you disobey."

"He is not going anywhere with you," Sebastian said.

"He is, or you will be imprisoned before the day is out," Fairfax replied curtly. "Is that what you want, Mr. Hall? After the scandalous events of recent years, do you want your family to contend with your arrest for abduction? Imagine what such gossip will do to your father's reputation. Not to mention his position with the Home Office."

A heavy stillness settled between them, as if even the air itself stopped moving. The edges of Clara's vision darkened. Fairfax clenched a hand around Andrew's arm and pulled him away.

As Clara reached to grab him back, Andrew yanked himself from Fairfax's grip and ran to Sebastian. He flung himself at Sebastian as if the man were a lifeboat in a storm-lashed sea.

Sebastian closed his arms around the boy. An expression crossed his face that Clara had never seen before—a wrenching combination of grief and hopelessness. Tears burned her eyes.

"If you let the boy go, Mr. Hall," Fairfax said. "I am willing to forget any of this ever happened."

Clara's gaze skidded to Rushton, her breath stopping as she silently prayed he would relent and intervene on their behalf.

Rushton watched his son holding on to Andrew. The earl's shoulders were stiff and his expression unreadable. Only a faint flicker in his eyes betrayed any emotion whatsoever.

"Please," Clara whispered.

Rushton looked away. He opened the carriage door. Fairfax took hold of Andrew and wrenched the sobbing boy from Sebastian's arms.

"No." Sebastian reached with his right hand to grasp Andrew's shoulder, but his hand froze into a clawlike position, his arm stiffening up to his shoulder. His curse broke like glass shattering through the air.

Clara ran to her son, her heart seizing at the sound of his sobs. Fairfax pushed out a hand to stop her. The impact slammed into her chest and set her stumbling back a few steps. Sebastian lunged forward and tried to grab Andrew again.

The groom sprang at Sebastian, catching him off-guard and bringing him to the ground. The two men fought, Sebastian's left fist flying upward to catch the other man's jaw. The groom jerked backward and raised an arm. Sebastian flung him off and vaulted to his feet just as Fairfax wrestled Andrew into the carriage. Rushton followed them, his back as rigid as a plank of wood.

The carriage door slammed. A cry lodged in Clara's throat. Sebastian started toward the carriage, but the groom had already clambered back to the bench. With a snap of the whip, the horses plunged forward.

Sebastian ran after them, his boots slamming against the dirt-covered drive. The carriage picked up speed, moving farther and farther away. After following it almost to the road, Sebastian slowed to a halt and braced his hands on his knees, his body heaving with exertion. The carriage rounded a corner and disappeared from sight.

Sebastian planned an immediate return to London. He sent word in advance for his house staff to expect them, then arranged for a carriage and train tickets. He went in search of Clara to tell her they would depart that very evening.

He found her standing at the window in her bedchamber, her profile etched against the cold glass. Regret wrenched at him, but he smothered it beneath an inflexible resolve.

He would not fail her.

He would not fail Andrew.

He would not fail himself.

"You'd best prepare to depart," he said. "Our train leaves at six."

She turned to him, her face schooled into an impassivity that did not conceal the grief burning in her eyes.

"There is nothing more we can do," she said.

He shook his head, hating the resignation in her voice. "You're wrong. There is always something more we can do."

"If not even your father will resist Fairfax, then what hope do we have of any success? And I will not drag you farther into—"

"Stop." Driven by sudden anger, Sebastian crossed the room to clasp her shoulders. "You are not dragging me into anything. If I thought you were, I *would* divorce you. We are in this together.

We have been since the moment I accepted your proposal. And we will fix it together."

She didn't ask how. Instead she folded herself into his arms and buried her face in his chest. Her arms tightened around his waist. He pressed his lips to the top of her head. For all his preoccupation with his family—Rushton, Jacob, Catherine, Alexander —he'd lost sight of the most basic premise of his marriage to Clara.

She was his family now. Clara and Andrew were his family. His to provide for, to cherish, to protect. He was bound to ensure their happiness. He alone could fight for their safety. He alone could keep them together.

And not even Fairfax could stop him.

The realization broke inside him like a comet racing through a dark sky. He'd spent so many months despairing the loss of his hand, the end of his career, that he hadn't realized the void was being filled with something so much more fulfilling. An abiding love, a sense of purpose that flared his blood with colors and happiness.

He grasped Clara's waist ignored the seizing of his hand, and lowered his head to kiss her. Her soft gasp slipped into his mouth, but her body curved against his as naturally as a leaf bows to a breeze. She parted her lips and smoothed her hands over his jaw and into his hair.

"I love you," Sebastian whispered against her mouth. "If you will but trust me, I will not fail you."

Tears slipped down her cheeks, salty against her lips. He brushed them away with his thumb and lifted his head. Though Clara might be correct that the core of his being remained the same, Sebastian knew he had irrevocably changed, and not solely due to the loss of his hand.

He had changed because of Clara, because she had shown him how to reshape desperation and use it as fuel. Because she, too, knew the black despair of having something taken away, and yet she had never wavered in her efforts to get Andrew back. If she would not waver, then neither would he.

"Your father is still in financial straits," he said. "And while we cannot rely on Rushton's help, I'm certain Alexander will give us whatever we need to appease him."

Clara shook her head. "It isn't about money. If it was, Fairfax would have made an explicit demand when we spoke with him about Wakefield House. I'm certain he would take whatever you offered, but I fear nothing will make him relinquish custody of Andrew."

"Yet it also isn't a question of Fairfax wanting to raise Andrew himself, is it? If it were, he wouldn't send the boy away for medical care. I don't imagine he would stay with Andrew in Switzerland, do you?"

"No." Clara bit her bottom lip. "He never thought Andrew would amount to anything."

So what else was there? Sebastian had the nagging sense that they were missing something important, and yet he had no idea what it was. On the surface, Fairfax was a grandfather committed to retaining custody of his grandson and putting him under the care of a physician.

Maybe the answer lay with the physician and the institution… if Fairfax chose not to stay with Andrew, which seemed likely, then Sebastian and Clara might have a chance to see the boy while he was under medical care. Fairfax would probably make arrangements to bar them from the institution as well, but money could work to unlock those doors.

And Sebastian would tell Alexander everything that had happened, if it would mean his brother's financial support. Alexander would be furious over the revelations about Catherine Leskovna and might very well renounce both Jacob and Sebastian for having associated with her again, but he would help give Clara the opportunity to see her son.

"I have an idea." Sebastian gripped Clara's shoulders, felt hope flow through him in a wave of sky-blue. "Will you trust me?"

"I do trust you." Her gaze searched his, her violet eyes filled with a mixture of warmth and sorrow. "And you have already proven your love for me. Now you must give me the chance to do the same."

$\mathcal{A}$ndrew did not want to return to London with his grandfather. That much was clear. Rushton watched as the boy all but cowered against the side of the railway car as they made their way back to the city. He looked at Fairfax.

"What was this talk about an institution?" he asked.

"Andrew has refused to speak since his father's death," Fairfax replied. "Several doctors have recommended I consult a Swiss physician who can help determine the cause of his affliction. I intend to leave Andrew with him until he is cured."

"You've no idea how long that will take," Rushton said. Unease laced through him as he glanced at Andrew again. If Fairfax abused the boy, then one would think Andrew might be relieved at the opportunity to get away from him. Then again, he'd have to consider an institution and a physician as the lesser of two evils.

"It does not matter how long it takes," Fairfax replied. "As long as Andrew is well cared for and cured."

"So your plan is to leave him in Switzerland while you return to London?" Rushton asked.

"Not London. I shall return to Manley Park for the remainder of the year."

Rushton narrowed his eyes. His unease intensified, alongside the growing sense that Fairfax was leaving something out of his story, some vital piece that might prove illuminating.

"If you don't mind my asking, Fairfax," he said, keeping his tone friendly and curious, "why exactly did your daughter leave Manley Park in the first place?"

"Oh." Fairfax waved a dismissive hand. "She too was distraught over the loss of her beloved husband. So distraught, in fact, that she was unable to properly care for Andrew. She thought it best if she went to London to recuperate from her bereavement."

A frown pulled at Rushton's mouth. If Fairfax indeed believed Clara had been responsible for her husband's death, why had he not accused her of the crime? And why would he concoct a tale of her grief driving her away from her own son? Which story was the true one?

Although Rushton possessed bitter, firsthand knowledge that a mother was capable of abandoning her children, he could not reconcile such drastic action with what he knew of Clara. So grief-stricken over the death of her husband that she would abandon Andrew, even if the boy was no longer her legal ward?

No.

The woman who had abducted Andrew in an effort to reclaim him, the woman who had begged Rushton for aid...such a woman would never leave her child behind. And even if Rushton was uncertain about his conclusion, he could rely upon his son's actions for confirmation.

Not even to defy Rushton would Sebastian have married a woman who had abandoned her child shortly after the death of the child's father. In a moment, Sebastian would have seen through to such coldness.

Instead Sebastian had married her partly to help her get her son back, obviously believing that Clara and Andrew should be together.

Rushton had never considered himself a man ruled by emotion. His anger toward his son was not so blinding that it obscured Sebastian's admirable qualities. Sebastian had always been the one most capable of understanding what people truly needed, often better than they understood themselves. It was but one of the reasons Sebastian had always been at his ease in the world.

"When do you intend to bring Andrew to Switzerland?" Rushton asked.

"I'd intended to leave last week, so all preparations have been made," Fairfax replied. "Provided I can change my tickets, Andrew and I should be able to leave for Brighton on Monday at the latest. We'll take a boat to Dieppe, then stay in Paris for a day or so before leaving for Interlaken."

Rushton tucked that information away in the back of his mind as he turned his attention back to Andrew. The boy stared out the window, his face pale but without expression.

Rushton had the upsetting thought that Andrew might very well try to run away at some point during his journey with his grandfather. Though likely Fairfax had also considered the possibility and would ensure the boy was well guarded.

Protected. Fairfax would ensure that Andrew was well protected.

Andrew turned his head and met Rushton's gaze. The sudden contact brought to mind an unexpected image of his sons. All four of them. Dark-haired boys whose eyes glinted with varying hints of mischief, curiosity, seriousness, glee. Boys who had grown into men of sharp intelligence and strong constitutions, despite the obstacles that had been thrown into their paths.

Men capable of teaching Rushton a thing or two about how to conduct oneself in the world.

Andrew Shepherd might become the same type of man, given

the opportunity to attend school, play sports, travel, work, marry. But such a future appeared in doubt, if his grandfather carried through with his plan.

Rushton tore his gaze from Andrew and looked out the opposite window. None of this was his concern, at any rate. Fairfax was the boy's guardian. And Rushton's sole concern was to prevent anything from further damaging his family's reputation.

By helping Fairfax reclaim his grandson, Rushton had fortified the walls around the earldom. That was all that mattered.

At the Paddington station, they procured two cabs to take them back to their respective residences. Rushton nodded a farewell to Fairfax and turned to ensure his luggage was loaded into his cab.

There was a quick, sharp tug at his sleeve. He glanced down. Andrew stood at his side, his shoulders hunched furtively.

"She didn't do it," he whispered, his voice hoarse with disuse. "Didn't."

Before Rushton could question the boy, Andrew darted back to his grandfather. Fairfax was speaking to the cab driver and appeared not to notice Andrew's short absence.

Andrew climbed into the cab and looked at Rushton through the window. He shook his head.

Disquiet tumbled through Rushton's chest. Was Andrew speaking of his abduction? Or Clara's involvement in Richard Shepherd's death? Although Rushton didn't believe her capable of murdering her husband, he hadn't discounted the potential of her accidental involvement. Fairfax would hold to his accusation that Clara was responsible for Richard's death.

But how did Andrew know she was not?

The familiar smells of paint and grease permeated the museum. In the front exhibition room, Clara pivoted on her heel and paced to the window. Her mind ferreted through all the tangles of the newest plan they had concocted since arriving back in London yesterday.

She could no longer afford to carry the weight of hopelessness and anguish. For the past year, such emotions had pulsed alongside her blood, fueling her desperation, but ultimately they were useless. She would never see Andrew again if she allowed despair to rule her heart.

And now, she was no longer alone. Even when faced anew with the loss of her son, even though darkness still fought to pull her downward, she reached for the light shining like gold coins on the surface. She and Sebastian had reclaimed Andrew once, and they would do so again.

She glanced to where her husband sat by the hearth, his brow creased as he studied the latest missives from his brother's solicitor.

"He didn't sign the deed of conveyance." Sebastian pushed to his feet and began to pace, latching a hand behind his neck. "That's to our benefit, at the least."

Jacob unfolded himself from a chair and approached to examine the papers. "Though there appears to be no possibility of Fairfax's willingness to settle."

"No." Sebastian shook his head. "We will not approach him again. I will write to Alexander explaining the situation and send the letter in Monday's post."

"I've the information about the institution here." Granville riffled through a stack of papers. "As well as all the papers pertaining to Wakefield House."

Relief eased some of the tension from Clara's shoulders. Wakefield House remained in Sebastian's hands, still useful as a point of negotiation should the situation arise, doubtful though that might be.

She met her husband's warm gaze, her heart fluttering again at the reminder that not once had he wavered in his determination to remain by her side.

The sound of the doorbell rang faintly in her ear. She went to the foyer to answer it, as both Mrs. Fox and Mrs. Marshall had left for the day. Clara pulled open the door, her breath stopping in her throat as she stared at the Earl of Rushton.

"Mrs. Hall." He gave her a stiff nod, his features set like stone. "Sebastian's footman said he was here."

"Yes." Confused and wary, Clara stepped back to allow him entrance. After he'd divested himself of his greatcoat and hat, she gestured to the drawing room. "Everyone is inside."

Rushton's shoulders tightened, but he nodded. Praying he would not throw yet another obstacle into their path, Clara preceded him and closed the door after he'd entered.

Silence crashed over the room. Jacob and Sebastian exchanged glances, their stances guarded. Apprehension flickered across Granville's face.

"Sebastian." Rushton nodded at his sons. "Jacob."

"My lord." Sebastian extended his hand to a chair. "Would you care to sit?"

"No." Rushton's gaze flickered to Sebastian's hand, the finger bent at a right angle. A shadow veiled his eyes for an instant. "I've come to ask about your intentions regarding Andrew."

Sebastian eyed his father warily. "We have no intentions. As you've proven, we have no further recourse."

"And yet I do not for an instant believe you will not attempt to find one," Rushton replied, folding his hands behind his back. "You've already gone to enormous lengths to reclaim Andrew, and I know there is nothing on earth that would stop either of you from continuing your efforts."

"Why do you want to know what they are, then?" Hostility threaded Sebastian's voice. "So you can relay the information to Fairfax?"

"No." Rushton cleared his throat, looking from Sebastian to Jacob and back again. "So that I might assist you."

Silence fell again. Clara's heart pounded inside her head as she struggled against the hope desperate to break forth. She met Sebastian's gaze and saw the same struggle in the depths of his eyes before he turned back to his father.

"Why would you assist us?" he asked. "All you've wanted is to avoid scandal."

"And up until now, I have had good reason to do so." Rushton turned to Clara. His brows pulled together with a faint sense of confusion. "Your son spoke to me."

Clara gasped, her hand going to her throat. "Andrew *spoke* to you?"

"He said, verbatim, *she didn't do it*," Rushton explained. "I assumed he was speaking of your hand in Mr. Shepherd's death."

Hope surged through Clara's blood, filling her heart. Andrew had believed her. No matter what Fairfax had said to him, no matter what lies he had slipped into Andrew's ear, her son believed her over his grandfather.

"Did he say anything else?" she asked.

"No. He had little time to speak at all." Rushton frowned, pinching the bridge of his nose between his fingers. "I was given to understand that Andrew had been rendered mute by the shock of his father's death. Yet if that is the case, why would he choose to make such a statement after all this time? And to me, no less? A stranger?"

"Perhaps he thought Fairfax would make the accusation public?" Jacob ventured. "And sought your help in denying it?"

"If Fairfax had intended to make the accusation public, he could have done so months ago." Sebastian raked a hand through his hair in frustration. "We must follow them to Switzerland. At least there, Fairfax won't have the weight of British law behind him should he start tossing threats about."

"Neither will we," Clara added, a fact which might be to their benefit.

Sebastian looked at his father. "Do you know anything else?"

"Fairfax plans to leave by Monday for Brighton," Rushton

said. "He might already be gone. I've procured tickets for our own travel. Jacob, you will remain in London in the event we need assistance here." He gave Sebastian a firm nod. "Bastian, Mrs. Hall, I suggest we depart immediately."

CHAPTER 35

*A*n amphitheater of green hills surrounded the town of Brighton, whose wide, paved streets enclosed the brisk sea air like the banks of a stream. Fashionable shops, theaters, and baths bordered the streets, and the royal gardens wrapped around the northern shoulders of the town like an ornamental cloak.

Sebastian procured two rooms at the York Hotel, an expansive hotel a short distance from the Chain Pier. After Rushton had gone to settle into his quarters, Sebastian pushed open the door to a clean, spacious room with a large bed, desk, and chest of drawers.

"There are refreshments in the coffee room," he said, but Clara shook her head. She hadn't been hungry for the past two days, her stomach tight with nerves.

She eased aside the curtain and looked out over the sweeping expanse of the ocean. Andrew could be out there already, carried away from her to a distant land where God alone knew what awaited him.

Sebastian's warm hand settled on her nape, his fingers working the knotted muscles. "I've sent word to a hotel in Interlaken for the reservation of two rooms. It's not far from the institution. We'll contact the director once we're there. I don't want him to say anything to your father about our correspondence."

The boat to Dieppe would leave early the following morning. It seemed an eternity.

A knock at the door announced Rushton's arrival. At his suggestion, rather than sit in the hotel room and worry about all the things that could go wrong, they went out to take some air. The cold, salt-tinged wind reminded Clara of Wakefield House, a memory that fueled her resolve anew. They walked along New Steine, past various shops and markets whose displays overflowed with fresh-caught mackerel and red mullet.

As Sebastian paused to examine the fish, Rushton glanced at Clara.

"Did he tell you what I asked of him?" he said.

"Your requirement that he marry?"

"My requirement that he marry a woman who makes him a better man."

Clara stopped and turned to face him. "No, my lord. He didn't tell me that."

"His brother Alexander did so, though I admit for a time we feared he would bring us all to ruination again," Rushton said. "And since my own marriage failed in an unfortunately spectacular fashion, I've come to the conclusion that unions of political or social ends matter far less than the moral quality of the woman involved and her ability to improve upon a man's own constitution. I told Sebastian as much when I insisted that he find a wife."

"I hope..." Clara swallowed past the tightness in her throat. "I hope you haven't been too disappointed with his choice."

"On the contrary, Mrs. Hall," Rushton replied. "I admit to grave misgivings when you told me of Fairfax's accusations, but such doubts have been overshadowed by your son's reactions to both Fairfax and Sebastian. Over the last year I have learned that children's true feelings are not easily concealed. Moreover, they often possess a very keen perception about the character of others. A lesson I failed to comprehend when my own children were young."

"Andrew took to Sebastian immediately," Clara said. "And though I'm biased, I cannot think of a better endorsement of your son's character."

Now she had to hope that Andrew would one day trust her again as he trusted Sebastian. Although she had sensed the breach between herself and her son begin to close during their last day at Floreston Manor, there hadn't been enough time to fully understand its formation in the first place.

All Clara had were speculations that Fairfax had poisoned her son against her. And all Andrew had were Clara's assurances that she had not been responsible for Richard's death, though the confirmation that he had *believed* her shone inside her like sunlight.

They continued walking as the sun began to sink, casting a reddish glow over the streets. Other people strolled along the streets as well, some peering into shop windows and others going in and out of baths and restaurants. Clara tilted her hat to block the glare of the sun just as she caught sight of two figures walking along the opposite side of the street.

She stopped. Her breath snared in her lungs.

"Clara?" Sebastian turned to her with a frown, sliding his hand beneath her elbow. "Are you all right?"

Clara pressed a hand to her chest. Her heart slammed against her palm. Across the street, a small, chestnut-haired boy walked a pace behind an older man clad in a dark blue greatcoat, his features concealed beneath the shadow of a hat.

Sebastian followed her gaze, his spine stiffening. Before Clara could stop him, he lunged across the street like a tiger attacking its prey and came to a halt in front of Fairfax and Andrew.

They both stopped in their tracks. Fairfax looked from Sebastian to Clara, his eyes widening with shock and anger. Andrew started forward. Fairfax threw out an arm to block his path.

"Get out of my way," he snapped at Sebastian. "Or I *will* have you arrested."

"You will not. Andrew, come here."

Andrew started toward Sebastian again. Fairfax grabbed Andrew's arm, wrenching a yelp from the boy. Several pedestrians paused as they sensed a brewing conflict. Fairfax pivoted to stare at Rushton as he and Clara hurried across the street to them.

"Rushton?" Confusion flared in the baron's eyes. "What...?"

"Andrew, explain what you said when you spoke to me at the Paddington station," Rushton said, without a glance at Fairfax. "What did you mean by that?"

The boy swung his gaze from Rushton to Clara. His mouth opened and closed. Tension squeezed Clara's shoulders.

"Andrew." She spoke his name in a hoarse whisper. She extended a hand and took a cautious step forward, her heart thudding. "You know I was not responsible for your father's death."

Andrew started to shake, all color draining from his face. He tried to yank his arm from Fairfax's grip, but Fairfax took a step back and pulled Andrew with him.

"Andrew, you know nothing of the kind," Fairfax said.

"I...I do," Andrew gasped, throwing his grandfather a terrified but determined look. "It...it wasn't M-mama."

Tears sprang to Clara's eyes at the sound of her son's voice, music that had been silenced for the past year. A cascade of relief burst through her fear. She took another step forward. Andrew suddenly wrenched his arm from his grandfather's grip and flung himself at Sebastian, the impact powerful enough to send Sebastian stumbling back. A collective gasp rose from the crowd of people who had gathered nearby.

"It was *him*!" Andrew pointed a trembling finger at Fairfax the instant before Sebastian's arm closed around his shoulders. "He k-killed my father. I saw him d-do it."

Clara froze, swamped with horror. She stared at her father, saw the truth of the accusation in the guilt that flared across his features before a shutter descended. His eyes hardened to ice as his gaze broke from hers. He darted forward to grab Andrew.

Sebastian stepped back, his hand curling around Andrew's arm. His grip faltered. He cursed. Fairfax hauled Andrew up and turned to flee. He staggered a few steps then, realizing the hindrance of the boy's weight, he dropped Andrew and ran.

"Andrew!" Clara hurried to her son and fell to her knees beside him, relief billowing through her as she gathered him into her arms. "Are you all right?"

He nodded, his slender body shaking with fear and exertion as he sagged against her. Sebastian passed them in a blur of speed. His boots slammed against the cobblestones as he gave chase.

Fairfax's dark-clad figure was halfway down the street when Sebastian caught up to him, both of them crashing to the ground with one lunge. A scuffle ensued as the two men fought, but Fairfax was no match for Sebastian's height and strength. Within seconds, Sebastian had subdued the older man and dragged him to his feet.

Still clutching her son, Clara turned to search for Rushton. For a moment, she couldn't find him in the growing crowd, but then he pushed past a group of people. Two police constables followed, their batons at the ready as they approached Sebastian and Fairfax.

Voices rose from the crowd in excited chatter. Clara tightened her arms around Andrew and led him to the safety of a doorstep. She pressed her cheek against his hair.

"I'm sorry," she whispered. "So sorry it happened this way."

One day soon she would ask him exactly what he saw happen between Fairfax and Richard, but that day could wait. Right now all she wanted was to hold her son again and get reacquainted with the boy he had become—this time, without the portent of fear hanging over them like a thundercloud.

They waited together, huddled close, as the crowd began to disperse and Sebastian returned to find them. He scraped a hand through his messy hair and crouched in front of them, balancing on the balls of his feet.

"You did the right thing, Andrew," he said. "No harm will come to you for having told the truth. Had you feared that it would?"

Andrew nodded. Sebastian lifted the boy into his arms, then extended a hand to Clara and helped her up. He pulled her to his other side, holding them close. A tremble shuddered through Clara as she embraced both her husband and her son. She and Andrew would always be safe at Sebastian's side.

Slowly, she turned to find Lord Rushton.

"Fairfax is in police custody." His face reddened from exertion and lined with concern, the earl stopped beside them. "Rest assured, Mrs. Hall, I will do everything within my power to ensure that justice is served."

"Thank you, my lord."

Clara didn't doubt his promise. Rushton was determined that nothing would shake the foundations of the earldom again, but he was not so uncompromising that he would allow a murder to go unpunished.

Her heart clenched. *Murder.* Richard had been murdered by the very man to whom he had entrusted his son.

As if sensing her thoughts, Sebastian lowered his head to whisper into her ear. "He will never harm you or Andrew again."

She tightened her hold on him. "I believe you."

Several days after returning to London, Andrew explained in slow, halting speech what he had seen that fateful day when his father died. They sat in the parlor of Blake's Museum of Automata—only Clara and Sebastian, as Andrew had said he wanted no one else present. He huddled in a chair before the fire, his hands cupped around a bowl of hot cocoa. Soon he would have to recount the events to the police superintendent, but everyone had agreed to give the boy a chance to recover.

"They were talking about business," Andrew said. Firelight flickered across his youthful features as he stared into the flames. "Grandfather and Papa. Railway stock or...or something like t-that. Then they started arguing."

He fell silent, a distance blurring his gaze as if he saw the scene anew.

"M-my grandfather accused my papa of keeping him out of a...a contract," Andrew continued. "Their voices got louder and louder. I'd gone into the woods a ways to follow a rabbit, so I don't think they knew I...I was there. Then I heard the sound of a slap and I went back to see what had happened. Grandfather had...had grabbed Papa and was shaking him. They were both yelling. Then he...he hit Papa hard enough that Papa f-fell off the horse. There was a...a horrible crack. Blood. Grandfather jumped down and ran to Papa, shouting at him to get up.

"He shook him again, then looked up and saw me. He l-looked awful...scared, like something was horribly wrong. I knew it too. The m-minute he shouted my name, I turned and ran. Just k-kept running until I didn't hear him anymore. I found my pony again and went back to the house to find Mama, but you weren't there."

"I'd returned to the woods to look for you." Clara brushed her hand across Andrew's hair.

"I...I didn't want to wait."

"Richard was dead by the time I reached him," Clara told Sebastian, an old horror pushing at her memory as she recalled finding Richard on the path. "I think my father had gone for help, but it was too late. And when he saw me with Richard, he obviously thought to deflect the blame."

"Why did you not tell anyone, Andrew?" Sebastian asked gently.

The boy's lower lip trembled as he stared down into the bowl. "H-he said he'd hurt Mama if I did. Said if I spoke a word, M-mama would be arrested and hanged. So...so I stayed quiet."

"Oh, Andrew." Clara struggled against the tears clogging her throat as she bent to embrace her son.

She understood now why Andrew had maintained a distance from her during their brief stay at Floreston Manor. He'd been afraid that if he let down his guard around her, he would say something to expose Fairfax, a confession that would then have repercussions for her.

"I'm so sorry," she whispered.

"You did the right thing, Andrew," Sebastian said. "Never doubt it."

Andrew looked at Clara. "Will I stay with you now?"

"Yes." She glanced at Sebastian. He returned her gaze, and a warm understanding passed between them. "You'll stay with both of us forever."

CHAPTER 36

*W*akefield House presided over the land like an aged matron who still retained vestiges of a youthful beauty. The sun cast a burnished glow on the rustic brown stones and the expansive gardens.

Red and orange leaves carpeted the grass, and the wind carried a fresh tinge of salt. The hills of Dorset rolled toward the sheer cliffs that plunged into the sea, foaming waves crashing at their base.

Sebastian took Clara's hand as she descended the carriage. He lowered his head to brush his lips across her cheek, pleasure warming his chest when she smiled at him. He then turned to help Andrew down the carriage steps.

"You've not been here before?" Sebastian asked.

Andrew shook his head. Since their return from Brighton two weeks ago, he still favored gestures over speaking, but slowly his confidence in speech was beginning to return.

More important, the haunted look in his eyes was lessening, eclipsed now by the curiosity and happiness every seven-year-old should possess.

Together they walked to the house, where a line of five servants stood waiting for them. Sebastian had arranged for the staff and the opening of the house prior to their arrival, though as he glanced at the cracks spreading through the window glass and the weeds in the neglected garden, he realized the extent of the work still to be done.

Anticipation lit inside him at the notion of restoring and repairing this property that meant so much to Clara. He would do it for her, but also for himself and Andrew, because he wanted Wakefield House to be more than a place for them to escape London. He wanted it to be their home.

Inside, the furniture and floors were worn but clean, the curtains parted to allow the late autumn sunlight to stream through the windows.

Sebastian stopped at the entrance to the drawing room. "Oh, no."

Clara paused to peer around his shoulder. She laughed. Strewn about the tables were machine parts, gears, and wires. Automata lined the walls—birdcages, mechanical animals, acrobats. A creature that appeared to be an elephant sat atop the piano.

"Did I forget to tell you?" Clara asked. "Uncle Granville spent a great deal of time with us when we stayed in Dorset."

"Yes, you forgot to tell me." He glowered at her. "And I neglected to consider the fact that your uncle is a consequence of marriage to you."

She shot him a smile. "Too late now, isn't it, husband?"

Too late, indeed. To his great good fortune.

Andrew darted forward to pick up a mechanical turtle, the shell a gleaming design of green metal. He turned the key and grinned as the creature plodded forward on thick legs.

"Oh!" Clara went to a large, closed trunk that sat near the windows. "I didn't think it would have arrived yet."

"I had Giles bring it directly from the museum," Sebastian said.

"Andrew, these are all for you." Clara unlatched the lid and opened the trunk to reveal the myriad of toys and automata inside. "Uncle Granville made most of them, and others were sent by fellow inventors."

Andrew hurried to peer into the trunk. Clara took out a wooden acrobat and demonstrated how it flipped into an intricate spin. The boy laughed.

"Isn't it wonderful?" Clara handed the toy to him.

Andrew dug into the trunk and began removing wooden trains and boats. Sebastian watched as Clara straightened and approached him again, a smile curving her mouth and a light glowing in her eyes.

His heart swelled, all the shadows of the past slipping away. The loss he had once considered so dire had become insignificant in the face of all he had found with Clara and Andrew.

Although he still could not fathom the extent of his mother's betrayal, he now understood both the strength and fragility of love. He would do anything to protect it, to ensure that nothing ever again came between him and his family.

He wrapped his arm around Clara's shoulders and pulled her to him, pressing his lips to the top of her head. She softened against him, one hand sliding over his back. For a moment, they watched Andrew as he began setting up the toys on the floor.

"Andrew, I'm going to talk to the housekeeper," Clara said. "We'll have supper in about an hour, I imagine."

Andrew nodded. Clara gave Sebastian another smile before she headed toward the kitchen.

Sebastian crouched down. He picked up a mechanical duck and set it waddling across the floor. He and Andrew both chuckled as the creature emitted a squeaky *quack* every step or two. Sebastian glanced at the boy.

"Would you like to continue your piano lessons while we're here?" he asked.

Andrew nodded, his assent bringing a welcome warmth to Sebastian's heart. After reviewing the charges against Fairfax, a judge had returned custody of Andrew to Clara and Sebastian, a situation that would be permanent as soon as the papers were drawn up.

"I want to make balloons again too," Andrew said.

"And I'll also show you how to make crystals using alum and hot water. Let's see if we can upset the housekeeper here as successfully as we did Mrs. White."

Andrew grinned. Sebastian reached out to tousle the boy's hair before he pushed to standing and went out to the garden. A fresh, cold wind swept through the trees. He breathed in the sea air, felt it swim through his veins and cleanse the dirt of the city from his lungs.

"It was once lovely," Clara said from behind him. She reached out to pluck a weed from a flower bed.

"It still is. And we'll restore it to its former glory." Sebastian tucked a stray lock of hair back behind Clara's ear. "Jacob has promised to visit prior to his return to St. Petersburg. And after he and Granville finish constructing the cipher machine, which they ought to do soon now that they have Rushton's patronage."

"When is Lord Rushton scheduled to present it to the Home Office?"

"Next month. Jacob is certain that the committee members will be highly impressed by the machine and Monsieur Dupree's unbreakable code. And if the Home Office uses it to further the British efforts in the war, then such an attainment will greatly enhance Rushton's political standing."

"And further diminish the effects of my father's disgrace upon the earldom," Clara added, a shadow darkening her eyes.

"As Jacob recently reminded me, the earldom is locked tight and secure," Sebastian said. "And trust me when I say that people are already talking about your courage in the face of your father's cruelty. Not to mention Andrew's."

"I can't believe we have him back."

"I can." Sebastian brushed his lips across her temple. "Nothing would have stopped you from saving him. Nothing. You have no idea how strong you are. Not even I could withstand you."

Clara smiled, her eyes crinkling at the corners. "Yet I surrendered my heart to you."

"And I will not return it." He turned her toward him and lowered his head for a proper kiss, heat coursing through his blood at the touch of her soft lips. "But you are welcome to keep mine in exchange."

"Gladly."

Clara's body arched against his, her arms sliding around his waist. Another gust of salt-fresh air glided in from the ocean, winding long strands of hair around her neck. Sebastian lifted his right hand and curved it around her nape.

Hope filled his veins alongside the realization that she had been right when she told him the core of his being would never change. He had just needed her to remind him how much joy there still was to be found in the world.

Although Rushton had settled Sebastian's medical debts and begun investigating possible doctors and treatments that might be able to help with his infirmity, Sebastian knew he would never regain full use of his hand. The thought didn't distress him nearly as much as it would have even a month ago, because so much more had filled the void of his loss.

And he was beginning to find his way back to music. He would find pleasure in teaching piano again. He would also continue his efforts to create compositions for the left hand only, a challenge that was already generating interest and speculation among his fellow musicians.

Another pianist had requested a demonstration of the composition, but Sebastian had declined. Soon enough he'd share his findings, but for the moment he wanted only to work alone and to be with Clara and Andrew.

He pressed his mouth to Clara's again, breathed in her orange-spice scent, and let her remind him of all they had together. All they would continue to have.

The rest of the world could wait.

ABOUT THE AUTHOR

New York Times & USA Today bestselling author Nina Lane writes hot, sexy romances about professors, bad boys, candy makers, and protective alpha males who find themselves consumed with love for one woman alone. Originally from California, Nina holds a PhD in Art History and an MA in Library and Information Studies, which means she loves both research and organization. She also enjoys traveling and thinks St. Petersburg, Russia is a city everyone should visit at least once. Although Nina would go back to college for another degree because she's that much of a bookworm and a perpetual student, she now lives the happy life of a full-time writer.

www.ninalane.com

facebook.com/ninalaneauthor
twitter.com/ninalaneauthor
instagram.com/ninalaneauthor
amazon.com/author/ninalane
goodreads.com/ninalane

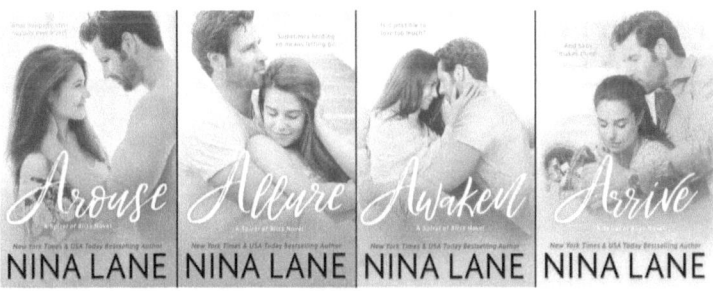

THE SUGAR RUSH SERIES

Sweet is the new sexy.

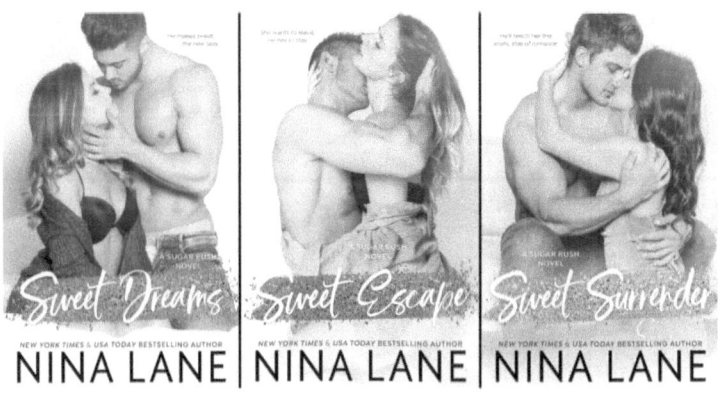

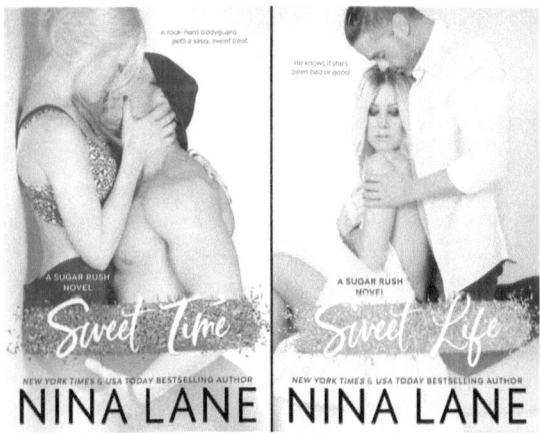

From the Stone family patriarch down to the youngest bad boy, follow the lives and loves of the Sugar Rush men and the women who bring them to their knees.

THE WHAT IF SERIES

First we fell in love. Then we fell apart.

Shattered by decade-old tragedy, two lovers fight the secrets that could destroy them.

THE SECRET THIEF

"This book is a work of art."

A woman fleeing scandal. A town's mysterious recluse.

Lust and secrets collide in this provocative romance.

THE DARING HEARTS SERIES

In bustling, colorful Victorian London, powerful lords and unconventional women battle scandal and secrets as they risk everything for love.